CW00602972

To Linda,
Happy Birthday
Love Brian and Sheila
x x

RESTLESS SPIRIT

Brian Rider

Bill Rider

MINERVA PRESS

LONDON

MIAMI RIO DE JANEIRO DELHI

RESTLESS SPIRIT
Copyright © Brian Rider 2000

ISBN 0 75411 383 3

First Published 2000 by
MINERVA PRESS
315–317 Regent Street
London W1R 7YB

Printed in Great Britain for Minerva Press

RESTLESS SPIRIT

This book is dedicated to my wife, Sheila,
for all her stalwart support and assistance in the research
and preparation of this book. Also grateful thanks to Geoffrey Lilley
for his assistance in proofreading the manuscript.

About the Author

Brian Rider, married with two children and two step-children, was a podiatrist (foot surgeon), who lived and practised in Hertfordshire. He has now taken early retirement to write full-time in the Cotswolds. A seasoned traveller, he would find it harder to tell you where he hasn't been than where he has. Both he and his wife love to explore the remoter areas of the world.

As an international lecturer, he has worked in many countries, including the United States, both in his own field of surgery and in research. He is an accomplished broadcaster with TV and radio experience over the past twenty-five years. Brian has already written a medical book and many magazine articles. He has written seven adventure thriller novels: *Snatched, Golden Inca, Dangerous Plateau, False Dawn, The Latin Mark, Saddlewitch* and *Restless Spirit*.

His many interests include drama, theatre, art, all forms of sport and he has a lively interest in history.

By the Same Author

Snatched
Golden Inca
Dangerous Plateau
False Dawn
The Latin Mark
Saddlewitch

Book I

Chapter I

Thebes, 1504 BC

The richly jewelled and ornamental bier, drawn by a retinue of thirty black Nubian slaves edged slowly forward. Borne on it was the body of Tuthmosis II, undergoing its last earthly journey. Immediately behind the Pharaoh's embalmed and mummified body, encased in its golden casket, came another elaborately throned plinth. This richly canopied conveyance was held aloft by a further twenty ebony-skinned slaves. Perspiration glistened on their labouring muscular bodies as they edged slowly forward, supporting the long shafts at front and rear. Seated on her throne high above them, a solemn expression on her strong face, Queen Hatshepsut looked neither to right nor left. At her feet, reclining on a mass of silken cushions and looking very bored, was a small chubby child, not yet five years old. He was the future Pharaoh of this very Egypt, and already well aware that he was to become Tuthmosis III.

In truth he felt little regret at the passing of his father for he had seen very little of him during his short life. His mother, Isis, one of the dead Pharaoh's lesser wives, had been a harem girl and was this day relegated to somewhere near the back of the funeral procession.

The regal-looking woman, now towering above him and seated on her richly jewelled and golden throne, was his stepmother, Hatshepsut. Already he had a dislike rather than a liking for her. Nevertheless he had been informed by the vizier, Hapi-soneb, that he must do as she so ordered, as his father had appointed her regent of all Egypt until he reached an age of maturity. Grudgingly he had to admit to himself that her own daughter, his half-sister, Neferure, was also relegated somewhere to the rear of the long column. She was only a little older than he himself, and would be accompanied by Senenmut, the queen's steward and Neferure's tutor.

He glanced up at the queen, who in her right hand held her staff of office. She was dressed in a long white gown, which would have left her shoulders bare but for the golden richly jewelled collar encrusted with inlaid malachite and jade, which reached down to almost the top embroidered band of the gown. Her black hair was arranged in elaborate plaits, and over it she proudly wore the vulture head-dress, the insignia of the queen; golden amulets encircled her arms and wrists. These were also richly studded with gems. Anyone else but the young child, Tuthmosis, would have been forced to admit that she cut an imposing and regal figure.

The solemn cavalcade stretched back for some two hundred metres and was made up of priests, nobles, army officers, lesser wives and slaves. Although it was now late in the day, the hot Egyptian sun beat fiercely down on the procession, which had slowly wound its way up from the Theban plain. A constant wailing from the rear of the column, as was the funereal custom, was accompanied by the monotonous solitary beat of a drum. The doleful sounds echoed from the barren and rocky walls of the sun-drenched cliffs. This was to be only the second burial of a Pharaoh in a place which had been designated the 'Valley of the Kings'. Tuthmosis I had already been buried here some fourteen years earlier, having previously selected his last resting place and decreed that it should be the future earthly abode of all Pharaohs.

Custom required that the dead Pharaoh must be buried at sunset. Already the high priest would have seen to it, that many of the great treasures and artefacts, which the Pharaoh had acquired during his reign, were already in place in the waiting tomb, together with all that he would require for his passing over into the next world. The high priest would have been given ample time to have completed all the arrangements for his sovereign's burial, as the embalming and mummification process alone would have taken all of seventy days from the Pharaoh's death. Wooden and stone carved *ushabtis* (effigies) of the monarch and his favourite retainers, who were to do his bidding in his afterlife, were already installed in the tomb, and the Canopic jars containing the Pharaoh's organs were travelling with the procession for final interment.

The sandy pathway was taking its toll of the slaves in the intense desert heat, and the procession's progress had substantially slowed by the time the valley entrance was reached. Hatshepsut impatiently brushed a fly away from her cheek, and beckoned for one of the handmaidens, supporting the canopy over her, to activate the ostrich-feather fan to encourage cooler air. The girl instantly obliged, wafting the designated article to and fro in front of her mistress's face. On up the dusty route, until the tomb entrance was in sight, the column continued.

Several royal guards and priests were standing sentinel outside the tomb and immediately fell to their knees in salute as the procession approached them. Hapi-soneb, the vizier, arrived to assist the queen as the slaves lowered the plinth conveyance for her to descend. The young child, Tuthmosis, scrambled down after her. The vizier signalled for the child's nurse to be brought forth to take care of him. Next he began to assemble the dignitaries who were to enter the tomb. Only the most important, the elite, were allowed to enter for the final interment. This matter concluded, the Pharaoh's body in the golden casket was ceremoniously removed from the bier by the Nubian slaves.

In orderly fashion, two by two, with Queen Hatshepsut and Hapi-soneb at the head of the column behind the casket bearers, a slow dignified entrance to the tomb was made. The walls and ceiling of the long entrance passage were decorated in a blaze of colourful murals and hieratic texts. Depicted were all the gods of Egypt and with them Tuthmosis II making and receiving offerings. Virtually everything the deceased Pharaoh would need to know for his journey into the hereafter was included somewhere, carved into the limestone. The whole ceremony therefore was not seen so much as a death, but of a passing over to a life with the gods. At sunrise the dead king would be reborn on the eastern side of the Nile and become immortal.

At the end of the long entrance corridor was another chamber filled with treasures, rich paraphernalia, domestic goods and even foods. Egyptian faith was such that they neither feared death nor the dead. More hieroglyphs covered the walls here too. From this chamber the now limited assembly followed the casket that was being carried by the slaves, into the final burial chamber. A huge stone monument was the immediate and focal centrepiece here. Hapi-soneb moved a lever on one of the side walls and part of the huge stone rolled away to reveal an open sarcophagus inside. He summoned the overseer of the slaves forward and gave final instructions. The man conveyed these to his workers, who reverently moved forward with the king's casket. This was carefully moved into the stone chamber and lowered into the sarcophagus. The high priest had personally supervised the final preparation of the mummy inside the golden casket. Between every layer of the bandages were gold and precious jewels, together with finely carved *ushabtis* of the Pharaoh.

Outside the tomb the wailing continued, accompanied by the steady beat of the drum, but only a faint sound penetrated the candlelit interior. The high priest went through several lamentations calling on Osiris, Horus and Anubis to receive this noble prince of Egypt. Earlier that morning he had supervised the ceremony of weighing the king's heart against a feather, to prove him worthy of joining the gods in the afterlife. Now all was ready for the new reigning Pharaoh to give a blessing for the departing monarch, and to give the order for final closure of the tomb.

'Who stands for Tuthmosis III of that name and Pharaoh of this very Egypt?'

'I do, as regent of upper and lower Egypt. I stand for the infant Pharaoh, Tuthmosis III, and so give the authority of Pharaoh,' said Hatshepsut in a firm and authoritative tone.

'So be it,' solemnly replied Hapi-soneb and indicated for everyone to leave the tomb.

All the occupants, including the queen, stepped forward to look into the sarcophagus one by one and then, walking backwards, slowly filed out.

The vizier and high priest then ordered the slaves to replace the heavy stone lid. Staggering under the massive and cumbersome weight they dutifully completed the manoeuvre. Hapi-soneb then dismissed them and offered up another incantation, before crossing to the wall of the burial chamber and pulling on the lever once more. With a rumbling, grating sound, the frontispiece of the huge stone monument rolled back into place, thus sealing the tomb.

However, he hadn't finished yet. Straining, he pushed the lever over even further. High up in the ceiling a stone panel slid back and sand began to pour into the chamber. His work done, Hapi-soneb moved to the outer storage chamber and repeated the ritual with another concealed lever. Sand began to flood in here too. Hurrying, he followed the last of the departing dignitaries from the entrance corridor into the brightly setting sun, sharply at contrast with the gloom in the burial chamber. Here he threw over one last lever, just inside the rocky entrance. From several stone orifices sand began to pour in here as well. He knew that by morning the entire three chambers would be totally sealed and rock solid with sand. Hapi-soneb congratulated himself on a task well done and joined the waiting procession for its return trip to the plains.

First, though, he must partake of a feast, together with the queen and other nobles. Slaves had laid all in readiness, whilst the ceremony had been in progress in the tomb's interior. A long table had been set up at the entrance. On it was a rich array of food and wine displayed on dishes and vessels of solid gold. Only the queen, himself and the most illustrious and the elite of the nobles would partake of the meal, considered by custom as a last salute to the dead Pharaoh, to his victory over death. The meal consisted of several courses. Sheep, duck of several species and goose. To aid its digestion, several jars of red wine had been provided. Hapi-soneb couldn't help but notice the queen ate but little. Then it was time to depart, the formalities complete.

To the rear of the departing column Senenmut accompanied Queen Hatshepsut's daughter by the dead Pharaoh, Neferure. He was anxious about her health, for she was a sickly if likeable child, having acquired none of her mother's, the queen's, robust health. Rather she had taken after her late father, who after suffering ill health, had departed his mortal coil while still in his early thirties. Senenmut realised the long arduous day with its intense heat had sorely taxed the little girl almost beyond her endurance. As her tutor, he felt responsible for her, but custom demanded she joined the procession for her father's funeral. She looked sadly up at him and his heart went out to her, as she was hardly able to drag herself along.

Seth's breath to convention! Senenmut, the queen's

steward, knew his head would probably roll for it, but he bent and scooped the tiny princess in his arms and carried her back to the river, where the royal barque was awaiting their return. A short journey down the Nile and across to the east bank, and he knew the little girl could be safely put to bed in the royal palace. Now that the ceremony was over there was no need to return to Tuthmosis II's temple on the Theban plain of the west bank. It was from that point that the day's ceremonies, and the procession, had begun. To Senenmut it now seemed hours away, and to the little frail child, Neferure, he knew it must seem like eternity.

By the time they reached the banks of the Nile the red disc of the setting sun was only just visible; only half of its circular shape could be seen over the western peaks.

As a privileged royal retainer, the queen's personal steward and Neferure's tutor, he was allowed a place on the royal barque. Others not so fortunate had to wait for the barque carrying the regent's party to leave the shore, before being allowed to board their own waiting vessels.

The straining slaves bent their backs to the overseer's whip as the banks of the Nile slipped by. Senenmut looked up at the raised deck above him where he could see Queen Hatshepsut. She was seated now on a richly carved chair of ebony, inlaid with ivory, near the stern of the vessel. He noticed that she looked relieved. The small chubby child, Tuthmosis III, was seated next to her on a small replica of her own chair.

Senenmut gazed over towards the west and marvelled at the already changing colours of the Theban hills that enclosed the valley. With the setting of the sun they had changed in minutes to a deep purple, which was in turn reflected by the waters of the Nile. Their vessel, with its Horus-figureheaded prow, knifed through the waters and left a frothy wake to the rear from the multitude of oars on the lower deck, disturbing the tranquil surface.

The little girl, Neferure, was asleep now in his arms. Had the queen noticed?, he wondered. Certainly Hapisoneb had. More than once the vizier had caught his eye and raised his eyebrows disapprovingly at this breach of convention.

By the time the barque had returned them to the east bank, and the waiting horse-drawn chariots had conveyed them to the royal palace, it was completely dark. Senenmut returned the sleeping child to her nurse and retired to his own quarters. He bathed and changed into fresh garments and settled down to study the *Amduat*, sometimes known as 'The Book Of The Secret Chamber' or 'That Which Is In The Underworld'. The work dealt with the sun god's journey through the twelve divisions of the underworld, which corresponded to the twelve hours of the night. Senenmut, as a commoner, owed his rise in prominence to education. His every waking hour was spent improving his mind; always he strove to learn more. He was an ambitious man, constantly striving for more knowledge.

After he had been so employed for about an hour, he was disturbed by a nearly nude Asian slave girl. This did not unduly surprise him for nudity and near-nudity had become quite fashionable by the eighteenth dynasty. The girl, slim, with long dark hair and almond-shaped eyes, informed him that the queen demanded his presence immediately. He dismissed her after requesting her to tell the queen he would come as quickly as he could. No sense in letting the girl know he was worried. These silly girls had nothing to do all day but prattle together, gossiping about everything that occurred in the palace. He waited for a respectful amount of time then, taking a deep breath, set off for the queen's chambers, which were on the other side of the palace. He realised his act in carrying the young princess that afternoon had probably brought about his downfall and ended his hard-won position.

He was shown into the queen's chambers by another young ebony-skinned handmaiden who, after requesting him to be seated, promptly left him on his own. He didn't have long to wait. Queen Hatshepsut soon appeared from her inner bedchamber through a beaded screen. She looked very stern indeed and was dressed in a long white gown. She had removed most of her jewellery, and her hair hung loosely round her shoulders, obviously having just been combed out by one of her maids.

Senenmut hurriedly rose to his feet and bowed low.

'Your Majesty requires my presence, I believe,' he exclaimed, trying to sound relaxed.

'You may be seated,' Hatshepsut replied curtly, as she herself lay back on a silken divan, arms behind her head.

Senenmut looked round for a seat of some sort. There was none. The queen, without saying a word, indicated the floor at her feet.

Somewhat dejectedly, he sunk to his knees and from there assumed a sitting position facing her. There was now a trace of a smile on her handsome face. Senenmut waited for her to address him. The queen took her time, her eyes slowly running over him as if to examine his very thoughts.

She saw before her a not unattractive man, deep of forehead, with a long aquiline nose, full lips and a firm chin. He hadn't been her steward for very long and had been recommended for the position by her vizier, Hapi-soneb. True, he wasn't attractive in a muscular manly sense, but his keenness of mind immediately drew one to notice him. Of just over average height, with slim hips and buttocks, a little more exercise wouldn't come amiss, thought the queen, noticing an extra inch or two around his waistline.

'Stand up, Senenmut,' she commanded.

Greatly puzzled as a moment ago she had ordered him seated, he slowly rose to his feet.

'Now turn round slowly... right round.'

Nonplussed, he did as Hatshepsut ordered until once again he faced her. To his amazement she patted the couch beside her.

'Come! Sit by me.'

There was an amused expression beginning to form round the corners of her full lips as she watched him. Rather like a cat playing with a mouse, he thought nervously, complying.

Once seated beside her, he watched her stroke the long black tresses of her now unbraided hair, which had fallen over her shoulders in attractive disarray. He found himself looking at the creamy alabaster-like skin of her shoulders and at the cleavage line at the top of her white gown. He forced his gaze up over crimson lips to where large brown eyes scrutinised him. Green eye shadow and dark-ochred eyebrows and lashes gave the whole face, tapering up to a broad forehead, a very pleasing effect.

'Do you like what you see?' she questioned. The light from the oil lamps and candles reflected on those deep-brown eyes.

He became aware that he had been staring, so entranced had he been with this unusual view of her. He stammered an apology.

'I… I am deeply sorry, Your Majesty, but I had never realised before quite how beautiful you were… until now, I mean,' he finished lamely.

Senenmut could see that she was pleased with this but, that she tried immediately to hide it, trying once again to make her face serious.

'You, Senenmut, although my steward, are a commoner and therefore in a very privileged position… Do you think you have the right to address me so? Perhaps you have forgotten today we buried my husband, the Pharaoh?'

'No, Your Majesty, I had not forgotten, but I fear that I was momentarily overcome by your beauty, for which I apologise.'

This time the queen ignored the apology and, switching to her stern face, went on the attack.

'Did you not think that I saw you pick up and carry my daughter, Neferure, both in the returning procession and on the barque this afternoon?'

'I am indeed sorry, Your Majesty, if in so doing I offended you.'

'Surely you realised that what you did not only offended etiquette, but contravened all that we stand for. Several of the priests have already made known their feelings to me, concerning your act of disregard for ceremony and convention.'

Senenmut now knew, or thought he did, that his head was about to roll. He threw caution to the wind.

'For that, Queen Hatshepsut, I make no apology. The poor little princess was almost in a state of collapse, so I saw nothing for it but to take her into my arms and carry her. This I did and I would do it again should the need arise.'

Quite suddenly the queen's face changed again, becoming quite beautiful with the radiance of her smile exposing a row of pearly-white even teeth.

'You are a brave man, Senenmut, and in the years ahead I shall need brave men around me if I am to govern this very Egypt during the new Pharaoh's childhood. I shall tell you now that your reply was what I would have expected of you, but I needed to test you.'

She clapped her hands together to summon the ebony-skinned handmaiden.

'Bring us drinks of honey and mead, and wine too,' she commanded. 'I shall this day drink with my steward and my daughter's tutor and to him I add one more title. From this day on he will be named Steward of the Barque Amen-userhet... the chancellor, Nehesy, shall be so informed of the appointment.'

'You do me very great honour, Your Majesty,' replied an amazed and overawed Senenmut.

Hatshepsut smiled and added, 'I will do you greater honour yet, should you serve me loyally and well, Senenmut.'

Chapter II

During the eighteenth dynasty Thebes had become the most important town not only in Egypt but of the civilised world. Gradually it had risen on the east bank of the Nile. Buildings were mostly made of mudbrick, stone being used rarely, except for temples. A royal palace had been built, where the queen and the boy king now resided, together with certain nobles, officials and servants, who were, in most cases, slaves. Other nobles and their families lived in villas with flower-filled and walled gardens. The plants and flowers and sometimes shrubs had been brought in from Asia. Roads were almost unknown, as the Nile, the great river, served as a perfect means of travel for the whole of Egypt. Wharves were built for trade on the east bank also. The manufacturing quarter was built on to these, where small houses of mudbrick sprung up with narrow lanes between them. These were in most cases well away from the houses of the great. There was a temple at Karnak, but it fell a long way short of the dimensions of later years. Sometimes the royal great wife of the reigning Pharaoh would act as high priestess for ceremonies there. This was something Hatshepsut had done on numerous occasions during the fourteen-year reign of her late husband, Tuthmosis II, with her as queen.

Theirs had been a strange marriage. She was, in fact, his half-sister. Their father, the great warrior, Tuthmosis I, had sired Hatshepsut by his chief and great wife, Ahmose, whilst Tuthmosis II's mother was only a minor wife, the princess Mutnefert, sister of Tuthmosis I's queen Ahmose.

Hatshepsut's husband, on his deathbed, had proclaimed

his little son of four years Tuthmosis III, with Hatshepsut acting as regent until his maturity. It still rankled with her bitterly. It wasn't that she disliked her stepson, but she felt hers was surely the stronger claim, and she was certain the great Tuthmosis I would have wanted her to succeed and rule. She was going to have to do it, anyway. Only Osiris and Horus knew for how many years, before the child could be expected to assume power.

It was early morning and she had risen early as was her wont. Summoning her steward, Senenmut, she had instructed him to arrange a sailing on the Nile in his new position as Overseer of the Royal Barque. Now, serenely in the early-morning mist, the prow of the barque cut through the water. Masses of tall papyrus reeds rose from the marshy banks. As they progressed, wild fowl of varied species took to flight, with a noisy fluttering of wings. Even the odd crocodile slithered into the water as the barque approached. How she hated the evil brutes, surely a hangover from the devilish Seth himself. Seated at the stern with Senenmut, her steward, at her side, she commented on her loathing of them to him. He commented that at least they cleared the great river of pollution and in fact provided food for the poorer classes.

'They do say, Your Majesty, that the underside of a crocodile's belly is very tasty.'

'Do they now... I think I shall stick with hippopotamus.'

He knew she referred to the soft succulent meat of the river horse, which was served as something of a delicacy. For some little while a pleasant and comfortable silence passed between them as each studied the river banks on either side. Here and there would be the odd peasant dressed only in a loincloth. He would be either fishing or, using a throwing stick, hunting small game in the reeds. Sometimes they would pass a group of happily chatting women, busily scrubbing on their washboards, at the river's edge.

'With all these crocodiles surely that must be a dangerous pursuit?' the queen enquired of Senenmut.

'If this is the life a person should be born to, then it must be as the gods will,' he replied, turning his palms uppermost.

'But surely you, who were once a commoner,' Hatshepsut said and paused before continuing, 'the loss of my subjects' lives does not concern you?'

'Indeed it does, Your Majesty.'

'Then, is there nothing that can be done about this needless loss of life?'

Senenmut was surprised by the question. No reigning Pharaoh in the past had ever been concerned with the lives of the poorer folk along the Nile's banks. He thought for a moment before replying.

'If it were my responsibility, Majesty, then, yes, I could do something, but it would cost much deben.'

Hatshepsut smiled.

'Then steward Senenmut, you have a new title to add to your array… "Chief Steward of the Fields of Amun". I shall give you one month to solve the problem of these needless deaths.'

At that moment Senenmut had little idea of what could be done, but he wasn't going to refuse this new high honour. In the next month he would doubtless come up with an answer.

'It shall be as you wish, Majesty,' was all he said.

Hatshepsut smiled indulgently, rather as a parent did to a favourite child.

'Good. So be it. I shall expect to see the results of your efforts. Meanwhile I shall advise Nehesy, the chancellor, of your new appointment and Thuty, the overseer of my treasury, shall make deben available for the project… Now, Senenmut, summon the captain for I would return up river to the palace.'

A week later, after much thought, Senenmut solved the problem of the crocodiles. With the monies furnished by Thuty he purchased thousands of hard wooden stakes. The lower half of these he had treated with a sticky resin gum. When he requested from Nehesy, the chancellor, at least one hundred slaves, the said official nearly suffered an apoplexy.

'Your position does not warrant such a number. I shall allocate ten,' he growled.

'I think you will find if you check with the queen my request will be granted,' exclaimed Senenmut firmly.

'Very well, I shall do so but I fear that will not be the case.'

Pompously he strutted off. Ten minutes later, looking very dejected and deflated, he returned.

'It appears that you may have the slaves you asked for.'

Senenmut smiled and graciously thanked the man. No need to make enemies needlessly.

Supervising the work himself, and labouring with the slaves for long hours at a time, he completed the work, just two days inside the time allocated by the queen. Every hundred metres along both sides of the river with a similar gap between them, he had rows of stakes driven into the shallows of the river. Each stake was placed with a man's hand length between them, thus making virtually a wooden screen, for washerwomen and fishermen at the water's edge to function safely behind. The crocodiles could still get to the muddy banks but only every alternate hundred metres. The poorer natives of Thebes were delighted with the result and praised the Queen Hatshepsut for her thought-fulness. Senenmut had taken good care to say, when questioned and whilst occupied in the construction, that it was the queen's idea, as she was so very concerned for her subjects' welfare.

The queen herself was delighted with the success of the project when he showed it to her two days later, and even more thrilled by the acclaim the deed brought her with the native population of Thebes.

'You shall be made Steward of Amun as well as of The Fields of Amun, I so declare.'

'To serve Your Majesty is reward enough,' Senenmut replied.

A few weeks after Senenmut's latest appointment, Hapi-soneb, the vizier and high priest, and Thuty, the overseer of the treasury, were deep in conversation in the temple of Karnak.

'The queen thinks well of the man, Senenmut,' exclaimed Thuty.

'It was I who first recommended him to her,' replied Hapi-soneb proudly.

Thuty stroked his short black beard thoughtfully.

'A wise choice, goodly vizier, for the man, although a commoner by birth, is well read and of keen wit.'

Hapi-soneb looked puzzled.

'This I know full well, Treasurer. However, I do not see the direction of your thoughts.'

'Have you not noticed how popular our queen is becoming with the populace of Thebes? Everywhere she goes the common people line the route to cheer her.'

'Is that then not as it should be, Thuty?'

'It is indeed, but did you ever see them do that with her late husband, or the great Pharaoh warrior before him, Tuthmosis I?'

'No, they were never that concerned with the people, only with conquests and wars. They had no time for internal affairs, like this queen.'

Still Hapi-soneb wore a puzzled expression. Thuty smiled craftily and touched his nose with his index finger.

'Can this very Egypt prosper with a child as its Pharaoh? Would it not be wiser and better for our queen regent to reign in her own right?'

Hapi-soneb considered the suggestion before replying.

'Egypt has never had a woman as Pharaoh and, in any case, the boy king has right of birth. Queen Hatshepsut would never go against her late husband's wishes.'

'Some say that the old Pharaoh, her father, would have expected her to succeed her husband, as he was her half-brother also.'

'The complexities of this are well known to me, and it may well be that the queen's claim to the throne is stronger anyway than the boy king's,' grudgingly admitted Hapi-soneb.

Thuty nodded, delighted that his argument seemed to be winning over the vizier, then resumed, 'This queen is immensely popular with the people of Thebes. If we can increase her popularity all over upper and lower Egypt we wouldn't have to do anything. The clamour for her to become Pharaoh in her own right would be enough.'

Hapi-soneb still looked doubtful.

'But we would still have to persuade the queen.'

'No, you are wrong. That is where your man, Senenmut, would come in. He is the queen's steward. She trusts and relies on him more each day. I am not suggesting that this could be done overnight, but over the next two years his influence could certainly change things – and it could only be good for our country.'

Hapi-soneb was gradually coming round to the treasurer's way of thinking.

'I shall speak to the man, Senenmut, and let him know he would have our support should he be prepared to help in convincing the queen.'

It was Thuty's turn now to look thoughtful. Again he stroked his little black beard before going on.

'Senenmut will need more authority. Suggest to the queen, in your capacity as vizier, that he should be made Overseer of the Granaries of Amun.'

'So be it... Let us hope this plan does not rebound on us,' concluded Hapi-soneb.

The boy king was now five and a half years old and was playing with his half-sister in the palace gardens. Neferure was only a year or so older. The two children had begun to squabble.

Little Tuthmosis stamped his foot angrily, shouting in a shrill voice, 'When I grow up I am going to be a great warrior like my grandfather, Tuthmosis I. I shall be Pharaoh and everyone will do as I say, or I shall have them thrown to the crocodiles... you too, if I want to.'

'No, you won't, because my mother is regent and she won't let you... nor will my tutor, Senenmut.'

'I hate your mother... My mother, Isis, should be regent,' screamed little Tuthmosis.

'No she shouldn't... Your mother is only a slave girl,' said Neferure, throwing her little shoulders back and standing up to her irate half-brother.

Not to be outdone, he shouted at the top of his voice, 'Anyway, you will have to marry me... My nurse says so, and my mother agrees.'

'I shall never marry you... you dreadful boy,' screamed the little girl.

'You will be made to. It is the custom in Egypt.'

Tuthmosis, who was wearing a miniature breastplate of golden armour beat his little knuckles upon it in temper. Neferure smiled knowingly and turned to leave him to his tantrum, tossing a last remark over her shoulders.

'Be careful not to stab yourself with that tiny sword,' she

said, referring to the miniature replica he was now waving madly about.

'That's right. Run off to your lessons. I'm going to play at soldiers,' he called after her…

The next day Senenmut was again summoned to the queen's council chamber. When he arrived he found her in consultation with Hapi-soneb, her vizier. She smiled warmly as he entered and invited him to be seated. As soon as he had done so she addressed him.

'The vizier and I are very impressed with your work on my behalf and I would like to show my appreciation… You are henceforth Overseer of The Granaries, from this day onwards, together with your other titles.'

Hapi-soneb nodded as if his confirmation were needed.

'See to it you serve the queen well in this, as you have in your other posts, Senenmut.'

The latter, ignoring the vizier's remarks, said to the queen, 'The harvest has been a very good one this year, Your Majesty, and the yield high. Have I your permission to donate a greater proportion to the populace of Thebes?'

'You are Overseer of The Granaries now, Senenmut. It is for you to decide,' exclaimed Hatshepsut.

'Just make sure that you do it in the queen's name,' put in Hapi-soneb. 'The people need to realise that she is indeed the living god and their benefactor.'

Senenmut smiled pointedly at both in turn.

'I have no doubt the people are already more than aware of the greatness of our beloved queen, but I shall take care to leave them in no doubt.'

'Very well said, Senenmut,' replied the queen. 'Now I think it would be expedient for you to sit in with the vizier and I. We are about to discuss the progress with the building of my tomb. You are aware of its location, are you not?'

'Indeed I am, Your Majesty, but I think it is a mistake.'

Hapi-soneb looked as if he was about to explode.

'Are you questioning the work of the architects, including the great Ineni, the favoured of the last Pharaoh, the living god, Tuthmosis II?'

'Not at all,' answered Senenmut quite casually. 'All I would say is that a hidden tomb some two hundred feet above the ground in a deserted valley is not a fitting memorial for a queen as great as ours.'

Hatshepsut blinked in amazement and for once appeared speechless.

The vizier sarcastically replied, 'You think you could do better than Ineni and his architects? Is there no end to your talents?'

'I did not say there was anything wrong with the tomb or its design... only its location.'

The queen recovered from the shock and said, 'Surely you know, Senenmut, that the work on this tomb began years ago... soon after I married my late husband, as was the custom.'

'This I know, Your Majesty. Surely now that you are regent of both upper and lower Egypt, a grander tomb in the new valley, selected for Pharaohs of your dynasty, would be more appropriate.'

The queen looked thoughtful and turned at once to the vizier. 'Is there any wisdom in Senenmut's suggestion?'

Hapi-soneb was visibly shaken but far from angry.

'I would need to discuss this with my fellow priests and your chancellor, Nehesy, before ruling on the matter, Your Majesty.'

'Then do so, Vizier, but remember that it is I who shall rule on this matter... You may leave.'

Both men rose to leave but the queen, with a smile, said, 'No, not you. I have further need of your thoughts, Senenmut. Kindly remain.'

Chapter III

No sooner had the vizier vacated the royal audience chamber than Hatshepsut moved much closer to Senenmut's side, so close, in fact, that her exotic perfume seemed to waft all around him.

'Your idea of a tomb in the valley greatly interests me, Senenmut... Enlighten me still further on this matter.'

'Think about it, Your Majesty. Who could gainsay such a plan? It will be many years before the new Pharaoh will come of age... You are the ruler both in theory and in practice. If all the kings of the new eighteenth dynasty are to be laid to rest there, then surely when your time comes you should be amongst them.'

Hatshepsut lent forward eagerly – strands of her long, luxuriant, black hair fell across Senenmut's hands and sent a shiver of excitement down his spine.

'But I am a queen, not a Pharaoh,' she huskily murmured.

Senenmut's eyes met hers and he could read the excitement in them. Was it him, or was it his plan that enthused and fuelled her interest?

Seizing his moment, he boldly continued, 'But what a queen, Your Majesty. No Pharaoh is your equal or ever was. Surely a title is in name only, and even in that, your claim to the throne is far greater than your stepson's. The people love you like a sister.'

In her excitement, Hatshepsut so far forgot herself that she placed a bejewelled hand on Senenmut's thigh. Senenmut pressed on with his narrative, although very aware of her physical presence.

'After all, you are, like your late husband, a true child of Tuthmosis I and the Queen Ahmose, whereas your stepson is merely the result of your former husband's liaison with a minor wife – the slave girl, Isis, from the harem.'

Doubt still showed on Hatshepsut's face.

Senenmut continued, 'Is it not true, Your Majesty, that the royal line always comes through the female heritage in this country of ours? Is that not why Pharaohs frequently marry their sisters to strengthen their claim?'

Senenmut looked alarmed at the example he had used for this was precisely what the queen's late husband had done. Would the queen now be greatly offended? She withdrew her hand from his thigh and he thought the moment was lost, but the act had only been to remove a strand of her hair that had fallen over one eye.

'It is true. Although you speak too boldly for a steward, not even my high priest and vizier would dare so address me.' The tone of her voice told him that she was not angry as much as amused at his audacity. 'And this new tomb in the valley…? Where would you have me interred?' she enquired.

'Should Your Majesty be interested, I could show you a drawing I have made of both the site and the tomb specifications.'

At this the queen threw back her head and laughed. It was a full, deep-throated and natural mellow tone that did much to reassure Senenmut that he had not overstepped the mark.

'Besides your other talents you are an architect?' she said incredulously.

'I always have been… in fact, I have drawn other plans for a magnificent mortuary temple to your honour.'

For once Hatshepsut looked quite thunderstruck. 'You have?' was all she could utter.

'Indeed I have. The tomb would be built in the valley

and a passage would run right through the rock to the new temple at Deir el-Bahri.'

The queen clutched at Senenmut's thigh in excitement.

'You have actually drawn the plans for such a project?'

'Most certainly, Your Majesty.'

'Where are they…? I would see them this instant.'

'In my quarters, but I can go and fetch them should you wish.'

'No. I shall come with you to your quarters,' the queen said and jumped excitedly to her feet. 'Lead on, Senenmut,' she commanded.

Half an hour later Hatshepsut was virtually glowing, having spent some twenty minutes studying Senenmut's plans which were drawn on papyrus. She questioned him at length on the feasibility of the project and then, standing back, viewed him with open admiration.

'This design is worthy of the great Inhotep himself and of our architect, Ineni.'

'No, Your Majesty. I think it will surpass anything that those worthy and talented nobles have ever achieved and it will be in your honour.'

Hatshepsut ignored the boast, so excited was she with the idea.

'You are hereby appointed Overseer of the Works and I command that the work shall begin at once, on the building of both my tomb and temple. You will report to me daily of your progress.'

'It shall be as you wish, Your Majesty, but what of your old rock tomb, where you were to be interred as queen?'

'Oh, that! Oh, I think we can leave that for the time being… Now be off with you and make your requisites known to the treasurer, Thuty. Tell him that no expense is to be spared. I shall dedicate the temple, when it is completed, to the goddess, Hathor.'

'It will, of course, take many years to complete, Your Majesty.'

'The sooner the work commences the quicker it will be completed,' enthused the queen.

The infant king, the young Tuthmosis III, was growing fast. Even at this stage of his life he was totally preoccupied with playing at battles and war games. When he wasn't so employed, he would spend every moment that he could away from his tutor, watching the royal guards drill, or the charioteers working with their horses. A bow had been specially made for him, and courtiers would frequently have to move with alacrity, as the youngster was not averse to using the less prominent nobles, and slaves, as targets.

These days he had little to do with his half-sister, Neferure, not that she minded, as the two had little in common. She had been upset enough to find that his words were, in fact, true and that she was contracted to marry him the following year. Neferure had bitterly complained to her mother when the high priest had informed her of the future ceremony. The queen, although sympathetic, had merely said that she shouldn't worry her head about it, as it was only a formality that was customary and expected. After all, hadn't she herself been forced to marry Neferure's father, her half-brother. The little girl wandered off, wondering just why that made it right. After all, she didn't even like little Tuthmosis and it was quite obvious that he had little time for her.

She was very happy to spend most of her waking day with Senenmut, her tutor, whom she simply adored. Sometimes he would allow her to accompany him when he was directing the building of her mother's new temple. Before her nurse prepared her for bed, she would sometimes sit on his knee and he would tell her the most wonderful stories about days gone by, and of the old

Pharaohs and queens of Egypt.

Everyone at the royal palace these days seemed very happy. Her mother had become very popular with both nobles and servants and everywhere she went in Thebes the people cheered her. One day Neferure asked Senenmut about this.

'Why was my father not as popular with the people as my mother is?'

'Queen Hatshepsut presides over an Egypt at peace, whereas your father and your grandfather too, for that matter, were frequently at war with our enemies. Perhaps it is because of the tranquillity the country has achieved under her regency.'

'People are saying that my mother should be the Pharaoh... I hear it everywhere,' whispered Neferure.

'There are certainly many who believe it so,' answered Senenmut.

'Can a queen rule in Egypt?'

'There has never been one that has. Perhaps in the future one will.'

'You mean my mother?'

Senenmut just smiled.

'We shall have to wait and see, won't we, little one.'

For the time being Neferure had to be content with this.

Thuty, the treasurer, raised one hand to his brow to shield his eyes from the glare of the setting sun. Together with Hapi-soneb, he was surveying the development of the new temple building at Deir el-Bahri.

'This is indeed a magnificent building, or will certainly be so when it is completed,' he exclaimed, admiration and awe in his voice.

'Certainly the progress made on it, by Senenmut and his workmen, in the last two years since its inception has been truly incredible,' affirmed Hapi-soneb.

'I have never seen the queen so excited about anything as she has been with this building,' added Thuty, 'although the cost of materials is proving phenomenal.'

'Trust you to think of that, Thuty.'

'It is my responsibility after all, but for such a work of art the expense is, I think, justified.'

'Senenmut seems to be the man the queen turns to for advice on everything these days,' remarked Hapi-soneb.

'Are you jealous? After all, you are her vizier and high priest.'

'I suppose I should be,' answered Hapi-soneb, 'but since Senenmut's arrival at the court, some three years ago, we have experienced only peace and harmony in Thebes... That can only be good for Egypt.'

Thuty glanced to left and right to make sure that he was not overheard.

'It is time, I think, for us to persuade the Overseer of Works, Senenmut, to convince the queen she should declare herself Pharaoh outright... The young boy, Tuthmosis, is but eight years old and thinks only of playing with his soldiers... Egypt cannot go on for another seven or eight years without a king.'

'Some would say you speak treason, Thuty.'

The smile on Hapi-soneb's countenance suggested that he wasn't one of them.

The following day the high priest and vizier summoned Senenmut to a meeting. When the latter arrived he found Thuty, the treasurer, and Nehesy, the chancellor, in attendance. Once all four occupants of the chamber were seated the vizier addressed Senenmut.

'We have summoned you here to commend you on your excellent work both on the mortuary temple and the tomb.'

Senenmut replied modestly that the work on the new tomb was largely the responsibility of his assistant, Amunhotep.

'True,' replied Hapi-soneb, 'but it is well known the plan and execution of the work is down to you.'

'Egypt owes you a great debt,' put in Thuty.

The chancellor, Nehesy, rose tall and dignified from behind the carved marble table. He cleared his throat before addressing Senenmut.

'We intend to recommend to the queen that you be appointed chief architect together with your other titles.'

Senenmut smiled knowingly and said, 'For the honour you bestow on me I thank you most sincerely... but do I suspect that you want something in return?'

All three men looked rather embarrassed. Hapi-soneb was the first to recover.

'It is plain that you are a very astute man, Senenmut. We want you to convince the queen that she should stand formally as Pharaoh of upper and lower Egypt.'

There followed an ominous silence.

'Egypt has never had a queen as Pharaoh,' said Senenmut, breaking the deadlock.

'This we know,' replied Nehesy, the chancellor, 'but the time, we feel, has arrived. Queen Hatshepsut is popular with the people and with the court. Egypt is ripe for change.'

'Why do you want me to speak to her, concerning this issue...? You are, after all, senior to me – all of you?'

Thuty smiled knowingly. 'It is well known that the queen is greatly influenced by you. Therefore the suggestion coming from you would be well received.'

'And you would certainly have the backing of us all,' enthused Hapi-soneb.

'Then I shall certainly give the matter some thought, although I make no promises,' remarked Senenmut, slowly rising. 'Now, if there is nothing else, gentlemen, I must be about my business. My workmen at the temple will be needing my directions.'

'That is all we ask of you. Think about it, Senenmut,' concluded Nehesy.

The following day Senenmut found his position of chief architect confirmed by the queen. It was with some sadness, for the first to congratulate him was the old and great architect, Ineni. Warmly, out of mutual respect, both men shook hands. Senenmut tried to explain the decision was not of his making. Ineni went on to say that every man had his day and that Senenmut richly deserved his promotion, for everyone accepted that the new mortuary temple was indeed the best in all Egypt. Nevertheless it was with sorrow that Senenmut watched the old man stumble away. He resolved then that he would always seek Ineni's advice on architectural matters, if only as a salve to the great man's pride. Senenmut's own conscience was troubled, as he had been giving the proposition of the day before, serious thought.

Over the years he had formed a warm affection for Queen Hatshepsut and virtually looked on his little pupil, her daughter Neferure, as his own child. At the back of his astute mind was the feeling that the three leading officials were right, and that Egypt needed a ruling Pharaoh, and not just a regent. However, should he persuade Hatshepsut to accept the throne, certain people of high rank would consider the act treasonable. The foremost of these would certainly be Thanuny, commander of the army, a traditionalist and supporter of the young Tuthmosis. A close second would be Rekhmire, the royal scribe. Senenmut knew he would have to take time to make his mind up carefully and weigh up all the options before deciding to talk to the queen.

Other problems troubled him greatly. His growing affection for the queen was one of them. He was constantly becoming more and more aware of her physical presence. She had begun to consult him on all matters of state, even to the extent of having him sit with her whilst she presided over the weekly court of grievances.

Under his direction the great mortuary temple of Deir el-Bahri was fast growing. Already the first and lower tier was complete and work had begun on the second level. Senenmut planned to build an avenue of sphinxes, each with the head of his beloved queen as an approach. Soon he would need to advise Hatshepsut to send an expedition to the land of Punt, to secure the shrubs and trees he would need to place around the lower steps and walkway ramps.

His assistant, Amunhotep, was experiencing great difficulty with the new tomb in the valley. Hard rock and bad air were only two of the difficulties. Tomorrow he must go down and see for himself. It had been Senenmut's original intention to cut a passage right through the cliffs from the mortuary temple to the tomb in the valley. Amunhotep had now said this was no longer feasible, the rock his men were coming up against was too hard. There was nothing for it but to examine the situation himself. Perhaps Amunhotep was right and the whole idea had been too ambitious. There were other aspects to consider too. If Queen Hatshepsut was to grow in popularity beyond the walls of Thebes, more must be accomplished in middle Egypt. Temples and monuments would need to be built there as well. If the work in the valley tomb was proving very arduous for Amunhotep, perhaps he would send him on a building expedition to middle Egypt and take over the work in the tomb himself. He could easily move between the temple and tomb, supervising each in turn.

Already he had plans for two large obelisks to be built at the temple of Karnak but he would need red granite from the quarries at Aswan if his queen's memory were to be perpetuated and prolonged into eternity.

Several days went by before Senenmut finally resolved to speak to the queen on all these issues. Hatshepsut seemed aghast at his suggestion of an expedition to the land of Punt (modern Somalia as we know it).

'I couldn't possibly spare you. Your presence here is vital.'

'Could your chancellor, Nehesy, not lead such an expedition? It would be merely to trade for the requisites we need?' Senenmut asked.

Hatshepsut seemed much happier with this suggestion.

'I do not see why not... What would we give in trade for the items we would need?'

'Beads, semi-precious stones, baubles, cotton... trivial things like that,' he replied.

'I shall speak to Nehesy and have him organise such a mission.'

For some time the two of them went on to discuss the development of the temple and tomb work, but finally came the burning issue of the succession. At first the queen was horrified by the suggestion of declaring herself Pharaoh outright, and Senenmut began to feel that he had gone a step too far. However, he pressed on with his argument reiterating the queen's superior heritage along the royal line. She grudgingly began to relent and became more amenable to his persuasion.

'We can even say you were not the natural daughter of your father, Tuthmosis I, but that your father was the god, Amun, himself.'

'Would the people believe such a story?' Hatshepsut enquired doubtfully.

'Your people love you, Your Majesty, even as I your subject love you... They will believe whatever we tell them.'

Hatshepsut looked visibly shaken at this declaration by Senenmut. Not about to lose his advantage, he pressed onward.

'You will be the greatest Pharaoh Egypt has or ever will

know, Your Majesty.'

The queen recovered her composure.

'Do my other ministers know of this?'

'All of them… We all want you to assume the throne.'

'Then I shall give the matter serious thought, even though my late husband had my stepson crowned at birth as Tuthmosis III, which means I shall be a usurper.'

'But a noble one, Your Majesty,' exclaimed Senenmut.

Chapter IV

Hatshepsut did indeed give Senenmut's proposal very serious thought. The idea of immaculate conception by the god Amun's visitation on her mother, Ahmose, resulting in her birth, greatly pleased her. After all, she knew, as did all Egyptians, that life here was but a preparation for the great after-life to come, for all eternity. Therefore she believed that her people would welcome such a statement. More and more she was becoming obsessed with the architect, Senenmut, and depended on him for advice, to a much greater extent than she did her vizier and high priest, Hapi-soneb.

It was now three years since the death of her late husband, Tuthmosis II. She had never welcomed the decision her beloved father had forced upon her to marry her half-brother. In fact, their marriage had been something of a sham, a sop to both custom and convention. The times that the two of them had cohabited could safely be counted on both hands, and once Neferure had been born even that ceased. Not that Hatshepsut minded. She was quite content that Tuthmosis should console himself with his harem girls, one of whom, Isis, had presented him with her troublesome little stepson. Hatshepsut counted herself lucky that, considering the number of harem girls at the palace, there were not more offspring of his loins. Hatshepsut herself had always been more interested in affairs of state than sexual relations. The idea of being unfaithful hadn't even occurred to her, until now, that was. Should she indulge her desire and begin an affair with Senenmut? She was certainly attracted to him more so than she had ever been, to any man since her father. One thing was certain. In her high and exalted position he would never dare to suggest such a liaison himself. Any overtures would surely have to come from her. There were times lately when she had felt very alone and in need of physical comfort. Spiritual comfort from her high priest and vizier, Hapi-soneb, were all very well, but that didn't satisfy a woman's inner need.

She looked at her reflection in the still waters of the palace pool. Was she not an attractive woman? Her long, black, silken hair hung loosely over her shoulders, and the chill of the cold spring water made her nipples stand out provocatively from firm, well-rounded, small breasts. Climbing from the pool, she looked down at a tight narrow waist, which accentuated the well-rounded hips, giving way to long, shapely, elegantly firm legs. Two handmaidens stepped forward to drape her wet dripping body with a decorative cotton towel. Gently, but firmly, they proceeded to dry her. This accomplished, Hatshepsut lay naked on a marble plinth covered with several layers of exquisite silk over a mattress of cotton, stuffed with goose down. The two handmaidens proceeded to massage their queen with aromatic and perfumed oils, until she glowed and purred with satisfaction. Finally, the two girls assisted her to dress in the finest satin and silk. After dismissing them, she was left again to her own thoughts, before another ebony-skinned handmaiden arrived to plait her long dark hair and apply her mistress's make-up.

Thus, another day for the queen was beginning.

Hatshepsut, although she probably didn't know it, had two very powerful enemies in Egypt. One was Thanuny, the commander of the army, the other Rekhmire, the royal scribe. Both men were staunch traditionalists and bitterly opposed to change. The very idea of a female Pharaoh wouldn't even have occurred to them. As far as they were concerned the queen was much too powerful already in her role as regent. Of course, there was little that they could do. After all, her husband had named her regent on his death-bed, so who could gainsay her? Whether they accepted it or not, Hatshepsut was the power in Egypt, as the new Pharaoh was a mere eight years old. Thanuny pointed out to Rekhmire that, as soon as the young Tuthmosis was old enough, he, Thanuny, would ask the queen's permission to have the boy king trained for army life. Rekhmire had laughed at this and agreed that the boy thought of little else other than soldiers and battles.

'One day he will make a fine Pharaoh, and therefore it is a military training that he will require, not the company of harem girls and simpering women... which is all he will receive at court,' remarked Thanuny.

'Will the queen consent to this?' asked Rekhmire, doubtfully.

'When the time comes I have no doubt she will be pleased to see the back of him. I am told neither has much love for the other,' said Rekhmire and laughed – a mirthless rattling sound.

'Well, what do you expect, when her husband preferred a harem girl to sire an heir?'

Thanuny snorted. 'It is said that our late Pharaoh was never very welcome in her bed anyway.'

Deep in conversation, the two men were strolling round the sacred lake of Karnak temple.

Rekhmire placed one finger alongside his nose before whispering, 'You would do well to mind how you speak of this matter. The queen has the power to remove you as commander of the army, should she so decide.'

'Why would she do that? Do I not keep her borders free from invaders, so that she may govern us in peace?'

'Surely the Hyksos (Asiatics) are long gone from our fair land, driven out by Segenence Tao and his son, Kamose, then later by Abmose I, who even pursued them to their own land of Palestine.'

'All of this is true, Rekhmire, but you too, as a scribe, must realise that there are always the Syrians and other border raiders.'

Rekhmire, a sardonic smile on his face retorted, 'You old warhorse. Sometimes I think you were born to fight.'

Thanuny raised his eyebrows.

'And to train Pharaohs to fight, don't ever forget that.'

Senenmut's propaganda machine was almost ready to launch the queen as outright Pharaoh. For the last few weeks he had cleverly been laying the foundations and acquiring support for Hatshepsut. Now all he was waiting for was the queen's assent. That evening at sunset he would go to see her. Such was his elevated position in the court of the royal temple that he no longer had to wait for the royal summons. The queen, it seemed, was always ready to grant him an audience. To his other titles she had now added Overseer of the Fields of Amun, Overseer of the Gardens of Amun, and Overseer of the Weavers of Amun. Only the vizier and high priest, Hapi-soneb, had more nominal power, but everyone was well aware that it was Senenmut who exercised influence over the queen.

Never had the time been more right for Senenmut's move to gain ultimate glory for the queen. Already in her early thirties and loved by the people of Thebes she was at the height of her ruling power as regent. He was confident that the population of both upper and lower Egypt would accept her as Pharaoh. His one obstacle was to overcome Hatshepsut's own resistance and convince her of the wisdom of his plan.

The sun was already falling below the western peaks when he set off for her quarters in the palace. An attractive semi-nude Nubian girl admitted him into Hatshepsut's audience chamber and then disappeared beyond the screened area in search of her mistress. A few moments later she reappeared and announced that the queen would be with him within a few minutes.

Senenmut settled down to await the queen's pleasure. It wasn't long before she appeared, looking very radiant in a long, almost transparent gown of silvery blue. Her brown shoulders were bare and her lustrous dark hair cascaded down over them. There was a pleasant rustling sound as she approached and even at a distance of a few metres, the exotic aroma of her perfume reached him. Senenmut could feel the warmth in his loins and the tingle in his spine, but tried hard to keep his mind on business. Stepping forward, he took her outstretched hand and raised it gently to his lips, his eyes never leaving the queen's deep brown ones. The greeting attended to, he lost no time in coming to the point.

'Has Your Majesty come to a decision yet regarding my proposal?'

Hatshepsut studied him coquettishly from beneath long dark lashes before replying, 'And what proposal was that, Senenmut, my steward?'

Senenmut realised she was playing with him, by deciding to be deliberately obtuse.

'I think Your Majesty is well aware of the love and respect her people hold for her... Will you now not declare yourself Pharaoh over all Egypt? This is a decision that could only be well received. Light of the world, chosen of the gods, guardian of all Egypt and protector of her people, I humbly beseech you to accept.'

Hatshepsut was astute, as well as beautiful.

'By what right do you offer this, Senenmut, my steward?'

She was, he realised, putting him firmly in his place. Maybe he had overstepped the mark and gone too far.

However, her smile reassured him and he pressed on.

'I act for the good of the people, my beloved queen. I speak for them.'

'And what of Hapi-soneb, my high priest and vizier. What says he of this plan?'

'Together with Thuty, your treasurer, and Nehesy, your chancellor, he agrees with me... Your Majesty should accept the crown.'

'Has the Pharaoh of Egypt not always been a man?'

'To date that is true, Your Majesty, but on all public occasions we shall have you dressed as a man, even to the point of you wearing a false beard for royal ceremonies.'

Hatshepsut chuckled.

'I hope it is a straight beard and not turned up at the end in a curve.'

Senenmut knew she alluded to the custom of dead Pharaohs being always depicted with a curved beard.

'Of course, Your Highness,' he responded. 'You would wear the full double crown of Egypt, with the cobra and vulture, the historic kilt pectoral, together with all the gold and jewels of your rank.'

Hatshepsut smiled and placed both hands over small breasts.

'And these? What do you and the rest of my nobles suggest I do with these?'

Senenmut showed his embarrassment and Hatshepsut was delighted to see him blush beneath his tan.

'You would only be a man metaphorically, my queen, and addressed as such. All would know that you were truly a woman.'

Laughing, she said, 'Well, that's comforting anyway, to know that you do not wish me to change sex completely.' She was quite enjoying Senenmut's obvious discomfiture.

He blustered on, saying, 'You would be far too beautiful, even wearing a false beard, to fool even a cretin.'

'You find me beautiful then, do you, Senenmut, my steward?'

'Your Majesty's grace is that of the swan in the water, the antelope in flight. Your radiance cannot be matched by the sweetest wild flower. Egypt has never seen such a queen.'

'And yet you would turn me into a man?' Hatshepsut, smiling, goaded him.

'Only for festivals and royal occasions of religion and justice,' Senenmut countered.

'Come, sit awhile here with me,' said Hatshepsut, seating herself on a silken divan. She patted the cushion beside her.

Senenmut saw that her dress had parted to reveal an elegantly shaped thigh. With greater alacrity than was necessary, he sat down beside her, finding it hard to remove his eyes from the shapely limb. Hatshepsut couldn't help but notice the direction of his eyes.

'Do you not have any harem girls of your own, Senenmut? I would have thought that with the high position to which you are now raised, you would have acquired some. Most of my officers and nobles do.'

'Your Majesty, my work on your behalf occupies my every waking moment and even the most beautiful Asiatic or Nubian wench would pale beside you. My service to you is my one desire.'

Hatshepsut looked pleased and made no attempt to conceal the exposed thigh, but rather drew attention to it further, by gently stroking the smooth skin with the backs of the fingers of one hand. She continued to grill Senenmut on the practicalities of accepting the crown, pointing out possible drawbacks. He defended her every objection with consummate skill, and frequently, being devil's advocate, turned her arguments back on herself. Finally, he could see that she was both flattered and almost converted to the idea.

Just when he thought he had won, Hatshepsut rose elegantly to her feet and looked down on him.

'You say my people love me, Senenmut, and you, would you do anything for me...? Would you support me in all things... whatever I ask of you, without question?'

'Until death, Your Majesty... I would give my very life for you.'

She smiled knowingly and turned towards her boudoir. At the curtained and beaded screen, she turned briefly to face him.

'Come back at twelve of the clock this night and I shall give you my answer.'

Almost before Senenmut could digest this latter remark Hatshepsut had disappeared from his sight through the screen.

Senenmut returned to his own quarters in the palace, his heart beating wildly. He knew that there could be only one reason for the queen's invitation to him. To pass the time, which seemed like eternity, he read, but finding it hard to keep his mind on his books, he gave up and bathed, finishing by applying a perfumed cologne. Dressing in his finest apparel, he awaited the hour of midnight. At five minutes to, he set off for the queen's apartment. Arriving in the outer chamber he found no guards at the entrance. This greatly surprised him but, on reflection, he realised the queen must have dismissed them. Passing on into the entrance hall he remained unchallenged. Even in the outer reception chamber he found no dusky Nubian handmaiden to greet him.

Standing alone there, he was uncertain about his next move. Moonlight flooded into the chamber, reflecting off the marble pillars. All the candles and oil lamps had been extinguished. He heard a faint rustling sound from the inner chamber. This was followed by a deep, husky whisper for him to enter. Senenmut tiptoed through the curtained screen, an area forbidden to all but the queen's personal maids and herself. Rooted to the spot, he gasped aloud. Silhouetted in the moonlit archway to the balcony was Hatshepsut, dressed in only the flimsiest of garments. From where he stood, he could see every sensuous curve of her finely formed body through her attire.

She turned towards him, arms outstretched. Through his excitement grave doubts assailed him. What if he failed to become aroused? What if he failed to satisfy her? Should he make the first move? Overawed, he wondered and agonised how one went about making love to your queen, the ruler of your country. After all, she had such power over all her subjects. Then a new confidence surged within him. After all, hadn't she chosen him as her lover, when she could have had anybody in her realm. Putting doubt behind him, he walked boldly towards Hatshepsut's open arms. She reached out, gripping his biceps.

Holding him at arm's length, she addressed him in a half-whisper, 'Earlier you said you would give your life for me.'

Senenmut tensed, wondering what was coming next. He swallowed hard and murmured, 'All that I have is yours, my queen.'

'For a woman widowed early in life by her husband's untimely death, life can be very lonely and for a queen doubly so,' Hatshepsut whispered. Her fingers were still holding his arms vicelike in their intensity. He sensed that she was as nervous as he.

'I do understand, my queen,' he repeated earnestly.

'Do you?' she countered. 'And do you also understand, if we are to be lovers, no one must ever hear of this...? Always you must return to your own quarters before dawn... I cannot afford to have you seen here... ever.'

'Yes, Your Majesty, all of that is clear,' he replied.

Hatshepsut gave a low, seductive and throaty chuckle.

'I think it will be appropriate for you to call me something else, other than my royal requirement, when we are alone. At other times, and in company, full ceremony must be observed… Is that clear?'

'What would you have me call you, Your M—'

The two of them, seeing the humour in this, broke into laughter. Senenmut was the first to recover.

'Hatshepsut, foremost of noble ladies, whose throne name is Maat-ka-re, which translated is "Truth is the Soul of Re", I shall call you Ka-re, for it seems to fit you well.'

'So shall it be. I like it well and you – who shall you be – I know… Djehutymes… I shall call you after my father.'

Senenmut inwardly winced at the connotation, and remembered an earlier comment about the queen, whom he once overheard two nobles discussing in the palace grounds. It was that Hatshepsut had a father fixation for her sire, Tuthmosis I. Immediately, he put it from his mind. Suddenly, he realised Hatshepsut had released her steellike grip on his upper arms and lowered her own to her sides. Turning, she retraced her steps, until she was silhouetted in the shaft of moonlight invading the boudoir from the archway. She turned slowly for his inspection, a seductive smile on her face.

'Do you like what you see, Djehutymes?'

Senenmut's mouth went dry. He could only murmur his assent.

'Then you may undress me, or would you rather I sent for my maids?'

With some alacrity Senenmut crossed the chamber to stand facing her. The exotic and erotic aroma of her perfume seemed to be everywhere. Somehow he instantly knew she would expect boldness from him. Given this opportunity, of which he had almost dreamed, he wasn't about to disappoint her. Reaching up, he sprung the gold clasp that secured her toga-like dress. With a soft swishing sound the garment slid, or rather seemed to slither, down her satiny skin to encircle her small dainty feet, leaving her totally naked except for her golden necklace and amulet.

Senenmut put his arms around Hatshepsut and pulled her firmly to him. The warmth of her naked flesh made his fingers tingle with excitement. Their lips met in a fierce hunger, accentuated by long abstinence. His every advance was returned with a warm passionate response. He turned his attention to her graceful neck, down over her shoulders to firm breasts, nipples protruding to meet his eager tongue. Suddenly, unable to control his anticipation a moment longer, he broke away and scooped her up in his arms, carrying her to the large canopied bed. Pushing the nets aside, he gently lay her on the satin counterpane. Quickly he disrobed and joined her on the bed. Hatshepsut's arms reached up to receive him. Their warm bodies interlocked. Her probing tongue forced his lips apart. His own tongue danced with hers before overpowering it and forcing it back between her strong, white teeth. Senenmut heard her gasp and drove his own tongue deeper into her throat. Hatshepsut's hips came up under him in her eagerness. Senenmut gripped her buttocks and pulled her onto his engorged member.

Already deliciously moist, he slid into her with ease and heard her moan with pleasure. She was his now. First he played her with slow, tantalising, exquisite movements, then gradually he quickened the pace. Gasping, she rose to meet each vibrant thrust from his loins. Then she climaxed in a glorious ecstasy of pleasure. Senenmut was only a split second behind her. Never had he known such a woman.

For a long while after, they lay in one another's arms, observing silence, neither speaking. Then her long delicate fingers were playing with him once more, and Senenmut was surprised how quickly he became aroused.

An hour before dawn Senenmut dressed, ready to leave for his own quarters in the palace.

'One moment, Djehutymes,' called Hatshepsut from the bed.

Senenmut halted at the beaded and curtained screen and turned to face her. The moon had long since gone. She was only a shadowy form on the bed now.

'Come back this afternoon and we shall discuss how you are going to make me into Pharaoh.'

Senenmut smiled, swept the curtaining aside, and left.

Later that same afternoon he was back with the queen in her audience chamber. This time they were accompanied by Hapi-soneb, the high priest and vizier.

Senenmut outlined the moves that should be made for the public to accept Hatshepsut as Pharaoh outright. Grants of land to certain individuals, more allocations of deben and grain to the poor. Promotion of certain individuals in influential positions and, above all, an increase in monetary reward to the senior priests and scribes.

At this, Hapi-soneb watched the queen's reaction with more than a little interest. When she didn't answer, he interjected, 'What thinks Your Majesty of Senenmut the architect's plan?'

'I agree to all these requests. You may have my chancellor, Nehesy, make the necessary announcements, Hapi-soneb. I am sure Senenmut, my personal steward, will give you the details.'

'Indeed, Your Majesty,' went on Senenmut, 'but there is more yet.'

The queen eyed him with renewed interest.

'Go on,' she said.

'Something memorable should be accomplished in your reign as Pharaoh, besides the battles and wars fought by earlier kings of Egypt.'

'What do you suggest, Senenmut?' she queried, moving forward, with excitement, on her throne.

'Allow me to lead an expedition by ship to the land of Punt, thereby to trade and bring back the goods of that land. I shall then have a record carved into the new mortuary temple, depicting the event to your honour, Your Majesty.'

Hatshepsut looked thoughtful and there was an ominous pause in which Hapi-soneb and Senenmut glanced at one another.

'The plan is sound, Senenmut, my steward, but I cannot spare you. Your work here in the valley and on my mortuary temple at Deir el-Bahri is too important for you to leave, not to mention the supervising of the red granite obelisks arriving from the quarries of Aswan for erection at Karnak... No, my chancellor, Nehesy, can lead the expedition to Punt.'

Although his request to lead the expedition had been quashed, Senenmut was not altogether put out. At least the queen favoured the mission. He nodded. 'It shall be as Your Majesty wishes.'

Hapi-soneb now put forward a plan of his own. It was for the queen to be dressed in the full regalia of Pharaoh whenever she appeared in public. At first Hatshepsut looked delighted, but then realised that the high priest expected her to dress as a man. She shook her head, but looked at Senenmut for support. He smiled reassuringly.

'Do not distress yourself, Majesty. I have a plan that I shall discuss with you in private at a more appropriate time.'

'Then I shall listen,' was all she would give either of them.

Chapter V

Nehesy, the chancellor, not the happiest man at this present time in Egypt, sat at the stern of an Egyptian ship. The vessel was making sluggish time in a southerly direction down the Red Sea. Only a light wind filled the sails, but Nehesy had no wish to use his several banks of galley slaves at the oars, unless the ship became completely becalmed. No doubt before this expedition was over he would have need of every man. The vessel sat low in the water, filled to the gunwales with items of trade, mostly semi-precious baubles, grain and rolls of material and suchlike. His orders were to sail to the land of Punt and trade them for the fragrant incense trees and spices that were indigenous to that land.

Why he had been selected as envoy to lead this voyage he couldn't even hazard a guess. One thing he did know was that it wouldn't be without its dangers and it would take some little time to accomplish and return home to Thebes, where at this time he would much rather have been.

As ordered, he had made the announcement that Queen Hatshepsut was now Pharaoh, but he had yet to see this very feminine-looking woman dressed as a man. The first ceremony of Amun was fully a week away, when she would make her primary appearance dressed in the full regalia of Pharaoh, at Karnak.

How would the people of Thebes and indeed Egypt accept her? True, she was very much loved and respected as queen, but, after all, the boy king Tuthmosis III was rightfully Pharaoh, as decreed by his father. It was said she was to be dressed as a male Pharaoh. He would have given his eye-teeth to have been there, but no, he had to lead this mission, simply because he had some knowledge of navigation and his exalted rank would make him a good envoy to the queen of Punt. That was Hapi-soneb's persuasive argument anyway, but the whole thing had been the idea of the architect, Senenmut. It was even whispered in the palace that Hatshepsut wanted to keep her steward with her.

Nehesy looked up at the sail, now hanging aimlessly from the twin masts. Even the light Red Sea wind had abated. He ordered the captain to put the galley slaves to work. The man relayed the order to the two whip-wielding overseers and the drum station took up its ominous beat. Dark-skinned, muscled backs were bent, the slaves straining at the oars, sweat running down their work-tortured bodies. Gradually the ship began to move again, increasing its pace slowly, ripples of foam showing at the blades of the oars and leaving a trail of froth in their wake. Nehesy shut his eyes against the hot sun and soon fell into a fitful sleep.

★

That night, after an hour of torrid lovemaking with Hatshepsut, Senenmut was ready to outline his plan to her. Elaborately he explained the details, and her eyes widened in both astonishment and horror.

'Impossible!' she exclaimed, the venom evident in her tone.

Senenmut caressed her cheek with the backs of his fingers.

'No, it is not impossible, and if we are to have people accept you as Pharaoh, then it must be done.'

'But surely what you suggest is physically impossible,' she protested.

Senenmut only smiled and produced a roll of silken material. Slowly and deliberately he unfurled it and handed the contents to the queen. It was a perfectly formed, hard, leather penis and it was attached to a complicated-looking hessian harness. Hatshepsut turned it over and explored the object, examining its every detail.

'Where did you get this, Djehutymes?'

'I made it with my own hands, fashioned it out of my love for you. The idea came to me from something you said to me last night.'

'Oh – and what might that have been?' she asked guardedly.

'I remembered you telling me how excited you became, when, one day as a young girl, you came across your father making love to a Nubian slave girl.'

'It is true. I stood and watched... Neither knew I was there. The girl was on all fours and my father mounted her from behind... She screamed and moaned with pleasure... It was then, I think, that I first became a woman. I remained in hiding, shaking with excitement until they left... I was no more than thirteen years at the time.'

Senenmut leaned forward and kissed Hatshepsut on the neck.

'It must be done, Ka-re... if we are to have people believe that you are the natural offspring of the god, Amun, himself, which is the story Hapi-soneb, Thuty, Nehesy and myself have put around.'

'Surely they will never believe this,' she protested.

'They will, for they will see the evidence for themselves and be convinced that you are a magical male Pharaoh when you choose to be.'

'Can we not wait and see whether people believe this first, before we...' She fingered the contraption once more with distaste and looked at Senenmut in hope.

'No, Ka-re, we cannot wait. It must be done before the

Festival of Amun in four days' time at Karnak.'

'Why?' she questioned him.

'Because the story must get around before that date, so it must be tomorrow night, for there will be an eclipse of the moon then. Just right for our little enactment.'

'Very well, Djehutymes. It shall be as you say, but by the goddess, Hathor herself, I hope that you are right for the sake of Egypt... Now, tell me again what I must do.'

'Neither you nor Egypt will ever regret it... Tomorrow night I shall help you into the harness. Then, when the moon is obscured and the light has gone, you will send for one of your handmaidens. You will order her to go down on all fours and you will mount her like you saw your father do all those years ago. She must know it is you... Be fierce and terrify the girl. Only stop when you are sure she has climaxed, then dismiss her, commanding her to send in the other girl. Repeat the same with her.'

'The idea of this greatly offends me,' protested Hatshepsut.

'Not when you see the result. You are well aware how these Nubian girls tittle-tattle. By the next night the story will be all over Thebes and you will be assured of acceptance by the public at the festival.'

'Even Thanuny and Rekhmire? You know they are hostile towards me,' she protested anew.

'Even so, they would not dare gainsay such a legend. All will believe you are the offspring of Amun himself.'

'And you? Where will you be during this... this thing that I must do?'

'I shall be with you at all times, although of necessity I shall remain hidden.' Seeing the doubt on her face, he tried to encourage her by adding, 'Try to think that you are your own father and they his slave girls. It may help.'

'And afterwards, what then?'

'Afterwards, Ka-re, I shall make love to you and there

will be no doubt that you are all woman.'

For the first time she smiled, saying, 'Well, that I can look forward to anyway.'

Together they laughed and she led him once more to the bed.

'You can show me now how you will do it,' she commanded.

'Certainly, Your Majesty,' he chuckled.

The following morning Thanuny, chief of the army, came to see the queen. With him was Rekhmire, the vizier of young Tuthmosis, her stepson. She received the two solemn-looking men in her audience chamber. Thanuny, fresh from exercise drill in the palace grounds, was still dressed in his battle armour. Rekhmire, as usual, stroked his small black beard and, after bowing to the queen, observed her through sharp deep-set eyes, from under bushy eyebrows.

'You wished to see me, gentlemen?' she ventured.

'Yes, Your Majesty,' answered Thanuny, in his deep, gruff and gravely voice. 'It is about your stepson, Tuthmosis. As you know he is very interested in the army.'

'I am aware that he spends much of his time, when he should be about his lessons, playing with soldiers and fighting imaginary enemies,' Hatshepsut countered.

'Enemies are not always imaginary, Your Majesty. A Pharaoh must learn to fight and lead his armies,' put in Rekhmire.

Before she could answer, Thanuny quickly broke in, 'The vizier is right. The boy king must learn the arts and secrets of armies. Martial arts are a must for all of Egypt's kings.'

Hatshepsut was well aware that this was a veiled insult to her as a woman. She ignored it, refusing to rise to the bait.

She replied, 'The boy, Tuthmosis, is but eight years old. What does he know of armies and war?'

It was Thanuny's turn to ignore the question this time.

'On the Nubian border I am training officers for the Egyptian army, under my deputy, Djehutymes*, a general appointed by you.'

'And?' said the queen, raising her eyebrows.

Thanuny glanced at Rekhmire for support.

'I think that what General Thanuny is asking, is if you will consent to having your stepson consigned to his care, at the army camp?'

'Have you talked of this to the boy, Tuthmosis?' queried the queen.

'Indeed, in the vizier's presence I have talked to the young Pharaoh and he is very desirous of joining the army,' said Thanuny.

Another veiled insult to Hatshepsut went ignored. She well knew he was trying to unsettle her, letting her know he recognised only the young Tuthmosis as Pharaoh. Hatshepsut looked from one to the other, letting the request and its possible complications sink in before replying.

'I shall discuss the matter with my own vizier and chancellor and let you know my answer.' She emphasised the word 'own', in retaliation of the insult to her.

'But, Your Majesty, your chancellor is on the Red Sea on a voyage to the land of Punt... He cannot be back for weeks. I beseech you – this matter is of the utmost urgency,' objected Rekhmire.

'I have appointed the chief architect, my steward, Senenmut, to deputise as chancellor in his absence... I shall let you know my decision by tomorrow morning. Now, will that be all, gentlemen?'

---

* Djehutymes bore the same name that Hatshepsut had chosen for Senenmut.

Thanuny gave a surly nod and Rekhmire an over-elaborate bow. A moment later, both men backed out of the audience chamber. Outside, and out of hearing of the two armed eunuchs guarding the queen's audience chamber, Thanuny turned to Rekhmire.

'You see what I told you. That upstart, Senenmut, again. The commoner is everywhere in this kingdom and he has the sole ear of the queen.'

'It is rumoured that that may not be all he has,' whispered the other, a crafty smile on his face.

★

The queen's young daughter, Neferure, was feeling very unwell, and earlier that day she had been violently sick. For some time now she had been losing weight and was beginning to look quite wan and emaciated. Of late, her appetite had deserted her and all she wanted to do was sleep. Both her tutor, Senenmut, and her personal nurse, Ermine, had expressed their concern to Hatshepsut. The queen had immediately called in the royal physician, About. After a lengthy examination, he had declared that it was the young princess's age. When Hatshepsut pointed out that the child was but ten years, he merely stated that she was passing early into womanhood. In a month or two her condition would stabilise, he said, by way of prognosis. She should be fed with goats' milk and fruit, he added.

Senenmut had recommended that a second opinion should be sought and that afternoon the queen, greatly worried, had consented. Senenmut lost no time in dispatching an envoy to Aswan, where he knew of a physician of high repute, named Tamer. Secretly he prayed to Amon that the man would arrive in time to save the little princess's life, for he had grown as fond of the child as if she were his own daughter. She no longer played with the other children at court in the palace grounds and kept to herself in her room for most of the day. Sadly, Senenmut could see that her life was gradually slipping away.

The young Tuthmosis, however, grew stronger by the day. Although not tall for his age, he was of a sturdy stature, which already showed promise of developing powerfully in later life. Busy with his martial games, he neither knew, nor cared, about his half-sister's absence in the palace grounds over the past few weeks. True to say that, if he had been aware of her illness, it would have remained extremely doubtful if he would even have enquired about her, let alone visited her.

The two of them had seen very little of one another since being united in a small private wedding ceremony six months earlier. His vizier, Rekhmire, had pushed the queen for the ceremony to go ahead and finally she had agreed. Tuthmosis knew, like everyone else at the court, that it meant very little. The marriage would aid his position as Pharaoh later on, Rekhmire had pointed out, and that anyway, it was his right.

Tuthmosis was much more elated at the thought of going to Thanuny's army officers' school, down on the Nubian border. The army commander had informed him that both he and his vizier had spoken to the queen and were apparently awaiting her consent. He had little time for his stepmother and bitterly resented her rule as regent over him. All that he could do now was pray to Amun that she would allow him to leave the court...

That night Hatshepsut and Senenmut waited in eerie silence in the queen's moonlit boudoir. All was in readiness. Senenmut had helped the apprehensive Hatshepsut into the male harness he had made for her. Together they watched through the marble-arched apertures for the beginning of the eclipse. Senenmut had worked out that it must be that night and prayed to the gods, Amun and Horus, that the queen would act out her part successfully. Given the astronomical phenomenon, and the superstition and beliefs of the Egyptian people, the story would be all the more readily believed when circulated.

Over the harness the queen wore only a light cotton shift. Once the girls backs were turned, all she would have to do to perform the subterfuge would be to gather it up round her hips. Senenmut had promised to stay nearby in hiding in the curtained alcove to give her support. This was the only way the heterosexual queen would agree to the act. She reminded him in no uncertain terms that it was for this very Egypt that she had consented to go along with his plan.

'Do this well, and your rule as Pharaoh will begin unopposed. I promise you, Ka-re,' he whispered as he slipped out stealthily to conceal himself in the alcove.

Already the eclipse had begun. The moon was nearly half obscured, something that rarely happened in anyone's lifetime, and only then, when the earth, sun and moon were in direct line with one another.

Hatshepsut steeled herself and strode purposefully across the chamber. Picking up a mallet made of oxhide and wood, she beat loudly on a gong of bronze, trimmed with gold, to summon her handmaiden of the bedchamber, Shazar. Some thirty seconds later, the lithe and pretty Nubian girl appeared, politely curtseying to her mistress. Although it was receding fast, there was still enough light for Hatshepsut to see the girl's face clearly. She had big, white, almond-shaped eyes and thick sensuous lips, which opened to expose a row of even white teeth. Shazar's high cheekbones and firm chin gave the girl a very attractive appearance.

'Disrobe, girl,' commanded the queen, trying to make her voice sound authoritative, although in this situation she felt anything but.

She found herself having to repeat the command, as her maid had obviously thought she meant for her to undress the queen. Rapidly, Hatshepsut took a pace backwards, and it was then that the girl's eyes alighted on the bulge under the queen's shift. Her gasp was audible and her large eyes opened wider still. Then the moon was gone, completely obscured. Hatshepsut heard, rather than saw, Shazar pull the cotton shift over her dark curly hair.

'On your knees, girl,' she commanded anew.

She sensed, rather than saw, the maid comply. Raising her own shift and arranging it around her waist she sunk to her own knees. Everything was by feel alone now. Hatshepsut grasped the girl below the armpits and slid her hands down to Shazar's naked hips, ordering her to spread her legs. The terrified slave girl, used to obeying instantly, accepted the command without question.

With one hand Hatshepsut explored between the girl's legs until she found Shazar's vagina. With some difficulty and fumbling, she succeeded in guiding in her imitation member. Grasping the maid by the hips she drove herself fiercely forward. Shazar screamed at the sudden shock rather than in pain. Hatshepsut suddenly had a vision of her father, Tuthmosis I, all those years ago with the slave girl. Suddenly, in her confused state, she became him, and pulling desperately at the girl's hips with her hands, she thrust violently again and again. Shazar was now moaning with pleasure and gasping with the effort of forcing herself back onto her mistress. Hatshepsut could feel the perspiration on Shazar's ebony skin.

Suddenly, the slave girl screamed with sheer ecstasy as she climaxed dramatically. A moment later, Hatshepsut was amazed at the violence of her own orgasm, shaking her out of her trance-like vision. The chamber now was once more flooded with moonlight; the eclipse had passed. Where had she been for the past few minutes? Pulling herself together, she realised Senenmut's plan would have to be revised... no time now for the second handmaiden, Mynha. Slumped forward, exhausted, her curly hair hanging in rivulets of perspiration, Shazar was still on all fours. Rapidly, Hatshepsut backed off her, thus withdrawing the instrument of pleasure to the accompaniment of a squelching sound. Rising quickly to her feet, the queen allowed her shift to fall down into place.

'Get up, Shazar, and return to your quarters.'

The girl, flushed with passion and excitement, obeyed, backing slowly out of the boudoir, her eyes never leaving the bulge under Hatshepsut's shift. She could hardly wait to tell her twin sister, Mynha, what had happened.

A few moments later, after her departure, Senenmut emerged from hiding. The queen addressed him in a low menacing tone, partly due to the embarrassment and shame she felt for her part in the plot, and not wanting to admit to her own confused emotions.

'This act you have had me accomplish had better prove worthwhile, Djehutymes... You have made me feel a traitor to myself.'

Senenmut took the queen in his arms and offered soft words of comfort.

'What you have done, you have done for Egypt. By tomorrow night all of Thebes will have heard of your magical prowess, and by the end of the month, all Egypt, to its very borders, will accept you as Pharaoh, unopposed.'

Hatshepsut replied, 'I trust you speak truly, Djehutymes.' Then, lifting the cotton shift, she snapped, 'Now help me out of this thing and make me feel like a woman. Afterwards, destroy the infernal contraption. I never wish to cast my eyes on it ever again.'

Chapter VI

A few days later came the great festival of Amun at Karnak. The high priest, Hapi-soneb, eagerly awaited the arrival of the royal entourage in the great hypostyle hall. The nobles and dignitaries of Thebes, together with other prominent citizens, were installed in their places, anticipating the arrival of the queen and her party.

A loud clamorous cheering broke out beyond the outer mudbrick walls. Hapi-soneb could hear several cries of 'The Pharaoh comes. Hail the Pharaoh, Hatshepsut.' The sound was not unexpected to his ears, for Senenmut had confided the plan of deception to both him and Thuty, but to actually hear the cry in reality told him the plan had exceeded their wildest dreams.

Now a hum of expectancy broke out in the Shrine of the Theban Triad, amongst the guards stationed there, just inside the entrance to the great temple. A few moments later, an armed guard of superbly muscled spearmen fell back respectfully at the temple entrance at the end of the long avenue lining each side. Hapi-soneb knew these to be forerunners in the van of the royal party.

Then, to the sound of trumpets and drums, appeared a canopied plinth held aloft by some twenty Nubian slaves. On it, seated on a throne of gold, was the queen, although had he not known it was she, he would have thought it was a new Pharaoh. She waved to the cheering crowds on either side and he saw at once that she was dressed in the full regalia of a Pharaoh of Egypt. She wore the double red and white crowns of upper and lower Egypt with both the vulture and the cobra. The false beard she wore looked strangely at odds with eye make-up and lip gloss. Her small breasts had been strapped tightly so that a golden embossed breastplate could cover them. Round her shoulders and neck was a gold-trimmed collar of jade, malachite and turquoise. To complete the ensemble, she wore the historic kilt of the Pharaohs, with winged sandals on her feet.

The Nubian slaves set down the plinth and stood to attention at its side. Hatshepsut smilingly alighted and immediately the high priest stepped forward, dutifully bowing to greet her. Hatshepsut proffered a bejewelled hand. Hapi-soneb took it and kissed the fingers, whilst still on bended knee.

'In the name of Amun I greet you, great Pharaoh, Hatshepsut,' he boomed in a loud deep voice for all to hear.

Cheering broke out again all around them, outside the mudbrick walls and further into the temple's interior. Hapi-soneb went on to greet the members of the royal party, who numbered about twelve. Sadly, he noticed the absence of Neferure, the queen's daughter, who was by then far too ill to attend. However, he was greatly relieved that the surly youngster, Tuthmosis, was not amongst them. The boy's presence could only have caused dissension and confusion in some quarters. He offered a silent prayer to Amun that Hatshepsut had shown the good sense to let the boy go to Thanuny's army officers' training school in upper Egypt.

Trying to look his most dignified, he led the procession through to the great festival hall. Once there, a fanfare of trumpets greeted them, and people threw bouquets of flowers in the queen's path to an accompaniment of loud cheering.

Once everyone was in place the ceremony began. Priests, led by Hapi-soneb, chanted the praises to Amun. This was followed by a doleful wailing from all present, a sign of assent. Then came an ominous pause with every eye turned on Hatshepsut. As was the custom, the high priest invited the Pharaoh to address the gathering.

Hatshepsut stepped boldly forward onto the raised platform. She tried to make her voice sound as deep-throated as possible, and yet penetrating. She went on to say that she was their Pharaoh, and, as such, would hear their grievances and disputes. With the help of the god, Amun, of whom she was the living image, she would rule upper and lower Egypt both justly and wisely. She would further protect them from their enemies and, above all, loved all of her people of this very Egypt.

At the conclusion, loud cheering again broke out, followed by more trumpets and drums. After this, Hapi-soneb escorted the royal party to a point within the temple confines where two large granite obelisks were to be erected in the queen's name. These were the ones Senenmut was arranging to bring up from the quarries at Aswan and would be in red sandstone. A dedication service took place, blessing the ground, in the name of Amun and Hatshepsut, on which they would stand. After this, according to custom, Hatshepsut and her party were led to the eighth pylon commemorating the reign of her late husband, Tuthmosis II, and herself as queen. This was a grand double-arched edifice covered in hieroglyphs and reliefs of rich colours.

Finally, the procession wended its long traditional way to the sacred lake of Karnak, where further dedications were made to Amun. From there one could see the sheer grandeur of the great temple of Karnak, and Hatshepsut felt a small tremor of fear run through her. Could she carry out in this great land that which she had begun? Anxiously, she glanced behind her, and was reassured to see Senenmut smiling adoringly at her, amongst the party of high priests and nobles to her rear.

He had said she would be the greatest of the Egyptian

Pharaohs. Well, she would, with his help and the guidance of Amun, be just that. This great temple of Karnak, with its wonderful hieroglyphs and reliefs, together with its great pylons, would be added to, by her. She would make sure that her reign as Pharaoh was a momentous one, and she would be remembered for all the wonderful buildings her architect, Senenmut, would build for her in the years to come. Egypt needed her much more than a boy king who thought only of soldiers. Of this she was convinced.

Her day's triumph was complete, when cheering hordes of ordinary Theban people followed her royal procession all the way back to her royal palace from Karnak at the completion of the ceremony. Shouts of 'Long live the Pharaoh Hatshepsut' greeted her all the way.

On her arrival back at the palace, cheering masses of people remained outside, calling for her. To appease them, she made several excursions to the gardened roof patio above, and from this vantage point she waved to the adoring crowds below. Finally, just before sunset, the last of them disappeared, and she retired to her own chambers, where she had her handmaidens prepare a bath for her, scenting it with delicious and exotic spices. After helping her step naked into the bath, Shazar remained, looking greatly puzzled.

'What are you looking at girl...? Go... I shall call you when I need you.'

Shazar looked disappointed and slowly left, her head downcast. Hatshepsut hardly noticed. She lay back, luxuriating in the warm, all-enveloping scented water. She realised Senenmut's plan had worked. Her country now accepted her as undisputed Pharaoh. It had been easier than she could ever have imagined and she could hardly wait for the night to discuss future plans with Senenmut. She would send for him even earlier that night.

Later that night, in the warm balmy atmosphere of an

Egyptian night and after another bout of boisterous and passionate lovemaking, the two of them discussed the events of the day. Senenmut had already congratulated her on the way proceedings had gone at Karnak, and now he was outlining his plans to make her into Egypt's greatest Pharaoh.

'I have despatched my colleague, Amunhotep, to middle Egypt with plans for the building of great temples in your honour and, in a week or two, the barges will arrive up from the granite quarries at Aswan with the red sandstone obelisks.'

Like a little girl, Hatshepsut clapped her hands in delight.

'And my mortuary temple, here at Deir el-Bahri, and my tomb in the valley, when will they be finished, Djehutymes?'

Senenmut placed a finger on her rouged lips.

'Patience, my love. All will be achieved in time, but, hard as I push my workers, everything takes time and to rush anything would not do my Pharaoh justice.'

'Am I truly Pharaoh?' she said, with a smile hovering round her dark-brown eyes.

'Indeed you are, Ka-re.'

'Then I command you to make love to your Pharaoh,' she murmured.

'Your wish is my command,' Senenmut said and laughed.

★

It was two weeks later, when Hatshepsut was called by the new physician, Tamer, to her daughter's bedside. She hardly recognised the poor, emaciated, skeletal figure, swamped by the giant bed in which she lay. Already the little girl's face was the deathly colour of chalk, with deep-blue circles around her eyes.

Hatshepsut knelt down at Neferure's bedside and held the frail little hand in hers. She had to bend forward to catch her daughter's words, for by now they were little more than a whisper.

'May I see Senenmut, my tutor?'

Hatshepsut was quite taken aback by the request, but instantly sent a servant to Deir el-Bahri, where she knew he would be supervising the building of her temple. She had to admit to herself to feeling a slight pang of jealousy, at her daughter wanting Senenmut and not her at such a time. Looking anxiously at the little girl, she wondered if Neferure could last until he arrived.

Tamer, the physician, stood by, awaiting the queen's wishes. For a moment Hatshepsut took him aside and whispered, 'What ails her, physician?'

'It is the wasting sickness, Your Majesty. I fear that there is nothing more that I, or anyone else for that matter, can do… She will be gone by morning.'

Hatshepsut wiped away a tear and whispered, 'I know that you have done all in your power, physician. No harm will come to you at my hand.'

Relief could clearly be seen on Tamer's face. It was not unusual for a physician in Egypt to be put to death if his royal charge failed to live.

'I think you should send for a priest… The princess's skull should be opened and I shall need his assent for this.'

Although Hatshepsut knew this was the custom when royalty were faced with death, she couldn't help an involuntary shudder. To her it had always seemed barbaric. She crossed to the bedside and picked up her daughter's frail hand once more.

'Be patient, daughter. I have sent for Senenmut, your tutor.'

Immediately, she sensed the relief in the princess.

Neferure sank back contentedly on the pillow, as if awaiting his coming. The queen told Tamer to send for the high priest. He left to do so. Hapi-soneb was already in the palace, so it wasn't long before Tamer returned with him. The physician outlined the situation to Hapi-soneb, who turned to the queen.

'The skull should be opened, Your Majesty, so that the ka may pass more readily.'

Hatshepsut looked determined and her eyes, although brimming with tears, held firm.

'Not until she has seen her tutor, Senenmut. He has been sent for and will be here soon.'

'To delay is bad,' urged Hapi-soneb. 'Are you sure that you don't want me to give the order, Your Majesty, for the physician to proceed?'

'I have said wait,' the queen reaffirmed resolutely.

Neferure's eyes had switched from one to the other. Although she couldn't hear their whispers, she seemed to sense the content of the discussion.

'No, Mother,' she said and managed to drag her head from the pillow and raise her voice above a whisper.

'Be still, my dear. No one will let anything happen to you,' comforted the queen.

Everyone settled down to await Senenmut's arrival. They didn't have long to wait. He had left the temple immediately he heard the news and rushed for the palace. Unceremoniously, he hurriedly entered the princess's bed chamber, virtually pushing everyone aside. The relief on the princess's face was clear to see. Hurrying to the bed, he placed an arm round the little girl's shoulders to support her. Gradually, he eased her forward and bent down to catch her whispers, after gently kissing her on the cheek.

'Stay with me, please, until I die, Senenmut. Don't let them hurt me,' she pleaded.

'I am with you, little one, and will see you safely into the arms of Isis. It is she who will be waiting to greet you in the hereafter.'

'And will it be like you have told me in your instruction, Senenmut?'

'This I can promise. Our life here is but a preparation for our eternal life to come.'

The others watched anxiously as Neferure clung grimly on to Senenmut's hand. She seemed to relax suddenly at his words and, for an instant, a sparkle seemed to enrich her tired eyes. Then a new doubt assailed her.

'Shall I have need of my body in this new land I am going to?'

'No, my dear one, for Isis will restore to you a new and healthy one. Soon you will run and jump and sing as you used to.'

Peace descended on her once more.

'That is good, for I fear this body is of little use. I grow weaker every minute that passes.'

Senenmut found it hard to stem his tears, but he mustn't let the little princess see his sadness. It was up to him to find peace for her and maintain his composure. He suggested to the queen that the physician, Tamer, and Hapisoneb should depart, leaving the little princess in peace. It was plain by the way her eyes kept shifting to them that she still feared what they would do to her. All her life she had heard of the death rites facing royals, and still remembered her own father's deathbed scene. Everyone had been present when the physician had bored a hole into his skull and, then when he was dead, they had taken him away to the House of Death. The thought of it terrified her.

The queen agreed to Senenmut's request, but Hapisoneb objected and only agreed to leave after offering a prayer to the gods, Amun and Anubis. Neferure visibly relaxed when left alone with Senenmut and her mother, although never once did she let go of his hand.

'I wish you had been my father, Senenmut,' she whispered.

'I always have been, in both thought and spirit if not physically,' he murmured, choking back the tears. 'I have loved you like a daughter.'

A faint smile broke out on her pale and ashen countenance and a moment later she broke into a paroxysm of coughing and Senenmut saw that there were traces of blood round her mouth and nose. Gently, he eased her back onto the pillow, for he could see the end was near.

'Sleep, little one. I shall not leave you.'

'Shall I see you again in the next world, Senenmut?'

He could hardly hear the words now, so faint was her voice.

'Most surely you will be waiting there with Isis to welcome me when my turn comes,' he whispered.

'I have always loved you like a father, Senenmut... I...' The sentence trailed off in a long sigh and the little princess was gone.

Senenmut felt her hand go limp and release his. Unable to contain himself any longer, he broke down and wept for the little daughter he had never had. Hands over his eyes, he slumped over Neferure's deathbed. A moment later he felt the queen's consoling hand on his shoulder. She said nothing, but she was there for him; in spite of her own grief she showed her enormous strength of character. Perhaps in that moment he realised he truly loved her. Finally, he stood up and the two of them were locked in one another's arms. He recalled later that it was probably as well that Hapi-soneb and the physician, Tamer, had left. When they broke away, their eyes were reddened and their faces tear-streaked.

'I should have spent longer with her when she was alive,' murmured the queen.

'You did your best considering all of your duties and

responsibilities as queen regnant.'

'And now I am Pharaoh, but I have no daughter, only a stepson who hates me,' she said, between tears.

'Then I shall love you as no man has loved you, Ka-re. Always I shall be at your side.'

Hatshepsut gave him a long lingering kiss on the lips and then, breaking away, said, 'Now I fear we must send for the official mourners and then tomorrow the body of my daughter must be taken to the House of Death for embalming.'

Senenmut knew, of course, that this entailed several old crones, who would enter the chamber and wail and moan with pretended grief for the dead spirit, and then the body would be taken away for the customary seventy days of mummification in the House of Death. He would make his stand on this now, before either of them left the chamber.

'No, Ka-re. She is your daughter and a royal princess… Have the embalmers come here and do what has to be done… And as for the mourners, let her own nurse and servants come and sit in… At least that way we shall have genuine grief for Neferure. Surely such a brave soul deserves that… Her life was, after all, only too short.'

Hatshepsut studied him. Did she really understand this man? Up until now, she had been convinced that she had fallen in love with a schemer, although a brilliant mind, but she had never seen him like this. More than ever her love went out to him.

Gently, she laid a hand on his bare upper arm and murmured, 'It shall be as you wish, Djehutymes.'

Together they walked, arm in arm, to the bed and each in turn gently kissed the lifeless face of the little princess, before silently leaving the chamber.

Chapter VII

With the land of Punt in sight for the first time, Nehesy ordered the captain of the expeditionary ship to halt the work of the men at the oars.

'We shall sail right into land and lodge the prow on the beach,' he instructed.

The captain, Mohammed, argued against such a move.

'Have you seen the reception committee on the beach, Chancellor Nehesy, Your Excellency... There are many, and we have no knowledge that they are friendly towards us.'

Nehesy surveyed the beach with a more detailed scrutiny.

'Have our soldiers armed and ready, but no man is to begin offensive action unless force is used against us.'

Mohammed looked far from pleased and muttered as he walked away, 'It may be too late for us all then. We are hopelessly outnumbered as it is.'

Nehesy heard the utterance and, although he smiled at its content, he was well aware that the next few minutes would be vital. As the ship, the *Light of Horus* nosed in towards the beach, literally hundreds of naked black people of both sexes ran down to the water's edge. Most of them seemed to be waving, but Nehesy was grateful that none seemed to be carrying weapons or looking in any way hostile towards the visitors.

Summoning the interpreter, Ayei, whom he had brought along with them, he exclaimed, 'As soon as we land, have one box of beads brought forth and scatter the contents on the beach for all.'

Ayei, a coal-black slave indigenous to Punt, tall and long of limb, smiled, exposing a row of pearly-white teeth.

'Here you will be welcomed, Excellency. Have no fear. My people are a peaceful race.'

Nehesy was relieved but still cautious.

'Nevertheless, have the chest of baubles ready for scattering amongst them.'

'It shall be as you wish, Excellency.'

Nehesy saw that the *Light of Horus* was about to strike the beach, prow first, and run aground. He prepared himself for the jolt, holding on to a thick wooden spar. As it came to rest, half on the shore, its stern in the shallow water, the natives fell back expectantly on either side, lapsing into a pregnant silence.

Nehesy had the trumpeter strike up a fanfare, supported by the drummer. To this accompaniment, he strode ashore dressed in his full regalia as chancellor of Egypt. With him went Ayei and six armed soldiers and behind them two Asiatic slaves carrying a chest of coloured beads.

The natives parted to let his party pass between them. At the end of the column of natives, Nehesy saw that a tall, fiercesome-looking character, with a plume of ostrich feathers on his head, awaited their arrival.

'Who is he?' Nehesy whispered out of the corner of his mouth to Ayei.

The interpreter replied, 'He will be your equivalent in this land of Punt, Excellency, but not the same man that I remember from long ago when I lived in this land.'

As they approached the tall, stern-looking warrior type, Nehesy said, 'Tell him we bring greetings from the queen… Hatshepsut of Egypt, she who is the most powerful of Pharaohs.'

Ayei translated. The man showed no emotion but addressed the interpreter in a tongue completely foreign to Nehesy.

'What does he say?' exclaimed Nehesy.

'He wants to know our purpose in his land.'

'We have come as friends and wish to trade with this fine land of Punt. Tell him we wish to see his king and queen to that effect.'

By now the two Asiatic slaves had emptied the contents of beads on the golden sands of the beach. Standing back they waved the natives forward with their hand, invitingly. There followed a human surge of people, almost treading on one another in their haste to secure the gloriously coloured beads for themselves. The two slaves were bowled over in the rush and disappeared under a heaving mass of naked bodies.

When the latest information had been given to the leader of this reception party, he replied at length to Ayei, who eventually got round to translating to Nehesy.

'It appears, Excellency, that we are to camp here on the beach and await the arrival of the king and queen of Punt.'

'How long will that be?' exclaimed Nehesy, impatiently.

In answer, Ayei shrugged his shoulders and upturned his hands.

'Nothing happens quickly in this land of Punt, Excellency. We must wait.'

And wait they did. It was fully two days later, after Nehesy had set up camp on the beach, that a commotion broke up further along the shoreline. Nehesy shielded his eyes with the flat of his hand against the glare of the sun. In the distance he could see a large gathering of people. Some of them seemed to be dancing and playing some sort of musical pipes. Others surrounded a platform which was being pulled along by two white oxen. One thing for sure, the procession, for such it was, was coming their way. Nehesy turned to Ayei, standing beside him, with enquiry written in his eyes.

'The queen cometh, Excellency,' affirmed the

interpreter.

Nehesy lost no time in preparing a welcoming party. In no time he had organised two rows of trumpeters with the drummer at their head. Behind them a row of soldiers stood to attention. Nearby stood his galley slaves under the command of the captain, Mohammed, and the two overseers still brandishing their whips.

Ten minutes later he was finding it increasingly difficult not to laugh. It was indeed the queen and also her husband, the king of Punt. They were both seated on thrones made of carved ivory and wood which were attached to the platform. When the courtiers set down the platform on the sand, Nehesy fought to contain his merriment. Never had he seen such a weird pair as the queen and king of Punt. The king, whose name was Perehu, was almost a stunted midget but he strode forward in an arrogant manner. Beside him waddled the queen and waddled was the word for it, for Queen Eti, the steatopygous ruler of Punt, was truly an amazing sight. A huge head and long torso ended in the most enormous hips and rear end that Nehesy had ever set eyes upon. Under these were short, thick, stumpy legs with large feet.

Nevertheless, he ordered his trumpeters to begin their salute, followed by the drum. It was plain to see that Perehu, at least, was delighted with his welcome and a broad smile changed his earlier arrogant expression. The stoic face of Queen Eti, however, remained unmoved. The tiny king gabbled something in his own language, which Ayei translated for his chancellor.

'He welcomes us to the land of Punt and would like us all to journey with them back to the royal palace... How shall I reply, Excellency?'

Nehesy smiled at the king and queen, and then instructed Ayei to thank them for their formal invitation, which he and his party would be pleased to accept in the name of Queen Hatshepsut of Egypt. Nehesy could see that Queen Eti was not overly impressed, so he decided, on a whim, to try and change this. From one of the large chests he produced a necklace of richly coloured stones of malachite, jade and turquoise. The queen's little piggy eyes followed his every move and changed dramatically when he stepped boldly forward to place it over her head. No sooner had it descended on her ample bosom than Eti began stroking it with podgy fingers, obviously delighted with the gift.

After a further exchange of words through the interpreter, the royal party, again seated on their portable thrones, set off inland for the palace. Nehesy and several of his soldiers, together with about half of the slaves carrying the trading goods, followed in their wake. Nehesy had left the captain, the two overseers, half the slaves and the musicians to remain with the ship and await their return.

Inland the scenery was quite barren, although occasionally interspersed with greenery. For some little way they marched onwards until they came to a rocky gorge with high cliffs on either side of them. When they eventually negotiated this natural canyon and exited the other end, Nehesy was amazed to see a green and pleasant land. Ahead of them was the royal palace, set against a backcloth of green hills. He didn't know what he had expected, but this certainly surpassed his imagination. The palace was not large by Egyptian standards but a large white dome glistened in the noonday sun. There were pillared columns supporting it, and behind them, a long, flattish, limestone building with round apertures, through which they could see grinning black faces. Palm and incense trees were everywhere, giving off a pleasing fragrance. From the central archway of the flat main building a reception committee came out to meet them.

Well, so far so good, thought Nehesy. We are here,

which I never thought to be possible. Let us hope we can trade well and safely return to our homeland of Egypt.

Nehesy and his party were installed in comfortable quarters and the king, through Ayei, informed them that he would consider trading requests at the end of the week. Until then, they were welcome to his and the queen's hospitality. In fact, there would be a feast in their honour that very night...

The feast came and went; by Egyptian standards it was not a particularly grand affair. The portly queen never took her eyes off Nehesy, and for fear of offending her, he forced himself to eat all manner of repulsive edibles offered to him. He found himself positively amazed at the quantities of food Eti and her tiny husband, King Perehu, pushed down their throats. Some respite was offered to both himself and his party by the arrival of the entertainers in the form of acrobats and dancers.

Nehesy was surprised to see that most of these were, in fact, colourful little dwarfs. After these came a tall willowy dancer, with coal-black skin and eyes as bright as the flaming torches she danced between. He found himself much taken with this performer, and try as he might, he couldn't take his eyes off her sensuous and suggestive movements. With her dark skin glistening in the firelight, she danced right up to where he was seated, in the place of honour next to the queen. Coquettishly she made mischievous eye contact with him and Eti turned, laughing at his embarrassment. The girl dancer was virtually naked except for bands of copper round her neck, wrists and ankles.

Nehesy became even more embarrassed when Ayei, the interpreter, conveyed the queen's next remark to him.

'Her Majesty is making a present of the girl to you, Excellency,' he translated.

Nehesy was about to refuse, but seeing the expression on the queen's face, realised that this would be foolhardy in the extreme. He quickly changed his first response to one of 'Tell Her Majesty that I graciously accept her kind gift.'

Nehesy watched whilst an animated conversation ensued between Ayei and Eti. The former then addressed him.

'The queen wishes to know what gift you will give her in return.'

Nehesy was quite taken aback but recovered quickly, ordering one of his servants to return to his quarters and bring back an amulet of Horus, carved in jade and suspended on a golden chain. When it duly arrived on the servant's return, the queen was obviously delighted with it and placed the chain over her head immediately, caressing the pendant with her thickly rouged lips. As the time wore on late into the night, Nehesy realised he was becoming quite intoxicated by the amber liquid with which the servants were constantly filling his goblet.

Eventually, the king and queen made their exits and, ever mindful of his duties and etiquette as a guest, he was at leave to depart for his quarters. Once there he was in for another shock. The tall willowy dancing girl, whom Ayei had earlier informed him was called Salui, was already there. She stepped forward, her beautiful white teeth flashing in a seductive smile.

Nehesy was already feeling quite inebriated with a goodly fill of the amber nectar. Salui gazed into his eyes knowingly and gabbled something in her own language. Nehesy spread his hands and shrugged showing her that he couldn't understand. This seemed to deter Salui not one iota and, almost before he realised it, she began to disrobe him. As chancellor he was, of course, an important man in the court and had his own harem back in Egypt. Why not add this beauty to it, he concluded. She would be quite a prize to take back to his homeland. Salui, having completely disrobed him, ran her hands appreciatively over his well-muscled body. Without more ado, he scooped her young nubile form up in his arms and carried her to the mattress provided for him in the corner of the bedchamber. Then and there he decided for the first time that he liked this land of Punt...

It was just as well that he did, for the king and queen kept him waiting fully three weeks and not one, as promised, before they consented to discuss the trading aspect of the mission and then only, after Nehesy had pointed out that the great Pharaoh Hatshepsut of Egypt would be very angry, should he tarry longer in this beautiful land of Punt.

Finally, in return for the jewellery, baubles and cotton he had brought from Egypt, he received a cargo of palm and incense trees, together with a variety of spices and some of the dwarf acrobats to entertain his queen. He had his new acquisition, Salui, the dancing girl, clad in a dress of plain hessian, not wishing to have her exposed to the crew of the *Light of Horus* in her natural state. He had, by this time, become quite fond of his new slave, and well knew the temptation his men would be exposed to on a long sea voyage back to Egypt.

Nevertheless, he was relieved when the barque once again nosed its way out to sea leaving in its wake this land of Punt. On the shore a multitude had gathered to witness their final departure, but the steatopygous Queen Eti and the tiny King Perehu were not amongst them.

They pulled away from the shore with every one of the barque's galley slaves straining at the oars against the incoming waves. When they were some four hundred metres from the beach, he noticed Salui standing at the rail watching the waving throng of people on the shoreline. Her pretty dark face was wet and there were tears in her eyes. He didn't quite know why he did it, but Nehesy went to her and placed a comforting arm about her shoulders. She looked up at him and smiled through the tears, snuggling up against his broad chest.

The sea voyage north was long and arduous. Sometimes winds and rough seas would force Mohammed, the captain, to reduce all sail and rely on the oars. Nehesy feared for his cargo, being well aware that the shrubs and young trees required regular water. Sea water was of no use, so he was forced to instruct Mohammed to ration everyone aboard to a share of the drinking water available.

To his eternal credit Nehesy subjected himself to the same vigorous punishment. When a man was caught stealing water, Nehesy, although he experienced no joy in doing it, subjected the man to a flogging. Two days later another did it; some of the men were becoming quite mutinous, so Nehesy had no option but to make an example of the fellow. He had him hanged from the mast for all to see. It was a cruel move but for the time being it worked. For the next few days the crew were quiet and subdued.

Nehesy was relieved when the barque finally rounded the point at Caluula, the northern tip of the land of Punt, and a new course could be set for Dibouti, heading westwards. Here the seas were much more tranquil than they had been in the great ocean. With a strong easterly at their backs, they made steady progress, the wind stirring and rippling in the great canvas sails either side of the main mast.

An altogether more relaxed atmosphere seemed to settle on the occupants of the ship. Even the galley slaves, freed of the burden of rowing, began to sing. A week later they were through the Bab el Mandeb Strait into the Red Sea.

Nehesy, however, was only too aware that acute problems lay ahead. Water was running perilously low and the young trees and shrubs must be kept moist at all costs. In truth he had been against this daring mission from the first, but the queen had been wildly enthusiastic about it and he had been faced with little choice but to accept. Ahead of them now was still a lengthy sail in a northerly direction up the Red Sea until they reached the narrowest point of the Nubian Desert. Here they would be forced to disembark and cross the vast expanse of arid desert until they reached the Nile. Somehow their cargo must be transported with them and kept in shape. If there was to be any hope of this, water must be found and quickly. Nehesy sent for Mohammed, the captain.

'Prepare to put into Mitsiwa. We must find water,' he commanded the latter.

'Is that wise, Excellency? The tribesmen may be hostile. Little is known of the land south of Nubia,' replied Mohammed.

'We have little choice. If we do not take on fresh water soon both the plants and the rest of us will die. Have the bowmen stand by when we land.'

Mohammed raised his palms to the cloudless sky from where the sun beat down unmercifully.

'I pray to Osiris that you are right, Excellency,' he said. With that, he turned to give the orders to the helmsman. 'Hard to port and due west, helmsman.'

Nehesy gazed at the distant horizon. He too prayed to Osiris.

Chapter VIII

Following the success of her appearance at the great festival
of Amun at Karnak several weeks earlier, Hatshepsut was in
a buoyant and joyous mood. She had so readily been
accepted as the true Pharaoh by the populace, that even she
was astonished. It was just as Senenmut had planned.
Hadn't he told her all would be well. How could she ever
have doubted him. For the first few days and then the next
few weeks she had waited for the voices to be raised in
protest, but not even a whisper had filtered back to her. She
found it hard to believe that not even Thanuny and
Rekhmire had raised any objection to her being proclaimed
Pharaoh, but then she remembered that both men were
down with the army on the Nubian borders.

With them was also the young Tuthmosis. Since the
Karnak festival Hatshepsut had taken great care to rule both
wisely and generously, ever mindful of her public image.
Work on the great mortuary temple at Deir el-Bahri and
her tomb in the valley was proceeding well. The new
temple was already being acclaimed as a masterpiece of
architecture. Senenmut had despatched his colleague,
Amunhotep, to the middle kingdom where other temples
were in the early stages of being built in her honour. Never
had Hatshepsut been happier. She felt, as Pharaoh, she had
reached her true destiny and with the physical love of
Senenmut she felt fulfilled as a woman. Only in the passing
of her little daughter, Neferure, did she feel sad. The
seventy-day period of mummification was up the next day
and the princess's funeral would take place then. She was to
be buried high up in a tomb situated halfway up a massive

cliff face, similar to the one that had been prepared for Hatshepsut herself as queen. Now, of course, all interest in this tomb had ceased, due to Senenmut's planned new one for her in the Valley of the Kings.

That night in her bedchamber after a lovemaking session, subdued, due to the pending funeral being uppermost in their minds, Hatshepsut and Senenmut discussed the happenings of the past few weeks, together with the following day's funeral.

'Be not so sad, Ka-re. Tomorrow little Neferure will take her place beside the gods. One day you will be united with her,' consoled Senenmut.

'I know what you say is true, Djehutymes, but it does not ease the pain.'

Senenmut didn't argue further. He wondered inwardly whether the fact that the queen now had no heir to the throne of Egypt bothered her. He knew better than to suggest this. Was it possible that the continued union between them might bring forth an heir? For a moment he felt elated at the thought of fathering a future king of Egypt, then found himself wondering why this hadn't already happened. After all, their cohabitation in apparent secret had been going on for some time now. He forced himself to think of other matters and suggested to Hatshepsut that she should consider replacing Thanuny as army commander and Rekhmire as Tuthmosis's scribe. He was surprised at Hatshepsut's naive answer.

'Why should I do that, Djehutymes?'

'Because, my beloved, these are probably the only two men in all of Egypt powerful enough to be a problem to you as Pharaoh, and your young stepson, Tuthmosis, is now encamped with them... Must I say more?'

Hatshepsut smiled indulgently.

'Methinks you are too cautious. My stepson thinks only of playing soldiers, not of revolt.'

'Maybe now, but it will not always be so. It is now, when he is young, that the seeds can be planted in his fertile mind. I am convinced that Thanuny is your enemy and remember, unless you remove him, he controls the army.'

Hatshepsut dismissed this warning out of hand.

'Thanuny is a good commander. I have no reason to dismiss him or Rekhmire for that matter… No – let them amuse my stepson. It keeps him out of my way,' she added.

'So be it, Ka-re, but don't say I haven't warned you.'

Hatshepsut leant forward and kissed Senenmut full on the lips, then withdrawing, placed her index finger on his mouth.

'No, I shall hear no more of this. I shall have peace in all Egypt, not war and revolt. That is my promise as Pharaoh of upper and lower Egypt.'

'And a good promise it is, Ka-re, my love… Peace it shall be.'

'Now, tell me of my new temple and of the obelisks from Aswan. I would hear more of this.'

Seeing that the subject of possible revolt was now closed to him, Senenmut had no choice but to update the queen on both counts.

'The temple goes well and the obelisks are already on their way up the Nile from Aswan. They are of solid red granite. Their actual transport has been a problem. Low rafts, one hundred metres long, have had to be built for each one. In width they are fully thirty metres. Because of the weight involved, progress here from along the Nile will be slow.'

'Wonderful, my good Djehutymes. Whatever should I do without you? Can we not record the deed in the granite quarries of Aswan in recognition of the work in their cutting and transporting?'

'It has already been attended to, Ka-re. The inscription is already in place there for all to see in your honour.'

Hatshepsut lay back relaxing happily on her silken cushions. She held out her arms to Senenmut invitingly.

'I am sure that the goddess, Hathor, will one day reward you, Djehutymes, but until then she will recognise you in the shape of her living image, Queen Hatshepsut of all Egypt...'

In more sombre mood, the following day at sunset, the little embalmed body of Neferure, together with the Canopic jars containing her organs, was interred high up in the rock tomb. A system of pulleys on the top of the cliffs hoisted the casket containing the body up to the tomb's opening in the rock face. Here slaves were already in position to receive it and convey the golden-faced casket to its last resting place. At the base of the cliff, Queen Hatshepsut stood, accompanied by Senenmut, Thuty and several of her nobles. They watched as Hapi-soneb was lowered from the top of the cliff down to the tomb's opening. Here the high priest was helped to gain a footing into the entrance where he would conduct the last rites of burial.

The sun, a great red ball of fire, was just descending over the western peaks. Behind the watchers the traditional feast was being prepared at the base of the cliffs. Senenmut remembered the little princess in life and was surprised to find his face wet with tears. He consoled himself with the knowledge that she was at peace now and would soon be amongst the gods.

He glanced across at the queen. She was remaining serene and quietly dignified as befitted a Pharaoh of Egypt. He was only too aware that publicly he must show no familiarity towards her. Senenmut would dearly have loved to have been able to place a consolatory arm round her shoulders, to comfort her in her loss. This he knew was impossible. Once he caught her eye. There was a mutual sympathy there between them. Both understood the restrictions imposed upon them by formality and etiquette.

Hapi-soneb's last incantations in the tomb finally reached them, but far below they were almost inaudible to their ears. The high priest's last responsibility now was to give ultimate orders for the closure of the tomb, this before descending to join them on his wooden platform, lowered by the pulleys.

Fifteen minutes later he joined them for the ceremonial meal. By the time this had been consumed dusk was falling. Finally, with the flaming torchlight casting eerie shadows, the royal party left the scene in a dignified procession. High above in the rock face the slaves worked for the final closure of the tomb for all eternity.

★

Meanwhile down on the Nubian border Rekhmire was in deep conversation with Thanuny. Both men were deeply concerned that Hatshepsut had proclaimed herself Pharaoh, thereby bypassing their prodigy, the young Tuthmosis III.

'It is the boy's right to reign over all Egypt. It was so designated by his father and reiterated on his deathbed,' complained Rekhmire.

'Although you speak the truth, scribe, you forget the queen was also appointed regent to act in his minority,' replied the commander of the army.

'Yet she rules as Pharaoh outright. It is as if the young Tuthmosis never existed,' Thanuny said scowling, his dark bushy eyebrows knitting together.

'This is of grave concern to me also, but it appears from all accounts, that the people of both upper and lower Egypt have most readily accepted her to their bosom.'

'Is there nothing we can do? After all, you control the army… Can you not march on Thebes?' urged Rekhmire.

'Have a care, scribe, such words are treason. You are fortunate that it is only I, who am in sympathy with your thoughts, who has heard them.'

Rekhmire was far from abashed and continued with his line of thought.

'Will you, as commander of the armies, stand by and see the young Tuthmosis's right usurped?'

Thanuny touched his nose with his index finger before replying in a low whisper, 'The time is not yet ripe for such a move. At the moment the queen rules sagely and wisely. She is popular with the masses.'

'Only because she gives them added grain and concessions,' protested Rekhmire.

'That may be so, but any attempt to overthrow her at this stage would go badly with any who tried.'

'I say that it is wrong for a woman to rule Egypt. Such a thing has never happened before.'

Thanuny laughed and said, 'It is said that it is her steward, the man, Senenmut, who pulls her strings and rules through her.'

Rekhmire snorted.

'From my spies at the palace it would appear that he shares the queen's bed as well as the council chamber.'

Thanuny flushed angrily.

'The man has been raised as a commoner. Now he has more titles of rank than the high priest, Hapi-soneb, himself. It is said the queen would rather listen to him than her vizier.'

'He becomes more powerful every day. I say we should act now before this man, Senenmut, installs himself further in her favour.'

'Caution, my friend. I repeat, the time is not yet right. Always remember we have the young Pharaoh here. We shall know when he is ready. What good would it do to overthrow her now? Even if we succeeded, the boy is not ready to rule,' warned Thanuny.

'So what do you suggest we do...? Nothing!' snorted Rekhmire, sarcasm evident in his whole manner.

Thanuny smiled and then looked to left and right in conspiratorial fashion before replying, 'Listen well... this is what we must do. You must spend your time equally here with the army and at the palace at Thebes. Take the young Tuthmosis with you when you are at Thebes. See that he is addressed by all the nobles, courtiers and slaves as Tuthmosis III at all times. Use your authority to deal severely with anyone who does not address him so. This way he will be a constant source of annoyance and embarrassment to Hatshepsut, and further, a reminder that she is a usurper.' Thanuny waited for this to sink in, then continued, 'Eventually, although it may take years, she will make mistakes, or the man, Senenmut, will become too powerful for even her liking... Patience, my friend, is the watchword... Tuthmosis's time will come, and we must make sure he is ready. Should you, however, see a way to discredit the man Senenmut, then take it, by all means. His fall can only help our final objective in restoring the true Pharaoh to the throne of Egypt.'

Rekhmire smiled and said, 'I see now why you are commander of Egypt's armies. There is more between your ears than I gave you credit for.'

'From you, a rare compliment, Rekhmire. I would suggest you leave at once for Thebes with the young king.'

'What reason shall I give Her Majesty when she questions me on our return?' enquired Rekhmire.

'Say that I, Thanuny, commander of her armies, feel that the boy should have a rounded education, with a share of palace life, for the day when he will be Pharaoh.'

Rekhmire smiled at the audacity of this.

'Very good indeed, Thanuny. Her reply will be most interesting.'

Two weeks later Rekhmire arrived back at court in Thebes with the boy, Tuthmosis, resentfully scowling at his side. No sooner had Hatshepsut received the news of their arrival than she sent for them, granting an immediate audience. Rekhmire, bowing low, entered the council chamber, but the young Tuthmosis simply glared insolently at her. Hatshepsut ignored the insult. She was dressed in her full regalia as Pharaoh, with the double crown of Egypt, historic kilt and false beard. Seated on her throne of carved ebony inlaid with gold and ivory, she made a regal and splendid spectacle.

'To what do I owe this honour? I understood I gave both you and the commander, Thanuny, leave to instruct the young Tuthmosis in martial arts. I believed you to be on the Nubian border where you requested my permission to take him.'

Hatshepsut addressed the remark directly to Rekhmire, purposefully ignoring the scowling Tuthmosis. He squirmed uncomfortably under her steady gaze, but tried as eloquently as he could to give the explanation Thanuny had suggested. When he had completed the statement he swallowed hard and waited. A long silence followed. He shuffled his feet, dropping his gaze, unable to meet the queen's clear piercing eyes.

'Very well,' she replied coldly. 'But you will remember in future to consult me before the child is moved from one place to another... Is that clear?'

'Yes, Your Majesty, perfectly. I am indeed sorry if either Thanuny or myself have caused offence.'

'I shall disregard it this time... See that there is no repetition... Now go with the boy and find a nurse. See that he is quartered and fed.'

Rekhmire backed out, bowing low, but Tuthmosis without a word turned on his heel and virtually stormed out. For a few moments the queen remained seated before slowly rising and summoning her maid. When the slave girl appeared, Hatshepsut ordered her to send for her steward, Senenmut, who was at that time occupied at the Deir el-Bahri mortuary temple.

'Have a messenger sent at once,' she commanded.

With a curtsey, the girl backed out and scurried to do her mistress's bidding...

Two hours later found Senenmut in the presence of the queen. As soon as he had received the message he had returned by horse-drawn chariot to be with her. Even the two eunuchs guarding the entrance to the queen's council chamber looked with distaste at his dusty and sweat-soaked appearance. Brushing past them, he strode into the inner chamber. Hatshepsut rose to greet him. In a loud voice, more for the ears of the eunuchs outside, he apologised for his disreputable appearance.

'I came with all haste, Your Majesty, just as soon as I received your message.'

Hatshepsut smiled indulgently, taking in his dishevelled state at a glance.

'It is of no matter, my steward. I know full well that you were engaged in the building of my temple.' Dropping her voice, so that the sentinels couldn't hear, she relayed developments concerning the return of Rekhmire with the boy king.

Senenmut rubbed a hand down the side of his tanned and dusty face, deeply engaged in thought. After a long pause, he whispered, 'It is plain Thanuny and Rekhmire are up to something. I have suggested to you before, Ka-re, that you would do well to discharge both of them. They are probably the only two enemies you have in this very Egypt and Thanuny controls the army.'

Hatshepsut looked pensive and carefully weighed Senenmut's warning before replying, 'Thanuny is a successful and popular commander, is he not?'

'True, Ka-re, but the man's intentions towards your reign as Pharaoh bode nothing but ill.'

Hatshepsut seemed to come to a decision and spoke at length, keeping her voice low so that only Senenmut could hear.

'My faithful Djehutymes, although what you warn me of I know to be true, to discharge Thanuny now without good reason, at this time, would only alienate the army of Egypt from me. Whatever both he and Rekhmire are conspiring to do against me, we must wait for them to show their hand. My vizier and treasurer have both warned me of the same, so with the three of you, besides my loyal chancellor, Nehesy, to safeguard my interests, I have no fear for my immediate safety. For the time being we shall keep a very close watch on them. Should either show open hostility I shall take your advice and remove them at once. A greater worry to me is the return of the boy, Tuthmosis. It is quite plain that he has an inborn hatred of me probably fostered by his mother, the harem girl, Isis.'

Senenmut scratched his head thoughtfully.

'From what I have seen of the boy when he was last at the palace, what you say is undoubtedly true. He shows an open hostility towards you, mostly in the form of dumb insolence... Why not have your vizier speak to him on the subject?'

'But I thought that you would remonstrate with—'

Senenmut cut in, pre-empting the queen's last sentence.

'I would suggest that it would come better from your high priest and vizier, Hapi-soneb. It is his right on your behalf, and we do not want to make enemies unnecessarily.'

Hatshepsut, seeing the wisdom of this, readily agreed.

'I shall instruct Hapi-soneb in the morning.' Then, quickly changing the subject, she raised her voice to a normal level once more. 'What of my temple at Deir el-Bahri? What progress there, architect Senenmut?'

Senenmut went into lengthy detail, clearly proud of his work and now in his element.

'Soon it will be completed and, when it is, it will be the most beautiful and wondrous building in all Egypt, both upper and lower, even perhaps in all the known world.'

'I shall ride out with you tomorrow and inspect this wondrous spectacle you speak of.'

'Will you not wait, Majesty, until Nehesy returns from Punt with the plants and shrubs? Once the trees are in place on the approaching ramps to the temple it will be even more splendid.'

'No, Senenmut, I shall not wait a moment longer. I am impatient to see your miracle that all my courtiers have told me of. It is only your wishes that have prevented me this long from inspecting the temple.'

Senenmut nodded, resigning himself to the fact. He well knew that Hatshepsut had been badgering him for months about a visit there, but he had continually advised against such a mission. Wait until it's finished to your glory, he had always urged. Until now she had always agreed. This time he knew that he had lost and must agree to her wishes. To press home her advantage, Hatshepsut pointed out that there was no certainty that Nehesy's mission to the land of Punt would be successful.

'After all, it is unknown territory. The expedition might not return at all from their long sea voyage and overland trek... No, tomorrow I shall accompany you to Deir el-Bahri and see for myself what wonders you have performed on my behalf.'

'So be it, Your Majesty. Tomorrow it shall be as you wish.'

Chapter IX

With the barque moored at Mitsiwa, Nehesy sent his
second in command, Panehsy, inland with a small armed
force, in search of water, the remaining drinking water
having been divided three ways. One third went to the
expeditionary force, another third to Nehesy and the men
remaining with the barque, and the last third was for the
precious plants and shrubs. Nehesy inwardly blamed
himself for his inadequacy in calculating the amount of
water that would be needed for the watering of the shrubs.
When they had taken water aboard before leaving Punt, he
had made almost the same calculation as for the outward
journey. Now he was only too aware that the expedition's
success depended on the results of Panehsy's task force.

The crew was becoming ever more resentful and mutinous at the enforced rationing of water. Unfortunately he
had been compelled to send most of the soldiers and
bowmen with Panehsy, as no one knew what resistance the
foraging patrol would meet in this land of Ethiopia.

In fact the young Panehsy trekked for two whole days in
the blazing heat, before reaching blessed water, in the shape
of a sparking waterfall cascading down the rocks into a
turbulent river below. It took another hour before they
were able to scramble down into the valley and begin filling
the casks. Most of the men fell on their bellies and lapped
the water directly from the river to satiate their immediate
thirst. Eventually Panehsy regained control and scolded
them for behaving like undisciplined animals, although
inwardly he had every sympathy with them.

He gave thanks to Osiris whilst the filling of the casks

was being completed and hoped that their return trek to the coast would be uneventful. Either Osiris wasn't listening, or Panehsy was plain unlucky. The last cask was just being corked when a loud shouting broke out above them. He gazed up at the rim of the cliffs, towering above the gorge, from where they had earlier climbed down. A party of tall coal-black warriors, ostrich feathers in their hair, was shouting abuse down on them. A moment later a spear clattered into the rocks, only a metre from where Panehsy sat. His men were thrown into momentary panic but, in spite of his youth, Panehsy was a trained soldier who believed that he should have been put in charge of the expedition in the first place. After all, Nehesy, although a likeable man, was the queen's chancellor, not a trained soldier.

Barking orders to his men, he ordered them to drag the casks into cover behind the rocks. The last thing he wanted now was to lose the precious water. More spears and rocks clattered down onto the rocks around them. Panehsy had no means of knowing how many their enemies numbered, but he intended to find out. Immediately he realised that his men were at a great disadvantage down there in the gorge, with the tribesmen above them. If they stayed in this position, their attackers could rain death and destruction down on them.

He must think of a way to bring the attacking warriors down to them. With this plan in mind, Panehsy ordered his men into hiding behind the rocks. He was the last to join them. If he could succeed in making the attackers think their adversaries were frightened of them, maybe they would be fooled into descending to finish them off. It worked. About thirty of the warriors, who appeared to be their entire force, began to scramble down the rocks towards them, gesturing and shouting abuse. Now they were playing into Panehsy's hands. Behind the rocks, he lined his Egyptian longbowmen up in two columns, ordering them to await his call to let loose their arrows. Patiently he waited until all the attackers were fully committed to the descent and about halfway down. Then quite suddenly he dropped his upraised arm. A shower of arrows fell on the unsuspecting enemy now trapped in no man's land between the river and the summit. At least four of the coal-black warriors plummeted downwards, plucked from the rock face by the Egyptian arrows. With a loud splash they crashed in turn into the river below. Two more huddled wounded against the limestone rockface.

Panehsy's second line stepped forward and fired to order. This time at least six of the attackers lost their tenuous hold on the rock face and plunged downwards head first into the river. A few moments later their bodies disappeared from view, washed round the bend of the river by the force of the swiftly flowing current.

If Panehsy had thought their comrades would retreat, he was made to think again. The slaughter only seemed to have renewed the resolve of the remaining warriors. Onward and downward they came, still mouthing oaths and obscenities. Panehsy was forced to admire the Ethiopians' courage and fighting spirit. There was time only for two more fusillades of arrows, which accounted for another six or seven attackers, before the remaining force of about twelve or thirteen was upon them.

Now it was the turn of the Egyptian soldiers armed with spears and rawhide shields. Experts at close combat and seasoned veteran campaigners, they scrambled over the rocks to close with the enemy. The entire battle lasted less than five minutes before all the Ethiopians lay dead, their short stabbing spears no match for their Egyptian adversaries.

Panehsy surveyed the carnage around him. There were bloodied corpses everywhere and even the river at the foot of the rocks was dyed red. A call to order showed that he himself had lost six of his expeditionary force. He had the bodies of his own men collected and he supervised whilst a cairn of stones was erected over the corpses. His remaining force raised their spears in salute, whilst he entreated Osiris to receive their brave souls in the afterlife.

He organised his men as quickly as he could for the return trip. There was no point in hanging about in this hostile territory probably to be attacked again. The ascent this time with the heavy wooden water-casks proved much more difficult than anybody had imagined, and it was fully two hours later when the last man stood on the rim of the gorge.

Back at the coast Nehesy had his problems. An argument had broken out about the amount of water being used to sustain the precious plants and shrubs. A low murmuring of dissent could be heard everywhere. Even the barque's captain, Mohammed, suggested to Nehesy that the plants should be allowed to die.

'After all, we have myrrh, ebony, malachite and ivory. Surely, together with the performing acrobats and dwarfs, the queen will be well pleased. What need have we for the greenery, Excellency?'

The next day the remaining water would run out and Nehesy knew they were doomed unless Panehsy's force returned with the valuable means of survival. Fresh food was not a problem, an abundant supply of fish and water-fowl being ever plentiful. Without water, survival was impossible.

Nehesy saw a group of the crewmen approaching – a delegation surely. His assumption proved correct. A wizened old salt stepped forward – obviously the spokes-man. Nehesy noticed that the man had a bad squint in one eye and a cruelly twisted mouth. He remembered him as the man who beat time on the drum for the oars of the galley slaves. Nehesy knew he mustn't let them see he was worried or indecisive or he was lost. The girl, Salui, clung nervously to him, her eyes locked on the leader of the delegation. Nehesy pushed Salui behind him, screening her from the delegation.

'Speak!' he ordered, staring straight at the wizened fellow's one good eye. The man scratched the ground aimlessly with one sandalled foot, then began his rehearsed address.

'Excellency, water being so short I thought, I mean the crew thought, that if you had no further use for the girl... as she is only a slave, she could be killed and her ration given to us.' When Nehesy eyed him coldly, without replying, he was encouraged to continue, 'In fact, the girl's blood could be drained together with that of some of the other slaves—'

Such was the disgust Nehesy felt that the man's next words were lost on him. Stepping forward, he drew his dagger and plunged it up to the hilt into the stomach of the leader of the delegation. With a low moan the fellow sank to the earth, clutching his stomach, and the remainder of the delegation took two visible steps backwards. Nehesy swung his attention round to them.

'If you want water, use his share. If you want blood, use his.'

With that he ushered the shocked Salui to the shelter of nearby palm trees. The last he saw of the delegation they were carrying their dead comrade away.

The following morning Osiris did indeed smile upon them for, just after dawn, the lookout reported Panehsy's returning expeditionary force had been sighted in the distance and, from their slow progress, it was obvious they were carrying heavy casks of water. Nehesy gave praise to Osiris and went out to meet them...

After warmly embracing and congratulating Panehsy on the success of his mission, Nehesy lost no time in ordering the barque's captain, Mohammed, to load all the water casks on board. At the setting of the sun he had all the shrubs and plants thoroughly soaked. Some were looking distinctly sorry for themselves, and Nehesy found himself wondering whether they would make it. The arrival of water had miraculously improved the mood of the men, who went to work with a will on their various chores.

Nehesy instructed Mohammed that they would up-anchor and sail at dawn. The savage justice administered by their leader on the spokesman for the delegation seemed to have worked. There were no further murmurs that night, and at the first light of dawn Nehesy was wakened by Panehsy, who folded back the flap of his tent to peer inside.

'Soon the sun will be up, Excellency. I would advise haste in case we are again attacked by the natives of this land of Ethiopia.'

'You speak with wisdom, Panehsy. Give the order to break camp at once. We sail within the hour.'

Panehsy hurried off to carry out his commander's orders. The sooner this expedition was over and he could return to Thebes the happier he would be. He had recently plighted his troth and broken a jug with a young widow and longed to return to her warm charms.

The process of breaking camp took less than thirty minutes. Tents were quickly taken down and packed away. The fires of the night were quickly extinguished and a hasty breakfast partaken of. The sun was just rising, a semicircle of crimson in an orange sky on the distant horizon of the Red Sea, as they left Ethiopia in their wake.

Nehesy felt now that his luck had changed. A light southerly breeze filled the huge sails, one on either side of the barque's mainmast. Once they had pulled away from the shore there was no need for the oars, much to the relief of the galley slaves. An inspection of the cargo of vegetation delighted Nehesy. Overnight, as if by magic, the trees and shrubs had revived beyond belief. A few more days now, if the breeze held, and they would have sailed far enough up the Red Sea to have passed the worst of the Nubian desert.

At its northernmost tip, Nehesy hoped and expected to meet up with a reception committee at an oasis there. The object of this second party was to provide transport for the long overland trek to the Nile at Aswan. It would consist of chariots and horse-drawn plinths to carry the barque's cargo and would be escorted by a supply train of provisions and a military escort. Nehesy knew only too well that a fierce ordeal still lay ahead of his party. From the time that the *Light of Horus* rendezvoused with the reception party, two hundred kilometres of angry, hot, dusty desert still had to be crossed before they reached the Nile at Aswan.

From there, the course would be comparatively easy. Barques would be waiting there to convey them up the river to Thebes and the conclusion of the mission to the land of Punt. By the time that happened several long months would have elapsed. During their overland trek there was always the possibility of their caravan being attacked by bands of desert nomads, hence the escort of fresh troops.

All that, however, was still ahead of Nehesy and his party. For the moment he stood proudly on the poop deck of the barque, and watched its carved prow cut through the waters of the Red Sea, the warm breeze caressing his tanned face and rustling his tunic as they beat a path northwards. Beneath him the galley slaves rested on their oars and gave thanks for the blessed wind that was doing their work for them.

A week later they had arrived at the rendezvous point. With relief Nehesy saw that the reception committee was there to meet them. A party of Egyptian soldiers, led by a young captain, and about thirty slave bearers waited to unload the cargo onto dry land. Mohammed sailed right in and half beached the barque on the sandy shore. The young captain, whose name was Umbu, introduced himself to Nehesy.

'We expected you earlier, Excellency, and have been encamped here for the past four weeks.'

Nehesy's first inclination was to take the young captain to task, but he realised that Umbu had no means of knowing the ordeals that had befallen them, since the expedition had left Thebes months earlier. He merely introduced the leader of the reception party to Panehsy and the captain of the barque, saying, 'My men are tired, captain, after a long sea voyage and an inland battle. We shall rest here for two days before beginning our trek across the desert... Kindly see to it that my men are taken care of, refreshed and quartered, and the supplies carefully unloaded and stored in a shady area.'

Umbu eyed him, questions written in his gaze.

'See that the trees and shrubs are well watered. I would hate to lose them now.'

He was too tired to explain to the young captain, who was plainly puzzled by the cargo his men were now bringing ashore. Jewels and gold, yes, Umbu had heard of these, but trees and shrubs? No one had said anything about these. He shook his head in disbelief. Still his job was to lend all assistance to the chancellor, not to ask questions.

★

Work on the queen's mortuary temple at Deir el-Bahri was nearing its end. Senenmut drove his workers on with a fervour unmatched by anything ever witnessed before. It was as if something possessed him, driving him on. From sunrise to sunset he threw himself into the work, labouring alongside the artisans and slaves employed there. Gradually the three great colonnaded monuments rose in three terraces from the desert floor, great sweeping ramps leading from each one to the next. The whole magnificent structure backed on to the sheer cliff face towering above it, the upper terrace being the actual temple.

The first court surrounded by pylons had an entrance avenue of sphinxes and obelisks. On the north-east corner was built the temple to Anubis with a hypostyle hall and three chapels. Within, to the south-west, was a temple dedicated to the goddess, Hathor. The week before, Senenmut himself had personally escorted Hatshepsut on a detailed inspection. As yet, of course, the walls were largely bare of hieroglyphs and decoration, but he had proudly outlined his plans for each area of the temple. The queen was clearly delighted and had to constrain herself not to throw her arms round Senenmut's neck. The latter forced himself to speak loudly and formally in front of the artisans and slaves.

'All we are waiting for now, Majesty, are the trees and shrubs from Punt, just as soon as the chancellor, Nehesy, returns from his expedition. When we have those, you will see such a transformation in the courtyards and in the approach to the temple. The very bareness of the sur-rounding area shall become as nothing.'

The queen clapped her hands in delight, her eyes verita-bly sparkling.

'You have done well, my loyal architect,' she said, loudly enough for all to hear. Then, in a private aside for his ears alone, she added, 'You shall reap your reward tonight, Djehutymes.'

Together they walked to a waiting chariot, where a charioteer of the queen's private guard waited to convey her back to the palace. Senenmut bowed low and kissed the back of the queen's hand, allowing his lips to remain perhaps a fraction too long. The charioteer stood to attention, holding the reins of two fine, black, Arab horses, as Senenmut assisted his sovereign up into the chariot. A few moments later he watched, as in a cloud of dust the horse-drawn conveyance with its royal cargo disappeared into the distance and was swallowed up by the desert haze. As he was standing lost in thought, he felt a tug on his sleeve. Brought back to reality he saw that it was old Ramose, a trusted and talented artisan and craftsman employed by him to oversee work on the temple in his absence.

'What is it, Ramose?' he snapped, irritated by the heat and numerous flies buzzing round his head.

The old man, with greying hair, beard of the same colour, and bushy eyebrows, addressed him in a low but dignified voice.

'I think there is something you should see, master.'

Knowing the old retainer well, Senenmut knew full well that the man would not have bothered him with a trivial matter. Immediately his manner changed to one of concern.

'Is there a problem with the temple, Ramose?'

'Not with the temple, master.'

'What then ails you, Ramose?'

'Nothing ails me, master, but there is something that I would show you… Will you be so good as to follow me?'

Senenmut nodded and fell into step behind Ramose. The old man led him up through the corresponding terraces of the temple and beyond, to where they came to a cavern in the cliff face. Stopping there, he lit a torch from the smouldering embers of a workman's fire at the rock face. Senenmut looked greatly puzzled and stated as much.

'But this is merely a cavern used by the workmen, a place where they take nourishment and rest from the heat of the sun at midday… What can this have to do with me,

Ramose?'

'If you will allow me, master.'

The old man, holding the torch aloft, stumbled onwards and led the way into the dark interior of the cave. A little way in he stopped and held the torch in such a way as to illuminate the cavern wall. Senenmut could see at once that a mural or engraving had been roughly drawn on the limestone fascia. It depicted a female form bending over. Behind her, obviously from his posture, was a man mounting her.

Senenmut laughed, and said, 'What has this to do with me, Ramose, you old rogue?' He used the term affectionately.

Ramose edged forward with the torch and said, 'Look closer, master.'

Senenmut peered closely at the graffiti. It was well done. He let out a gasp. There was no doubt about it. The caricatures were of himself and the queen, Hatshepsut. A sudden thought struck him. If old Ramose had realised this, then others must, too.

'Shall I have it removed, master?' enquired Ramose.

Senenmut thought for a while before answering. Was it such a bad thing if the public were aware he was the queen's lover? Surely, in a way, the caricature was something of a compliment. To suppress it might make things worse. No, he would pretend he hadn't seen it. He turned to Ramose and addressed him in a dignified voice.

'This is of no matter, Ramose, and has nothing to do with me. It's nothing but a workman's imagination working overtime. No, we shall let the drawing remain. Let the men have their fun... You haven't seen it. Do you understand?'

Ramose looked puzzled, but nodded his head. 'If that is what you wish, master,' was all he said.

Without another word the two men took their leave of the cavern in the rock face. That night, in the queen's bed,

Senenmut said nothing of the incident to Hatshepsut. There was no sense in worrying her unnecessarily. After all, it was nothing but a workman's prank.

Chapter X

In spite of Senenmut's exalted position within the queen's court and his many titles of rank, it was the responsibility of the vizier, Hapi-soneb, to supervise the taxation system of the country. Much of the country's prosperity came with the agricultural yield, and this depended largely on the Nile's annual flood. Along the course of the great river were sited Nilometers. These were but a flight of steps on the bank of the Nile. From these could be determined the water level at each flood. Hapi-soneb, when the levels were reported to him, could estimate the extent of the inundation within a given period. With this information, he could set the taxes. Small wonder then that it could be said that Egypt was but a gift of the Nile. Without the great river she would have been unable to survive.

It was fortunate for Hatshepsut that in the early years of her reign the flood was good, richly endowing the surrounding land. Senenmut, keen to take advantage of such prosperity, allowed the story to circulate that it was because of his royal mistress – surely the god's choice – that such prosperity ensued. He had his underlings harness this gift of nature, building embankments and dikes to both protect buildings and land, channelling the flow of water into the fields. After the inundation, when the flood waters receded, silt would leave the land richly fertile. Senenmut saw to it that the queen appeared on a regular basis dressed in the full regalia of Pharaoh. Rich and poor alike began to acclaim her, none openly declaring animosity. Gradually, it became as if the young Tuthmosis III never existed. Not even Thanuny or Rekhmire dared to speak openly against

Hatshepsut so popular had she become.

Then came the harvest – surely one of the best ever. Cereal crops of barley and wheat were harvested in abundance. Labourers in the fields used wooden sickles with teeth of flint. Grain was carried away in large baskets to the villages. Here, after the stalks had been removed, oxen and donkeys drove over the grain, trampling it to a fine powder. From there it would be taken to the granaries and the amount recorded by a scribe who would have to report the total to the vizier.

Bread and beer were the staple diet of the multitude and these were made from the cereals harvested. The rich grasslands of the delta were thriving too. Here great herds of cattle were raised and the people also ran pigs, goats and sheep for meat. The size of the herds was calculated every two years and the value of the estate for taxes calculated upon it by Hapi-soneb. Cattle were kept for dairy produce and as beasts of burden. The poor did not eat meat and only the elite would eat beef on special occasions.

The building of the queen's mortuary temple at Deir el-Bahri was just about complete as far as the actual building went. Senenmut had just commenced the great work of recording the murals, reliefs and hieroglyphs to honour the reign of his mistress as Pharaoh, a labour that was to take many more years before its completion.

Working hand in hand with Hapi-soneb and Thuty, the treasurer, Senenmut made the best use of Egypt's abundant mineral wealth, which included gold, malachite, alabaster and copper. As well as using limestone and granite in a gigantic scale of building, they freely exported surplus stocks to Egypt's neighbours. Gold was rated as a divine substance. The bones of the gods were thought to be made of silver and their flesh gold. The goddess, Hathor, was even called 'The Golden One', whilst the sun-god, Re, was known as the 'Mountain of Gold'. At Senenmut's instigation, Hapi-soneb saw fit to build up large reserves of gold for Pharaonic government.

'If we are to build in middle Egypt to the queen's glory, funds must always be available,' he urged the vizier.

So began a period in Egyptian history that has never been equalled for wondrous architecture and majesty. Egypt was at peace under its queen Pharaoh, and only mild skirmishes by border raiders tested its armies. These were easily put down by Thanuny and his well-drilled and trained soldiers. He was ably assisted in this by his deputy, Djehuty, later to become one of Tuthmosis III's greatest generals.

The piety of the land was upheld by Hatshepsut. Offerings were made three times daily on her behalf in all the temples in both upper and lower Egypt. The high priest at each would recite to an effigy of the god, 'It is the king who sends me', thus serving his royal Pharaoh. The high priest would then light a torch, which supposedly awoke the god and symbolised the rising of the sun. He would anoint himself with water and oils to an accompaniment of singing priestesses, wash the effigy of the god, and after purification with incense, dress the statue in clean clothing. Finally, the god would be further anointed with perfumes and cosmetics and presented with gifts, before food would be set in front of him.

Hatshepsut encouraged poets and musicians, together with artists, mathematicians and students of medicine. Dancers and magicians performed regularly for her pleasure.

One evening, however, she conveyed her anxiety to Senenmut that nothing yet had been heard of the expedition she had sent to the land of Punt.

'It is several months since their departure from Egypt. I fear they must all have perished or surely they would have returned by now.'

Senenmut tried to reassure her. After all, the expedition had been at his suggestion and he, too, was by this time very worried.

'Nehesy and Panehsy are able men and they have a strong force with them. Although we know little of this land of Punt, I am sure they will prevail and return in due course with rich gifts for you, Ka-re.'

'I pray to the goddess, Hathor, that you are right, Djehutymes, and that they will return safely to us soon.'

★

It was true to say that the worst of Nehesy's expedition to Punt was now over. Although ahead of them lay a two-hundred-kilometre trek across the desert, their depleted party was now reinforced with a martial escort. In the event, Nehesy, on consideration, gave his men a four-day rest at the rendezvous point, before setting off into the desert. The caravan of men, baggage carts and chariots was heavily laden and progress would be slow across the desert. Nehesy planned to achieve a target of about ten kilometres a day, resting overnight as and when they reached various oases. He was aware that an attack on his party was not only possible but highly probable. Several nomadic tribes habited the rocky and sandy terrain and were not averse to attacking caravans, no matter how heavily armed. From the Red Sea coast to the Nile, travellers were frequently ambushed and attacked by the minatory hordes of nomads.

Nehesy deployed his men on the advice of Panehsy and Umbu. After all, both were military men of experience and he was only too glad to bow to their superior knowledge of such tactics. On either side of the main baggage train were two columns of Umbu's men. The rear of the caravan was protected by what remained of Panehsy's soldiers. Nehesy sent two of the chariots ahead to scout for likely dangers.

Forewarned was forearmed. If they were going to be attacked he wanted to know about it in advance. In any event the worst enemy was the almost phenomenal heat of the desert at midday, dehydrating the body and searing the skin.

After four days, Nehesy realised his daily target of distance was falling short and, at this rate, they would take a good week longer than his estimate to reach the Nile. He decided to adopt a drastic change of plan, something that was bitterly opposed by both Umbu and Panehsy. They pointed out that it would be much more difficult to protect the caravan by night, which was Nehesy's alternative plan. It would be cooler for the men and horses. (Camels had not yet found their way into the Egyptian way of life.) It would be more difficult too for any enemies to see them, so Nehesy reasoned with his two subordinates.

They, in turn, pointed out that the reverse also applied. An enemy would be amongst them before they could properly deploy. However, on that day's march the elements came heavily down on the side of his arguments. At about halfway through a blisteringly hot afternoon a warm breeze began to get up, strangely cooling at first, but then gradually particles of sand began to sting the skin and irritate the eyes. Visibility was lessening by the minute and even that weird heat haze that rose above the desert had disappeared, lost in an ever-approaching dust storm.

Almost without warning it was upon them. The screeching of the wind was like a thousand banshees. Nehesy turned to walk backwards into it, hugging his long white cloak up round his face. Sand was everywhere. Pandemonium reigned. Horses and donkeys neighed and brayed in a blind frenzy of panic. It was almost impossible to see a man a few metres away. The sand bit at men's throats. A canopy ripped loose from one of the baggage carts and was hurled away into the vastness of the desert by the angry wind. Almost choking on the continuous and venomous particles of driven sand, Nehesy seized Panehsy's arm, shouting at the top of his voice, which was almost inaudible to his companion against the force of the howling gale.

'Have the baggage carts unharnessed and lined up in a tight row. Then get all the men and horses behind them for shelter.'

Panehsy told him afterwards that he had only caught the last word – shelter – but he had guessed the rest. To give him eternal credit he did his best to achieve an end result, but faced with such an appalling adversary of such gigantic proportions, his success could never be more than minimal. Ten minutes later a mere handful of men, some twenty in all, huddled together with a few horses, behind a makeshift screen of baggage carts. For some three hours the storm never abated, deafening them in its hellish fury. Sand was everywhere and even piling up in a huge drift on the far side of the wagons.

Nehesy found himself wondering what had become of the columns of men on either side of them, and to their rear. Several of the horses, once released, had bolted in fright. There were not enough left now to even pull the baggage carts. It was impossible to see any distance at all.

Nehesy realised there was nothing anyone could do but sit tight, accepting their meagre shelter, remaining where they were until the wind blew itself out. It was impossible to hear oneself speak. Best, he concluded, to not even try. The most important thing was to try and keep the mouth and eyes shut. Even so he could feel the sand in his mouth and throat and his eyes were red-rimmed from the stinging particles.

Panehsy huddled down in a ball next to him feeling even worse. He felt doubly guilty, knowing that many of his soldiers were missing and had probably perished without cover. And what of the scouts in the van of the column? He wondered what had become of them. Everyone suffered in silence, alone with their thoughts. To have come this far only to lose everything in a dust storm, mused Nehesy. The gods could be cruel, he concluded, probably reminding him of his frailty and their own immortal power. An object – he didn't know what – flew off one of the baggage carts, catching him a glancing blow on the shoulder, before whipping away in the gale, lost from his sight in the dust.

Just before sunset, almost as suddenly as it had begun, the storm blew itself out. Nehesy tried to blink the particles of sand from his sore eyes and extricated himself from the cover of the wagons, in an effort to take stock of the damage. In the distance he could see two or three loose horses lying down on the sand. He hoped they were still alive. Of his missing columns of men there was no sign. Panehsy joined him, after having surveyed the baggage carts. He addressed his leader.

'We have been fortunate, Excellency. Most of our trade goods have survived.'

Nehesy looked more pessimistic.

'It was as well, Panehsy, that we had the carts so well battened down, but I do not think that we have been fortunate. Most of our men have disappeared, we know not whether they have even survived.' He paused, a gloomy expression on his usually affable countenance, before adding, 'We have the carts and chariots but not enough horses now to pull them.'

Panehsy gave a knowing smile before replying. He spoke calmly.

'A thousand pardons, Excellency, for addressing you so, but it is clear that you have little experience of the desert.'

'That is so. I am the queen's chancellor, not a soldier, but I fail to s—'

Panehsy cut him short before he could finish the sentence.

'I have no wish to offend, Excellency, only to give you the wisdom of my experiences in desert warfare.'

'Go on,' replied Nehesy, indulgently.

Panehsy glanced towards the western horizon. It was perfectly clear now. Only half of the crimson sun remained above the horizon, in a red, orange and purple sky.

'Soon, Excellency, it will be dark. We should remain here and camp for the night, lighting the biggest bonfire possible. In the desert at night, this will be seen for many kilometres. Our missing men, wherever they are, will see it and be guided to us. Even the horses as they grow hungry will return from afar, sensing human presence and food.'

Nehesy's smile returned then disappeared almost as quickly.

'But we have nothing to burn, my loyal friend,' he sadly replied.

'Two of the chariots will have to be expended together with some of our spare clothing. The fire must be a good one to be seen from afar.'

Nehesy slapped his companion on the back.

'Brilliant! The chariots are made mostly of wood and will burn well. See to it, Panehsy, whilst I check on every-one here.'

He found his slave girl, Salui, given to him by the queen of Punt, cowering under one of the baggage carts. As gently as he could he extricated her. Wiping her tears away, he did his best to console her. It was plain the storm had greatly frightened her, but on seeing him, her recovery was swift.

Evening gave way to night and Panehsy was proved right. Gradually their men, lost in the fury of the earlier storm, began to return to them, some in ones and twos, others in parties of six or more. For long distances they had been able to see the fire beacon in the clear and cold desert night. At night in the desert, the temperature falls like a stone. Horses too, hunger gnawing at their bellies, began to return. When the sun rose the next morning, all but six of their men and two of the horses had returned. Nehesy felt this was nothing but miraculous and immediately gave thanks to Osiris for their deliverance.

The reunited party broke their fast with a form of beer and a cereal made from wheat and maize. Half an hour later the whole reorganised columns were again on the move. Nehesy told Panehsy that they would push on to the next oasis and camp there to recuperate. After that they would travel only by night, sheltering from the blistering heat of the day.

Four days later, whilst they were sheltering at midday in one of the oases, one of Nehesy's outrider scouts brought alarming news to his leader. It appeared a large party of desert nomads were assembling out in the desert, some two kilometres away, obviously with the intent of attacking them at the oasis.

'Surely,' argued Nehesy, 'if they were that close we could see them from here? How many?'

'No, Excellency. They are assembling over that rim, about forty or more, all mounted.'

The outrider pointed in the direction of the sand dunes. Nehesy noticed that the man's horse, a black Arab, was considerably lathered and sweating badly.

'You have done well. See to your horse and send the Captains Panehsy and Umbu to me.'

The scout turned his horse about and rode off into the rich green vegetation of the oasis. Three minutes later the two subordinates joined Nehesy at the perimeter, where he was scrutinising the distant rim of the desert.

He informed both men of the imminent attack, adding, 'The defensive deployment I shall leave to you, Panehsy. With Umbu's men to assist you I am confident we have little need to feel alarmed.'

Panehsy's face was wreathed in smiles. Now, as a soldier, he was in his element.

'This oasis, with its cover, should be a simple matter to defend from an attack from the open desert.' Ignoring Nehesy, he rattled off a string of orders to the young Captain Umbu, then, remembering his commander, added as an afterthought, 'As a non-combatant, Excellency, I think you should remain with the baggage train in the centre of the oasis. I shall leave a few men with you in case they break through.'

Nehesy, at once, bridled at this.

'I may be a politician, Panehsy, but that doesn't prevent me fighting alongside my men. I shall remain alongside you throughout. Do you understand?'

'Yes, Excellency. I hadn't realised that you would want to fight the enemy with us… I thought only of your safety.'

During this discussion, Umbu had hurried off to carry out Panehsy's orders.

Ten minutes later the nomadic raiders swept down upon them, urging their galloping steeds at a headlong pace towards the oasis. Some twenty metres out from the oasis Umbu had stationed himself with some twenty spearmen to face the oncoming enemy. Concealed behind them to the rear of the baggage carts, which had been brought up to the edge of the verdantly green area, were Panehsy's bowmen.

On came the nomads, some standing in their stirrups, brandishing long curved swords, the sun glinting off the raw metal. With blood-curdling yells they swept down, on what they obviously thought was the full force opposing them. Umbu and his men held firm. When it seemed the oncoming horde would simply mow them down, trampling them under hoof, Panehsy dropped his right arm, the signal for his bowmen. From behind the baggage carts a stream of arrows was released skywards, high into the clear blue sky and descending in a rain of death upon the attackers. At that time there was no greater fighting force than the bowmen of Egypt. Within seconds half of the attackers lay writhing or dead upon the desert sands. Many of their horses perished with them, which made the watching Umbu – a lover of horses – very sad indeed, but he had no time to dwell upon the matter.

After the first shock the nomads wheeled about in confusion, then began to reassemble for another charge. A second cascade of arrows fell upon them, diminishing their numbers still further. If nothing else the nomads did not lack courage. The remainder, several of them now on foot, charged Umbu's spearmen, engaging in hand-to-hand contact. At this Panehsy sent his bowmen forward to join Umbu's spearmen. This time the bowmen carried short stabbing spears and rawhide shields.

The battle was fierce but soon over, and the survivors, six in all, prostrated themselves on the ground in surrender. Nehesy, who to Panehsy's surprise, had rushed forward, joining in the thick of the battle, had the six nomads immediately taken captive as slaves.

The battle over, he quickly renewed his authority by organising burial procedures for his own men. The dead nomads he had carried out into the desert.

'We shall leave them for their bones to be picked by the kites and jackals and to bleach in the sun. It will act as a warning to all the enemies of Egypt,' he exclaimed.

The remaining trek to the Nile at Aswan was made by darkness. They were guided by moonlight, travelled in the comparative comfort of the desert nights, and a further ten days saw the expedition's arrival at Aswan. They were greeted joyously by the people of the area, but Nehesy cut short their rapturous welcome, rapidly transferring his precious cargo and men onto the barques and barges awaiting them there. Within a few short hours they began the journey northwards up the Nile towards Thebes.

If the welcome at Aswan had been impressive, it was as nothing to that which awaited them at Thebes. Word had gone ahead that they were on their way, and a great cheering multitude saw them come to anchor. The Queen Hatshepsut, herself, together with her steward, Senenmut, accompanied by the high priest and vizier and a party of nobles, were heading the reception committee to receive them. After the queen, in her full regalia as a male Pharaoh, had made her speech of welcome, she issued an invitation to Nehesy and his captains to join her at the palace that evening for a celebratory feast.

A tired but deliriously happy Nehesy graciously accepted. It was good to be home again in Thebes, and to return as a hero was something else he hadn't expected.

Chapter XI

Hatshepsut was delighted with the trade goods brought back from the land of Punt, and that night had the dwarf acrobats perform at the feast for her court's entertainment. The plants and young trees were all arrayed in large earthenware pots, around the perimeter of the banqueting hall, for everyone's appreciative scrutiny. Nehesy's personal gift from the queen of Punt, the slave girl, Salui, also performed an erotic dance by way of entertainment for all. Also on display was the gold, malachite, ivory, myrrh, ebony and other commodities brought back from Nehesy's expedition.

Nehesy revelled in the adulation showered upon him and was inwardly relieved that the plants and shrubs had survived their long land and sea trip from that faraway land. He openly blushed when the queen teased him about the girl, Salui. Only Senenmut seemed agitated, lest his precious plants should come to harm before they could be formally planted on the approach and terraces of the queen's mortuary temple at Deir el-Bahri.

An almost continuous line of coal-black Nubian slave girls waited on the seated guests with courses of fish, goose, goat, mutton and wild fowl. This was followed by an assortment of sweetmeats and washed down with heady wine or crude beer. Then came the fruit – figs, palm nuts, melons and young shoots of several other plants. At the completion of the meal, Hatshepsut gave an official vote of thanks to Nehesy and Panehsy for the success of their expedition. Then there was more entertainment and dancing, which went on almost until dawn.

The following day Senenmut began the supervision of the installation of the young plants and shrubs at the mortuary temple. By sunset the last of them were in place and he saw to it that all were well watered in. He stood back to admire the finished work and, even if he said it himself, surely the temple had no equal in the known world. Tomorrow the work to adorn its walls with murals, relief and hieroglyphs would continue. Although well under way, he knew this work would take several years to complete. What a showpiece it would all make for visiting dignitaries. That night he sat up late, making calculations on how long the work would probably take. He concluded that by the eleventh year of the queen's reign all would be in place. Satisfied with his findings, he left his own quarters to visit Hatshepsut.

After an hour of passionate lovemaking he discussed the details of the temple decoration and his plans for further building in middle Egypt.

Hatshepsut listened attentively before enquiring, 'And what of my tomb in the valley, Djehutymes? What progress are you making there?'

Senenmut smiled.

'It goes well, Ka-re, my love. Do you want me to take you there and show it to you?'

'No, I shall go to the valley and inspect the tomb when it is complete, not a moment before. I plan to have my father's mummy moved there and I shall be buried next to him, when it is my turn to cross the river and live with the gods for all eternity. I have instructed the high priest and vizier, Hapi-soneb, to this effect.'

Senenmut showed the hurt on his face that this fact should have been relayed to the vizier before him. After all, he was the queen's lover and her architect.

If Hatshepsut noticed his look of dismay, she pretended not to. Showing all the enthusiasm of a little girl, she exclaimed, 'You shall make it the biggest and longest tomb in all Egypt to honour both my father, Tuthmosis I, and myself.'

Senenmut merely replied, 'It shall be as you wish, Ka-re. No Pharaoh will ever have a more magnificent tomb from which to embark upon their eternal journey.'

Later that night he retraced his steps to his own quarters feeling both used and sad. He knew it was quite unreasonable to expect to be buried with his queen, or Pharaoh as she was now. He might be her lover in secret and even her adviser, but he was, after all, a commoner. No matter how exalted his position at court had become, there could be no escaping that one fact.

Senenmut fell asleep wishing Hatshepsut had considered his own feelings in the matter. She hadn't even asked his opinion. Surely she knew that he would have done anything for her, he loved her so much. Could she not have expressed some regret that they couldn't be together in eternity? Was that too much to ask?

Perhaps on looking back, years later, he was to realise that the thoughts he then had were to shape future events in Egypt's eighteenth dynasty. Even in his dreams, he felt resentment as well as love. Surely she realised it was he, Senenmut, who had made it possible for her to assume the mantle of Pharaoh. Without him and his propaganda machine, it would be the young Tuthmosis III who would now be acclaimed as Pharaoh of upper and lower Egypt. Perhaps the time had come when he should be thinking more of his own future. Up until now his every waking moment had been for her, his queen, his Pharaoh, his Hatshepsut, his only love.

Hatshepsut had given him a slave girl named Meteri. It was not fitting, she said, for a man of his rank not to have at least one. Furthermore, such a move would allay any suspicion falling on their own liaison. Senenmut had

122

argued that it was not necessary, but the queen had insisted. The girl, Meteri, plainly adored him, but Senenmut barely gave her a passing glance. His eyes were for Hatshepsut alone.

However, it was certainly time to think about his own tomb, the one previously prepared for him being now not nearly grand enough for a man of his position. Tomorrow, he would draw a plan for his own last resting place. The tomb already prepared for him was of the normal T-shaped plan of the New Kingdom and was situated in Sheikh Abd Al-Quarnah, with those of other nobles. For the new one Senenmut's notion was much more ambitious. He would make an entrance to it by cutting into a quarry face on the approach road to the Deir el-Bahri temple itself. A deep entrance would head north-west, finishing up under the outer court of the temple.

Ideas began to flood his brilliant architect's brain. He would have an image of himself depicted on the northern wall of the stairway entrance. Why not, he thought, I am, after all, the architect and builder of Deir el-Bahri and as such should be represented in effigy. His ambition and pretentiousness went even further and he sat down to draw on papyrus another rough sketch. This one depicted himself with the late little Princess Neferure sitting on his knee. Discarding this for later, he began another, showing him kneeling in prayer. This he would have done in a relief, concealed behind the opened doors of one of the small shrines in Hatshepsut's upper sanctuary in the main temple.

So intent was Senenmut with his thoughts and drawings that he forgot the passing of time and worked late into the night.

★

Nehesy, as chancellor of Egypt, grew greatly in stature as the result of his successful expedition to Punt. He experienced a new-found popularity with both the nobles at court and with the ordinary people of Thebes. The expedition to the land of Punt was by far the most auspicious and daring expedition ever attempted. Earlier Pharaohs had never attempted such a project. Even so, Nehesy was glad to be back at court again in Thebes. In future, he would leave such trading missions to the young Panehsy, a military man. He, too, had benefited from the queen's favour. From captain, he had been made a general, the youngest in the Egyptian army. Thanuny, the commander of the army, had protested violently to the queen, but she had obviously enjoyed overruling him.

Nehesy had installed Salui, the slave girl, as his number one wife and spent as much time with her as his high office allowed. Clearly infatuated with the dark willowy beauty, he begrudged every minute away from her.

In these early years of Hatshepsut's reign, Egypt prospered and by and large its people were happy and better off than in earlier times. The great inundation of the Nile flood was in these years generally high, and the rich silt it left behind favoured the crops, and the granaries were full and well stocked. Trade, too, was exceptionally good, and in the treasury Thuty was kept busy recording the monetary dealings.

Hatshepsut herself continued to prosper, always appearing in public dressed as a male Pharaoh. The people accepted her laws and disregarded, or rather forgot, about the young Tuthmosis III in her shadow. Tuthmosis himself, however, was growing up, ever more resentful of his strong, wilful and beautiful stepmother. One day the time would come when he would be of age. He promised himself a reckoning with her; meanwhile his hatred grew ever stronger...

And so the years passed. Few voices other than those of Thanuny, Rekhmire and the young Tuthmosis were raised against the queen. Egypt went on contentedly, Hatshepsut gaining in stature with every passing year, no longer a youthful radiant beauty but somehow just as attractive to Senenmut in a different way. With her broad forehead and strong features she had matured in her late forties into a remarkably handsome woman. Her dark eyes had lost none of their old fire and her passion for him still burnt as fiercely as when they had first come together, all those years before. Senenmut loved her beyond life itself. There wasn't anything he wouldn't have done for her.

The day came when all the reliefs and hieroglyphs at Deir el-Bahri were finally completed, besides his own tomb and the queen's. It was, of course, considered impolite to stop work on a Pharaoh's tomb until the monarch died, so further refinements and hieroglyphs would always be added there. To all intents and purposes, though, Senenmut's work there was over.

In middle Egypt several fine buildings and temples had sprung up in Hatshepsut's honour, built by Amunhotep, Senenmut's assistant. The great temple of Karnak had been added to and the two huge granite obelisks stood proudly there, a testimony to Hatshepsut's reign over Egypt.

No man in all the land was more important, or of higher stature, than Senenmut with his numerous titles bestowed on him by the queen. Even the high priest and vizier, Hapi-soneb, took second place to him in all but name. It was fortunate for Senenmut that the vizier was a good friend and not susceptible to jealousy or things might have been very different.

One man, however, who was very jealous of Senenmut's influential position, was Rekhmire, vizier to the young Tuthmosis.

Imagine, then, Senenmut's surprise when one day

Rekhmire approached him saying, 'It has come to my ears that your great masterpiece at Deir el-Bahri in the queen's name is now complete. I wonder whether you would do me the honour of escorting me round the temple, that I might appreciate it more than if I were to visit it on my own.'

Senenmut shrugged, greatly surprised. He had always been aware of Rekhmire's hostility and animosity towards him. Could it be that the man now wanted to bury the sword he had always carried? Senenmut decided to give him the benefit of the doubt.

'Certainly. It would be an honour to so escort you round the temple. Shall we say tomorrow morning at eight of the clock?'

'I shall await you at the temple entrance,' exclaimed Rekhmire. With that he turned on his heel and strode off.

The following morning Senenmut conducted Rekhmire on a guided tour of the mortuary temple. At various points he stopped and explained in some detail to his guest, who would merely grunt in a disinterested way. Senenmut could feel his own temper rising. Why had the man asked for the tour when he clearly wasn't interested? It wasn't until they reached the inner sanctuary and Rekhmire saw the relief depicting Senenmut that his whole demeanour changed. He became positively excited.

'You have had yourself depicted here in the queen's inner sanctuary, architect Senenmut!' He virtually fired the remark at Senenmut.

'That is so, Rekhmire. I am, after all, the queen's steward and would be expected to look after her on this earth after death. She would need me in the afterlife.'

Rekhmire grunted.

'In the tomb I would have expected this, but here in the mortuary temple... surely the height of presumption on your part... don't think I didn't notice the earlier reliefs of you at the entrance… Does the queen know of this?'

'I shall not deign to converse further with you, Rekhmire. It is clear you are not interested in architecture of the highest calibre.'

Senenmut about-turned, leaving Rekhmire standing gazing at the relief on the temple wall. As he marched out of the temple, he nevertheless felt an uneasy sensation somewhere deep down inside himself. Had he stayed to see the self-satisfied expression on Rekhmire's face he might have been even more troubled.

At about the same time Egypt began to experience its own difficulties, a growing unrest along its borders and, worst of all, severe drought. The Nile's inundation that year had been almost non-existent. The annual crops had largely failed and for the first time stocks in the granaries were low. Poorly fed, because of famine in the land, the people had little resistance to the new pestilence that seemed to be engulfing middle Egypt. Thousands had died and the malady had now spread into Thebes itself.

Rekhmire was smugly confident. The opportunity he had been waiting for had come his way. Tuthmosis was now a young man and he, Rekhmire, had carefully groomed him for the role he was to play. Together with Thanuny, the commander of the army, he began putting his propaganda machine into effect. A paid mercenary force of troublemakers roamed the countryside spreading stories of discontent and unrest.

It was all because Egypt was ruled by a female Pharaoh that this had come about. The people with hunger gnawing at their bellies were ready to listen to anything. Few of them realised that all these things had happened many times before, in other dynasties. The problems were all heaped on Hatshepsut's doorstep. The queen herself had become depressed of late and greatly concerned about the circumstances that had befallen the land. Even her beloved

Senenmut had been unable to come up with a solution or panacea.

Rekhmire now knew this was the time to play his ace in the pack. He sought an audience with the queen. After a cautious and polite beginning he gradually eased into his reason for requesting a hearing, using all his consummate cunning.

'In the mortuary temple is depicted what we know as the "birth relief", is it not, oh mighty Majesty?'

Hatshepsut knew full well that he referred to a scene where she was conceived and chosen by Amun himself to be king. Her large dark eyes narrowed suspiciously, questioning his motives.

'Do you dare challenge that which Amun himself has decreed?' she exclaimed.

'On the contrary, Majesty, no one doubts it for even a minute. It is your right as the god's living image.'

Hatshepsut began to wonder where all this was leading. She well knew that Rekhmire, her stepson's vizier, was no friend to her.

'So what purpose has this visit?' she fired at him.

'Would you say, Majesty, that such scenes, so depicted, should be reserved for Pharaohs and the gods themselves?'

Hatshepsut was puzzled and more than a little annoyed but she was no fool. It was obvious that Rekhmire was up to some trick and laying a trap for her.

'Get to the point, Rekhmire, your audience is nearly at an end.'

'In such an esteemed sanctuary as your inner temple, oh mighty Pharaoh, you would not expect to see a commoner amongst Pharaohs and gods.'

'I say again, Rekhmire, make your purpose here clear.'

'On the walls in the mortuary temple at Deir el-Bahri, both at the entrance and in the inner sanctuary, are reliefs of your steward, Senenmut, a commoner.'

Hatshepsut was profoundly shocked. Senenmut must have added these since her last visit there, but she wasn't about to let Rekhmire see that he had shocked her.

Quick to recover, she countered, 'What of it? Surely you know he is both architect and builder of this masterpiece?'

Rekhmire smiled secretly, delighted with his strategy. Now for the *coup de grâce*.

'And what thinks Your Majesty of his new tomb?'

Hatshepsut knew nothing about any new tomb. Senenmut had never even mentioned it to her.

'What new tomb is this you speak of?'

Rekhmire gloatingly went on, in his most oily vein, 'The tomb for Senenmut your steward, which has its final burial chamber in the very approaches of your wonderful temple. Surely this is presumptuous in the extreme?' When Hatshepsut didn't respond, Rekhmire went on in detail, finally getting round to the illicit carving of Senenmut and herself in the cavern above the temple. He could see immediately that she knew nothing of this, and try as she might, she was unable to hide the shock his disclosure had caused her. Clearly at a loss, she rose slowly and serenely from her throne of audience and, in an effort to regain her composure, addressed him in a tight-lipped manner.

'Your audience is at an end, Rekhmire. The news you bring me is old and withers with the leaves of autumn. When you have something new to relate, request another audience with me... Now, begone from my presence.'

Rekhmire, a satisfied smirk on his face, bowed low and backed out of the reception chamber. He was well aware that, whatever the queen had pretended she already knew, his news was a great shock to her.

No sooner had Rekhmire vacated the palace than Hatshepsut sent a slave hurrying away to summon Senenmut to her side. She awaited his arrival, pacing up and down, ringing her hands together in consternation, and every so often stamping her foot angrily. Hadn't she enough trouble already, without this new turn of events to worry about!

Chapter XII

Senenmut came as quickly as he could, but due to the distance involved, it was fully two hours before he was ushered in to see her. During this time Hatshepsut, worried and anxious beyond belief at the growing problems of ruling in Egypt's dire predicament, was almost beside herself. No sooner had Senenmut appeared than she began to verbally attack him with accusations concerning the building of his tomb on the extremity of the temple. Before he could even begin to defend himself she began a new verbal assault about the reliefs depicted there. In all their years together, hardly a cross word to him had escaped her lips. Senenmut was quite shattered by the animosity and fury she was venting upon him.

'You, a commoner, thought fit to be buried with your Pharaoh?'

'No, Ka-re, only to be near you always, to serve you in death as I have in life.'

'Use not that ridiculous title to me, steward. You have betrayed me!'

Senenmut hotly denied the accusation.

'I would never betray you, Your Majesty. My life has been for you. Always I have only thought to serve you. Gladly would I die for you.'

Hatshepsut was in no mood to listen. In full flight of temper she laced into him.

'How could you, my steward, on whom I have bestowed every honour, raising you to great heights in my land, so deceive me, saying nothing of this new tomb of yours, and further depicting yourself in relief in the holy temple? May

Hathor forgive you and your vain presumption.' She then went on, complaining about the ribald carving in the cavern above the temple. 'You must have known of this for you are at the temple every day, yet you said nothing of this.'

Senenmut countered, 'I thought only to protect your feelings so I said nothing.'

'Why did you not have the carving defaced?'

'Because so to do would have convinced workmen that there was truth in the drawing. Better to leave it and say little.'

'Better for your vanity, you mean,' ranted Hatshepsut.

Senenmut realised that, in this mood, there was little use in trying to reason with her. In a firm quiet voice, he said, 'If I have offended Your Majesty do with me what you will. I sought only to serve. I beg your forgiveness. You are my only love and I would pluck out my eyes and cut off my right hand, rather than displease you in any way.'

Hatshepsut looked at him coldly. Senenmut had never before seen such hurt in anyone's eyes. She wiped away a tear, anxious that he shouldn't see it. Turning her back on him, she whispered, 'Go, Senenmut. I may send for you again, I may not.'

Senenmut couldn't believe the words he had heard.

'No, Ka-re, not like this. Don't send me away from you,' he almost pleaded.

In a louder voice she commanded, 'Begone from my sight, betrayer!'

It was almost too much for Senenmut to stand. Sadly, he turned and slowly, head down, trudged out from her audience chamber, through the palace and out into the blistering heat of the day. Tears stabbed at his eyes and ran down his face in rivulets.

Back in his own quarters that night he consoled himself with the thought that Hatshepsut would get over her fury with him, and her love for him would return in plentiful abundance. The slave girl the queen had given him, Meteri, seeing his distress, offered herself to him but he brushed her aside roughly. Tomorrow Hatshepsut would send for him. He knew she would…

The next day came and went and the next day and the one after that, but no call came. Senenmut stopped eating and wallowed in his distress. He didn't even go to the temple and forgot about his drawings for further building in middle Egypt. Recently he had been restoring temples destroyed there by the Hittites. Now all but his misery was forgotten. Senenmut had nothing left to live for without his queen, his Hatshepsut.

On the fourth day he left his quarters, saying nothing to the girl, Meteri, of his intended destination and walked off, a broken-hearted man towards the barren desert. The fierce heat of the noonday sun at its zenith beat down upon him. Senenmut felt none of it, so engrossed was he in his own misery. Nothing mattered anymore. All his wonderful architectural works were as nothing. His mind was numb. The one person who meant more to him than all the world had rejected him.

Like a man in a trance he trudged ever onwards deeper into the desert, leaving Thebes and all he loved behind him. Soon he was totally alone, a distant speck on the horizon. His eyes and throat burnt, but he carried no water nor wanted any. On through the unrelenting and unmerciful heat he trudged. Finally the sun sank over the western rim of the desert in a fiery crimson ball; dusk and then night descended upon him, the temperature dropping like a stone, such was the contrast to the day. His teeth began to chatter with the cold and he started to shiver and shake. Overcome with fatigue he fell to his knees in the sand and rolled over onto his back. Not even aware of the myriad of stars above him, he fell into an exhausted sleep.

It was the spiteful rays of the sun the next morning that

awoke him, although he could barely see it through the slits that passed for eyes in his face. His tongue was swollen to twice its size and his skin was dry like papyrus. His body craved water but in his numb state he cared little. Death would be a merciful end. Dragging himself to his feet he forced himself ever onwards. High in the blue cloudless sky a group of vultures endlessly circled above his solitary form, shadowing his every step. Through nearly closed eyes he saw their shadow on the sands next to him. Looking up he screamed up at them like a madman possessed.

'Soon, my black-feathered sons of Seth... soon.' His voice tailed off in a half cackle, because his throat was so dry.

Senenmut staggered on throughout the day, falling every few metres and somehow miraculously rising again, to totter on once more. Noon came and went. He could hardly breathe now in the intense heat, more and more vultures closed in, sensing the end. Once one of them landed next to him after one of his falls. Scooping up a handful of sand, he threw it at the trespasser in his space. With a squawk the giant bird became airborne once more.

It was just before sunset when Senenmut sank to his knees and pitched forward onto his face to move no more. Unconsciousness claimed him and death was not far away. His only companions, the vultures, descended onto the desert floor, encircling his lifeless prostrate form. Ominously they waited, their beady eyes focused on the man's still form. Gradually first one, then another, became bolder until one landed on his back. There was no movement to disturb the scavenger as his vicious curved beak tore at the man's neck. The rest of the flock moved in. Soon all a passing Bedouin would have seen was a black mass of feathered birds gathered round something on the ground.

★

For the first week after her confrontation with Senenmut the queen had remained in her chambers, attended only by her maids. She had cancelled her daily grievance hearings, which were her usual custom, until further notice. At first she had been furious with Senenmut for his presumption, but gradually her mood changed to a morose sulkiness. Let him suffer for a while, it will remind him of his place, she told herself. At the end of a week, however, she was missing him dreadfully. She concluded that Senenmut had suffered enough. Time to forgive him; besides his presence was vital to her. His brilliant probing wit and sound advice she depended upon. Besides, she loved him greatly, otherwise she would never have reacted as she had. Even the thought of recalling him to her presence made her heart jump with ecstatic joy. Soon they would be as one again. Without further ado, she sent one of the slave girls off in search of him.

'Tell him to come at once, girl,' she commanded.

She waited impatiently for Senenmut's arrival, having spent an extra-long time with her make-up and attire. An aroma of exotic perfume lingered around her as she drummed her fingers on the ebony arm of her chair. Why was he taking so long to come to her? One hour passed, then two and it was almost up to the third hour when the slave girl returned in tears.

'Wherever have you been, girl? And stop that snivelling at once! Where is my steward and why have you returned without him?'

The girl fell at her feet and in between sobs gasped out the explanation.

'Forgive me, Your Majesty, but I have searched and asked everywhere… H… he is nowhere to be found and hasn't been seen for the last three days.'

Hatshepsut rose from her chair and placed a hand under the girl's chin, forcing her head upwards.

'You are a stupid girl. Somebody must know of his whereabouts. Perhaps he has journeyed to the middle kingdom to supervise the building projects there,' Hatshepsut exclaimed, which was more a case of convincing herself than Shazar, the slave girl.

Shazar began to cry and on her knees kissed the queen's feet. Hatshepsut pushed her roughly aside and issued another command.

'Have every slave in the palace go out and search for him and send the captain of my personal guard to me at once, girl.'

Shazar leapt to her feet and rushed out, in her haste forgetting to retreat backwards and bow. The queen was so agitated that she didn't even notice. Three minutes later the captain of her guard arrived, bowing low.

'You ordered my presence, oh mighty Pharaoh. Your wish is my command.' Hatshepsut nodded before responding, 'It seems my steward, Senenmut, has disappeared. Despatch the entire guard and search until you find him.'

Re-ar, the captain, protested, 'But Your Majesty, if I do that the palace will remain entirely unprotected. I cannot allow y—'

Hatshepsut, beside herself and for once losing all dignity, screamed at Re-ar.

'I have given you an order. See it is carried out and don't return without my steward.'

The captain, a hurt expression on his usually genial face, bowed low and backed out saying, 'It shall be as you wish, Your Majesty.'

The next few hours in the palace seemed like eternity to Hatshepsut. With all the servants and guards out searching for Senenmut, the whole building throughout its marble and alabaster halls seemed both lonely and silent, like death itself. The day wore on ominously; neither guards nor servants returned with news. Were they all so frightened to face her? Surely someone must know what had happened to Senenmut.

At sunset a nervous Re-ar returned. The look on his face confirmed for her that he and his men had failed in their search.

'Well?' snapped the queen, impatiently.

'I am sorry, Your Majesty, but of your steward, the architect Senenmut, there is no sign. No one has seen him for the last three days.'

Now the queen's temper turned to acute anxiety.

'Three days, you say?'

Re-ar nodded in confirmation. A silence reigned between them, the queen seeming to be deep in thought. Suddenly an idea struck her. She turned again to Re-ar.

'His slave girl, Meteri, is she in his quarters?'

'Yes, Your Majesty,' said Re-ar, puzzled.

'Very well, have her brought here immediately,' commanded Hatshepsut, coming to a sudden decision.

Ten minutes later the girl, Meteri, was prostrate on the marble mosaic floor in front of her. Hatshepsut commanded her to rise. The girl was red-eyed and had obviously been crying. Dark circles under her eyes showed an obvious lack of sleep. Hatshepsut tried a kindly tone, one which she would not normally have used to a servant.

'Now, Meteri, when did you last see your master, the architect Senenmut, my steward?'

'Three days ago, Your Majesty,' Meteri said and rubbed both eyes, clearly distressed.

'Do you know where he is?'

'No, Majesty, only where he was going… the direction, I mean.'

The queen's face lit up expectantly.

'Go on, girl, go on,' she said, impatiently.

Meteri stifled a sob before continuing her narrative.

'Three days ago, just before noon, he left the palace, saying nothing to anybody. He was in a very strange mood.'

Hatshepsut interrupted, 'What sort of mood, Meteri?'

'Strange, moody, silent. He just walked out and headed straight for the desert. I called out to him but it was as if he couldn't hear. I followed because I was so worried he would come to harm.'

'And?' prompted Hatshepsut.

'He walked to the edge of the desert and then just carried on walking into the wilderness. I kept on calling, but all to no avail. I stood and watched until he was but a speck on the horizon.'

'Why didn't you do something, girl? Fetch somebody or something?'

'I did. I became so worried that I went to find the royal guard to see Captain Re-ar, in the hope that he would do something for my master.'

The queen looked flabbergasted.

'And Captain Re-ar did nothing?' she said, hotly.

'I never saw him, Your Majesty. The sergeant said I was a bad girl and beat me. Told me not to bother them with such wild stories.

'This sergeant – would you recognise him again, Meteri?'

'Certainly, Your Majesty, a large brutish man with a black beard.'

'When you leave here, go to Captain Re-ar and let him have you identify the man. He will be severely punished for his folly. Now, girl, was your master carrying food and water into the desert?'

'No, Your Majesty, nothing… If he had been I would have seen as he was only lightly dressed.'

Hatshepsut's distress showed on her face. No one could live in the desert without water. She knew that as well as anybody. Coming to an instant decision, she ordered

Meteri to go and find Re-ar.

'Take him to where you saw your master, Senenmut, disappear into the desert. Tell him to lead a detachment out into the desert for a full-scale search. He is to leave immediately and take as many men as he needs. Now go at once, Meteri. There is not a moment to lose.'

Meteri scrambled to her feet and scurried off in search of Re-ar.

Hatshepsut, looking strained and wan, exclaimed aloud, 'Pray to Osiris that we are not too late. I shall go to the temple of Hathor and pray for his survival.'

Pulling on a dark cloak over her apparel she hurried from the palace, never giving a thought for her own safety.

Chapter XIII

For the following week Hatshepsut sent search party after search party into the desert, but as Captain Re-ar informed her, 'Looking for one man out there is like looking for a specific fish in the Nile.' Again and again she forced him to return until, taking his courage in his hands, he exclaimed, 'If he is out there alone with no water then he has long since joined Osiris in the hereafter.'

At this the queen flew into a rage and ordered him out. After his departure she fell on the counterpane of her bed in a flood of tears, and remained there for several hours. The following day she made a determined effort to pull herself together, resuming her daily audiences where she listened to the grievances of her subjects. After a while, though, she found it quite impossible to concentrate on what she was hearing. All she could think of was Senenmut's disappearance. Why? she asked herself. Surely he knew she would forgive him. She had only meant to punish him for a while. Now whatever would she do without him? Never had she felt so utterly alone.

Suddenly, she was aware of her vizier's voice, requesting her decision on some mundane matter. Jolted back to reality she looked down on Hapi-soneb from her throne. He was standing expectantly with the plaintiff, an elderly noble. Hatshepsut realised she had been so deep in thought that she hadn't heard a word relating to the man's case.

Quietly she rose from the richly carved throne and, looking at them both in turn, exclaimed, 'I think it best, Hapi-soneb, if you decide the matter. In fact, you can stand in for me for the rest of the day.' With that she marched out of the chamber.

Hapi-soneb coughed with embarrassment. 'The Pharaoh is unwell.' He then went on to arbitrate on the matter that had been raised before the queen.

Over the next few weeks the daily routine of the palace fell into disarray. Hatshepsut found herself shelving every matter that the vizier put before her. Even the mild-mannered vizier was becoming exasperated. He discussed the matter with the chancellor, Nehesy.

'It seems the disappearance of our architect friend has affected the queen so badly that she can think of little else.'

Nehesy sympathised.

'It would be easier if we knew what had happened to the man. Not knowing makes it worse for the queen.'

'She obviously blames herself for whatever happened to make him act in the way that he did,' put in Hapi-soneb.

Nehesy gave a poor imitation of a smile, more like a grimace really.

'Well, it's no secret that they have always been lovers,' he said. 'The problem is, Nehesy, that if she doesn't pull herself together I fear her enemies will capitalise on it.'

'That is true. She has always ruled with strength. Indecision will be seen as weakness. Can you not make her see this? You are, after all, her vizier and adviser?'

'Do you think I haven't tried? However, I shall try again.'

The two men wandered off, going their separate ways. Hapi-soneb went to see the queen, who reluctantly agreed to see him. Making his boldest effort yet, he stated the grim facts to her, realising that if he incurred her displeasure he could be sealing his own fate. Much to his amazement, however, Hatshepsut listened to all he had to say, showing very little, if any, emotion at all.

At the conclusion of his long speech she merely replied, 'Do as you think best, vizier... Will that be all?'

Totally amazed at the queen's response, which was nothing like he had expected, he could only answer a meek, 'Yes, Your Majesty.'

As if in a trance, she rose, looked into an unseen distance beyond him and vacated the chamber. Hapi-soneb shook his head in nonplussed disbelief. Was this the beginning of the end for Hatshepsut, he wondered.

Rekhmire and Thanuny were in conference with the young Tuthmosis, now a young man of fine stature, broad of shoulders and deep of chest. Although of only average height, he was possessed of terrific strength. His ambition still lay with the army rather than politics. Handsome of face, he had already excelled as a soldier and his conquests amongst the fair sex had been many. His nature, however, was rather cold and uncaring. He considered women were to be conquered, rather like his country's enemies.

'Now is the time, Majesty,' urged Thanuny.

'The time for what?' queried the young monarch, as he tested the edge of a newly sharpened sword with his moistened finger.

'For you to take your rightful place as the true Pharaoh designated by your father, Tuthmosis II,' urged the commander of the army.

Tuthmosis swung the sword in a great arc narrowly missing Thanuny's nose. The latter, pulled his head back in an involuntary manoeuvre. Tuthmosis laughed loudly at the other's discomfiture.

'I am already the king, the mighty Tuthmosis III, everyone knows this.'

Risking his young protégé's displeasure, Thanuny argued, 'It is true that you are the Pharaoh, but I fear everyone does not know this. You have been pushed aside, Majesty, by your stepmother. She has usurped your rightful place as Pharaoh of upper and lower Egypt.'

Tuthmosis, with a sly look, responded by saying, 'You, Thanuny, are the commander of the army. Rise against her on my behalf.'

'It is not quite as easy as that. Although she is fast losing ground, many of the people still love her. The time is not yet right, but we must be ready for the moment when it comes. The queen must be discredited still further in the eyes of the multitude.'

'Then what are you waiting for, Thanuny? It is for you and Rekhmire to spread the word amongst them that the queen is no longer fit to rule.'

It was Thanuny's turn this time to give a sly smile.

'It is being done, Majesty. Even as we speak, our agents are active everywhere.'

★

Out in the desert a hunting party had penetrated deep into the wilderness, their purpose to capture as many animals as possible to tame for domestication. Having lassoed them without harming any, they would be driven back to civilisation for training to plough, or as beasts of burden.

When a royal party such as this one ventured forward to hunt in the desert, it was more for sport. Sometimes the Pharaoh, or one of his high nobles, would lead the expedition, and the animals would already have been driven to a makeshift enclosure for the Pharaoh's entertainment and to demonstrate his courage. Arrow after arrow would be handed up to him and he would merely have to fire and despatch the luckless animals, which would then go to provide meat for the royal court. Hatshepsut never took part in these barbarous encounters and had little interest in hunting or blood sports of any kind.

Today was no exception, and she had remained at the palace whilst one of her nobles, one Harkhuf, led the hunting party. Far out in the desert, whilst driving the captured animals homewards, they came across a skeleton of a man, half buried by the wind-driven sand. Harkhuf would not have bothered to have descended from his chariot, had a glint of gold from around the skeleton's neck not caught his eyes. Such bony remains were often encountered in the wilderness, frequently the remains of some poor traveller or nomad, who had run out of water and died of thirst. Climbing down from his chariot, he advanced to the half-covered remains. Examining the gold pendant round the neck of the gruesome skeleton, he almost jumped back in shock.

'What is it, my lord?' enquired his slave and chariot driver who had accompanied him.

'The cartouche... see this, round his neck... It is the cartouche of Queen Hatshepsut,' gasped Harkhuf.

Shreds of clothing still hung round some of the bones, although most had long since disappeared. Harkhuf could see from the remaining material that it had once been of excellent quality. Carefully he removed the golden pendant with its royal cartouche from around the poor unfortunate's neck and then, borrowing his slave's dagger, cut the remaining shreds of cloth away from the bones.

'It is plain that this man, whoever he was, had a position and standing, therefore we shall bury him here.' Turning to his slave he instructed him to organise a party of bearers to pile the sand up over the skeleton. 'At least we shall stop the jackals feasting on the poor fellow's bones,' he said, before offering a prayer to Osiris for the dead man's soul.

Back at the palace, Harkhuf immediately sought an audience with the queen. She had him admitted but showed little interest at his arrival saying, 'If you have come to tell me how well you have done with your hunt, I do not wish to hear it, for I have little heart or appetite for such ventures.'

'No, Your Majesty, I would not have bothered you, but for this.'

He stretched out an arm, holding forth the golden pendant. Hatshepsut's interest was immediately aroused. She reached eagerly for it, recognising it instantly.

'Where did you find this? It belonged to my steward, Senenmut, who, as you know, disappeared some time ago. See, it bears my cartouche.'

Harkhuf related solemnly where he had found the golden piece and the circumstances. The queen's face went literally grey through her tan, and he thought that she would faint from shock. Producing the remnants of material from a hessian bag he handed them over to her.

'These, too, I found nearby.'

Discretion told him not to say he had cut them from the bones.

Hatshepsut, hardly able to speak coherently, so great was her shock, strung a few words together.

'And... the r... remains? Did you... bring them back f... for burial?'

'No, Your Majesty. We knew not whose they were, so we buried them there in the desert.'

Hatshepsut leapt to her feet, fury replacing shock. 'What!' she screamed. 'This was undoubtedly my steward and architect, Senenmut, for whom we have long been searching and you chose to leave him in the desert?'

Harkhuf backed away. The queen in this mood was decidedly formidable.

'I did not know, Your Majesty. I thought only to give him burial whoever he was.'

Hatshepsut looked at him in cold fury.

'You will return this instant with a party of slaves and recover the body. Do you understand?'

'But it is almost dark, Your Majesty, and the desert winds are rising. It will not be possible to relocate the place where we buried him.'

Hatshepsut's beautiful dark eyes narrowed menacingly.

'You would do well to leave at once, Harkhuf... Return without the remains and pray to Osiris for your own safety.'

Harkhuf, fearful for his own life, departed post-haste to raise a search party.

Harkhuf had always known the search would prove fruitless. The dunes and valleys of the great desert changed endlessly with frequent dust storms. The undulations of the wilderness were never the same two days running. After two days and nights, with their supply of water running low, he was forced to call off the search, but it was more than he dare do to return to Hatshepsut empty-handed. Leaving his second in command to report back to her, he made good his escape, leaving immediately with his belongings and family for the border. Convinced that the queen's retribution for his failure to locate the remains would result in his own death, he was taking no chances.

Hatshepsut was indeed furious when his second in command, Mose, reported the failure to her and even more so with Harkhuf's cowardice in not facing her. She sent charioteers out in pursuit immediately, but already too much time had been lost and together with his family he had made good his escape.

Alone that night, she turned the gold pendant, taken from the remains, over and over in her hands. She had recognised it immediately as the one she had given to Senenmut many years earlier. Raising it to her lips, she kissed it, the memories of many nights of bliss returning nostalgically to her. It, together with the remnants of cloth, convinced her that it was Senenmut's remains that they had found out there in the wilderness. Disturbed by guilt, she lay awake that night. Why had she acted so? He hadn't deserved such punishment. She realised that the reliefs and inscriptions in the mortuary temple were as nothing, compared to the loss of him. Even in the building of his tomb, he had only wanted to be near her in death, as he had always been in life.

Unable to face life without her, he had obviously just walked into the desert to die. There was a lump in her throat and her eyes were sore from crying. She was to blame for losing the only man she had ever really loved, besides her father. Now she would never see him again and would have to govern alone. Until recently she had never realised just how much she had depended on his wise judgement and decisions. No longer would he be there to advise her. Now when she needed him most of all, with her kingdom falling into disarray with famine and insurrection. How long could she go on with all the forces beginning to stack up against her? She well knew that Rekhmire and Thanuny were deliberately pushing her stepson's rights down the throats of the people. Dissatisfied and hungry people would be apt to believe them.

Thanuny controlled the army. How long before he led it against her? Hatshepsut was aware that of late, desperate with grief, she had let things go. Tomorrow she would start reasserting herself as the living Pharaoh. She owed it to Senenmut's memory. He was right. He had made her into what she was, and she must not let him down. One day they would be reunited in the afterlife. Until then, she must rule wisely and well. If only she didn't feel so tired…

The next morning she renewed her grievance audiences in the great chamber, aided by her vizier, Hapi-soneb, at her side. To say that he was relieved at her new attitude would have been an understatement. Loyal to her through-out, he had found it a great strain of late, making excuses for her apparent lack of rule. Now she was back, the old Hatshepsut once more. Perhaps it was not too late to re-establish her in the eyes of the disbelievers.

The following day she even toured the poorer areas of Thebes, dressed in her full regalia as a male Pharaoh. Hapi-soneb accompanied her. She listened with patience to the problems facing her subjects. She sent her own physician to those who were suffering and had extra grain issued to the starving. Gradually, over the next few months, she began, greatly to the consternation of Rekhmire and Thanuny, to regain her erstwhile popularity with the multitude.

Inwardly she remained guilt-ridden and disturbed. She found it harder to sleep at nights, and her physician constantly prepared sleeping draughts for her. Even her dreams were interrupted by restless nightmares. Always she blamed herself for Senenmut's death. If only she hadn't been so hard on him. Why hadn't she forgiven him at once? Now it was too late.

During her waking hours the sparkle had gone from her beautiful eyes and the lithesome bounce from her step. Suddenly it seemed as if age was catching up with her. Constantly she would look to left and right, as if expecting an enemy.

More and more, she became aware of Rekhmire's skulking presence, always watching her, waiting for her to make that one major mistake. The boy king, Tuthmosis, was no longer a boy, and bitterly resented her rule over Egypt. Hatshepsut was sure that both were hatching plots against her to place Tuthmosis on the throne, aided and abetted by Thanuny.

There was no one, with Senenmut gone, to whom to air her suspicions. When she tried to talk to her vizier, Hapi-soneb, all the loyal little man would say was, 'Your Majesty has no need to fear as she is greatly loved by her people', and that was the end of the subject. Hapi-soneb, steadfast vizier and high priest, wouldn't have recognised intrigue if it had risen up and hit him in the face. More and more she realised that the years ahead, whatever remained to her as Pharaoh, without Senenmut at her side, would be ridden with difficulties.

Chapter XIV

1483 BC

Four troublesome years had passed since the untimely death of Senenmut, years in which Hatshepsut hung tenuously to her crown during famine, poor floods and insurrections.

Along Egypt's borders new enemies were massing, gradually encroaching onto Egyptian soil. Sadly Hatshepsut knew little of war and the people who should have been supporting her, namely Thanuny and the army, by design, were doing nothing. On the contrary, Thanuny, with the help of Rekhmire, was spreading rumours that soon, due to Hatshepsut's incompetence, Egypt would be overrun, much as it had been years before by the Hittites.

'What Egypt needs is another Ahmose, who swept out the Hittites,' he said. 'If we only had Tuthmosis III in power, he would know what to do.'

Very little of this reached the ears of Hatshepsut. Once a week she would make a pilgrimage to her mortuary temple at Deir el-Bahri. It was the only way in which she could still feel near to Senenmut. In this beautiful temple that he had built, she could still feel his presence. She would gaze up at his effigy behind the inner sanctuary and reaffirm her love. Then, offering up a prayer to the goddess, Hathor, she would remain on her knees for several minutes in penitence.

By the time she had returned one night to the palace from one of these weekly excursions it was already dusk. Dismissing her escorting guard, she decided on an early night. The day had been long and arduous, unusually hot, even for an Egyptian summer, the evening little better. Hardly a breath of air disturbed the drapes in her boudoir. She beat the gong for her maidservant and was surprised when it was answered not by her handmaiden, Shazar, but by a strange girl. Becoming alarmed, she enquired of the newcomer, 'Where is my handmaiden, Shazar?'

'She has been taken ill, Majesty, and confined to bed by the physician, who has sent me in her place. My name is Alysha.'

Hatshepsut became suspicious.

'When Shazar is not available her sister waits upon me. Where is Mynha?'

'She is ill also, Majesty, and confined to her bed.'

'This all sounds very strange. How can it be that both are ill at the same time? I shall go to the servants' quarters and see for myself.'

The girl, Alysha, stepped boldly into the queen's path, saying, 'The physician said that you would probably be concerned for them, but that they are both suffering from a contagious disease and you must not, as Pharaoh, be exposed to it... I beg of you, Majesty, remain here and I shall serve you.'

Hatshepsut looked far from convinced but, if it were true, supposed the physician's reasoning was sound.

'I shall talk with him in the morning about this matter.'

'Very good, Majesty... Shall I serve you your evening meal now?'

'No, it is too hot to eat. I wish only that you bring my nightly sleeping potion. I intend to rest early.'

It was perhaps a pity that Hatshepsut couldn't see the girl Alysha's smug face as she left the boudoir. Ten minutes later she returned with a golden goblet.

'Will you partake of this now, Your Majesty?' she said, proffering the queen the goblet.

'No, set it down on the marble table, there by the bed, girl,' commanded the queen, without giving the receptacle another look.

It was about an hour later, an hour she spent studying sheaves of papyrus brought to her earlier in the day by Hapi-soneb, that she sat down fully clothed on the edge of the great bed. Reaching for the golden goblet, she sipped its contents, so preoccupied that she hardly noticed the extra-bitter taste of the liquid as it slipped down her throat. She was already taking her second swallow when she felt a tight burning feeling in her throat and chest.

Gasping for breath, she dropped the receptacle which clattered to the marble floor. Air – she must have air. Dragging herself across the room, she tore at the huge drapes which kept at bay the night air from the archway to the veranda. The pain in her chest was unbearable. It was reaching right down to her stomach now. One of the hanging drapes came down on top of her and she fell in a writhing heap on the floor, trying to disentangle herself from the cloth.

Once free, she crawled on hands and knees towards where the great oxhide gong hung. Somehow she must summon help. Suddenly, the realisation hit her that she had been poisoned. Whoever had done this to her had seen to it that all her loyal staff had been removed. The girl, Alysha, was all part of the plot. Suddenly, amidst her terrible suffering and pain, she remembered where she had seen the girl before. It was amongst the harem of Rekhmire, her stepson's vizier. Now she knew who had poisoned her. A black mist was coming over her eyes. She wasn't even going to reach the gong, let alone have the strength left to beat it to summon help. Her whole body was consumed with unbearable burning pain. She opened her mouth to cry out.

'Senenmut, my love, help me,' were the words that came out of her parched and fiery throat. A moment later she pitched forward, writhing in agony on the cold marble floor.

Through a crack in the curtain the girl, Alysha, watched the queen's distress, a satisfied expression on her face. When the queen finally lay still and hadn't moved for fully five minutes, Alysha entered and collected the golden goblet. Taking it out onto the veranda, she poured the remaining contents out over the terrace down to the rocks far below. She rinsed the goblet in the fountain and refilled it with water, leaving it by the queen's bedside once more. With a final sideways look at the prostrate body of Hatshepsut, she left to find her master. Ten minutes later she was relaying to him all that had happened.

'Shall we now sound the alarm?' she enquired.

'No, girl. We shall wait. Let her own people find her in the morning. Nobody must suspect us. It will look like she has had a heart attack and died a natural death,' exclaimed Rekhmire, an evil grin on his face.

The following morning Shazar woke beside her sister, Mynha. She felt heavy-headed and her throat was dry. The sun was already shining through the arch leading to their little room. The sisters shared the large truckle-bed. Quickly she shook Mynha awake.

'Whatever has happened, sister? The sun is already high in the sky. I can remember nothing since early last evening.'

Mynha rubbed her sleepy eyes.

'It was that drink the merchant offered us. He said it was nectar from the gods.'

Realisation and remembrance came back to Shazar. She recalled the smooth-talking merchant who had made the acquaintance of both girls during their off-duty hours.

'Quick, we must attend the queen,' cried Shazar.

'But she has not sounded the gong for us or we would have heard it,' pointed out Mynha.

'Strange, considering the hour,' agreed Shazar. 'But then, if we were drugged, would we have heard it?'

'If we hadn't, the queen would have come to remonstrate with us,' argued Mynha.

Holding hands, and still in their nightshifts of white cotton, the two girls, sensing something was very wrong, hand in hand, set out for the queen's boudoir. A few moments later they both screamed in unison at the sight of their beloved mistress lying, fully-dressed in her male Pharaoh's attire, prostrate upon the marble floor. It was Shazar who was the first to recover, and she bent down beside her mistress. 'She's quite cold and dead,' she screamed.

'Whatever shall we do, Shazar?'

'We must fetch the vizier, Hapi-soneb. Go get him at once, sister, while I stay with the queen.'

Ten minutes later Mynha returned with a deeply shocked Hapi-soneb. He knelt beside the prostrate form of the queen, ascertaining that she was indeed dead.

'Go fetch the chancellor, Nehesy – a proclamation will have to be issued – and then send for the royal physician. The queen's skull must be opened immediately,' he commanded Mynha, who scurried off to do his bidding.

By the time that Nehesy and the physician had arrived, word had already leaked out of the queen's death. Several courtiers had assembled in the outer chamber, all asking questions of each other. Nehesy pushed his way through with the physician into the inner sanctuary. With the physician had come two old crones, paid professional wailers. As the physician took out the necessary instruments in preparation for opening the queen's skull, they began their doleful chants of lament.

Kneeling down, the physician supported the queen's lifeless head in one hand and reached for a boring tool. It was then that they heard the commotion outside in the audience chamber. A moment later those present in the inner sanctum were amazed as Rekhmire, Tuthmosis III and Thanuny, together with two of his army captains, burst in upon them.

'Stay your hand, physician, if you wish to live,' commanded Rekhmire.

The physician began to protest.

'According to custom I must open the queen's skull or she cannot enter the afterlife.'

'You are in the presence of the true Pharaoh, Tuthmosis III. He will decide what is to be done with this usurper of his crown,' exclaimed Thanuny.

'Indeed I shall,' growled Tuthmosis. 'Let all here listen to me.'

Every eye turned upon him.

He continued in a low but authoritative voice. 'My word as Pharaoh is law. I am your rightful monarch, Tuthmosis III of that name. This woman, my stepmother, was a usurper. Not only has she died in this world, but life in the hereafter shall be denied her by my hand. She shall be buried in a secret place, without her skull being opened, and without the seventy days of mummification, it will be impossible for her to enter the hereafter and be amongst the gods. Forever she shall be damned. Furthermore, her name shall be erased from lists of the royal kings and all her works and effigies destroyed for ever.'

Hapi-soneb attempted to protest.

'But, my lord, this is not a just sentence. She has been a great and honourable Pharaoh and w—'

'Silence!' boomed Tuthmosis, looking as if he would strike down the little vizier and high priest.

The two girls, Shazar and Mynha, began to cry, drowning out the two old crones. Nehesy stepped boldly forward to support his friend, Hapi-soneb.

'What right have you to decree such an inhuman

sentence?'

'Seize him, seize them both,' Thanuny ordered his two army captains.

Chancellor and vizier were both held in restraint by the two guards, Nehesy, by his size and strength proving the more troublesome. Tuthmosis looked coldly at both, no mercy or pity in his eyes.

'Tomorrow both of you will be fed to the crocodiles for your part in assisting this usurper.' Roughly he kicked the lifeless form of the prostrate queen, which brought further screams of anguish from Shazar and Mynha. Rekhmire's evil grin showed his appreciation of his young protégé.

'What of Thuty, the treasurer, Your Majesty? He was one of them too.'

'Yes, Thuty too. Send men to arrest him. He shall die as well as these two, and anyone else who aided and abetted her wicked reign to usurp my place as Pharaoh,' commanded Tuthmosis.

Shazar and her sister watched in horror as Nehesy and Hapi-soneb were roughly marched away in captivity.

Tuthmosis ordered out the two old crones, both protesting at being done out of their official fee. Then, turning to Shazar, he commanded, 'Move the body onto the bed. Strip it of all refinements and jewellery. Clothe her in a plain black shroud. Tonight we shall take her away and bury her where none shall find her. Do you understand, girl?'

Shazar, devoted to her late mistress, tried to protest.

'But, my lord, she has a fine tomb prepared in the Valley of Kings. Will you not allow her to rest there?'

Tuthmosis threw back his head and laughed uproariously.

'Insolent girl. She will rest where I say, not in an elegant tomb way beyond her station. That will be reserved for my grandfather, Tuthmosis I.'

Rekhmire, who had remained behind with his master when Thanuny and his armed escort had left with their captives, stepped forward and slapped Shazar's face.

'How dare you address your Pharaoh, girl. You are but a slave girl of little merit.'

Shazar's dark eyes flashed momentary defiance. Tuthmosis smiled and reached for the hem of her cotton shift. Raising it, he ogled her firm young legs.

'A comely wench is she not, Rekhmire?' Then, pushing her roughly at his vizier, he roared, 'There – I give her to you as my first gift as Pharaoh.'

A protest gained Shazar another slap from Rekhmire.

'In fact, Rekhmire, you can have both of them. The queen will have no further use of them,' laughed Tuthmosis.

Rekhmire smiled. A sadistic twist to his lopsided mouth made him look even less attractive than usual.

'You heard the Pharaoh, girls. Attend the body of the queen as instructed, then report to my chief eunuch. You are both to be allowed to join my harem. A very great honour indeed.'

Turning, he followed the chuckling young Pharaoh from the chamber, leaving the two distraught young girls alone with Hatshepsut's body. Gently they laid her on the canopied bed, tears running down both their young faces.

'When they come to take my mistress away at dusk I shall follow,' whispered Shazar.

'Have a care, sister,' urged Mynha, 'or you will be fed to the crocodiles. The new Pharaoh is warlike and full of hate for all who love Hatshepsut.'

'He is the living brother of the god, Seth, himself,' hissed Shazar contemptuously.

Just after dusk an ox cart rumbled out of the palace court-yard. It was drawn by two white oxen and escorted by a party of soldiers. On it lay the darkly shrouded body of the queen. Tuthmosis, of course, had not wanted to soil his hands with the deed so had sent Rekhmire to supervise the burial party. Hidden behind a tall granite pillar, Shazar watched the macabre procession pass out from the palace's interior. When enough distance between them had elapsed, she set out, using the shadows to follow them and keeping well out of sight.

Shazar had little doubt what her fate would be should she be spotted.

It was soon obvious that their intended direction was Sheikh Abd Al-Quarnah. Shazar well knew that most of the nobles were buried there. She had first thought that perhaps they were going to bury her mistress in her original tomb, prepared for her as queen, in the time of her late husband, Tuthmosis II. She soon realised that this was not the case. Once or twice the sounds of Rekhmire's voice floated back to her on the night wind as he cursed one or other of the soldiers. It was plain that he wanted to have the deed done with as quickly as possible.

Progress was slow. The wooden wheels of the cart frequently bedding into the sands forced the soldiers to put their shoulders to the cart in an effort to assist the oxen. Shazar felt bitter resentment at her mistress being dealt such a shameful and inglorious end. That such a mighty queen should come to this, denied the hereafter and buried in an unmarked tomb.

At times Shazar was forced to crawl on hands and knees to avoid detection as she followed in their wake. Finally, after what seemed hours, the undignified procession came to a halt before a cliff face. Fortunately some large rocks had fallen nearby and provided the watching Shazar with some cover. At Rekhmire's command a party of soldiers took up the queen's body and stumbled with it over a mass of rocky outcrops towards a cave entrance. Another produced a blazing torch and held it aloft at the cavern entrance. The men bearing the body shuffled past him and some time later returned without it. Shazar heard Rekhmire call out to them.

'Fill the entrance for all eternity. Not even a rat must get in.'

The work party set to work with a will using crowbars of iron to dislodge rocks and limestone above the entrance. After two hours a great wall of rock and sand had engulfed the cavern's entrance. To anyone passing, it just looked like a continuance of the quarry face. Rekhmire seemed satisfied and ordered the men back whilst he made a closer inspection. Finally he turned to face the assembled men.

'You men are all sworn to secrecy. If any of you divulge what you have seen here tonight your eyes and tongues will be pulled out. Now return to Thebes all of you and forget this night.'

Some left for Thebes with the now empty ox cart, others departed in twos and threes. Soon only Rekhmire was left. Shazar, from her place of hiding, watched him verbally chanting aloud and cursing the dead Hatshepsut. Through pursed lips, she found herself doing the same to him. She waited a good five minutes, until after he had left, before coming out of hiding. The moon was up now, casting eerie shadows amongst the rocks and crevasses of the limestone cliffs. She edged forward towards the concealed entrance and produced a knife from her belt.

Silently she scanned the cliff face for a solid surface and finally found what she searched for, low down amongst the fallen rocks. With dexterity she began to carve away at the tough limestone. It was hard work and took several hours into the night, but at last it was finished. Shazar stood back to admire her work, a perfect replica of Queen Hatshepsut's cartouche. Her task completed, she gathered a further supply of rocks and stacked them to conceal her handiwork. One day someone would find it, but not now and not for a long while.

Wearily, she trudged homeward, reaching the palace just before dawn. She was met by a tearful Mynha, who explained that Rekhmire had come for her during her absence and was quite furious at not finding her. Mynha had been forced to oblige him, after making excuses for her sister.

'I told you, sister, he is the brother of Seth himself,' Shazar consoled her, wiping the tears from Mynha's face.

Shazar gazed out at the reddening of the dawn sky, orange streaks preceding the sun's appearance.

'Soon they will be taking out their Excellencies, the chancellor, Nehesy, the treasurer, Thuty and the vizier, Hapi-soneb to cast them to the crocodiles.'

Mynha stopped crying and began to chuckle.

'I think not, sister.'

'Whatever do you mean? It is this morning they are to be executed,' exclaimed Shazar.

Mynha whispered in conspiratorial tone. 'When you left last night to follow the burial party, I took a cask of drugged wine to the guards who were in charge of all three. An hour later I went back, took the keys off the sleeping guard commander and released them. When Rekhmire comes for them this morning he will find the birds have flown.'

Shazar embraced her sister.

'You are a brave girl, Mynha, but when the guards awake they will tell Rekhmire what you have done and we shall take their place feeding the crocodiles.'

'I think not, Shazar. You see, when I released the chancellor, Nehesy, he richly rewarded me. Look at this.'

Mynha produced a purse of gold. Shazar gasped. She had never even seen such riches.

'This being the case we must leave at once. I have little wish to spend the rest of my days in either Rekhmire's harem or a crocodile's belly... We must head for the Nile and secure a passage north,' urged Shazar.

Ten minutes later, the two girls, shawls covering their heads, crept from the palace and headed in the direction of the great river.

Too late Rekhmire discovered that he had been outwitted and his prisoners freed. He ordered the guards who had been duped to take their place at the crocodile pit. By the time he had revelled in this grim orgy of blood and threshing foam, he was somewhat satiated. Now for those two slave girls. He would teach them once and for all. One had the audacity to disappear for the night from his harem, to only Seth knew where. The other had obviously been the one, from the guards' description, before their untimely death, to free the prisoners. How he would make them suffer. Seth's breath, he would flay the very skin from their bodies and then have them boiled in oil. Ten minutes later he found even they had flown the coop. Stamping and raving in fury, he went in search of Thanuny.

A widespread search was instigated by Tuthmosis, the new Pharaoh, for any nobles who had assisted with his stepmother's reign. When they were found, they were quickly put to death, and even nobles, who were dead already, had the stela on their tombs defaced.

Nearly all of Senenmut's wonderful works honouring Hatshepsut were viciously hacked and erased. Even at Deir el-Bahri a great pile of smashed remains lay in the dust outside the temple. Unable to topple the great red granite obelisks at Karnak, Tuthmosis had them walled up, to hide them from view. Curiously enough this was to preserve one of them for all time, although this had certainly not been the Pharaoh's intention at the time.

During Hatshepsut's later reign as Pharaoh, Egypt's control of Syria and Lebanon had slipped away. Their local princes had switched allegiance from Egypt to a new powerful rule in the kingdom of Mitanni. Once the hatred in his soul for his late stepmother and her courtiers had waned and he had defaced everything to do with her, Tuthmosis turned his attention to military matters. With the bitterness now expunged from his soul, he began a series of warlike campaigns against all of Egypt's enemies, securing great victories against all comers. His military upbringing under Thanuny stood him in great stead for the battles that were to take place during his reign, and he often marched at the head of a column with complete disregard for his own safety.

At a much later time in history, he was to be called the Napoleon of ancient Egypt by the American Egyptologist, Breasted. His reign was also noted for its opulence and nothing reflected this more than the tomb of his vizier and high priest, Rekhmire, magnificent in its grandeur.

The great eighteenth dynasty went on for another one hundred and fifty-seven years, until the last of their line, Horemheb, another great general. It included the heretical Pharaoh, Akhenaten, and the boy king Tutankhamun, but none matched the architectural vision of Hatshepsut, or the incredible courage she showed as Egypt's only truly ruling queen. She ruled as Pharaoh against all the odds, a colossus whose memory will never die. Denied everlasting life and a place on the carved list of kings by Tuthmosis, will she one day return to exact her vengeance?

Book II

Chapter I

Egypt, 1997

At early dawn and some distance north of Aswan, Elaine Gilroy watched the dark waters of the Nile slip away from the stern of the *Enchantress*. It was the last day of Elaine's cruise down the great river. A week earlier, together with her employer, archaeologist Paul Stanton, she had boarded the cruise ship at Luxor. For several months they had been working together on a dig at Saqqara; now they had completed the work and tomorrow would be heading home. It was the last day of a six-day cruise and later that morning they would disembark at Aswan. Elaine had left her cabin early and ventured on deck to watch the sunrise. Already the sky was lightening to the east and she could see flecks of orange tinged with strips of pink.

She had only been working in Egypt for the past six months, but already she loved the country and its traditional way of life along the Nile. The atmosphere and the warmth of its people seemed to have found a place deep within her heart.

Now twenty-eight, she had qualified two years earlier in archaeology at Oxford and had been fortunate indeed to secure a post with her present employer, the celebrated archaeologist of world renown, Paul Stanton, some fifteen years her senior.

Elaine both admired and respected him and at times felt quite in awe of his immense depth of knowledge. It was said that there was no greater expert concerning the eighteenth dynasty of Egypt. Elaine for one never doubted

165

it. She sought only to gain the maximum knowledge that he could pass on to her. Their working relationship was a good one; both were passionately involved with their work, but each had an individual and keen sense of humour, one complementing the other.

In the time that they had worked together Elaine and Paul had become firm friends, often able to rib one another about various things, in the way that only true friends can. Secretly Elaine wished that they could be more than just friends, but Paul had never shown her any encouragement in that direction. She supposed that, having had a failed marriage, he considered, once bitten twice shy. Anyway she certainly wasn't going to be the one to make the first move, and was happy that she could call him her best friend as well as her employer.

She was tall for a girl, at five foot eight inches, with shoulder-length blonde hair, small firm breasts and long shapely legs, tanned a rich brown from six months in the Egyptian sun. Bright blue eyes highlighted attractive features in an equally tanned face, that needed little make-up to enhance its natural beauty.

Possessed of a keen enquiring mind, she had earlier broken off her engagement to David Bannon, a lawyer, to follow her career in archaeology. David had been quite unable to understand what motivated her. Grubbing about in dirt and sand, he had accused her of. After that she had given him back the ring. It was simply no contest. Elaine had never regretted the decision and in truth had never been happier than during the time she had just spent in Egypt with Paul Stanton.

If she was honest with herself that was why she was feeling sad and nostalgic now, standing alone on the deck of the *Enchantress*. Tomorrow, their work done in Egypt, they would board a plane in Cairo for London. Angry at her own feelings of weakness she brushed away a tear at the corner of her right eye. Don't be stupid, she told herself, you can't always do everything in life you want to. Perhaps one day the Egyptians would invite Paul back and she could accompany him once more to this land of her dreams.

She consoled herself with the thought that the next day she would see her parents who lived in Sussex. Her father was the local village rector at Buckchurch, and her mother the pillar of the community, president of the Women's Institute and Mothers' Union. It would be nice to spend some time with them again. Elaine had one brother ten years older than herself, Clive, who had followed their father into the church and now at thirty-eight was actually, strange as it seemed, based in Egypt, the leader of a mission on the borders of Cairo.

Elaine had always been close to her brother and they were constantly in touch on the telephone. In short, Clive was everything a big brother should be to Elaine, both protective when she had been younger and supportive now she had matured. She wished sometimes that he had married. He deserved someone nice, but then he helped so many people, so she supposed in a way that was his reward in life. Anyway he seemed happy with his lot, so what business was it of hers? He had been simply delighted when she had come out to Egypt to work, and they had been able to spend quite a lot of their spare time together.

Sadness hit her anew, as to the east the first rays of the sun on the horizon preceded its actual appearance. Everything took on a soft golden glow, made more apparent by the darker diminishing purple of the sky above, the last remnants of the departing night.

Suddenly she was startled by a hand laid gently on her shoulder and a firm strong voice saying, 'A penny for them.'

Half turning, she saw that it was Paul who had joined her at the stern rail of the *Enchantress*.

'You quite startled me, Paul,' she said softly.

'A thousand pardons, fair damsel. I guess I had the same thought as you… to come up on deck and take my last look at Egypt before we return to foggy London town.'

Elaine turned to face him and said, 'I'll miss it terribly, Paul… Do you think we shall ever come back? Sometimes I feel that I really belong here.'

The upper crest of the fiery red sun appeared over the edge of the horizon. Almost immediately the entire Nile valley seemed to lighten. Elaine watched the sun's rays reflected in the waters of the great river and saw that they seemed to bathe Paul's tanned features. From the river bank came the sound of wild fowl taking to the air, and of a donkey braying. Somewhere far off, they could hear the first call to prayer from a distant minaret.

'Ah, a magical land indeed,' agreed Paul. 'Sometimes I feel that I could just stand here for ever watching the world go by. Nothing seems to have changed along the Nile for thousands of years. It's as if time has stood still.'

'Yes, it's only in the cities that time has changed, Paul, and for the worst I fear.'

Elaine was quite surprised when Paul took her hand and gave it a gentle squeeze. He wasn't usually so demonstrative. She gazed up into his hazel eyes, looking for something, she knew not what.

'One day we shall return if time doesn't run out on us first,' he said softly.

The moment was broken by a shadow flitting between them and the rising sun. A red kite spread wide its wings as it glided in on the rising thermals and scanned the waters below.

'Looking for his breakfast, I guess,' put in Paul. 'See how beautifully he moves.'

He transferred his hand from hers to around her slim waist and the two of them stood side by side, watching the large bird's progress downriver.

Elaine could feel the warmth of Paul's arm round her, and nestled in closer to him. There was something so comforting about the man, an honesty and steadfastness of security she couldn't quite explain. Although there was nothing sexual about the move, she immediately felt as one with him.

They remained on deck for the next half-hour, taking in the joy of a Nile sunrise together, and the passing scenes on the banks to either side of them. Finally their blissful unspoken peace was broken by a family of tourists arriving on the top deck, alongside them. The little group chatted noisily, laughing merrily, and the moment was gone.

After speaking politely with their new companions, Paul indicated to Elaine that he would see her at breakfast and left for his cabin. Five minutes later she took her last long look at the river and she went below herself to her own cabin. After a refreshing shower she dressed in a white cotton sundress and sandals and passed the rest of the time until breakfast reading, needless to say about Egypt and its mythology. Later she joined Paul for a leisurely breakfast in the ship's dining room. Together they chatted amicably to the other diners, which stretched the meal out until well after half past nine. Finally Elaine excused herself, saying that she still had a few more things to throw in her cases. She well knew that the *Enchantress* was not due to dock until eleven o'clock, but she hated to be hurried, always worried that she would forget something or other.

Time passed all too quickly now the end of the cruise was in sight, and no sooner had she put both her cases outside her cabin door than the steward collected them. With a finality she realised the next time she saw them they would be on the quayside waiting to be transferred to the airport with the rest of the luggage.

Noises outside shook her out of her reverie. Glancing

out of her cabin porthole, she was surprised to see that they had arrived at Aswan half an hour early and were in the process of docking. Several turbaned figures were scampering about on the quay below ready to catch the ropes thrown to them. Oh well, thought Elaine, I guess this is it. The cases have gone. I may as well go on deck and watch the mooring. After a final check of the cabin to ascertain that she had left nothing behind, she blew a farewell kiss to the empty cabin, closed the door behind her and went topsides.

Most people were already there standing at the ship's rail looking down. Paul was amongst them. She squeezed in next to him, as he turned and smiled at her.

'Everything packed and all ready to go?' he asked.

'Yes, but I don't want to, really,' she answered.

'You will be all right once you get home and see your parents,' he consoled her.

'I expect so,' Elaine said, without a great deal of conviction in her voice.

Then she thought about Paul. What would he do when he arrived home? Although still on friendly terms with his ex-wife Helen, he had no family and his parents had both died a few years earlier. As far as Elaine knew, there was no current girlfriend in the picture. Divorced from Helen five years earlier, he bore no malice towards her. True, he said, she had gone off with a young racing driver, but the fault had been his. He had been much too immersed in his work, he had admitted to Elaine. She knew that he had written several books on the eighteenth dynasty and confessed that Queen Hatshepsut was his favourite. Elaine had often teased him that he bore a remarkable resemblance to statues and reliefs of Senenmut, who had generally been believed to be the Egyptian queen's lover. Paul would always argue that he couldn't see this resemblance himself.

'People never can see likeness of themselves,' Elaine

would laughingly point out.

'Well, I'm taller than he was,' Paul would argue.

'Yes, but you have the same features, the nose and eyes are identical… Why, even the hairstyle is identical.'

Paul would run his fingers through his dark hair, which was fast silvering at the temples.

'You are talking nonsense, Elaine, which is worthy of rebuke. You are supposed to be a seriously minded archaeologist.'

The laughter lines at the corners of his mouth and eyes belied the words and showed that he really didn't mind the comparison.

What a pity he hasn't got somebody back home waiting for him. He's such a lovely man, thought Elaine. From what he had told her in a conspiratorial moment between them, his ex-wife, Helen, had loved parties, dancing and socialising, for which he had really little time. She had also been a good ten years younger than himself. The fling with the racing driver hadn't lasted for more than a year, but although Paul had remained good friends with Helen, they had never got back together again. He had showed Elaine a photograph of her once. She was very sophisticated and beautiful, with auburn hair.

'I guess it was a complete mismatch from the start,' he had concluded.

Finally, with the *Enchantress* firmly moored they watched the cases go ashore and saw them stacked on the quayside. Ten minutes later all the passengers were assembling below decks at the entrance to the companionway. Paul heard someone calling him and saw that one of the ship's crew was parading up and down with a board bearing his name.

'Over here,' he called, raising his right arm above the assembled throng of passengers. The crewman pushed his way through to them.

'Meester Stantone?' enquired the man, heavily accentuating the e's.

'That's me. What's the problem?' enquired Paul.

'No probleem, Meester Stantone, just meesage.'

The fellow pushed a sealed letter into Paul's hands and departed quickly with his board, before Paul could enquire who had delivered it. Shrugging his shoulders, Paul raised questioning eyes to Elaine.

'Suppose I had better open it,' he said.

'I suppose if you want to know who it's from you should. Obviously an admirer you didn't know you had,' laughed Elaine.

Paul tore it open and read it slowly, a puzzled expression on his face. Without saying anything he read it again and then handed it to Elaine.

'What do you make of this?'

The message had clearly come direct from the ship's radio room. Elaine read it slowly.

Dear Mr Stanton,

Please delay your flight to London later today, until you have considered a proposal the Egyptian Ministry of Antiquities wish to put to you. Should you be interested I can arrange to meet you at the Cairo Hilton tonight at eight. We have taken the liberty of reserving two rooms at the above hotel for you and your assistant for tonight (at our expense of course). After listening to my proposal, should you not be interested in helping us, we shall be happy to reserve and pay for your first-class flights to London.

Hoping to see you tonight at eight when I shall explain more fully.

I remain, sir, your respectful servant,
Ali ben Mustapha

Elaine could feel the excitement running through her. 'Perhaps they are going to extend our stay at Saqqara,' she ventured.

'No, it's something else, or they would have already said

before we left Saqqara,' said Paul pensively. Then, reflecting on the situation, he came to a decision. 'Look, I'm quite happy to cancel my flight from Cairo to London tonight, but you, surely you were looking forward to seeing your parents?'

'Do you need to ask, Paul? Surely you realise I would do anything to stay in Egypt.'

'But won't your parents be disappointed?'

'Of course they will, but they will understand when I telephone and explain.'

Whilst this discussion had been going on, the rest of the passengers had filed off the ship, down the companionway and were being escorted to taxis to take them to Aswan airport for their flights to Cairo and elsewhere. Paul took Elaine's arm.

'Come on, then. We can ring though from Aswan to Cairo and cancel tonight's home flight if you're sure about this?'

'I've never been surer about anything in my life, Paul. Lead on.'

Once on the quayside a representative from the ship obtained a taxi for them and gave orders to the driver. Turning to Paul he said, 'Your cases will follow on, sir, and be tabbed through to Cairo airport.'

Paul tipped the man and climbed into the car beside Elaine. 'Let's hope we won't regret this hasty decision,' he remarked.

'Things done in haste are more fun,' laughed Elaine.

On the taxi ride to the airport they passed the great, higher and lower dams and marvelled at these great feats of engineering. They were both aware that due to this the great flooding inundations from the Nile were a thing of the past. Sitting in comparative silence both took in the scene through their respective sides of the vehicle.

There over on the west bank were the rock tombs, dating back to the Old Kingdom, cut for the nobles of the period. They could see the numerous feluccas sailing on the Nile, tacking criss-cross in the morning breeze, across the great river, and beyond them, the Botanical Gardens on Elephantine Island. There was the famous Cataract Hotel. The great attractions of Aswan to tourists was the magnificent temple of Isis at Philae and the unfinished obelisk which, if it hadn't cracked in its fabrication, would have been the largest ever made, forty-three metres in length and four point three metres wide at its thickest end.

By the time they had arrived at the airport it was midday and the tourist flights from Abu Simbel were arriving back. These flights left Aswan just after dawn and returned at midday. Both Paul and Elaine had visited the spectacular temple before, the former many times. Each time he had marvelled more and more. Some people said the moving and resiting of it was as wonderful as the original building of it.

The airport was busy and, as usual, the Cairo flight was delayed. By the time they took off it was already an hour and a half late and the flight to Cairo took about the same time. Another taxi from the airport there took them through the streets of Cairo, as always teeming with people, a somewhat strange mishmash of ancient and modern. Everywhere vehicle horns honked belligerently at all and sundry, but nobody seemed to take any notice, not even the odd oxen pulling a cartload of fruit, or a camel weighed down with a gargantuan load of rugs. Old battered buses, looking beyond service, still toiled on, heavily overloaded. Several times the traffic ground to a halt, completely gridlocked. The sprawling suburbs of the great city now reached out almost to the pyramids at Giza. New high-rise buildings were oddly at contrast to the mosques and minarets. To their left was the city of the dead, an old network of catacombs and graves, but even here life went on. Several people had made their homes beyond its grim walls.

At last the taxi swung into the Hilton and a doorman stepped forward to assist, summoning a porter for the cases. Soon they would find out what this mysterious invitation was all about.

Chapter II

They didn't have long to wait for the answer. First having booked into their respective adjoining rooms, they were able to have leisurely baths and change for the evening. At eight, in the lobby downstairs, they met up with Ali ben Mustapha.

For Paul, this was not the first meeting with the man from the Ministry of Antiquities, but Elaine had never seen him before. He was a polite and dapper little man, with a sallow complexion and a large walrus-like moustache, which seemed somehow too large for his face and frame. Immaculately dressed in a pale-grey, double-breasted suit, he shook hands warmly with Paul and kissed the back of Elaine's hand, whilst peering up at her from under bushy eyebrows. She was forced to smile at the too obvious complimentary endearments that followed.

The introductions completed, Mustapha formally invited them to join him for dinner and escorted the pair into the dining room. He made an effusive display of ordering wine but noticeably ordered fruit juice for himself. Obviously a devout Muslim, Elaine decided. Everyone ordered from the extensive menu and Ali ben Mustapha continued to chat about everything but that which they expected. Would he never come to the point, thought Elaine, trying not to show her curiosity. Paul had met Ali before and wasn't going to give the little Egyptian the satisfaction of raising the matter himself. Finally, on the dessert course, Ali came to the point of his invitation.

'I expect you are both wondering what this meeting is all about?' he said.

Paul raised his eyebrows at this and retorted, 'Well, it's obviously important to you, or you wouldn't have gone to all this trouble on our account.'

Although this was said quite light-heartedly, Ali looked somewhat put out.

'Oh, I assure you, it is both a pleasure and honour to be able to entertain you.'

Paul laughed and said, 'I suspect that there is a lot more to it than that.'

Ali coughed, a little embarrassing sound issuing from his throat before he addressed them again.

'You are right, of course, Mr Stanton, and it may well be, what with the recent massacres here in Cairo and in Luxor by the Fundamentalists, that you may not be interested in the ministry's offer to you.'

Both Paul and Elaine knew that he alluded to the killing of a busload of German tourists at the Cairo museum and of the even worse slaughter of visitors to the temple at Deir el-Bahri, shortly afterwards.

Paul smiled, trying to hide a slightly suspicious expression from showing.

'Suppose you make your offer and we can be the judge of whether we accept it or not.'

Elaine, bursting with anticipation and curiosity, remained on the edge of her seat but she felt it wasn't her place to comment at this stage.

'Very well,' exclaimed Ali, taking a deep breath and watching the face of each in turn. 'I shall tell you of a discovery that has been made in the Sheikh Abd Al-Quarnah.'

There was another pause as he waited for a reaction.

'Go on,' exclaimed Paul, being careful not to show too much interest.

'We are sure that a new tomb has been discovered.'

'Surely in Egypt that can hardly be surprising,' put in

Elaine, breaking her silence.

Ali turned his attention from Paul to her and went on excitedly, 'We have reason to believe that this tomb is a very special tomb indeed.'

Paul looked pensive and fingered his chin, a habit he had when thinking.

'A special tomb, in the Valley of the Nobles?' he enquired.

Ali continued, 'It has escaped discovery all of these years due to a heavy rockfall long since obscuring its entrance.'

'Any idea who the tomb might belong to?' exclaimed Elaine, excitedly.

'Yes, as a matter of fact, we have,' answered Ali, enjoying his moment of supreme mystery.

'Well, are you going to tell us or not?' said Paul, matter-of-factly, shooting the Egyptian ministry man down.

'I am empowered to tell you that the cartouche of Queen Hatshepsut has been discovered at what we think is the entrance.'

'Good heavens!' gasped Elaine, 'Not another one, surely?'

Ali looked somewhat put out by this, and was relieved when Paul cut in with, 'In the three tombs attributed to Queen Hatshepsut, two of which are in the Valley of the Kings, the remaining one in the Queen's Valley, no mummy was ever found. Nor did they ever find her in the two great caches of mummies discovered in 1881 and 1898.'

'This is entirely true, Mr Stanton,' agreed Ali. 'She had indeed three tombs, KV20 and KV38 in the Valley of the Kings and her old one, never used, in the Queen's Valley.'

Elaine knew that KV was an abbreviation for the Kings' Valley. She edged to the rim of her chair in excitement.

'Yet, Mr ben Mustapha, you think you have located another?'

'At this stage it is much more than a possibility, Miss

Gilroy.'

Paul still looked unimpressed.

'This cartouche you say that has been discovered... of Queen Hatshepsut, you say...? Has it been authenticated...? Could it not be a modern forgery?'

Ali ben Mustapha looked Paul straight in the eye.

'No, Mr Stanton, it could not be a forgery. It was discovered quite by accident, due to a landslide and has been validated as eighteenth dynasty by our experts... There remains not a shadow of doubt that the cartouche is genuine.'

Ali watched him, awaiting his further response. Paul did not disappoint him.

'Has the tomb been opened?' was his next question.

'No, as you yourself were in Egypt and are a greatly respected archaeologist specialising in the period, we... I mean, I am empowered to seek your help in the matter.'

Paul was showing much more avid attention now.

'What exactly did you have in mind, Mr Mustapha?'

Ali threw wide the palms of his hands in a theatrical gesture.

'If you accept, you will, together with an archaeologist of our choosing, be responsible for the excavating and opening of the tomb.'

Paul looked suspicious. He knew Ali's tricks of old.

'Another archaeologist...? Am I to be told who?'

Ali smiled.

'Why, of course, Mr Stanton, if you are to work together you must know.'

'So, who is it?'

'Chantal Shariffe.'

Paul's face turned as black as thunder. 'Chantal Shariffe,' he echoed. 'No way!'

'I am sorry, Mr Stanton, but that is the way it must be. I am well aware that Miss Shariffe and yourself have had your differences.'

'Differences you call it. I would call it a little more than that,' retorted Paul.

Ali gave another embarrassed little cough before continuing, 'You will forgive me, Mr Stanton, if I say you are considered to be biased on the side of Hatshepsut, in all your writings of the period... Miss Shariffe, on the other hand, comes down heavily on the side of Tuthmosis III, does she not?'

Paul clamped his teeth tightly together. Elaine could sense he was in one of his stubborn, I-shall-not-be-moved moods. She tried to ease the tension by suggesting to Ali that he obviously thought both attitudes would strike a healthy balance.

'Of course, my dear. We thought it to be an excellent liaison of two great learned minds,' Ali replied.

Paul looked him straight in the eye and asked, 'Who do I take it would be in charge? Chantal or me?'

'You would both have equal powers of authority. I—'

'No way!' cut in Paul. 'I'm not interested in working with Chantal Shariffe... not this year... not any year... not ever!'

Ali ben Mustapha sipped his coffee.

'I am disappointed to hear you say that, Mr Stanton. We had very much hoped to have you working with us on this.'

Elaine could see Paul had that defiant look on his face and wasn't about to change his mind. She felt bitter disappointment. Her chance of staying in Egypt was fast slipping away. Desperately she searched her mind for a solution. If only she could change Paul's mind. Ali was rambling on again.

'Well, it's your decision, of course, Mr Stanton, but I must say that I am sorry you are not prepared to give it a try.'

Elaine, of course, had heard of Chantal Shariffe and read

one of her books, but Paul had never spoken of her before, yet it was clear he felt great animosity towards the woman. Why? she wondered. She could see the stubborn set of Paul's mouth and jawline, but decided upon a tack of her own.

'Look, Paul, if you give this woman her head, as you say she is anti-Hatshepsut, might she not come up with pro-Tuthmosis answers?' she urged.

'I'm not giving her carte blanche to do anything,' snapped Paul, irritably. 'It's our Mustapha here who's doing that.'

'Now, now, Mr Stanton. We are offering you the same chance as we are offering Miss Shariffe, are we not?'

Paul saw that he was cornered.

Ali went on, regardless, 'If you choose not to accept, that's up to you... I can tell you Miss Shariffe already has accepted our offer. I'm sorry if no is to be your last word.'

Elaine looked pleadingly at Paul.

'Surely she can't be that bad, Paul, and think of the thrill you will get if it really turns out to be Hatshepsut.' She could see he was beginning to waver. 'I'll be there to help you negotiate with her. You won't even have to talk to her if you don't want to. I can act as intermediator for you.'

Ali swept his gaze from Elaine back to Paul.

'Well, Mr Stanton?'

'I expect I'm going to regret it, but very well, I accept.'

Ali ben Mustapha beamed from ear to ear.

'You won't regret it, I'm sure, Mr Stanton. Now it only remains for me to go through the details with you.'

'When do you want us to go down to Luxor?' enquired a resigned Paul.

'As soon as possible. If you could agree to meet up with Miss Shariffe, I shall arrange a get-together for all... say at the Winter Garden Palace in Luxor, at the end of the week?' Without waiting for an answer, Ali went on, 'Now as to financial details…'

For the next fifteen minutes Ali went on with the itinerary in minute detail and concluded by saying, 'One word of warning I must give both of you. We can give no assurances or guarantees against the Fundamentalists.' There was an ominous pause.

'You, of course, know what happened a few weeks ago at Deir el-Bahri.'

Both Paul and Elaine nodded.

'I guess that's a risk we shall have to take,' said Paul.

'You are, after all, foreigners,' pointed out Ali.

'Guess that depends on where you live in the first place,' exclaimed Paul.

Ten minutes later Ali ben Mustapha took his leave of them, saying to both, 'Stay on here. Your rooms are booked and I shall be in touch tomorrow or the next day.'

'Very sure of himself, wasn't he, that I would accept,' Paul said to Elaine.

Everything, in fact, seemed to happen very quickly. Ali ben Mustapha, true to his word, rang Paul at the Hilton later the next day. He wanted to know if they could go down to Luxor the day after tomorrow and meet up with himself and Chantal Shariffe for a final briefing. When Paul confirmed that they would be able to manage this, Ali said he would make the necessary arrangements for their overnight stay at the Winter Garden Palace. The meeting was to take place in the lounge there at eight.

Paul replaced the phone and relayed the details to Elaine, who was in the process of doing some work for him on her laptop. As well as assisting him with the archaeological work, she also acted as his secretary.

'I'm quite intrigued to meet up with this Chantal Shariffe, whom you seem to dislike so much,' she said, with a twinkle in her eye.

'Well, don't hold your breath,' replied Paul. 'She's not worth it.'

'I've heard of her, of course, as an archaeologist, but nothing about the woman herself. You make her sound as if she breathes fire and has horns.'

'Well, she certainly breathes fire – or is it acid? – but I don't know about the horns,' laughed Paul.

'Tell me about her and why you dislike her so?'

'My fault really, I expect,' said Paul, modestly. 'It just seems we have clashed several times over recent years, both in person and in the press. I can't think of a more unlikely alliance than Chantal Shariffe and me working together on anything. Whatever I am quoted as saying, Chantal will say the opposite.'

'Isn't that bound to happen when she's so pro-Tuthmosis III and you so supportive of Queen Hatshepsut?' ventured Elaine.

'Somehow it goes deeper than that. I can't explain.'

'Try… What's she like… to look at, I mean? I picture her as a shrewlike, little emaciated lady, with spectacles and a walking cane. A real old spinster.'

Paul laughed aloud.

'Then you'd be entirely wrong. She is quite attractive, with very dark hair and eyes to match, eyes that seem to pierce your very soul, seeking flaws in your character.'

'Sounds like she has you rattled, Paul.'

'She will you too, when you meet her… You just see if she doesn't. She has that effect on people.'

'How do you mean?'

'Analyses your every thought and deed.'

'Is she Egyptian?'

'Yes, but her mother was French, although her father was an eminent Egyptian archaeologist in his day.'

'What sort of age would she be?'

'Mid-thirties, why?'

'I'm just intrigued by the sound of her I guess. I pictured her older,' said Elaine.

'You will meet her quite soon enough,' laughed Paul.

Two days later Elaine glimpsed Chantal Shariffe for the first time. At least she was aware of someone's eyes on her as she entered the lobby of the Winter Garden Palace with Paul. She had that strange feeling of being watched and found her eyes drawn to the watcher. A tall attractive woman, dressed in a two-piece, oatmeal-coloured suit. Her hair was a luxuriant coal black and shone like satin, but it was the woman's eyes that struck Elaine. Never had she seen such dark hostile eyes in a face. She was standing talking to Ali ben Mustapha but her eyes never left those of Elaine, who tried to look away but found herself drawn to them like a magnet.

Paul nudged Elaine's arm as they approached. 'The vixen herself,' he whispered.

Elaine was still trying to drag her eyes away from Chantal's when Ali ben Mustapha effected the introductions. Paul and Elaine offered their hands but Chantal just inclined her head slightly by way of greeting. Suddenly Elaine saw what Paul had meant. This woman had the ability to make one feel uncomfortable and at a disadvantage. Ali ben Mustapha enquired whether everyone was ready to go into dinner, as he had been informed their table was ready.

Elaine, always sensitive to atmosphere, sensed all through the meal the vibes of animosity between Paul and Chantal. It was fortunate that Ali was both garrulous and informative, so much so that he obviously failed to notice the undercurrent between them. If it was acceptable to them, he would take them to the site first thing the next morning, he explained. After that, it would be up to them to hire the men needed to assist with the excavation and opening of the tomb. Only when both parties had accepted and agreed to the proposal did Chantal glare across the table at Elaine.

'What's *she* here for? I don't recall any mention of having to share this project with an unknown. It's bad enough having to work with *him*,' she said, jerking her thumb in Paul's direction.

Up to now he had kept his temper in check, but the verbal attack on Elaine was just too much.

'Miss Gilroy is a qualified archaeologist and my assistant. Where I go, she goes. Is that quite clear, Chantal?'

Chantal shrugged her shoulders, never taking her piercing gaze away from Elaine.

'Oh well, if you need somebody to hold your hand,' she exclaimed, her voice dripping with sarcasm.

Paul ignored the last remark and said cuttingly, 'I suggest if we have to work together we try to co-operate and make the best of things.'

'So be it,' snapped Chantal, then turning to Ali and ignoring the other two, she said, 'I'm off to get an early night. What time do you want to leave for the site in the morning?'

'I thought about six, before it gets too hot in the valley,' Ali responded.

'Suits me... see you then.'

She turned abruptly on her heel and walked briskly out of the dining room.

Elaine couldn't resist it. 'What a pity her manners don't match her looks.'

Ali smiled, saying, 'You will get used to her, Miss Gilroy, I promise you.' Then he quickly changed the subject, turning back to Paul. 'Once I've taken you all to the site tomorrow, I shall leave you to it, as I must return to my work in Cairo.'

Paul nodded. 'I know a good fellow here in Luxor who

would make a good foreman... I used him once for some work in the Valley of the Kings... Once I tell him how many men we shall need, he can hire them for us.'

'Fine,' replied Ali, 'just as long as you remain within the Ministry of Antiquities' budget that I outlined to you. Also I would point out Chantal would have to agree to the man.'

'If she doesn't like the idea, she can damn well do the hiring herself. I shall simply wash my hands of it,' snorted Paul.

Ten minutes later Ali took his leave of the pair, although a lot more graciously than Chantal had done.

Once on their own, over a second cup of coffee, Paul said, 'I can't help but feel this is going to prove a serious mistake, working with Chantal again.'

Elaine was quick to home in on his last word.

'You've worked with her before, then?' she enquired.

'Only once... a long time ago. It proved a disaster then, too.'

When it was obvious that Paul wasn't going to elaborate, Elaine didn't press him. He would tell her in his own good time.

'Come on,' he said, 'let's go and drown our sorrows in the bar.'

After a couple of dry Martinis, knowing that they had to be up early the next morning, both left for their respective rooms. Once ensconced in her bedroom, Elaine put a call through to her brother, Clive, and was disappointed when there was no answer. Either he had given himself an early night or had been forced to go out on some business or other. She listened hopefully to the ringing tone, and when it was obvious there was going to be no response, hung up. It wasn't really important, but she just enjoyed a chat from time to time with Clive. They had always been very close and usually discussed their problems to mutual advantage.

The bedroom was air-conditioned, but the noise of the

fan always kept her awake, so she turned it off and opened the window. There was almost no breeze at all and the warm, balmy, night air instantly invaded the room. Then she remembered the mosquito problem and rapidly closed it.

After a refreshing shower she lay naked on top of the bed and read for a while. When her eyelids became heavy and the print blurred, she put down the book and turned onto her side. Within a couple of minutes she was asleep, but it proved to be a fitful and restless slumber and she drifted off into a nightmarish dream.

Chantal was astride her, hands around her throat. She could feel the fingers tightening, but it was the eyes that really terrified her, those beautiful, almost black eyes that bore down on her, piercing her very soul. She seemed to be held in a hypnotic state unable to shake off the assailant's grip. Then just when she thought she would choke, she awoke in a mass of cold perspiration, amazed to find that she had been only dreaming and was alone.

Gradually getting over the shock, she went through to the bathroom and had another shower and then, after thoroughly drying herself, put on a light cotton nightie. Finally she turned back on the air-conditioning, as the heat in the room was stifling, and reluctantly got back into bed. For the rest of the night she didn't sleep very well, and was relieved when the alarm went off at five o'clock.

Chapter III

Elaine found the dream of the preceding night was still on her mind and the reappearance of Chantal for an early Continental breakfast did little to dispel it. The hotel had laid on an early sitting for them by special request and by six, the four of them were on their way to the site by taxi. Paul, because he was the tallest, was given the front seat beside the driver, whilst Elaine found herself squeezed in between Ali and Chantal in the rear of the vehicle. The three archaeologists were all dressed in khaki shirts and shorts made of cotton, as were the socks they wore under strong chukka boots. From long experience they knew strong boots were essential against both the rocks and heat of the sand. Ali, as usual, was immaculately dressed in a finely cut lightweight suit.

Elaine, next to him, began to feel quite nauseous with the strongly scented aftershave he must have bathed in. They needed to cross from the east to the west side of the Nile, but unable to use the ferry, they first had to negotiate a few miles, to cross by the new bridge. It was going to be impossible to reach the site by car and the last section would have to be traversed on foot. Finally, the taxi put them down at the nearest point. Having carefully extracted their belongings and armed themselves with canvas backpacks, the quartet set off on foot. Ali was careful to instruct the driver to wait for his return.

It was early dawn, and not yet too hot for the arduous trek between the barren and rocky hills, stretching between Hatshepsut's temple at Deir el-Bahri and the Ramesseum, the Valley of the Nobles, with its myriad rock tombs honeycombing the cliffs. In this early-morning light, casting a slightly purplish shadow from the limestone cliffs and rocks, Elaine felt quite overawed by the almost living presence of ancient times. Here countless important courtiers and nobles, together with lesser ones, were buried, all of them having their place in millenniums of Egyptian history.

Ali interrupted their onward trudge across the sandy dunes and indicated the cliff face to their right. Elaine could see several gaping caverns in the rock face, some of them even quite near the top. She found herself wondering how past generations had been able to cope with such precipitous burials. He halted them at a massive pile of heaped rocks at the base of the cliff. An elderly Arab was sitting cross-legged on the topmost boulder. He scrambled down to meet them with an alacrity that belied his years.

'Hassan, the night-watchman,' said Ali, introducing the man to them.

Hassan, clutching a heavily knotted wooden staff, gave them a toothless grin in return.

'We have had the area guarded day and night since the discovery was made,' proclaimed Ali proudly.

Chantal, who hadn't said a word during the long trek, impatiently questioned Ali.

'Show us this cartouche you talk of. It may well be a fake and we could be wasting our time here.'

'I assure you, Madame Shariffe, it is no fake, or we would not have sent for you, or Mr Stanton. It has already been verified as of the period.'

Chantal dismissed his explanation with a somewhat derogatory sound, something between a grunt and a cough.

'I shall see for myself and then I shall judge.'

Elaine caught the look Paul gave her, almost as if to say, 'See what I told you. She's quite impossible.'

'Come this way then, all of you. Soon you will see for

yourself.'

Dressed in his suit and highly polished hand-cut shoes, Ali attempted to climb over the boulders towards the cliff face. Several times he almost slipped. Chantal pushed forward, determined to be the first to see.

'There,' exclaimed Ali proudly. 'The cartouche of Hatshepsut.' He pointed at a carved relief on the limestone in the typical oval shape of a cartouche.

Chantal pushed past him and scrambled up onto another boulder to inspect more closely. There wasn't room for any one else, so all Paul and Elaine could do was to wait for her to finish her inspection of the carved design. Finally, after what seemed an age, she turned and scrambled back down to them.

'I am not convinced the inscription is genuine,' she said to Ali, ignoring Paul and Elaine.

'Oh, and why do you say that, when it has been verified by our experts?' retorted Ali, hotly.

'Because such an inscription could not have lasted, cut into limestone, for three and a half thousand years. Long since it would have crumbled.'

Paul, who hadn't as yet had a chance to examine the cartouche, scrambled over the boulders for a closer inspection. From his pocket he produced a small battery microscope with which he proceeded to examine the carving. In the background below he could still hear Chantal arguing with Ali. After carefully studying the cartouche, he switched his attention to the cliff and rock face and then scrambled down into a gully between the rocks. The sand at the base was very loose with considerable hard deposits of limestone. Several times he sifted handfuls of it through his fingers. Finally, satisfied, he clambered out from the hollow and up and over the surrounding boulders to join the others. Chantal was still arguing with Ali. Elaine was looking embarrassed and the

Arab, Hassan, was sitting cross-legged on the sand, an amused expression on his face.

Ali, looking rather hot and bothered, turned to face the returning Paul.

'I suppose you think it is a modern fake too, do you, Mr Stanton?'

Paul gave a wry smile at the sarcastic note of the question, probably reinforced by Chantal's hostility.

'On the contrary, Ali, the cartouche is definitely genuine,' he replied.

Chantal swung round to Paul, exclaiming, 'You would say that because it's your precious Hatshepsut!' Before he could reply, she went on, 'There is no way the pushy woman would have been buried here in the Valley of the Nobles in an obscure tomb. She would have been far too grand for that... In any case, the carving would never have lasted in the limestone over all these centuries,' she said smugly.

Paul smiled.

'The reason it has remained intact was due to rockfall. It has been obscured by sand and rock for centuries. A recent further landslide has exposed the cartouche. I am sure what we have here is a genuine tomb.'

Ali beamed, showing a row of gold fillings, but Chantal was not to be appeased. For some reason beyond Elaine's understanding, Chantal glared at her, before continuing her reasoning.

'Oh, and I suppose he is going to find his precious Hatshepsut all nice and wrapped up, mummified inside, waiting for him.'

Paul didn't rise to the bait, but merely stated that no mummy of Hatshepsut had ever been found in any of the tombs attributed to her, or in the caches of mummies of Pharaohs found later in the last century. Ali turned on Chantal.

'Do I take it you wish to back out of this project?'

Paul and Elaine waited with bated breath, hoping she would, but they were soon to be disappointed.

'I shall stay on, if only to protect the memory of Tuthmosis III, and see that no false claims are made by either of these two on behalf of the usurper.'

Paul couldn't help but laugh out loud before countering, 'Why do you have to take this so personally, Chantal? You are a respected archaeologist, are you not? Can you not remain objective and open-minded?'

'Can you?' she snapped.

'Now now, please, you two. Can we not have a truce here? After all, you are going to work together on this,' said Ali, trying to pour oil on troubled waters.

'That's okay by me,' agreed Paul, immediately.

After an embarrassing pause, Chantal answered, 'Very well, but nothing must be done without my agreement.'

Elaine, who had felt totally out of her depth in this argument between the two more experienced archaeologists, broke her silence.

'It seems to me that there won't be any decisions to make until we are ready to go in, and there is a lot of work to do before then, clearing this lot.' She waved a hand at the pile of rocks and sand.

'Correct,' agreed Paul. 'First we have to hire a few workers.' Turning to Chantal, he enquired amiably enough, 'Have you any objection if I go into Luxor today and hire a crew and we make a start tomorrow?'

Chantal looked as if she would object again but, after a pause and another glare at Elaine, she replied, without looking at Paul, 'No, you can go ahead if you like. I shall remain here and poke around a bit.'

Elaine found herself wondering how anybody could look so attractive, and yet be so objectionable. Was it just with Paul, Ali and herself, or was she like this with everyone?

Ali suggested that Paul and Elaine were welcome to go back to the east side of Luxor with him in the taxi if they so wished. Paul accepted and intimated that besides hiring a crew he would have to acquire a vehicle, equipment and secure some accommodation for them all. Ali laughingly agreed that the Ministry of Antiquities certainly wouldn't wear them staying on for a lengthy period at the Winter Garden Palace Hotel.

'Would you mind awfully, Paul, if I stayed on at the site here and did a little investigating myself?' asked Elaine.

Chantal watched her from under long eyelashes with those dark unfathomable eyes, before interjecting, 'If you are staying on here, don't get in my way, that's all.'

'I wouldn't dream of it,' said Elaine, sarcastically.

A further discussion followed concerning the require-ments the explorers would need, then ten minutes later, Paul left on foot with Ali, to retrace their steps to the waiting taxi, having told Elaine he would come back for her later. She wandered off along the foot of the cliffs, leaving Chantal on her knees, rooting around in the sand, in front of the boulders bordering the suspected tomb.

In Luxor, Ali handed Paul a card, saying that if he experi-enced any difficulties to let him know. He seemed anxious to get back to Cairo, and before leaving Paul at the kerbside in Luxor, he reminded him that whatever they found must be handed over to the Egyptian Ministry of Antiquities. Handing Paul an envelope, he exclaimed, 'We shall, of course, expect you to keep to budget for the project, although reasonable advances will be forwarded to you within the week, to tide you over for personal expenses... Let me know the forwarding address as soon as you have secured some accommodation for yourselves. I shall attend to it personally.'

Before Paul could question him further, Ali wound up the window of the taxi, waved a silent goodbye and gave instructions to the driver to take him to the airport. Paul watched the car disappear into the distance and then set off to find Ibrahim, an Arab who had worked with him in Luxor a few years earlier. The fellow lived in a broken-down, adobe-type dwelling some two hundred yards inland from the east bank of the Nile with his wife and children. When Paul arrived, he found that Ibrahim was out, ferrying people, tourists mostly, across the river in an old broken-down boat. Meir, his wife, remembered meeting Paul in the past and made him very welcome.

'My husband will be very pleased to see you, Mr Stanton. Work is very scarce in Luxor now. You are very welcome to wait here for him.'

Meir looked older than her years and was dressed in the traditional black garb of an Egyptian wife. Paul thanked her and seated himself on an old box that served as a seat. Meir's two young children, the oldest of whom couldn't have been more than five, watched him from a dark corner of the shack, their large, round, brown eyes full of wonderment.

Luckily Paul always carried some wrapped boiled sweets for such an emergency. He produced a paper bag and offered them to the children, a raggedly dressed boy and girl. The elder, the little girl, took a tentative step towards him, then looked expectantly at her mother for confirmation that it was all right to accept.

Meir smiled and nodded. This encouraged the little boy to emerge from his hiding place and reach for the proffered sweet. He retreated with it shyly, holding it in his small grubby hand. Meir offered Paul a drink in return, but he declined. These people had little enough for themselves to live on, but he did it graciously, saying that he had just eaten and drunk liberally and couldn't possibly manage another thing.

Fifteen minutes later, Ibrahim arrived, with a great smile on his face when he saw that he had a visitor. Recognising Paul at once, he shook him warmly by the hand saying, 'Greetings, effendi. What brings you to my humble dwelling?'

'If you are not regularly employed, Ibrahim, I have work for you.'

'There is not any work so important that I would not put it off for the honourable Mr Stanton,' exclaimed Ibrahim, effusively.

'Good man. Then I shall outline what is required. We are to commence unearthing a suspected tomb in the Valley of the Nobles.'

Ibrahim puffed up his skinny chest, saying, 'There is no one better suited to this work than I, effendi.'

Paul smiled. He remembered Ibrahim from old, but in spite of the man's boastfulness, he knew him to be a good honest worker and reliable to the core.

'I know this very well, Ibrahim, and that is why I am here to secure your help. Together with another archaeologist from your own country, I am entrusted with this project. Can you secure the services of another three men to assist with the work? You, of course, will be my foreman.'

'Thirty-three men, if you wish it, Mr Stanton.'

Paul laughed. 'No, three will do, I think.'

Then began the haggling over wages. Always it was like this. Ibrahim would ask for a mountainous sum. Paul would offer him a molehill in comparison. In the end, as always, they settled the deal with an amount fair to both parties.

'The men you hire will all receive fifty per cent of that paid to you, Ibrahim. Do you consider that fair?'

'Very fair, effendi. Boss man always gets more.'

Paul laughed.

'And now, where can I hire a jeep or something for the duration of the work? Plus we are going to need tools and equipment – sieves and vacuums, and so forth.'

'Ah, you come to the right man, Mr Stanton. I shall take you to see an emporium where all these things can be arranged.'

'Is now as good a time as any, Ibrahim?'

'Now is as good as any other time, perhaps better,' said Ibrahim, with a smile.

Paul took his leave from Ibrahim's little family, minus the remainder of the packet of sweets which he left with the children's mother. Waving goodbye, he set off with Ibrahim on foot.

First the Arab took him to a tented market place where he haggled with a fat oily individual for the hire of a jeep. The vehicle looked as if it had seen better days and reminded Paul of a United States army jeep. However, when the engine was run over, it sounded sweet enough and the heavy-duty tyres would prove a bonus.

The tiresome and usual haggling went on. How Paul wished sometimes that these people would state a fair price and then the purchaser could pay it, but no, it always had to be like this and you lost face if you didn't haggle. Finally, after the owner had called him all the names under the sun, including a camel stealer, horse thief and the seventh son of a bandit, a satisfactory deal was struck. The vehicle was then fuelled up with petrol from a supply of jerrycans stacked against a corrugated-iron shed. With Paul at the wheel and Ibrahim beside him, they drove out onto the road.

Giving him directions, Ibrahim took him across town to a much more dilapidated establishment than the one where he had secured the vehicle. Once again the process of sharp bargaining commenced, this time with an elderly emaciated-looking fellow minus his front teeth. The end result was the same and Paul and Ibrahim drove off with the supplies needed for their work.

'Now, Ibrahim, last of all, we need good clean accommodation for myself and the two ladies. Do you know of anywhere…? We don't want to pay hotel prices as our budget is tight.'

Ibrahim smiled knowingly.

'Ah, you are lucky, effendi. You have two women to choose from… one each night, yes?'

Paul smiled.

'No, it's not like that. We shall require three separate rooms. Do you understand, Ibrahim?'

Ibrahim looked somewhat amazed.

'If that is what you wish, Effendi Stanton, I will see what I can do.'

Meanwhile, back at the valley, Elaine was beginning to wish she had gone to Luxor with Paul. Once the sun began its daily rise into the heavens, the heat became intense. Already at this early hour, Elaine could feel the reflected heat coming off the cliff face almost like a physical force. The only shade in the valley was behind the isolated rockfalls. She concluded that if Paul didn't return until lunchtime, or even later, if his business arrangements took longer than expected, she would have to beware of heatstroke. Removing her backpack Elaine produced a high-factor sun cream and liberally covered her face, neck, arms and legs with it. Extracting a battered old baseball cap and a large white handkerchief, she donned it in such a fashion that the handkerchief hung down protecting the back of her neck under the cap. Together with her curved sunglasses, the peak would protect her eyes from the fiercely reflected glare. She reminded herself of the need to drink plenty in such a hot climate and on repacking her backpack left her water flasks out, clamping both, one each side of her belt, with Velcro strips.

Thus prepared, she returned to the tomb site to find Chantal still scratching about on her hands and knees in the sand between the boulders. Trying to be friendly, she enquired whether Chantal would like to borrow her sun cream. All this brought forth from the Egyptian woman was a contemptuous look and a sarcastic retort.

'If you blonde European women can't stand our climate you should stay away.'

Elaine thought of a sharp reply, but chose not to rise to the bait and have an argument. After all, whether she liked this woman or not was beside the point. Both she and Paul had to work with her. Ignoring the other's hostility, she changed the subject.

'Found anything interesting?' she enquired.

There was an uncomfortable silence, in which Chantal fixed those unfathomable dark eyes on her before replying, 'What did you expect me to find?'

Elaine shrugged her shoulders.

'Just thought you might have some early thoughts on the possibilities.'

'If I had I wouldn't share them with a blonde bimbo now, would I?' exclaimed Chantal, her expression turning to one of amusement.

Elaine felt like walking forward and slapping Chantal's face, but she resisted the impulse. If this was the way this bitch wanted it, then she was fed up with trying to be polite and friendly.

'What's with you, Chantal? We have to work together, so even if we don't like one another, we can at least be polite.'

Chantal arose from her exploration and crossed over to where Elaine stood. She insolently ran her eyes up and down Elaine's trim figure.

'I didn't say I didn't like you, did I?' she ventured.

'It would seem you made it pretty obvious,' Elaine replied.

'I wouldn't say so. If I really took a dislike to you there wouldn't be any doubt in your mind.' With this she reached out and squeezed Elaine's upper arm.

The sudden change of tack took Elaine completely by surprise. Chantal's unwavering gaze studied her with amusement.

'Come and have a look at the cartouche with me, Elaine, and I'll explain a few things that may be useful in your career.'

Oh well, thought Elaine, why not indulge her, and followed Chantal back over the rocks and boulders to the cliff face. The morning passed quite quickly with a much improved rapport between them. Chantal passed on the benefits of her superior experience as an archaeologist to her junior colleague. At lunchtime the two women sought some scanty shade behind some boulders and, in companionable fashion, ate the packed lunch the hotel had put up for them. Chantal, who obviously had a great pride in her country, relayed stories of Egyptian mythology, which quite enchanted and fascinated Elaine. So captivated was she that she hardly heard Paul and Ibrahim return in the jeep.

After introducing Ibrahim to the two women, Paul brought them up to date on all that he had accomplished during the morning, the latter part of which being the accommodation that he had secured for them all – three single rooms in an inexpensive guest house in Luxor. Although Chantal had immediately reverted to open hostility at Paul's arrival, even she agreed that these would be acceptable.

Finally, Paul invited them all to help him unload the supplies and equipment out of the jeep. After this was accomplished and all was safely stowed away from sight behind the rocks, Elaine enquired, 'Will all this stuff be safe here?' As she said this she glanced across to where the ancient and toothless Arab, Hassan, was seated on the rocks some hundred metres away.

'If you mean are we going to solely depend on him during the night, the answer's no.'

With this Paul turned to Ibrahim and said to the women, 'One of Ibrahim's men will be here each and every night to back up the watchman… Now, if you are both in agreement, I suggest we return to the Winter Garden Palace and collect our personal belongings. We can then move into our new lodgings.'

After general agreement, Paul called over Hassan to explain about the extra watchman and told him that they would be starting early the next morning. Everyone clambered into the ancient jeep and they were on their way back, bumping and rolling over the sandy base of the valley. Elaine found herself looking forward to a refreshing shower. Hassan watched the vehicle until it was out of sight.

Chapter IV

At this time, many miles away down on the Nubian border, an exercise was in progress, in truth an illegal exercise, but nonetheless a studiously carried out rehearsal. A group of Fundamentalists were being given a blow-by-blow account of how to assemble and fire a Sten gun. A powerfully built South African Boer mercenary was the instructor, and his trainees consisted of six men and a girl. All were dressed in khaki denims similar to military issue. Each and every one had one objective in common, and that was to bring down the Egyptian government by any means possible.

The exception to this was the huge Boer. He couldn't have cared less, and his only interest was money. When he had passed on his knowledge and experience to this bunch of Egyptians, he would be on his way to Central America and his next employer. Wilhelm Snoek was his name, and his face and frame looked as if they had been hewn out of granite. He stroked the barrel of the completely assembled and loaded Sten, as if it were a woman's breast, whilst at the same time going on with his lecture to the terrorist group. He had been hired to hone them into a tough unit and that was exactly what he was doing. Snoek was proud of his pupils, particularly the leader, a tall swarthy individual with an eyepatch covering his left eye. Khaled was quick to learn and seemed to hate everybody, even his trainee colleagues.

Definitely an asset for a terrorist, thought Snoek. A man without a conscience, tell him what to do, and he would do it without a backward glance or a second thought. The other trainee to impress Snoek was the woman, Fatima. With short cropped hair which was as black as the ace of spades, she was not unattractive, although there was a flinty hardness about the eyes that seemed to give warning of an inner strength. She was a woman who knew exactly what she wanted and was going to take what she wasn't freely given.

Khaled, thought Snoek, was probably about thirty but he doubted the woman, Fatima, was more than twenty-five. It amused Snoek sometimes to watch the antics of his trainees, hell-bent on bringing the Egyptian government to its knees by targeting the foreign tourists. That way they hoped to prove that the authorities were powerless to protect the visitors to Egypt and the country could be brought back to its old ways. Snoek smirked at the thought of Fatima going back to wearing a veil. She had certainly been liberated enough in his bed last night. Khaled was another matter – the worst sort – a religious fanatic who would stop at nothing.

'Now pay attention and watch this, all of you,' snapped Snoek. Immediately, running low in a zigzag path, he fired the Sten from the hip at a line of dummy figures to the left of the little group. Chunks flew off the plaster replicas of people. Finally, throwing himself forward on his belly, he shot the head off the most distant dummy.

Slowly he rose to his feet, gun in hand, to face his pupils. He could sense the awe and esteem in which they held him. Throwing the gun at Fatima, he ordered her to firstly strip and reassemble the Sten, then load and emulate his feat with the models. Methodically Fatima complied and taking only a few seconds longer than Snoek had taken, repeated the demonstration which culminated in the upper torso of the last figure being blown away.

'You didn't leave me the head,' purred Fatima in a voice that was both deep and sexy. Snoek threw back his head and roared with laughter.

'Some woman, this. Let's hope you men can do as well.'

Khaled grabbed the Sten from Fatima and in no time had broken it down and reassembled and loaded it.

'Ready when you are,' he snarled, his one eye looking menacingly evil.

'Go to it, man,' Snoek retorted, which was precisely what Khaled did with a first-class display of marksmanship every bit as good as Fatima's.

'Not much more I can teach you two about Stens... Let's hope the rest of you are as good,' Snoek said, running his gaze systematically over each in turn. Methodically he ran them all through their paces. Not a bad bunch really, although not nearly as efficient as Khaled or Fatima. 'Now for grenades,' he snapped.

Walking over to a metal box he removed the padlock and opened the lid. Dipping his hand inside he produced a grenade and flipped it into the air, letting it fall on the ground. Two of the trainees threw themselves down on the sand. Snoek gave a deep rumbling laugh that seemed to come from his very belly.

'Harmless... see, harmless... At least they are until you pull the pin.'

He walked over and picked up the grenade, extracting the pin. He appeared to count, then hurled it at a stone wall, built for the purpose, some forty metres away. As the missile hit the wall it exploded, and as the smoke cleared the watchers could see that the structure had sustained considerable damage. Snoek turned back to the small group.

'Remember always to count three before you throw the grenade after you have pulled the pin. That way no one is ever going to get the chance to pick the damned thing up and toss it back at you.'

One of the trainees, a young fellow named Wael, chuckled before commenting, 'You're joking, of course.'

Snoek went over to the ammunition box and produced

another grenade, then deliberately he slowly walked over to where Wael stood and looked down on him from his immense height. Wael failed to match his gaze and averted his eyes.

'Here, take this, Wael,' snarled Snoek, handing him the grenade.

Reluctantly the young terrorist recruit took it. Snoek turned and walked about ten metres, then turned back and faced Wael again.

'Pull the pin, man, and toss it at me. Aim for my middle.'

Wael hesitated, looking nervous.

'If I do that I may kill you,' stammered Wael.

'Isn't that what you want to do, man... kill people?' goaded Snoek.

Still Wael hesitated.

'Come on, man. Do it!' roared Snoek. 'What are you – a jelly-livered camel driver?'

At this, Wael pulled the pin and hurled the grenade at Snoek, before throwing himself face down on the sand and covering his face and head with his hands. He never even saw what happened next. Snoek, agile for a man of his immense height and size, caught the grenade in one huge bucket-sized hand. Then turning slowly, he took careful aim and hurled the small missile at the already broken wall. Again it exploded on impact.

Snoek turned back to the shocked group and, in a very calm voice, explained, 'You see, five seconds is a hell of a long time. To do the most damage, remember, always count to three before you throw.'

Everyone but Khaled watched in awe; that worthy only nodded, his one eye fixed on Snoek. 'We shall take a break for lunch now. Reassemble here at two thirty,' exclaimed Snoek.

Wael had only just found the courage to scramble to his

feet, but again he protested.

'That's going to be in the full force of the sun out here, Mr Snoek. Don't you think a little later might be better?'

'Isn't it now, man… See you all at two thirty.'

With that Snoek turned on his heel and made for his quarters, part of an old World War Two Nissan hut. The group stood and watched him go, two or three of them bemoaning the training programme in the heat of the day. Khaled swung round on them.

'If we are to free this country of the usurpers, all is necessary.'

None but Fatima could match the fierce glare of his one fanatical eye. All she said was, 'You are right, Brother Khaled. It is necessary.'

She detached herself from the group and wandered over to Wilhelm Snoek's quarters, knocking softly on the door and waiting. When no answer came she thought she could hear running water and knocked again, still no answer.

Turning the handle, she found that it wasn't locked and opened easily. Fatima let herself in and closed the door behind her. At the far end of the makeshift hut was an area screened off as a temporary washroom and shower. She tiptoed towards it and peered round. Snoek had his back to her and was soaping himself down, naked under the shower. Fatima watched the muscles ripple in his broad back and shoulders as the water ran down from his massive neck. Almost as thick as a tree trunk, she thought. He was totally unaware of her watching him, as standing with his powerful legs astride, he vigorously soaped his hair. For fully a minute Fatima watched, remaining silent, until, seeming to sense her presence, he slowly turned round to face her.

'How long have you been there, girl?' he enquired roughly.

'Long enough to appreciate the scenery,' Fatima replied,

watching him from under long dark lashes.

'Did you think I didn't know you were there?' laughed Snoek, throwing back his huge head and making no attempt to cover himself.

Fatima's eyes were immediately drawn down to his maleness and remained riveted there.

'Want some more of what you had last night, woman?'

Fatima, for answer, said nothing, but slowly advanced towards him, a lustful expression in her dark-brown eyes. Suddenly Snoek's arm shot out, a huge hand restraining her.

'Get those dirty denims off first, woman. I've just showered and I don't want those filthy things rubbing against me.'

Slowly, never taking her eyes off Snoek, she totally disrobed. He reached out and pulled her roughly in under the shower that was still running. Producing the soap once more, he began soaping her hot body, rolling her ample breasts in one large hand, the other one reaching round her bottom which was towards him, and through her legs.

'Good, eh?' he enquired.

'You are very rough with a lady, Wilhelm,' she said, pretending to object.

'Just the way you like it, woman,' snapped Snoek, forcing her to her knees, the water cascading down her back.

He knelt down behind her and forced her knees apart with his own. Within a few seconds she gasped with simulated shock, as he forced his way into her.

'Not like this, Wilhelm,' she protested, meaning it this time.

Snoek cared little and savagely thrust at her, intent only on his own pleasure.

'This is what you came for, girl, and I'm giving it to you.'

Fatima's hands were slipping on the wet floor of the

shower and it was almost impossible to resist the huge bulk of the man. She had wanted it to be like the night before, not like this. Snoek became rougher and rougher, pulling her back onto his huge frame by sweeping his hairy arms up under hers, until there was nothing left but to totally submit to his fierce desire. Finally he climaxed, leaving her bruised and used, but totally unfulfilled. Landing her on her knees, he turned off the shower, picked up a towel and towelled himself dry. Nobody spoke. When he was dry he flung the towel at her. Fatima was just getting to her feet.

'You didn't have to be like that,' she protested. 'You were like an animal.'

Snoek snorted, 'Oh yes I did. All part of the training. If you are going to be a good terrorist, and stay alive, that what's you do... You use people the way you want to... No time for sentiment or attachments. Life's too short for that mush.' He began to dress without a second look at her.

Fatima wasn't about to let him see her cry and somehow choked back the tears. She had thought, after last night, that he really wanted her for herself. Now she knew she had been no better than a whore to him.

With no further word, Snoek wandered round the screen, dressed in only his denim overalls, and shoeless. Fatima dried herself, angrily and vigorously rubbing her skin red with the towel. When she had dressed, she produced a knife from her belt and tiptoed round the screen. Snoek again had his back to her, lying back in one wooden chair, with his feet on another. He was reading a newspaper. Gripping the knife tightly, Fatima crept silently up behind him and pulled his head backwards with one hand, whilst pressing the knife across his throat. Fatima held him like that for fully ten seconds before removing the knife's pressure and standing back.

'Think yourself lucky I didn't kill you, Wilhelm Snoek,' she snarled, venomously.

Snoek stood up, visibly shaken, and then, recovering, laughed before saying, 'I always knew you'd be the best of the bunch, girl... One thing, though, whenever you draw a knife on someone, finish the job... Remember that. There are no second chances in the work you are preparing for.'

Through slit eyes, Fatima retorted, 'And you remember you owe your life to me. I could have finished you.'

'That you could, too,' laughed Snoek. 'Damned if I'm not impressed. Come to me tonight and I'll treat you like a lady should be treated.'

'Go to hell and back, and may it freeze over before you ever have me again,' exclaimed Fatima. Turning on her heel she stormed out of the hut, leaving Snoek tracing the blood pattern round his throat with his fingers.

'That's sure some woman,' he said aloud to the walls of the hut, there being no one else to hear him.

★

Work had been going on for fully two days at the site in the Valley of the Nobles. The area around the suspected tomb had been cordoned off, and Ministry of Antiquities' notices attached at various points on the posts to keep everyone at a distance. The writing was in Arabic for the locals and English and French for the tourists. A watchman was also in attendance day and night. Paul, Elaine, Chantal and the men Paul had hired had begun work two days earlier, clearing the rubble and piles of boulders, sand and rock from the front of the cartouche.

It was slow arduous work in the heat and all of them were forced to take numerous breaks throughout the day. Everything that was being moved and taken away was carefully scrutinised in case anything of relevant importance should be missed.

Whenever Paul was around, Elaine noticed that Chantal

was openly hostile but the Egyptian woman was now much more openly friendly to her. It appeared that Chantal now realised that she, Elaine, was only Paul's assistant, and that the pair were not an item, although quite what difference that made was beyond Elaine's imagination. At least with Chantal being nicer to her, life was somewhat easier.

The third day was a Sunday, a holiday for all. Paul invited Elaine to go with him to have another look at the Valley of the Kings.

'I want to have another look at Hatshepsut's official tomb. It's years since I saw it and maybe I've missed something.'

Elaine jumped at the chance and agreed to accompany him.

'I've seen it scores of times so I think I'll hire a felucca on the river. Sounds more enjoyable to me,' Chantal said.

When Paul and Elaine arrived at the valley on the Sunday morning, Elaine was surprised that there were so few tourists. Paul reminded her of the terrible massacre a few weeks earlier at Deir el-Bahri, where sixty-odd people had died, killed by the Fundamentalists.

'Even the Nile cruise ships are half empty or not running,' he had pointed out.

Elaine was cross with herself for not remembering. How could she have forgotten such a terrible crime against humanity? All those people killed, whole generations of families wiped out and for what, she wondered. Was it just to satisfy the beliefs of a minority of terrorists? Thinking of the magnitude of the disaster sent a cold shiver through her whole body. It had happened not that far from where they were standing now, in the Valley of the Kings. She knew full well that at the other side of the cliffs lay Deir el-Bahri.

Elaine tried to bring her mind back to the present. It was quite early on the Sunday morning and the stallholders and numerous postcard vendors had gathered already, quite outnumbering the few tourists. The entrance-way from the coach park right into the neck of the valley was literally full of them. Paul told her that it was something they would have to put up with, running the gauntlet of the traders and pedlars.

'With so few tourists about they are having to work much harder to survive,' he commented.

Luckily Paul spoke Arabic and once they knew that all but the most persistent ones gave up. However, apart from one stop, which Elaine requested Paul to make so that she could purchase some postcards, ten minutes took them to the head of the valley. Here they were clear of the pedlars. Dotted around the valley were the concrete tomb entrances, leading to, she well knew, a magical world of the past with all its mysteries and wonders.

'The tomb I'm going to show you is way up there over to the left,' explained Paul, pointing upwards. 'Don't expect it to be richly decorated with hieroglyphics and reliefs, because I'm afraid it isn't. Very few tourists, unless they are dedicated Egyptologists, ever bother to trek that far in this heat. It's going to take us a good half-hour,' Paul added.

Elaine found that he hadn't exaggerated and she was glad that she was young and fit. An older person would have probably found it beyond him or her, she concluded.

The trek was up long, winding, sandy and rocky paths, and when they finally arrived at the tomb entrance, they saw that it wasn't guarded as were most of the other tombs.

'KV20,' said Paul, standing by the entrance. 'It's said that this tomb in the eastern corner of the valley was supposed to go clear through the cliff face and end up with its burial chamber actually in the mortuary temple at Deir el-Bahri.'

'Weren't they supposed to have hit bad rock or something that prevented that happening?' asked Elaine.

'When we get inside I think you will see for yourself,' said Paul, producing a torch. 'Come on, I'll show you.'

He led the way through the entrance; the dim lighting from outside soon failed and Paul switched on the torch. Elaine could see the first turn in the rock face and soon they had rounded it, totally dependent on the torch beam. All it revealed was another turn, and so they progressed slowly downwards, twisting and turning. Once Paul pointed out a column of steps on the left side of the passage.

'This would have allowed the sarcophagi to be slid down more easily to the final burial chamber,' he commented.

As Paul had warned her, the walls were quite rough and undecorated. After more steps and turns, he pointed out some slots which had been made for beams.

'What would they have used them for?' enquired Elaine.

'To slow the descent of the sarcophagi, almost certainly,' he whispered.

It was a weird feeling, this feeling of a need to whisper.

Paul continued his narrative, 'This tomb was originally cut for Hatshepsut's father, Tuthmosis I. When we get to the bottom you will see the two sarcophagi, one for him and one for her.'

They were now standing in the undecorated antechamber and a further descent took them down to the final burial chamber. Paul shone the torch about and Elaine could see three storerooms, going off the central chamber.

'Where are the yellow quartzite sarcophagi now? I've read about them being here.' enquired Elaine, feeling like an intruder in somebody else's family grave.

'One's in Boston, the other's in Cairo,' he replied.

'Do you think she was ever buried here, Paul?'

'Remains a mystery. Nobody has ever found her mummy. It is claimed that a box found in 1881, with her name on it, in the discovered royal cache of that year, contained a mummified liver or spleen. It was said to be salvaged from the debris here... Who knows for sure...?

We do know, however, that the body of Tuthmosis I, buried in here, was removed, for some reason, to KV38.'

'Isn't that attributed to Tuthmosis III…? The moving of it, I mean?' said Elaine.

'Almost certainly,' he answered.

Elaine began to feel herself shiver and clutched her bare arms with her hands.

'Cold?' enquired Paul. 'Not surprising really, when you think we are just on three hundred and eighteen feet down from the surface and some seven hundred feet in from the entrance.'

They spent another good ten minutes exploring, with Paul doing his best to answer all of Elaine's questions. Finally, he noticed that the torchlight was not nearly so bright as it had been.

'Come on, Elaine. We had better make our way out. It wouldn't do to be stuck down here with no light.'

Slowly they retraced their steps to the surface, the bright sunlight quite hurting and stinging their eyes as they emerged.

'I wouldn't have missed that for anything,' enthused Elaine.

Chapter V

It took a good two weeks of painstaking work clearing the approach-way to the cartouche. Over the centuries numerous rockfalls had littered the base of the cliffs. Paul had insisted, and for once Chantal had agreed, that everything must be carefully examined before being removed. Ibrahim and his three workers, Ashraf, Ahmed and Sabar, all seemed to respect Paul and worked well for him but they seemed to resent any orders given by Chantal.

There were no short cuts and Paul and the two women pitched into the task, getting equally hot and dusty. Elaine smiled to herself. It was a good job they were all wearing khaki shirts and shorts; any other colour would have been a total disaster in all this sand. The biggest luxury to her was a nice hot shower and hair wash every night when work for the day was finished.

Finally the day came when they had effected a clearance right up to the edge of the cliff. If indeed there was a tomb, it was either behind the cartouche or to the side of it, Paul had said. Chantal, as usual, had disagreed and said that all she expected to find was solid rock. Elaine, in a quiet moment with Paul, enquired how they were going to find out.

'After all, we can't just dig half the cliff face away, even if we could,' she added.

Paul explained at length.

'No, it's going to be a little like drilling for oil. We sink a number of rods lengthways through several drill holes, above and below the cartouche and to each side of it. With any luck one of them hits an empty space and we at least know that, if not a tomb, there is an opening behind the rock face.'

'But surely,' argued Elaine, 'if there was a cave or something, wouldn't it be exposed like all these others?' She pointed further along and above them, to where caverns showed gaping exits high up the cliff.

'No, not if that too had been filled up over the years by subsequent falls of rock and sand. Most of these others', he said, pointing to where she was looking, 'were too high to be affected by the landslides of time.'

Elaine could feel a tingling in her spine. Was there really something behind the cartouche? Maybe they were going to make another find, like Howard Carter did, when he unearthed Tutankhamun on 4 November, 1922.

The following day, in spite of Chantal's cynicism, work of boring through the limestone began. It was laboriously slow as only hand drills could be used, the authorities having banned any form of power tool, in case other tombs were damaged by the vibrations. Most of the time whilst Ibrahim and his crew, together with Paul and Elaine, took turns with the elongated brace contraption, with its ridiculously long burrs, Chantal watched them, seated upon a boulder, a look of bland indulgence on her face.

It was towards the evening of the third day when Ibrahim thrilled everyone with an excited exclamation in Arabic. Paul left what he was doing and rushed to his foreman's side.

'The drill has gone right through, effendi... Look! Not very far in, either.' He moved the piece backwards and forwards quickly to show how easily it moved.

'Good man, Ibrahim. Pull the drill right out.'

While Ibrahim obliged, Paul hunted round and found one of the long steel rods. By the time he rejoined Ibrahim, he could see that Chantal had arrived and was trying to peer through the small borehole with a torch. The exercise proved useless. She turned it off and pocketed it. Paul waited for her to get out of the way so that he could try with the steel rod. After another derogatory remark she reluctantly stood aside.

'Be my guest,' she said, sarcastically.

Everyone else had now gathered round and was looking expectantly at Paul. Gradually he fed the slim steel rod in through the drill hole. In no time at all he felt the difference in resistance and the others could see by his face the excitement there. He withdrew the rod, and turning to Ibrahim, asked him to make the hole bigger by using a much larger bit. With bated breath everyone watched the agonisingly slow progress as the burr bit deeper into the rock face and existing minute hole. Then, with a rush, it went through. When the drill was withdrawn it was still impossible to see anything with Chantal's torch.

'That's the largest burr we have, effendi,' said Ibrahim, apologetically.

'Never mind, we shall go to work with a chisel and make the hole bigger all the way in until we are able to see. I don't think we shall have to go very far before we are through,' said Paul.

Ibrahim and his men took turns, as working with the chisel was hard work. It was Ahmed who finally broke through. Now the incision in the rock face was cone-shaped, going down to about a two-centimetre hole into whatever lay behind. The hole was less than a metre into the rock.

'We shall still need to make the entrance bigger on the cliff face if we are going to be able to see anything with a torch.'

By the time this had been done, sunset was fast approaching. Chantal roughly pulled out of the way Sabar, who was the one working with the hammer and chisel at the time. Pushing her head and shoulders into the outer recess he had made, she shone her torch in through the small hole.

When there was no response, Paul said, 'Well, can you see anything or can't you?'

She withdrew and handed Elaine the torch, saying to Paul, 'It's a cavern all right. Nothing more,' she exclaimed, before walking away.

Elaine, with the curiosity borne of woman, was already peering into the dark recess. She gave Paul, who was standing behind her, a running commentary.

'It's a cave… Goes a long way back… Appears to be only boulders and rocks lying around… Can't see the back of it… Just seems to disappear in the darkness, only a blur.' She extricated herself and handed Paul the torch. 'Here, you have a look for yourself.'

Paul took it eagerly and took her place, hoping to see something else. Finally, after a long scrutiny, he withdrew, congratulating the men.

'Well done, men. It's already sunset so there's no more time today. Tomorrow we shall break through, but I shall have to let the Ministry of Antiquities know, as they will probably want to send someone down for the opening. I think the best thing is for you four men to start early tomorrow, making an entry point, but not breaking right through until we arrive at about noon with the ministry man. Do you understand, Ibrahim?'

'Yes, effendi. Do not break through until you and ministry here… Yes?'

Chantal had rejoined them.

'Why wait for the ministry? Why not just go in ourselves?' she retorted.

'Because, my dear woman, if there is anything in there, we need to protect ourselves against any claims or accusations of theft on our part,' Paul replied.

'I am not your dear woman… but I suppose you are

right, otherwise.'

Paul turned to Ibrahim.

'Perhaps you and your men can take turns tonight standing guard. We can't afford to rely on one night-watchman at this stage. Obviously I shall see that you receive added compensation for the overtime.'

'Certainly, effendi. I shall see that nobody interferes.'

Chantal again walked off, saying, 'What harm can come to an empty cave?'

Elaine couldn't resist it. She ran after her and caught hold of her arm.

'We don't know yet that it is an empty cave,' she exclaimed.

'I wouldn't get my hopes up too high if I were you, Elaine,' whispered Chantal, placing her hand over Elaine's. 'I think tomorrow we shall all find that we have been wasting our time here in the valley.'

Elaine felt quite deflated and watched Chantal walk towards the jeep.

That evening, whilst they were eating dinner at their lodgings, Elaine tactfully began probing Paul about Chantal's obvious hatred of him. It was one of the few times she found herself alone with him, as Chantal had gone out to dinner with friends, so it seemed as good a time as any. The bottle of Chardonnay that they shared put both in a garrulous mood and the atmosphere was suitably relaxed to broach the subject that had been bothering her for some time.

Paul explained that Chantal's belief and allegiance to Tuthmosis III was almost bordering on necromancy. He went on to say that, because he took the opposite view and supported Hatshepsut's cause, she made it personal and hated him equally as much as the strong queen she had deemed a usurper.

'No, Paul. There has to be more to it than that. Think about it... I'm your assistant and therefore obviously sympathetic to your beliefs, which means I come down on the side of Hatshepsut also.'

'So what are you saying?' asked Paul.

'Well, she now seems to be quite friendly with me. It's noticeable that it's only when you come around that her hostility emerges.'

Paul gave an embarrassed cough, before trying to explain.

'You are a very perceptive young lady for an archaeologist, and yes, you are right. As you may or may not have gathered, Chantal is a very mixed-up lady.'

Elaine leant further forward on her chair, as Paul's voice had dropped to no more than a whisper.

'What do you mean, mixed-up? Surely she is as respected in her field, just as much as you yourself are?'

'Quite so, but I wasn't referring to professional standing or qualifications,' said Paul, clearly embarrassed. He fingered his collar and gave another little cough. 'Sexually, I mean... She is somewhat confused as to her sexuality.'

'Surely not, Paul, I can't believe that. She must be one of the most attractive women I've ever seen.'

'Did I say she wasn't?' countered Paul.

'No, you didn't, but...' Elaine's voice tailed off.

'I see that I shall have to tell you, as you are rather like a terrier with a bone. You're not going to let this drop, are you?'

'Well, as we are all working together, I think you owe it to me,' argued Elaine.

Paul blurted it out.

'Well, apart from her obsession with Tuthmosis III, who unfortunately time denies her and she can't have, Chantal prefers women. No other man is good enough for her.'

'How do you know all this, Paul? You do know something about her, don't you?'

Paul looked to right and left, to ascertain that none of the other guests in the boarding house were within earshot, before beginning.

'Yes. I first met Chantal ten years ago when we were both working on a dig up near Alexandria. My ex-wife, Helen, was with me then. We hadn't been married above two years and were pretty close in those days.' Paul paused for breath, still not very happy with what was being dragged out of him.

'Go on,' prompted Elaine, leaning further across the table in her impatience to hear more.

'Chantal Shariffe was only about twenty-five, a year or so younger than Helen. My wife, as I've told you before, had no interest in archaeology, but she was very happy to socialise with everyone in the evening, and that included Chantal. They became good friends but then one evening when they were alone she made a move on Helen. It appeared our Chantal wanted more than friendship. Helen, however, whatever else she might have been, was entirely heterosexual and was appalled. This did not deter Chantal, however, who continued to pursue Helen, making herself into quite a nuisance. Finally, Helen confided in me and asked me to warn Chantal off. This I did in no uncertain terms. The stalking and bothering of Helen stopped, but the lifetime hatred of me began and you see it for what it is today.' Paul looked almost relieved at getting this off his chest.

'It explains a few things anyway, Paul. I suppose I should have suspected.'

'What do you mean?'

'Of late she seems to find reasons to touch me more and more, nothing improper you understand,' added Elaine.

'I'm not surprised. You are a remarkably attractive woman, Elaine.'

219

Elaine found herself blushing at this unusual and unexpected compliment from Paul. She tried to cover up her confusion by saying, 'Ahmed and Sabar are very attractive young men, but she never gives them a glance, so I think what you are saying is probably true as they continually watch her.'

Paul laughed.

'That's true, when they are not watching you.'

'They never watch me,' Elaine denied hotly.

'Not when you are looking, they don't. Other times their eyes never leave you. They like blondes in these eastern countries.'

'There are times, Paul Stanton, when you talk rubbish,' countered Elaine in light-hearted vein.

'What me? Never,' laughed Paul, then changed the subject to a more serious one. 'I rang through to the ministry and told them we plan to open the tomb, if tomb it is, tomorrow at noon, and they said that they will be sending someone down from Cairo, probably Ali, I expect,' he added.

'You sounded, then, as if you had doubts yourself. Do you think we won't find anything tomorrow when we open it up?' said Elaine, disappointment creeping into her voice.

'Well, we mustn't build our hopes up too high... Only time can give us the answer.'

'I can't help but wish we had worked all night and gone in. I won't be able to sleep tonight for excitement... Noon tomorrow can't come quickly enough for me,' exclaimed Elaine.

However, the morning did come round just as it always did. Paul joined Elaine for breakfast at eight. Both had asked for late calls, as there was no need to get to the site before noon. Ali had telephoned the night before, very late, and left a message that he would meet them at the lodgings at eleven and travel with them to the site. By the time they had finished a leisurely breakfast and read the morning papers Chantal had still not arrived for her breakfast.

'I expect she's taking advantage of the late start and having a lie-in,' ventured Paul.

'Unlike her, though. She's usually up before either of us,' replied Elaine.

Neither said any more about it until around ten thirty when Paul, looking at his watch said, 'Perhaps you had better go up and give her a call. She must have overslept, or worse, be ill.'

Elaine laughed.

'Perhaps, under the circumstances, it would be safer if you went up there to knock on her door.'

'Chicken!' said Paul.

Elaine made a rude sign and got up and left the room. Two minutes later she returned looking very puzzled.

'What's wrong?' Paul shot at her.

'No answer. I knocked three times, still no answer, so I opened the door and went in. Her bed had been slept in all right, but of Chantal there was no sign.'

'Very strange… Perhaps she went out early, shopping or walking or something,' added Paul as an afterthought.

'Possibly, but somehow I doubt it. I'll go and see who's around. Perhaps someone has seen her or knows something.' With that Elaine left to make some enquiries.

Ali arrived early at about ten fifty and a few minutes later Elaine returned looking somewhat disturbed.

'What's up?' questioned Paul.

'That's what I'd like to know. It appears she left this morning early, about an hour before we got up. The caretaker saw her get into a taxi.'

'The blazes he did,' exclaimed Paul and his face showed annoyance. 'Did he say how she was dressed?'

'Same as us, shorts, shirt, boots and backpack and carrying a tote bag,' responded Elaine, then, watching Paul's face she added, 'Are you thinking what I'm thinking?'

'You bet I am. It's a pound to a penny she's gone down to the site, planning to go in before we get there,' snapped Paul. Turning to Ali, he exclaimed, 'And you asked me to work with her. The woman is quite impossible.'

'Oh, come now, Mr Stanton. We don't know for sure that's where she's gone to… She could be anywhere.'

'Do you want to have a little bet, Ali?' said Paul.

'I'm not a betting man, Mr Stanton.'

'Just as well, because I'm quite sure you'd lose your money.'

'Are we going to wait here in the cool for Miss Shariffe to return?' asked Ali.

'The hell we are,' snapped Paul, then, turning to Elaine, he said, 'Get everything together, Elaine. I'll go out and fetch the jeep and bring it round.'

Within five minutes, the jeep had been brought round, loaded and was on its way, with the three of them on board. Paul drove like a madman. Twice Elaine shut her eyes as the end looked inevitable, but somehow he managed to squeeze the jeep through between a bus and a lorry going in opposite directions. She gave him an old-fashioned look, on opening her eyes and finding that they were still in one piece.

In his heart Paul was only too aware of what had happened. Chantal had stolen a march on them, and had gone down to open the tomb on her own. It wasn't the loss of any possible glory that he minded, although that was bad enough. It was the fact that the woman had openly deceived them by going alone. He was inwardly seething with pent-up fury and rage. Elaine sensed it, and sitting in the front, placed a restraining hand on his thigh.

'Calm down, Paul. I think we would all appreciate getting there in one piece.'

He forced a wan smile. 'Sorry. I guess I let it get to me.'

Making a conscious effort, he reduced his speed.

Soon they left the road and began the bumping and rolling through the sandy valley. He could see the site long before they reached it. Of Chantal there was no sign, but he could see Ibrahim and the three men hired by him, standing around the rocks near the tomb.

Perhaps he had misjudged her and she wasn't there at all. It was then that he saw it, a gaping black hole, where the sealed entrance to the tomb had been, to the right of the cartouche. Elaine saw it too and he felt her hand tighten on his thigh. He slammed his foot hard down on the accelerator pedal and the jeep careered forward. A minute later it came to rest in a cloud of dust a few yards from Ibrahim and the men. Paul leapt out and stared straight at the opening in the rock face.

'What in hell is going on here?' he demanded of the foreman.

'I thought you knew, effendi... Madame Shariffe, she arrives this morning early and said that you had given orders for the tomb to be opened, so I gave orders for the men to create an opening.'

'Where is the bitch?' roared Paul.

Again, he felt Elaine's restraining hand, this time on his arm. Ibrahim explained that the opening had finally been made about an hour earlier and Madame Shariffe had gone straight in, armed with two torches.

'Did you accompany her, Ibrahim?'

'No, effendi. She say we are to wait until she returns. We are still waiting. She no come out again.'

'Come on, Elaine,' exclaimed Paul. 'We are going in.'

With Elaine in his wake he headed for the entrance. Ali stood with the workmen watching from the rocks.

Chapter VI

Fatima was feeling bitterly resentful. She had topped Khaled by two clear marks in the report Wilhelm Snoek had handed to the leaders of the Fundamentalists. Two days earlier the recruits had completed their special training course and Snoek had congratulated her when he had read out the marks. Now she had just been told that she was to be made second in command to Khaled, in a special armed unit to work in the Luxor area. She realised that she might have expected such a decision, as the Fundamentalists would probably draw the line at following a woman or accepting orders from her. It was Khaled's gloating that she found hard to take.

She was to pull out for Luxor with the unit in two days' time, part of a special hit team aimed at exterminating all foreigners. One of the hierarchy had come down to talk to them on their graduation and give a final briefing. At that stage, Fatima had still nurtured a hope that they would make her the leader. Now she knew differently. They should all be prepared to die for their country if the need arose, and be proud to do it. The aim of the movement was to bring down the government at all costs, and they must consider themselves expendable in the doing of such deeds to this end.

The elder had gone on to say that the government must be shown to be inept, and unable to protect visitors to the land of Egypt. 'In this way we shall bring them down and put our own leaders into power. Only by this action can we restore the greatness of our land.'

The elder had then left after shaking hands with all the

graduates. Tonight they would be outfitted for their mission, which would include, besides a new denim boiler suit, a pistol, Sten gun and two grenades each. Earlier Wilhelm Snoek had said his goodbyes to the squad. His work done, he was returning that night to his homeland in South Africa. Already Khaled was throwing his weight about, leaving no one in doubt that he was in total command.

'Any minor grievances that you men may have, take them to my second in command, Fatima, here,' he had exclaimed, jerking a thumb in her direction. 'Of course, if it is an important issue, you should bring it to me.'

Fatima had caught her tongue between her teeth and bit it. In her fury she could taste the salty blood in her mouth. She knew it was something she would have to get used to, but it needled her nonetheless.

Two days later they left for Luxor, all travelling separately on the train. It had been considered far too risky, given the maximum security now in force after the massacres that had taken place, to travel in one band. Fatima herself was dressed in the traditional garb of the long black dress and headgear of the married woman, and with her she carried a large, strong, cardboard box with a rope handle. In it, unseen, were the merciless tools of her new trade.

All the squad had been given a rendezvous point, once they reached Luxor. It was a house on the borders of the town, owned by a sympathiser of the Fundamentalists. Here they would be given their orders. Sitting back in her carriage seat in the train, she seethed at the thought of having to receive them from Khaled. Some men she could have accepted, even Snoek, brute that he was, but... She knew she was better. Hadn't she proved it to them? Perhaps he would fail and they would make her leader; until then, she consoled herself, she would have to go along with it.

An officer in the Egyptian army sat down in the seat

opposite her, a handsome fellow… Twice he smiled at her and the third time struck up a conversation, or tried to. Inwardly she felt very satisfied at the thought of what the man didn't know or even suspect. Just as well for him, she thought, for if he suspected what was in her large cardboard box, she would have to shoot him. A pity that, for he was quite young and good-looking. However, it didn't arise, as he got out at one of the stations on the way to Luxor and she was left alone.

★

Shining a torch in front of him, with Elaine bringing up the rear, Paul entered the tomb. Of Chantal there was no sign. In spite of the heat outside there was an eerie cold clamminess about the cavern. With only the torch to guide them, the beam of which wasn't very bright, progress was slow. The cavern floor was uneven and rocky. Stalagmites and stalactites had formed in several places. Elaine reached for Paul's hand to guide her as the light barely reached back to her.

Even when they whispered to one another their voices seemed to echo and come bouncing back to them. The roof was surprisingly high and the cave went deeply into the rock. Once they had made a turn, all the light from the entrance was denied them. The torch beam seemed to flicker, then went out and they were left in total darkness. Paul gripped Elaine's hand more firmly and drew her tightly into him.

'Keep in contact. I'll strike a match,' he whispered.

'A match,' came back the echo.

Elaine gave an involuntary shudder. Paul sensed it and gave her a comforting squeeze. A moment later he struck a match which illuminated the scene around them. Moisture dripped from the ceiling and there were huge limestone columns to either side of them. Another turn in the cave lay ahead and they could see that they were standing between two bends, a small plateau of some three metres. Some broken rocks lay on the floor, and something glinting reflected the flare from the match. As Paul bent down and grasped it, the match went out, leaving them once more in a black void.

'Listen, it's no good going on like this. One of us is going to fall and get hurt. We'll retrace our steps and get some hurricane lamps lit and come back,' said Paul.

'Come back,' said the echo.

'First we had better call out just in case Chantal is in here and hurt and can't move.'

'Chantal! Chantal! Are you in here? Shout if you can hear us,' Paul called. Only the echo floated back. 'Hear us.'

They waited with bated breath. There was not a sound, only the gloomy noise of dripping water in the darkness. Elaine called out, her more highly pitched voice rebounding back to them. Paul struck another match and in its glow they retraced their steps. Long before they were out, the draught extinguished the match, but by now the light from the entrance guided them clear.

Ibrahim rushed forward.

'What did you find, effendi? Was Madame Shariffe in there?'

Paul spread his palms wide in a noncommittal gesture.

'Nothing as yet, but we need more light. Can you get three hurricane lamps lit, then you can come in with us whilst we look round.'

'The hurricane lamps, yes, effendi… Come in with you – no… I tell Madame Shariffe the same,' said Ibrahim, backing away.

'What nonsense is this, Ibrahim?' Seeing that the foreman was not going to budge on this he exclaimed, 'Very well. I'll take one of the men in with us then.'

'They no come either. There are bad omens here. We feel it.'

Elaine, in spite of the heat, felt herself shiver once more.

'Very well, Ibrahim. The lamps, please, three of them.'

When the foreman hurried away to attend to the lighting of these, Elaine questioned Paul. 'What are they frightened of, Paul? Do they know something we don't?'

'Not you, too! Don't get your knickers in a twist. These guys are just very superstitious. Probably Howard Carter had the same problems back in 1922.'

Elaine couldn't help it, she just had to say it. 'But that was followed by the stories of the curse and people died.'

'Circumstances, Elaine, and anyway we don't even know this is a tomb yet, do we?'

'It is. I'm sure I could feel it somehow when we were in there just now... These fellows can even feel it without going in,' she said, looking towards the men lighting the lamps.

'Don't tell me you don't want to come back in with me?' said Paul, crossly.

'Oh no. I'm scared stiff, but I'm still coming back in with you. Anyway, we've got to find Chantal. If the men haven't seen her come out she must still be in there somewhere.'

Ibrahim and Ahmed returned with the hurricane lamps. Suddenly Paul remembered the item, still clenched in his fist, which he had picked up from the cavern floor. Opening his palm, he examined the object. He recognised it at once, so did Elaine, who excitedly pulled his open hand towards her for a closer look.

'It's Chantal's golden ankh, which she wears on a chain round her neck,' gasped Elaine.

Paul examined it closely. He knew it to be an Egyptian cross, the symbol of eternity, similar to a Christian cross, apart from the large loop at the top. He was far more interested in the piece of chain still attached to the top of the loop, which had clearly broken off. The gold ankh, with diamonds set into the crosspiece, reflected the fierce heat of the sun. Turning it over, he examined the reverse side. Apart from the gold standard marks, there was no clue to how it had become detached from Chantal's neck. And where was the rest of the chain? The concern showed on Elaine's face.

'Do you think she has come to harm in there, Paul?'

'Only one way to find out,' he exclaimed, taking two of the lamps from Ibrahim, after having safely pocketed the ankh.

Elaine took the other from Ahmed and followed Paul, who was striding purposefully back towards the cave entrance. Things were much easier this time and the three hurricane lamps gave good light, apart from the eerie shadows the flickering flames gradually exposed. Elaine kept close to Paul and could almost feel her knees knocking. Again she gave an involuntary shudder. They advanced slowly, examining every nook and cranny before proceeding on to the next. Soon they were round the first turn and eventually round the second, further than they had been before. Here the cave widened into a large chamber, with both the floor and the roof undulating downwards.

To either side were large rocks and boulders. A detailed inspection behind all of them revealed nothing. Everything seemed to have been undisturbed for centuries. At the end of this large chamber there was yet another turn, and having made it, they were immediately confronted by three separate wide tunnels, two of them high enough to walk through. The other would necessitate them almost crawling on their hands and knees.

Paul whispered that they would try the two easiest ones first and they took the one to the left. It soon petered out and they came up against a solid rock face. They retraced their steps and tried the second. It went further than the first but ended in a small antechamber which revealed nothing but more boulders, some of them shaped quite grotesquely. Elaine thought them quite sinister and threatening and couldn't rid herself of this feeling of dread. Gradually they retraced their steps yet again to the entrance to the low tunnel.

'You can go back if you want, Elaine,' whispered Paul, sensing her fear.

'No way! I'm staying with you,' she answered.

The thought of returning alone through those dark passages frightened her more than staying with Paul. After all, hadn't Chantal disappeared in here somewhere?

On hands and knees, holding one of the lamps in front of him, Paul crawled forward into the tunnel. There had been nothing for it but to leave one of the lamps behind as he would need a free hand. They could always pick it up on the way back.

Elaine found that, not being anything like so tall, she could get through in a half-crouch, and in this position, with her lamp, she followed him. To their surprise the low narrow passage quickly opened up into a larger chamber, but half barring their way was a large hole some metre and a half across. Paul stopped dead, having nearly pitched headlong into it. Elaine almost crashed into him.

'What is it?' she asked, unable to see past him.

Paul shone the lamp over the edge and gasped. Elaine, from the rear, gripped his ankle, aware of sudden alarm.

'What can you see?'

'It's a deep well, natural by the look of it. I can't see the bottom… Hold on a minute.' He scratched around on the floor of the tunnel and found a loose rock and dropped it over the edge of the black hole. Several times they heard it strike the sides, then nothing. 'Holy Moses, it must be one hell of a depth,' exclaimed Paul. 'I didn't hear it hit the bottom.'

'Do you think Chantal could have fallen in?' asked Elaine, nervously.

'It's possible. I nearly did, but there's only one way to find out.' Leaning over the forbidding black opening, he called as loudly as he could. 'Chantal! Chantal! Can you hear us?'

The echo came booming back from all sides and even up out of the seemingly bottomless abyss. Elaine's hands moved up to around Paul's waist and she nearly burnt him with the lamp she had forgotten she was carrying.

'Hey – be careful, love. I can do without being roasted.'

'Roasted,' came back the echo.

Again Elaine shivered. 'How are we going to get past this obstacle?' she said, trying hard to make her voice sound normal as she couldn't see past Paul.

'Follow me and for heaven's sake be careful,' he urged.

Hugging the side of the tunnel, there was just room to squeeze past the gaping abyss. Once through, he found he could stand up, and was able to hold out a hand to assist Elaine past the obstacle. A moment later, she had joined him on the other side. Holding their lamps high, they were amazed to see how high the roof was. Again there was an abundance of limestone stalagmites and stalactites every-where. There was even a small underground stream, which disappeared from sight somewhere down under the rocks.

Systematically, they began to explore. Elaine began to establish a greater control of her fear and searched with her lamp on one side of the chamber, whilst Paul explored the other side. Somehow the sound of the trickling water seemed to restore her confidence. They were nearly at the end, when Paul made the discovery of something bright jammed between the rocks and exposed by the flickering lamp.

'Over here, Elaine,' he called.

'Elaine,' called back the echo.

She hurried over. He pointed to the object half buried by slimy algae on the rocks. He realised that the moss and algae must be caused by the moisture from the underground stream. Gently he prised away at it with his fingers as Elaine peered over his shoulder, holding her breath in anticipation. Finally it came away. He set the lamp down on a smooth piece of rock and held the object as near as he could. Producing a handkerchief, he gently rubbed it. Gradually, through the stain of years, a distinct pattern began to show.

'It's gold anyway,' he whispered. 'There's a design on it.' He continued working away with the handkerchief, which was fast becoming a grubby rag.

'Here, take mine,' called Elaine, proffering her own handkerchief.

More diligent work with the help of some spit revealed a carving or inscription. Finally Paul almost yelled with delight.

'It's a cartouche and it's that of Hatshepsut.'

'Hatshepsut, Hatshepsut, Hatshepsut,' echoed the chamber.

Elaine found herself almost looking round expecting the eighteenth-dynasty queen, of three and a half thousand years earlier, to reappear, so loud had been the reverberation in the chamber.

'Are you sure, Paul?' she found herself whispering, not wishing to waken the echo once more.

'No doubt of it. It's the royal cartouche of Hatshepsut and it's the kind a Pharaoh would have worn, either pinned to them, or on a chain round their neck.'

With great care he wrapped the golden object in Elaine's handkerchief and carefully placed it in the breast pocket of his shirt. Elaine wandered off and gazed down into the shallow gully where the stream trickled away into the rocks.

It was no more than about twelve centimetres deep. She held her lamp aloft, to see where it disappeared into the rock face.

Something was wedged there, where the water rushed through a tiny crack. It glinted as she held the hurricane lamp nearer. She reached down and fumbled for the object and came up with a golden chain. Immediately she thought of Paul's words and dismissed them as quickly. This was a new and sparkling gold chain. Hurrying over to Paul, she showed him her find.

Producing the ankh that belonged to Chantal he compared the two and then exclaimed, 'It's Chantal's all right... See here, you can see the broken link where the ankh broke off.'

'Then she must be here somewhere, otherwise she really has fallen down that horrible place.' She looked back towards the abyss.

'I don't think so. I think she is too experienced to have made such a mistake,' mused Paul.

'But you nearly did,' put in Elaine.

'True, but I still think she has to be here somewhere. We haven't looked over there yet,' he said and indicated the far end of the chamber... Come on.'

Further exploration showed where a shelflike rock had an underside that dropped away into a hidden recess going down at quite a steep angle. With difficulty Paul lowered himself down and disappeared from sight. Elaine felt dreadfully alone and isolated and shivered involuntarily again. She heard Paul's voice floating up to her.

'It's okay, come down. There's another narrow passage going on down.'

Elaine squeezed through under the rock and joined him below. She saw at once she was in a narrow passage, but through the rock face. Gradually, due to the confined space, they edged forward. A final turn brought them into a tiny chamber and it was then that they found Chantal.

Both Elaine and Paul let out an involuntary gasp. There, spread-eagled on the cavern floor, was Chantal. Her usually lustrous black hair was damp and matted, and her khaki shirt looked as if it had been roughly torn open, exposing a white half-cup bra. Paul rushed forward and bent down beside her. One glance told him she was either dead or unconscious. If she was breathing at all, it was only shallowly, as no chest movement could be discerned. He reached for her wrist, searching for a pulse, as Elaine joined him on her knees besides the comatose form.

Elaine waited with bated breath, anxious not to interrupt his investigation. When finally he laid the slim wrist back on Chantal's stomach, she whispered, 'Is she?' and was almost afraid of what she might hear. Was this to be the curse of the Pharaohs all over again.

'No, she's alive, but her pulse is very faint,' he replied.

'Whatever can have happened to her? It almost looks as if she's been attacked or something,' ventured Elaine.

'Could be a fall, I suppose. We had better check that nothing's broken before we try moving her out of here.' Gently he ran his hands over Chantal's unconscious body, paying particular attention to the neck region. Slowly he stood up, looking down on Chantal with a puzzled expression. 'I'm fairly certain that nothing's broken, but we have got to get her out and to a hospital fairly quickly... She's obviously been here for some time and her body temperature will be way down.'

Elaine climbed to her feet and nervously faced Paul.

'Just how are we going to get her out of here? I mean it was difficult enough us getting ourselves past that black hole.'

Paul looked thoughtful.

'We shouldn't move her without expert help, but obviously we can't leave her down here, even if she does deserve it.' He couldn't resist adding the final few words.

'So, what do we do?' enquired Elaine, bending down again and trying to make Chantal's shirt close a little more respectably.

'I'm sorry, love, but one of us will have to go for help while the other stays here with her.'

Elaine looked aghast.

'I don't think I could stay down here on my own, Paul, but on the other hand I don't fancy the trip out alone either.'

'Well, I'm afraid it's got to be one or the other... All I can do is give you the choice. I should have thought to have brought my mobile with us and we could have called for help... But then I don't suppose it would function right down here in the earth anyway,' he added as an after-thought.

Elaine took a long last look at Chantal's comatose form and thought, That could be me lying there needing help. Quickly she came to a decision.

'I'll go back and fetch help,' she said, bending down and picking up the lamp.

Paul tried to smile and gave her a hug.

'Good girl, but for Christ's sake be careful getting back past that hole.'

Bravely she tried to return his smile, and turning, edged her way back up the tunnelled incline to the edge of the black abyss. With difficulty she got past it and called back to reassure Paul she was on her way.

Left alone with the unconscious Chantal, Paul's thoughts began to race. Whatever had possessed the woman to steal a march on them, and come in alone, and whatever could have happened to her? He didn't see from where she was lying how it could have been a fall and no bones seemed to be broken. He bent and felt her skin; it was cold and clammy. There was no means of knowing how long it would take Elaine to fetch skilled help. Somehow he knew he must do something or hypothermia would set in.

Nothing for it but to risk moving her. The cavern floor where she was lying was quite damp.

As gently as he could he raised her head and shoulders and then placed an arm under her knees. She was fairly light and he had no difficulty carrying her to a dry area over by some rocks. Slowly lowering himself with his burden to the rocky floor, he cradled her slight form in his arms, pulling her in towards his warm chest. If he could only keep her warm until help arrived.

Slowly the minutes ticked by, seeming like eternity. Only the trickling sound of the underground stream broke the interminable silence. Slowly Chantal opened her eyes and blinked. She gave a smile of recognition and then spoke the words that shook him to the core.

'It is indeed you, my love, after all these years. You have returned to me.'

With that her eyes closed and she again fell into unconsciousness. These words, from a woman who had always hated him, shook Paul rigid, until he put it down to obvious delirium due to shock or something. Then he realised, with something like horror, that the voice that had come out of Chantal was not Chantal's. True, it was a very female voice but much deeper of tone, husky and sensual. He convinced himself he must have imagined it. After all, the situation in which he found himself was both extraordinary and bizarre. The mind could play strange tricks in this semi-darkness.

Chapter VII

Fatima and Khaled were reconnoitring the valley, both with field glasses to their eyes. High up in the cliffs they could see the full scenic panorama unfold below them, Deir el-Bahri and the Valley of the Nobles and behind them the Valley of the Kings. It was possible to ride on donkeys right over from the Valley of the Kings to the mortuary temple on the other side of the cliffs. Fatima had argued against this; the fewer people who saw them the better. For once Khaled had seen reason and agreed with her. The rest of their detachment had been left in their base camp in Luxor. Since the last massacre at Deir el-Bahri, there were understandably few tourists about and down on the valley floor they could see several detachments of troops and a few civil police.

'We shall have to take great care, woman,' snapped Khaled. 'It would be foolish to attempt something on the scale of the last tourist executions.' Khaled, like all fanatics, did not see the recent massacre as anything but a military exercise. Execution of the infidels, he called it.

Without looking at him, but with her eyes still glued to the field glasses, she retorted, 'Then why try it when there is bigger glory to be won?'

'What mean you, woman?'

Khaled rarely gave his second in command a name. To him she was always woman and therefore inferior. In fact, he had already told her that he couldn't understand why she had been chosen to second him. Fatima hadn't deigned to answer but had just given him a contemptuous look. She was sure that when the time came she could put ideas into the man's head and let him think they were his own.

'Down on the valley floor over to your right in the Valley of the Nobles, do you see three men, Khaled?'

'These I see, but they are not tourists, but Egyptians. Anyone can see that, woman, by their clothes.'

'Exactly, but I have been watching them. They are part of an archaeological investigation. Do you not see the roped-off area?'

'Yes, I see it,' snapped Khaled. 'But we are after tourists, not Egyptians.'

'The Europeans are in the cave behind the roped-off area. I saw them go in earlier,' stated Fatima.

'Ah, infidels, but with all these troops and police about it will be impossible to shoot them,' argued Khaled.

Now was the time for Fatima to exercise her wiles on the unimaginative Khaled.

'You are no doubt clever enough, Khaled, to see that, so you will also realise that if we follow these people back to wherever they are residing, we can capture them and hold them to ransom.'

Khaled's slow mind worked its way round what she had proposed.

'I see, woman, that you are only one step behind me. I, too, had thought of that. If they are important enough, the Egyptian government will pay us much for their return. Is that not so?'

'Far more profitable and of more use to our movement than killing them. No profit in that, is there, Khaled?'

Khaled gave her a cunning smile and then a hearty slap across the backside.

'Then after we have the money, we kill them anyway.'

The statement was followed by a hearty laugh. Fatima ignored the sting on her buttocks and kept her gaze fixed on the cavern entrance.

'We shall watch their movements for a day or two then move when you say so, Khaled, is that not so?'

'My very words, woman. Why must you repeat what I am thinking…?'

Twenty minutes later an old army ambulance with very thick tyres on the front and a half-track at the rear, swung off the track and headed for the Valley of the Nobles. Fatima watched its progress and was surprised when it finally drew up at the roped-off area she had been watching. Three men alighted with a sense of urgency, one of them was soon in conversation with a blonde European woman who had emerged from the cavern only ten minutes earlier. This man turned to the others, obviously calling out instructions.

Fatima, of course, couldn't hear as they were well out of earshot. She could, however, sense their urgency, and watched with interest as a stretcher, ropes and medical bag, together with what appeared at that distance to be an oxygen cylinder, were extracted from the interior of the vehicle.

'What's going on down there?' snapped Khaled.

'Looks like there's been an accident,' she confirmed. 'We can hang on and see what happens.'

'We can, if I say so,' exclaimed Khaled, indignantly.

Fatima realised she had forgotten the golden rule. All ideas must come from him.

'I naturally assumed you would want to, as you are so astute a commander, Khaled.'

'That is true anyway. We shall stay and watch what develops.'

They watched the men follow the blonde woman into the cavern and settled down to wait.

★

Paul Stanton would have been even more concerned had he been aware of the fate that had befallen Chantal earlier that day. Determined to either seize all the glory for herself, or disprove the existence of the possibility of it being Hatshepsut's last resting place, she set off from the lodgings soon after the crack of dawn. Ibrahim and his men were already at the site when she arrived.

'Open it up at once,' she ordered the foreman.

'Not without Effendi Stanton, Mademoiselle Shariffe. I take my orders from him.'

Chantal had suspected that Ibrahim would be difficult, so she had prepared a typed note in Arabic and forged Paul's signature. Ibrahim took the note and read it and appeared bemused.

'This is very strange, Mademoiselle... Mr Stanton, he say none of this to me last night.'

'Well, as you can see he is saying it now,' snapped Chantal, impatiently.

When Ibrahim still delayed and stood his ground, Chantal stamped her foot in the sand. 'Come on, man. I've given you his written instructions... Now get to it... Mr Stanton and his assistant will be joining us later.'

Ibrahim shook his head, doubt was in his every movement.

'This is not like Mr Stanton... I have worked with him before, and—'

Chantal cut him short.

'Do you want to lose your job and those of your men? Now, do as I say at once.'

Ibrahim scrutinised the note once more before saying, 'Well, I suppose it must be all right, as he's signed it, but I don't understand this change of plan.'

'You don't have to... I would remind you that you are only an employed worker here. The requirement is for you to do as you are told... Now open it at once.'

Ibrahim shrugged his shoulders and called over Ahmed.

'Get the others together. Bring hammers, picks and shovels… Mademoiselle Shariffe is going in just as soon as we open the tomb.'

'We don't know that it is a tomb yet. It may be nothing more than a cave,' snapped Chantal.

'Oh, it's a tomb all right,' exclaimed Ibrahim with a strange expression on his face.

'That remains to be seen. Now get to it, man… Hurry and get it open.'

The work took a good two hours with all four men slowly breaking down the limestone resistance. Even before they had finished, Chantal took a lamp and squeezed through the incomplete opening. Ibrahim, watching, saw her disappear from sight round the first bend.

Once inside Chantal didn't really know what to expect, or what she might find. She hoped against hope that it would be nothing. That really would be one in the eye for that biased Hatshepsut fan, Paul Stanton. By having a look first for herself she could come out and confront him with the fact that he was wrong. The cartouche outside was just a red herring. She knew the cave for what it was, just another cavern obscured by the rockfalls of centuries. How she would laugh when she saw his handsome face with disappointment written all over it. Pity about the girl, though. Elaine Gilroy was quite nice, but she would soon get over the false hopes.

Holding the lamp out in front of her, she rounded the second turn and studied the stalagmites and stalactites with professional interest. It was whilst she was thus occupied that she first experienced a feeling of unease, nothing she could explain really. It was as though something or some-body was watching her.

It's just the eerie loneliness of the cavern, she told her-self, not given to fantasy or phobias. Still the strange feeling persisted and she found herself nervously looking to left and right. Suddenly she felt like turning and running back the way she had come. An inner strength fought back the desire and she pressed onwards.

It was then she felt that some unseen thing was walking with her; the flesh on her face burnt and tingled as did the skin on her back. The temperature seemed to be getting colder. Her scientific mind told her that it was because she was descending further down into the earth as the cavern floor sloped continually downwards.

She was now in a large chamber, rocky boulders and ledges on either side, with more grotesque stalagmites and stalactites reaching to the roof. Chantal could feel her own heart pounding and her breathing sounded heavy. She made a conscious effort to regain control and held her breath. Then, with horror, she realised that the breathing sound was right there beside her and it wasn't her breathing. She wanted to scream, but her throat was dry and she couldn't utter a sound. Tentatively she reached out to the right and left of her, expecting to touch a tangible presence… There was nothing but thin air.

Once more she fought down the panic that had assailed her and pressed onwards to the end of the chamber, where a passage took another turn. Chantal now felt as if the very walls were closing in on her. Turn and run, she told herself, get out of here and wait for the others. There would be safety in numbers.

It was then that sheer terror took over. Having convinced herself to return to the entrance, she turned to leave. At the far end of the passage, from which she had just left the large chamber, was a wraithlike apparition blocking her retreat. Chantal froze in trepidation and abject horror. Even in her terrified mental state she knew at once with one glimpse that it was the figure of a woman in the clothes of a Pharaoh of the long distant past.

She forced herself to shut her eyes. It was only her imagination… When she opened them it would be gone and everything would be normal. With a tremendous effort she forced her eyes open once more, then screamed with terror as the figure was nearer and coming towards her. She could see the amused look in those deep dark eyes, the slow sensual advance of the apparition. Turning, Chantal ran towards an area where three passages converged. Thinking only to escape and hide, she ducked into the low one, almost a tunnel. Perhaps the apparition wouldn't be able to follow her there.

Catlike, on all fours, she scampered along the low passageway, half dragging the hurricane lamp with her. Suddenly her right hand, the one with the lamp, struck empty air, and she saw from its light a deep opening into which she had nearly pitched.

In her fright she released the light-giving object, which tumbled into the abyss. She heard it go crashing on its way down, striking the sides as it went, until there was nothing, only total darkness and a deathly, all-pervading silence. Expecting any minute to be grabbed from behind, she scrabbled in the dark with her fingers to find the edge of the black hole. They came in contact with solid rock to her left and, driven by blind panic, she flattened herself against the rock and worked her way along, every so often feeling with the sandalled toe of one foot to see if she was past the abyss.

Then she remembered the torch in her pocket. Fighting desperately to gain control of her shattered nerves, she fumbled with the buttons of her khaki shirt and eventually produced a little flat torch. She switched it on and immediately shone it behind her. Nothing! She had escaped the apparition. Maybe it had been her nerves and she had been hallucinating. Yes, that was it. Pull yourself together, woman. There's no such thing as ghosts.

She had, by the time she had reached the next chamber, almost regained control of her shattered nerves, but worse was to come. She heard soft musical laughter, like that of a woman, from somewhere behind her. Chantal froze on the spot where she stood and then backed away across the chamber. Her fingers sought for the ankh around her neck, something she always had a habit of doing when under stress. It wasn't there, only the gold chain remained round her slim throat. She tried to reason that it must have come off somewhere in the cavern.

Then again came the soft feminine laughter. At any other time it might have been pleasing to the ear, like water running over pebbles. Now it struck sheer cold terror into Chantal's very being. She felt herself breaking out in cold clammy perspiration. Her throat was so dry she couldn't even speak or scream. She shone the small torch beam back in the direction of the laughter, but it was so feeble that its range soon gave way to the all-engulfing blackness.

Desperately Chantal tried to channel her fear into rage, to meet the thing, whatever it was, head-on. She opened her mouth to call out. Her voice croaked and almost broke, like an old woman's.

'Who are you? What do you want?'

'Want, want, want,' echoed the limestone walls, then silence.

Now she was aware of a presence very near to her, but the little torch showed nothing. Then there was a violent tug on her neck and she felt the golden chain part company with her person. It seemed to have been torn off by an unseen hand with such violence that Chantal nearly pitched forward on her face. Fighting to regain her balance, she clutched at her neck. She heard again the lilting laughter, which seemed to come from all around her now. If only she hadn't dropped the hurricane lamp down that accursed abyss. The torch was proving worse than useless. She shook with terror; everything around her seemed ice-cold. It was as if she was in a vacuum or void.

Still holding the back of her neck where the chain had dug in before it had broken, she cried out, 'I said, Who are you and what do you want with me? I have done you no harm.'

An eerie blue-green light, seemingly transparent, appeared no more than two metres in front of her. She fell back in alarm. A deep husky voice, unmistakably a woman's, answered her from somewhere within the transparency of the ghostly light.

'Is it not enough that I am denied everlasting life and a rightful place on the roll of kings carved for all of time?'

In some small way the voice seemed to calm Chantal's highly frayed nerves. At least she could talk to the apparition.

'Who are you?' whispered Chantal, nervously, although her professional knowledge gave her a good idea.

'It is no matter who I am. You are the first person to trespass here in over three millenniums.'

'You must be the spirit of the usurper, Queen Hatshepsut,' replied a shaking Chantal, still hardly able to believe what she was hearing. She was soon to realise that using the word usurper was a dreadful mistake and one she was about to deeply regret. She felt a great wind wafting all around her.

The spirit's voice replied, fury in its tone, 'I am that I am and soon you will be me.'

Chantal felt herself gripped by some hidden force and gradually propelled backwards, the blue-green light moving slowly after her as if tied to her person. The feeble torch was dashed from her hand, and she watched with horror as it disappeared down a crack in the rocks. Only the mysterious light remained, but it seemed to be an entity and illuminated nothing around it.

Suddenly, only for an instant, she saw a woman's face within the light, then it was gone. It was a woman's face, beautiful with large, dark, ochre eyes. On her head she wore the double crown of Egypt with the heads of the cobra and vulture. Beautiful it might have been, but cold fury and vengeance were indelibly written on every feature.

Chantal staggered back, unable to cope with something beyond her belief and totally outside her experience and education. The laughter came again, a cold mocking laughter. Chantal's shirt was ripped open down the front by an unseen hand and a moment later she felt a tremendous pressure on both her upper arms pinning them to her sides. Her mouth opened to scream but nothing came out and, then to her horror, she couldn't close it again.

The icy temperature around her seemed to be warming up and her skin began to feel as if it were on fire. An object seemed to fill her mouth. She tore one arm free and tried to extract the unseen object from her mouth. There was nothing there and yet she still couldn't close her mouth.

Chantal staggered backwards and tripped over a rocky shelf of rock. Over and over she rolled, ending on her back down a slope. She struggled to rise, but some tremendous force was holding her down. Again the laughter echoed in the coal-black tomb, mocking her vain efforts. An unseen force propelled her onto her knees, and a moment later down onto her back. Chantal felt the cold of the cavern floor against the heat of her skin. She struggled to no avail, sensing that further struggle was useless against this apparition. Gradually she could feel her whole being becoming overpowered. Now her legs were being forced apart, until she felt she would be split in two. A great unseen weight descended on her torso, a force so great that she thought the tomb floor must surely open and swallow her.

She tried to squirm and roll free but the weight on her

was growing even heavier. She pummelled the air with her fists but it was like a force field and her knuckles were physically skinned and bled from the exertion.

Now her mouth was being forced even further open and she thought she could taste and smell burning. Gradually Chantal felt the last of her strength failing. It was as if she were being taken over by an unseen presence. There was a pounding in her ears and she could hardly breathe. Just before she lost consciousness, she thought she heard that female laughter again and a voice saying, 'Now I have you.'

Chapter VIII

Elaine and Paul followed the ambulance in the jeep, there not being enough room for them with the patient and attendants in the recovery vehicle. Getting Chantal out of the tomb had been no easy task. Fortunately the paramedics did not share Ibrahim and his men's fear of the unknown and had accompanied Elaine back into the cavern. To say that Paul was pleased to see them, when he first saw their approaching lights and heard their voices, would have been putting it mildly. Chantal had remained unconscious, hence the problem in getting her out without harming her further, but at last they had achieved it. Now they were following on behind the hospital-bound ambulance.

Elaine broke the silence as they bumped along in the jeep.

'Whatever do you think could have happened to her, Paul?'

'Search me... Apart from the odd bruise and scratches she doesn't seem to have broken anything. Perhaps when they do a full examination in the hospital they will know more,' replied Paul.

'She was still unconscious when they put her in the ambulance... It doesn't look too good,' put in Elaine.

Paul didn't reply, but she was aware that the way his knuckles whitened when he gripped the steering wheel showed his obvious concern.

'It is indeed you, my love, after all these years. You have returned to me.'

Hardly aware that he was talking out loud, Paul recited Chantal's words to him in the tomb.

'Pardon?' exclaimed a surprised Elaine, thinking that he was talking to her.

'Sorry, I didn't realise I was talking aloud. Those were the words Chantal used to me when I was alone with her in the tomb.'

'I didn't know she had recovered consciousness... You didn't say,' Elaine ventured.

'It was only momentary before she lapsed into a coma again,' he added.

'Still, it sounds hopeful if she recovered, even for a minute, doesn't it... But why would she say that to you when she hates you?'

'Delirium, I expect, but one thing was rather odd, though.'

'Odd? What do you mean, odd?'

'Well, the voice that came out of her wasn't hers, it was much deeper. Feminine, mind, but much huskier and richer in tone.'

Elaine felt that cold shiver go through her once more quite involuntarily. She tried to establish down-to-earth reason.

'Don't you think you could have imagined it? There, in the darkness of the tomb... It wouldn't be surprising if your mind played strange tricks now, would it?'

Paul gripped the wheel against another bump of the jeep's wheels as they neared the approach road. He shrugged his shoulders in a non-committal fashion.

'Yes, I expect that's what happened. I mean, after all, it had to be her voice... Chantal's I mean.'

Neither spoke again until they followed the ambulance into the hospital courtyard. The paramedics had radioed ahead and the staff were ready and waiting for them with a stretcher on wheels. Chantal was carefully transferred from the vehicle to the mobile bed, and wheeled in through the double doors. Elaine and Paul followed at a respectful distance. It had been obvious to them that she was still unconscious.

Once they were inside, a nurse conveyed them to a small office, and when they were seated, she requested details concerning the patient. Paul relayed them as best he could. Some of the personal questions, like the next of kin, he couldn't answer. The nurse introduced herself after taking down the basic details.

'My name is Heba and I shall try to find out how the patient is progressing. The doctor is examining her now,' she stated in a very businesslike manner.

'Shall we be allowed to see her when he has finished the examination?' enquired Elaine.

'The doctor will probably want to talk to you both before you leave the hospital anyway,' replied Heba.

'We shall help in any way we can,' put in Paul.

'There is little that either of you can do at present but wait patiently here.'

With that Nurse Heba turned on her heel and left them both alone. It was about half an hour later that she returned with the doctor whom she introduced as Doctor Garnal. He shook hands with both of them before bringing them up to date with Chantal's condition. With a slightly embarrassed expression on his face, he tried to explain.

'Your friend, Mademoiselle Shariffe, is still in a coma. We have found no evidence of physical injury, but obviously will have to conduct further tests to be sure. Did she have a fall of some sort?'

Paul tried to explain that she had been exploring alone and it was possible, but neither of them knew for sure.

'Hmmm, there are some strange things about her condition that we cannot fully explain,' went on Garnal.

'Such as?' enquired Paul.

'Temperature for one, abnormally low.'

'Wouldn't hypothermia account for that?' ventured

250

Elaine.

'It would, but she has none of the other symptoms,' replied Garnal. Then, as if to change the subject, he said, 'Nurse Heba here will take you to see your friend now… She is still in a coma but you are welcome to see her. She is in a small intensive-care private ward.' He gave another embarrassed cough. 'I understand the Ministry of Antiquities will take care of her treatment here… Yes?'

'Correct. Insurance with them will attend to that,' confirmed Paul.

'Ah, good… Take them to see the patient, Nurse.'

Heba led them down a long corridor and round a corner where they turned into a small unit marked 'Intensive Care'. It was partitioned into cubicles and in one lay Chantal. Her tanned face now drained of its colour looked almost as white as the bedlinen. She was lying on her back but breathing easily, although shallowly.

Elaine had expected to see Chantal with tubes up her nose, but all that was attached to her was a heart monitor. Two wavy lines ran across it, both totally similar in pattern. She bent down and whispered in Chantal's ear… There was no response. She tried several times in the half-hour that they remained with her. Finally Garnal returned with Heba, the nurse.

'I suggest you leave now. We have your telephone number and shall contact you if there is any change in her condition. There is nothing else you can do for her here, so you may as well continue with your work, whatever it is.'

After Elaine and Paul had departed, Garnal turned to Heba.

'I said this case was strange, Nurse, but I have never seen a heart monitor registering two completely separate heartbeats from one body.'

'Perhaps the machinery is faulty, Doctor Garnal,' prompted Heba.

'It has to be; there is no other possible explanation, Nurse. Fetch another.'

'There isn't another available, Doctor. They are all in use.'

'Oh, well, never mind. Both lines are the same, so we shall assume the machine is duplicating itself. I'll have the engineers have a look at it when they come round.'

★

Khaled and Fatima sat watching the hospital entrance from their parked car. From their vantage point earlier, high up on the cliffs, they had seen the ambulance leave the site and guessed, quite rightly, that it would be going to the hospital, with the two Europeans following in the jeep. It had taken them some time to descend from the high peaks and pick up their vehicle, but Fatima had pointed out there was no hurry.

'Why do you say that, woman?' Khaled had retorted.

'Because obviously one of their party has been injured and it will take time for the doctors at the hospital to examine the casualty. Almost certainly the other two will wait there until the injured one is settled in.'

Finally Khaled had seen reason, but now, after a long wait in the car, he was growing impatient again. Taking a pistol out of his inside pocket, he spun the chamber and began inserting shells.

'What in the name of Allah are you doing?' gasped Fatima, looking to left and right to see if they had been observed by anyone.

'I have waited and listened enough… Better that I shoot the infidels when they emerge from the hospital.'

'Our leader will think that foolhardy of you, Khaled,' reasoned Fatima.

'Why? These infidels would ransack our country and

grow rich at the land's expense… They deserve to die,' argued Khaled.

'Shoot them if you must. You are the leader, but I shall say in my report that there were richer pickings to be had here.'

Khaled eyed the pistol longingly then laid it down on his lap.

'Speak, woman. What devious thoughts go round in your stupid head?'

'Think about it, Khaled. These people – these foreigners – are exploring a roped-off and guarded site in the valley. Obviously they are archaeologists so the Ministry of Antiquities must have hired them to work here.'

'So?' interrupted Khaled.

'So there must be something for them to find. We should keep them under observation until they find whatever it is, then move in.'

'And shoot them,' said Khaled, eagerly.

'Yes, after we have taken whatever they have found for our Fundamentalist movement. Then we shall have no further use for them… unless, of course…' Fatima let the sentence tail off.

'Unless what?' snapped Khaled.

'Well, I mean, if they are important archaeologists, perhaps their government, or our own for that matter, will be prepared to pay a ransom for them.'

'Methinks you are not as stupid as you look, woman.'

Khaled replaced the pistol in his inside pocket, having ascertained the safety catch was on. Fatima smiled to herself and thought, Even you, Khaled, are not quite as stupid as I imagined. However, she wisely kept her thoughts to herself.

It was fully another half an hour before two Europeans emerged from the main gates of the hospital. Fatima nudged Khaled and directed him with a movement of her eyes.

'Is that them? I have never seen them close-up,' grunted Khaled.

'Nor have I, but I recognise the blonde woman from watching her through the field glasses earlier.'

The two terrorists watched as the pair reached the jeep parked by the roadside and climbed in.

'The woman is very attractive,' exclaimed Khaled.

'Does that mean that you won't shoot her when the time comes?' asked Fatima, goading him.

'One of us will, that's for sure,' he growled through tight lips.

The jeep edged away from the kerbside and edged out through the hospital gates, passing close by the vehicle containing the two terrorists. Khaled allowed a reasonable lapse of time before pulling out to follow them. Through the back streets of Luxor he managed to keep at least one or two cars in between them. When the jeep swung off into a small courtyard, Khaled drove by and parked round the corner well out of sight. Turning to Fatima, he instructed her to walk back and investigate.

'Knock on the door and say that you are interested in renting lodgings, woman… Find out what the setting is back there… How many people are residing in the building – things like that.'

Without a word to indicate whether she had heard Khaled or not, Fatima got out of the vehicle and, closing the car door silently, she walked off slowly round the corner and disappeared from his sight. Fortunately she was dressed in European-style clothes that day, a light cotton dress and sandals. Advancing through the courtyard, she climbed the steps to the front door, rang the bell and waited. Several seconds ticked by with no response. She rang again. This time, after about half a minute, the door was opened by, to her surprise, the blonde girl, who enquired politely what she wanted.

'I wondered if there was accommodation to be found here. Are you in charge of these apartments?' Fatima asked.

'No, we only rent. The housekeeper is out shopping at present... You would have to see her, I expect,' replied Elaine.

Fatima's agile brain was working overtime. Maybe she could actually get accommodation here. What a wonderful chance to know what was going on.

'Do you think it would be worth my while returning to see her? I mean, are there any rooms to let or have they all gone, do you know?'

'Well, there are certainly three of us staying here. We all have bedsits and use a communal kitchen and bathroom. I know one bedsit is still empty. Maybe the housekeeper would let you have that, but I really can't say,' said Elaine, trying to be helpful. After all, the girl looks respectable enough, she thought.

They continued to chat for a while, Fatima putting herself out to be charming.

'I tell you what. Why don't you come in and wait? I'm sure the housekeeper will be back within the next half an hour or so,' offered Elaine.

Fatima said that was extremely kind and she would accept the offer, but first she must go and discharge her taxi which was still waiting. Elaine looked over her shoulder.

'I don't see any taxi,' she said, surprised.

'Oh, no, you wouldn't. He has stopped just round the corner... I won't be a minute.'

Fatima turned and skipped down the steps and disappeared out of the courtyard. Elaine was left waiting, standing at the front door. Strange, she thought. I would have thought her taxi would have stopped outside. Then she assumed that perhaps they had overshot and the girl had walked back.

Fatima raced back to Khaled's vehicle and opened the rear door. Quickly she withdrew her tote bag and at the same time said, 'I think I'm in here... Drive off and leave me. I'll be in touch after I've found out what's going on.'

Before Khaled could offer an argument, she had slammed the door shut and scurried off.

'Stupid woman,' mumbled Khaled.

Then after a few moments, he let in the clutch and moved into reverse. Backing out of the cul-de-sac, he straightened up the car and left in a flurry of dust. Fatima rejoined the waiting Elaine at the top of the front door steps, an attractive smile on her face.

'Come in,' Elaine welcomed. 'I'm sure my friends won't mind me inviting you in to wait for Noha... That's the housekeeper's name.' In the communal kitchen, Elaine introduced the girl to a surprised Paul, who was reading a book. 'This is...' Suddenly Elaine realised that she didn't know the girl's name.

'Fatima Sherin,' volunteered the new arrival.

Paul rose and offered his hand, saying, 'Pleased to meet you, Miss Sherin.'

Fatima took it and gazed into his eyes, warmth exuding from her.

'My, you European men are so handsome and strong.'

Paul, obviously flattered, offered a chair by pulling it out from the table.

'Fatima is looking for lodgings,' Elaine prompted.

'Well, I'm sure we can help her by putting in a good word for her with Noha. Tell us a bit about yourself, Fatima,' urged Paul, obviously taken with the Egyptian girl's dark looks.

Fatima laid it on good and thick. She was a past master at this sort of thing. In no time at all she had both her listeners feeling very sorry for her. Fatima's parents had both died from cholera when she was still a child and she had been brought up in an orphanage. She had been forced to run away when one of the helpers had tried to abuse her, and for years had survived on the streets by begging. Finally she had been taken in by a religious order, but now, because she was nineteen, she had to leave the convent and must get a job to survive. Perhaps the handsome Englishman and his beautiful wife could help her? Fatima watched them both with large beguiling eyes. Actually she was twenty-five but she wasn't about to tell them that. Paul asked her several questions and she seemed well read.

Elaine remembered thinking at the time that this was strange, considering the girl's past. She was even more surprised when the kind-hearted Paul suggested that maybe they could find her a position with them at the site.

'What's your handwriting like, Fatima?' he enquired.

Without a second bidding, Fatima picked up a pen lying on the table and proceeded to write on a notepad. After a minute or so she handed this to Paul. She had written a sentence in a beautiful copperplate style. Paul handed it to Elaine, excitedly.

'Look at this, Elaine. We can certainly use her for notes and the like.'

Elaine coughed.

'I rather thought that was what you employed me for, Paul.'

Paul recovered quickly.

'Of course it is, Elaine, but Fatima can always help you, can't she? Especially at the moment, now that Chantal is out of action and we don't know how long it will be before she is well enough to return.'

Any further discourse was interrupted by the arrival of Noha, the affable and rotund housekeeper. Paul introduced Fatima to her and ended by saying she needed a room. Affable the housekeeper might have been, but she was shrewd enough.

'You have references, of course?' asked Noha.

'No, but I can obtain them. I mean, I don't have them with me.'

'They will be necessary. The owners will not entertain anyone living here without them.'

It was said pleasantly enough, but firmly. Then Noha stated the weekly rent required. To Elaine's surprise, Fatima unzipped a pocket on the side of her tote bag and produced a leather pocketbook. She counted out some Egyptian pounds and handed them to Noha, who carefully counted them.

'There is still the matter of references,' she reiterated.

Paul interrupted.

'How about I say I shall personally guarantee the young lady until she has been able to produce the necessary documents to satisfy your employers, Noha?'

'If you will do that in writing, Mr Stanton, I suppose that will be in order.'

Paul reached for the writing pad and began to write. Elaine pointed out that Fatima hadn't even seen the room yet and maybe she wouldn't like it.

'Oh, but I shall,' confirmed Fatima, enthusiastically.

'Okay then, I suppose Noha had better show it to you. When do you want to move in here?' asked Elaine.

'Oh, right away… now, if that's all right.'

Elaine shrugged her shoulders. She was trying not to show it, but how could Paul do this to her, without even asking her opinion on the matter? Tight-lipped, she left for her own room. Paul continued to scribble the temporary guarantee for Fatima. He didn't even see her leave the room. Men! Show them a pretty face, and give them a hard luck story.

Chapter IX

The following morning, after an early breakfast, for which Fatima had joined them, Paul rang the hospital to enquire about Chantal. He nearly dropped the handset in shock when the nurse on the other end of the line gave him the news. Apparently not only had Chantal recovered consciousness, but she had discharged herself and left the hospital.

'Discharged herself?' echoed Paul in disbelief.

'Not even that really,' replied the nurse, indignantly. 'Miss Shariffe has simply gone – disappeared completely. No one here saw her go but the heart monitor has been disconnected and her bed was found empty this morning.'

Paul, shocked to the core, mumbled some ineffective remark, thanked the nurse and hung up. Turning to Elaine, he relayed the information.

'But last night she was still unconscious. Wherever can she have gone?' mused Elaine.

'Maybe she's coming back here, or gone on back to the tomb,' suggested Paul.

Fatima looked wide-eyed at him.

'You have a friend and she is missing?' she enquired innocently.

Elaine explained the situation and what had happened to Fatima, who listened intently, before replying, 'Then it is indeed fortunate that I have arrived to help you.'

Elaine couldn't quite see what was so fortuitous about it, but she supposed the girl's intentions were well meant. Paul looked thoughtful, obviously weighing up the situation.

Finally he declared, 'Look, I'll go on to the tomb site and see if she's turned up there. Ibrahim and the men will be wondering what's happened to us all anyway, so I'll put them in the picture. You had better hang on here, Elaine, in case Chantal shows up. Could be she's lost her memory or something and will need help... Anyway we have to get on, our permit only allows us a month for this work, and I need to do a far more detailed inspection of the cavern with more light, especially that black hole.'

'I shall come with you, Mr Stanton. I am sure I can be of help,' exclaimed Fatima, jumping up.

'I'm sure you can,' Elaine muttered under her breath.

Out loud she simply concurred with Paul's suggestion. If Chantal returned here she might be in a bad way and need help. Elaine realised that equally as much as Paul. She watched them leave together in the jeep. Fatima was hardly dressed for the work in hand, wearing a cotton dress and sandals. Elaine felt cross and left out of things, but she realised under the circumstances, somebody had to stay and Fatima wouldn't know Chantal, even if she did turn up. Paul had taken his mobile and promised to telephone Elaine if Chantal was at the site. If nothing had happened by lunchtime she was to take a taxi and join him.

At the site Ibrahim and the men were idly hanging around, smoking their long pipes, in what shade the rocks offered. Ibrahim, on seeing Paul, rushed forward. Ignoring Fatima, he exclaimed, excitedly, 'Mademoiselle Shariffe, she is back, Mr Stanton, only she is not her.'

'What in blazes are you babbling about, man? What do you mean it isn't her?'

'Well, it is and it isn't, effendi. She looks the same, only now she smiles instead of scowls, and her voice is different.'

'Where is she now, Ibrahim?' asked Paul, trying to keep his voice level and hide his concern.

'She go in cavern half-hour ago. Ask for you and I say

260

you no here. Mademoiselle Shariffe she smile and say when her steward come, send him into her. I say who? Steward? She say you, not by name, but she describes you exactly, effendi.'

'Have you got over your ridiculous fear of the cavern yet, Ibrahim?' enquired Paul.

'I would rather not go in, Mr Stanton, but I shall, if you insist,' said Ibrahim nervously.

'Somebody will have to carry another couple of hurricane lamps and some rope,' affirmed Paul.

'I shall,' exclaimed Fatima, pushing herself forward.

Ibrahim looked relieved.

'Are you sure you can cope, Fatima?'

'Oh yes, I am very sure. I work for you now, Mr Stanton, and shall do anything you wish.'

'Very well.'

Turning to Ibrahim, he instructed him to bring two coils of ropes, four hurricane lamps, fully fuelled. Then he rang through on the mobile to tell Elaine what had happened, and that he was going in again. 'Come on over right away, Elaine.'

Before she could remonstrate and say, 'Wait for me before you go in,' the line had gone dead. She replaced the receiver, picked it up again, and dialled for a taxi. Ten minutes later it arrived.

Fatima kept close behind Paul's broad back, holding one of the lamps in each hand. Round both their necks, leaving their hands free for the lamps, were the coils of ropes. Round the first turn Paul called loudly for Chantal.

'Chantal – are you in here?'

He didn't know why, but he was surprised, when a voice came floating up out of the inner depths of the cavern, a woman's voice, but definitely not Chantal's.

'This way, my love.'

'Love, love, love,' echoed from the walls.

He turned to look at Fatima. She looked as surprised as he, the lamps illuminating the strong features of her face and the whites of her eyes.

'Come on,' was all he said, turning once more and pressing onward.

'This way,' echoed the voice, again from deeper within.

Finally, rounding the turn that led to the large chamber, they both stood stock-still in amazement. There, between two gigantic stalagmites, was Chantal, one arm reaching out to touch the pillars on each side of her. Paul was at once captivated by her appearance. Gone was the normal bush shirt, shorts and chukka boots. In their place was the full regalia of a Pharaoh of Egypt, the short, kilted, historic skirt, bare midriff and wraparound silk over her breasts and one shoulder. A large golden necklace studded with jewels covered both her neck and part of her shoulders. On her raven-black hair was the double crown of Egypt with the vulture and cobra evident at the front. But it was not only the apparel she wore that astonished him, it was the woman herself. Oh yes, it was Chantal Shariffe all right, but she was radiantly beautiful and heavily made up, a serene smile on her face.

She studied each of them in turn, then in that rich, husky, mellow voice which was not one bit like Chantal's, she addressed Fatima.

'Ah, my loyal slave, Shazar. You have brought my only love, Senenmut, back to me. Lost through the centuries you have searched and found him.' Then a puzzled expression formed on Chantal's face. 'But why are you dressed so... both of you?'

Paul's first reaction was that Chantal was playing some ghastly joke upon him. She held a hand out to him, beckoning him forward. He could sense Fatima shaking, pressed up against his back. Surely nobody, even an actress of consummate skill, could effect such a performance.

Chantal advanced on him, her deep dark eyes engaging his. He could feel himself becoming hypnotised by a power that he couldn't explain. He tried to tear his eyes away from hers, to no avail. It was as if he were being drawn into the very depths of those oh-so-dark, beautiful pupils. Her hands came up and gripped his shoulders. He could feel the warmth coming through the thin cloth of his shirt, sending a pleasant tingle from his shoulders right down his spine.

Up to now he hadn't uttered a word and felt powerless to do so. This couldn't be happening to him. What cruel joke was this? Yes, that was it. Chantal was paying him back for what she called his obsession with Hatshepsut. She had somehow dressed herself as the queen to mock him. Suddenly he sensed, rather than saw, some of the light growing dimmer and instantly realised that Fatima, intent on getting away, was retracing her steps. Chantal noticed it and her tone became commanding.

'Return here at once, Shazar. Why are you cringing back there in the shadows?'

Fatima edged forward. If Paul had any doubts about the situation, Fatima certainly did not. She fell on her knees at Chantal's feet, kissing the sandalled foot.

'Get up at once, girl,' commanded Chantal.

Fatima gradually uncoiled her sensuous body to stand before Chantal, who shot out a hand and gripped the front of Fatima's cotton dress between her breasts.

'What is this ridiculous apparel, Shazar? Why are you not properly dressed?'

With one downward sweep of her right hand Chantal ripped the flimsy dress from hem to hem, leaving the frightened girl in her undies.

'I am sorry, Your Majesty, I have always said Egypt shouldn't have changed and have done my best to see that it didn't.'

Chantal's puzzlement showed in her eyes.

'Of what do you speak, girl?'

'The government here is corrupt, Your Majesty, not as it was in your day.'

'I know not of what you speak, Shazar, but it is enough that you have returned my love to me.' Chantal turned again to Paul, saying, 'And you, my love, what have you to say to me?'

Paul, for once in his life, was dumbstruck. Chantal, with a knowing smile, interpreted his expression wrongly.

'Now that you are reunited with me, I see that after all these centuries you are lost for words.'

Struggling with his reason and desperately trying to hold on to his sanity, Paul tried to counter and said, 'What foolishness is this, Chantal?'

Even Fatima looked at him with something like horror in her eyes. Given her Fundamentalist upbringing, it was so much easier for her to accept the return of the queen.

Chantal's face creased in a scowl of displeasure.

'Who is this Chantal you speak of?' she fired at him.

Paul was taken aback.

'You, of course. You are Chantal or have you lost your memory?'

This was greeted by a throaty laugh from the beautiful woman confronting him.

'Oh, you mean this woman whose body I occupy… This Chantal you speak of… perhaps you prefer her to me, my love?' The last remark was said with a teasing and coy smile.

With horror Paul was being made to face the obvious. Chantal had been possessed and he realised that it had to be by the ka of Queen Hatshepsut, she who had been denied a place on the carved list of Pharaohs. Then this cavern really must be her last resting place. Until this moment, he had completely forgotten the golden cartouche that he had found on the limestone floor. Pulling it from his pocket, he held it up in the light for her to see.

'So you will be able to tell me what this is?' he said, to test the woman, whether she be the Queen Hatshepsut or Chantal. If it really was Chantal, playing some cruel joke, this would be the final proof. She would never be able to resist coming forward to examine it in detail. In point of fact, the woman, whoever she was, dismissed it offhandedly.

'Of course, I recognise it, Senenmut. It is my own cartouche. Do you doubt it? You had it struck for me yourself on my thirty-fifth birthday.'

Paul's mouth opened wide. All this was quite beyond his comprehension. Then a strange thing began to happen. Right before his and Fatima's eyes the queen's physical appearance began to change. Gradually the magnificent raiments of the Pharaoh queen were fading and the drill shirt and khaki shorts of Chantal were reappearing. The jewelled sandals were changing into suede chukka boots. The queen's voice grew ever fainter.

'Farewell, my love, the transformation is not yet complete. This Chantal you speak of is a strong one. Her mind is not yet completely mine, but soon...' Her voice tailed off.

A few moments later, Chantal, dressed in her usual working apparel and with her usual disagreeable expression, faced them.

'Why are you staring at me, Paul Stanton, and who is that half-dressed girl with you?'

There was no doubt that the real Chantal was back amongst the living, bad-tempered and with a scowl on her face. Paul still couldn't understand what had happened but at least now he had no doubt that for a time Chantal had been possessed by a spirit. He tried to explain and watched for Chantal's reaction. It was plain that she remembered nothing. Long before he had finished he sensed that it was useless trying to rationally explain this impossible phenomenon. Chantal looked from him to Fatima in her torn dress.

'It is plain that you are under the influence of alcohol and presumably have brought your Egyptian whore with you. Well, I won't keep you from your debauchery.'

Chantal gave them both another contemptuous look, picked up one of the hurricane lamps and stalked from the chamber in the direction of the entrance.

Fatima was, if anything, even more visibly shaken than Paul, who was making a tremendous effort to pull himself together. He replaced the cartouche in his breast pocket. The enormity of the situation was still dawning on his numb brain. Chantal had been possessed by a queen from three and a half thousand years earlier. Impossible as it might seem, it had happened because they had obviously uncovered her long-lost tomb. Fatima began to chatter, firing questions at him which he couldn't explain. Slowly and deliberately he did his best to tell her what he thought had happened. At the end of it she did, however, seem to grasp what he was trying to tell her.

'If you are right, then this queen is what Egypt needs to right our present-day wrongs,' she exclaimed.

'Hold on, hold on. Whoa... not so fast. If it is the ka of Hatshepsut, and I have no doubt that it is, it does not belong in the body of Chantal Shariffe. I don't like the woman one iota, but we have to try and help her.'

'The queen is much nicer', argued Fatima, 'and she is what Egypt needs.'

'Perhaps, but not in somebody else's body.'

'Anyway your Chantal is back!' said Fatima, hotly.

'More's the pity.'

'Yes, but for how long before the queen's ka takes over again?' said Paul. Their conversation was interrupted by footsteps echoing through the tomb. Their immediate thought was that it was either Chantal or the possessive spirit returning. But, in fact, it was a surprised Elaine Gilroy who emerged into the chamber, holding a hurricane lamp in front of her. When she saw the dishevelled state of Fatima in her torn dress her face fell.

'I thought when I met Chantal outside that there must be some mistake, Paul. She shouted something about you fornicating with your Egyptian whore and then jumped in the jeep and drove off.'

Paul seemed not to hear and asked a question of his own.

'Did she look normal?'

'Well, yes, if you call being irate and glaring at everybody normal, I suppose she did. Why?'

Paul crossed over, put his hands gently on Elaine's shoulders, and pressed her down, until she was seated on one of the numerous boulders within the cavern.

'This is all going to sound crazy, but I assure you every word is true,' he began.

Elaine replied, 'When anybody tells you something beginning with true or honestly, it's usually a lie.'

'Think what you like, Elaine, but what I am about to tell you is the stark truth. You can take it or leave it.'

In as much detail as he could remember in his confused and bewildered state, he brought Elaine up to date with the recent happenings in the tomb. Where he forgot something, Fatima was quick to jump in with the missing details. If anybody but Paul had described such a narrative, Elaine would have been forced to laugh out loud. She had never believed in the supernatural, and as far as she knew, nor had Paul. As he neared the end, relating all that had happened, Elaine's concern grew. She looked from one to the other, unsure of their next move.

'It is plain that when Chantal entered this tomb, she disturbed a presence that had been walled in for three and a half thousand years,' mused Paul.

Elaine ran her fingers through her blonde hair.

'Do you think the queen's ka, or spirit, whatever you like to call it, sensed that she was antagonistic and took its vengeance by possessing her body?' ventured Elaine.

'What do you mean? Why would this woman, Chantal, or whatever her name is, be antagonistic?' enquired a bemused Fatima.

Elaine explained that Chantal was pro-Tuthmosis III and anti-Hatshepsut. To both Paul and Elaine's surprise, Fatima obviously knew a lot about the history of her country, and went into a lengthy discourse on the subject. Paul cut in eventually, although he was obviously impressed with the Egyptian girl's knowledge.

'The plain fact is what are we going to do about the situation...? I mean we can't have Chantal wandering about not in control of her own movements,' said Paul.

'If the authorities get to hear of this, they will want to detain her in a mental institution or something of the sort... No one who hasn't seen it will believe our story,' exclaimed Elaine.

'You did,' put in Paul, dubiously.

'Only because it's you and I know you... Besides, it's just too impossible for anybody to have made up,' she added, to conceal her embarrassment at her trust in him.

'The point is we have to act quickly,' decided Paul. 'Get an exorcist or something... but how in blazes do we do that, without alerting everybody to what has happened here?'

'How about I ring Clive, my brother, at the mission in Cairo?' suggested Elaine.

'Wonderful idea, Elaine, I remember you introducing him to me once. As well as being a minister of the church, I remember he was telling me that he had made a study of the occult... Could be just the man to advise us. Once we get out into the open air you can telephone him, using my mobile, but don't let anybody overhear you talking to him.'

Suddenly remembering Fatima, he addressed her. She was still clutching her torn dress around her to hide her nakedness.

'I trust that we can rely on you, Fatima, for your discretion in not talking to anybody about this?'

She looked him straight in the eye.

'The golden cartouche… Have you told anyone about it yet?'

Paul patted his breast pocket and replied, 'No, I had quite forgotten it until a while back… Why?'

'Because, if you had, we would be in trouble and the authorities would come sniffing around as the interest in the tomb would undoubtedly escalate,' explained Fatima.

'She's right, Paul. You haven't said anything about it other than to us, have you?' asked Elaine.

'Only to Chantal. Only she wasn't Chantal then, was she, so obviously she won't remember it,' he answered.

Everyone silently weighed up their own thoughts. The silence was broken by Paul who removed his khaki shirt and held it out for Fatima to put her arms through.

'By the time you do this up, it will look like a dress on you, Fatima, because you certainly can't emerge from this cavern looking like that or you will be shamed in the eyes of your own people.'

The gratitude showed in her dark eyes which expressed their own thanks. He was quite right. As he was so much taller it reached almost down to Fatima's knees. Her own torn dress hung below it like a ragged petticoat.

Slowly they retraced their steps until they stepped out from the tomb into the heat of the day. The strong sunlight hurt their eyes and it took a few moments for them to accustom themselves to the brightness after the dusky depths of the cavern.

Paul led Fatima away from Elaine, leaving the latter to make the telephone call to her brother. Together they joined Ibrahim and his men, who were huddled together in the shade of the rocks. In an effort to establish normality, he addressed the foreman.

'We are calling it a day for now, Ibrahim, but tomorrow morning I want to explore the cavern at length, and I shall expect you to overcome your fear and accompany me. There is a deep abyss in there that goes down to I know not where, and in the morning I shall want several coils of rope, as I intend to descend and explore it.'

'Is there nothing to fear, Effendi Stanton?' asked Ibrahim, his eyes going back automatically to the entrance to the tomb.

'Fear? What can there be to fear, when you have seen these two women go in with me? We have all come out again, haven't we?' Paul said, indicating Fatima and then letting his eyes travel across to Elaine still on the phone.

'Tomorrow I shall accompany my friend, Effendi Stanton, and my men will do as I say,' said Ibrahim, puffing out his chest, not wishing to be outdone by the women.

'Did Mademoiselle Shariffe return to our lodgings, do you know, Ibrahim?'

'She no say… just get in jeep and drive off,' confirmed Ibrahim.

Paul inwardly cussed. The woman had taken the jeep. Now they would have to ring for a taxi and walk some distance in the midday heat, to pick it up at the end of the heat-scorched valley.

When Elaine finished the call to her brother, he called out for her to telephone for a taxi, then, turning to the foreman, he instructed him to arrange for the guard on the cavern to be doubled day and night.

'Let no one pass without me, and that goes for Mademoiselle Shariffe, if she returns. Do you understand?'

Ibrahim nodded.

'It shall be as you wish, effendi.'

Chapter X

Back at their lodgings, in answer to their enquiry, Noha, the housekeeper, informed them that Chantal had returned some time earlier and gone to her room, saying that she didn't wish to be disturbed. That fact was confirmed by the presence of the jeep parked outside the apartment.

After some light lunchtime refreshments and a further discussion between the three of them, Fatima said that, if they had no further use for her that afternoon, she would go out to visit some friends. Neither Paul nor Elaine objected, so at about two o'clock she took her temporary leave of them, promising to be back before nightfall.

In actual fact, she summoned a taxi and headed for the terrorists' apartment in the back streets of Luxor. No sooner than Khaled saw her, than he began, as usual, to berate her. What had kept her? Why hadn't she let him know? As leader he should be kept informed at all times. These were just a couple of the questions with which he confronted her.

Fatima didn't know why, but she told him only what she wanted him to know, which didn't include anything about the appearance of the spirit queen, or the finding of the golden cartouche. By the time she had finished her explanation, all Khaled knew was that she had installed herself in the midst of the enemy – the foreign infidels – and knew all their plans as they trusted her implicitly.

'Is there anything of value where they are exploring in that cavern?' he fired at her. 'If there is, we shall move in and take it before they hand it over to the authorities. Then we shall have no further use for the infidels. We can then exterminate them.'

'Yes, but wait patiently, Khaled. I shall be exploring with them. If there is anything of value I shall know immediately and let you know.'

'See that you do, woman.'

Khaled eyed her with his one piercing good eye, the black eyepatch concealing the other empty socket, destroyed in a knife fight years earlier in Aswan.

'Have I not said that I would?' Fatima exclaimed hotly.

'I do not entirely trust women, least of all you. Most are only good for whoring and lying and will steal your money as soon as look at you.'

Fatima laughed.

'Then, friend, Khaled, methinks you have known the wrong kind of woman.'

Encouraged by this, Khaled reached for Fatima's breasts.

'Come, comfort your leader.'

Almost as if by magic, a knife appeared in Fatima's right hand. Like lightning she struck with the speed of a cobra to press the blade against Khaled's throat and check his impetuous advance upon her.

'Not part of the bargain, Khaled,' she hissed through clenched teeth.

Khaled, with the steel pricking his scrawny neck, replied nervously, 'See, woman, I was only testing your reflexes.'

'So, you will know that they are good and ready and able to repel all but the strongest,' said Fatima in a half-laugh devoid of mirth.

Khaled drew his lips back over uneven teeth and growled. 'I trust, woman, that when the time comes, you will remember where your loyalties lie.'

'Like yourself, Khaled, I never forget that I am a follower of the Fundamentalists.'

'See that you don't, woman. When I give the orders, you will be ready to wipe your new friends out. Is that clear,

Fatima? I wouldn't want you becoming too attached to them.'

Fatima bit her lip and let the matter rest there.

★

Around midnight or just after, Elaine thought she heard a noise on the landing outside her bedroom. Everyone had turned in earlier, except Chantal, who had never even emerged from her room since returning that morning from the tomb. As quietly as she could, Elaine got out of bed and tiptoed to the door, opening it just a crack. To her horror she saw Chantal with her back towards her, standing outside Paul's door. The reason for her surprise and shock was Chantal's apparel. She was dressed just as Paul had described her earlier, in the clothes of an Egyptian Pharaoh. Elaine stifled a gasp and watched half mesmerised as Chantal grasped the door handle to Paul's bedroom and slowly turned it. A moment later she had disappeared inside, closing the door behind her.

Elaine tiptoed along the landing, without waiting to don even a dressing gown over her short nightie. Her first thought was that Chantal, in whatever guise she was now in, was about to do Paul harm. She pressed her ear up against the thin wooden door, but not a sound came from within. If only Clive, her brother, was there. She was sure he would know what to do. Unfortunately he wasn't going to be able to arrive before the next night. There was still no sound from within...

In the pitch-dark room, Paul was half-awakened with what he thought was a fly settling on his cheek. Irritated, he brushed at it with his hand, but it was no fly. It was the sensuous lips of a woman, her long dark tresses brushing across his face, and he was aware of a rich exotic perfume in the room, something he recalled smelling only once before, that morning in the tomb.

Fighting down the feeling of blind panic, he scrabbled about for the pull-on light switch over the bed and yanked it on. When the light came on, there stood Chantal, dressed just as he had seen her earlier in the full regalia of a Pharaoh of Egypt. She was smiling down on him from the side of his bed. He found his eyes riveted on hers, held there like a rabbit caught in the headlights of an oncoming car. He seemed to be drawn towards them, as if compelled by an irresistible force. Without being aware of his actions, he sat upright in the bed. Chantal reached for the bed-clothes and drew them back. It was then she spoke, followed by a rich mellow chuckle from deep within her.

'What strange apparel is this?' she asked, alluding to his striped pyjamas. When he didn't reply, she went on, 'Once you came only to my boudoir, now it seems I must come to yours, my love.'

Paul could only manage a gulping sound from his throat. Chantal pirouetted in a full circle before facing him once more.

'Do you not find me beautiful, as once you did, my love?'

She watched him from under long dark lashes, inviting comment. Paul, gradually recognising the situation having been awakened from a deep sleep, sought to humour her.

'You are truly as beautiful as ever you were.'

He saw by the flash of temper in those dark eyes that he had said the wrong thing. She stamped her foot in fury.

'How dare you compare me with this hateful woman, within whose body I am forced to reside.'

Paul was quick to recover and exclaimed in his most charming voice, 'Surely you realise, my queen, that I see beyond the frame of this human woman the true beauty that is yours for all eternity?'

Instantly her rage was gone, as suddenly as it had

appeared.

'Then through this earthly body you can again enjoy me as once you did,' she said and, stepping boldly forward, she took his hand and placed it on her left breast. 'Can you feel my heart beat for you, Senenmut?'

Paul didn't know why, but it came as a surprise to find that she was flesh and blood and not an apparition. But then, why wouldn't she be, for this was Chantal facing him.

She bent and encircled his neck with her right arm. Coming down to his level on the bed, she kissed him on the lips – a long, lingering kiss. Paul felt himself stirring, and tried to tell himself this was the Chantal with whom he shared a mutual hatred. How could he possibly, even to humour the spirit queen, make love to the hated Chantal? If the situation ever resolved itself, both he and Chantal would have to live with it.

Just when he thought he was winning the battle of wills, those dark, beguiling and beautiful eyes met his and he felt as if he would surely drown in their hidden depths. He was dimly aware of Chantal undoing the buttons of his pyjama jacket and running the palm of her hand sensuously across his chest. With her other hand, she tore off the silk sheath that encased her rose-tipped breasts. Paul found his eyes now riveted on nipples that hardened and projected invitingly forward from firm round breasts.

She took his hand and sucked his fingers, a deep look of longing in her eyes, then ever so slowly, she lowered the hand and placed it over her left nipple. Paul could feel it hard and urgently pressing into the palm. He was only human and losing the battle fast, aware of desperately wanting this beautiful spirit woman, whose flesh and blood was real enough. He was so absorbed and losing his reason that he didn't hear his bedroom door open and someone slide in, closing it behind her.

Elaine had entered and stood stock-still, with her back to

the closed door facing them. She watched mortified as Chantal eased off over her hips the historic kilt of a Pharaoh and let it slide noiselessly to the bedroom carpet. Chantal's back was towards her and she could only imagine the view Paul was receiving. She was totally nude now, except for the gold collar, richly studded with jewels, and the Pharaoh's crown of red and white on her head. Elaine watched with horror as Chantal pushed her naked breasts into Paul's face. She felt a pang of jealousy to which she would never have admitted. It grew within her into a cold anger as Chantal in all her nakedness, climbed onto Paul's bed and sat astride him.

Elaine knew that somehow she must stop this. Paul couldn't be in command of his senses, the woman had clearly bewitched him. In a loud voice she cried out, 'Enough of this, Chantal. Go back to your room.'

Without moving from her position astride Paul, Chantal turned her head and torso from the waist, to see the intruder.

'Who are you and how dare you enter my steward's chamber? Can you not see, slave, that he is engaged in matters most private?'

The intrusion thankfully brought Paul back to reality and an embarrassed grasp of the situation. In horror at what he might have done, he roughly pushed Chantal off him and onto the floor. Both he and Elaine watched in amazement as her naked form, with its collar and head-dress, began to fade, leaving the figure of Chantal looking dazed and dressed in a long, white, satin night-dress. She rose from a crumpled heap, stretched her arms out in front of her, and without a word to anyone, like a sleepwalker, walked out. Elaine rushed to the door and watched her silently go down the landing, back to her own room. Closing the door, she faced Paul, who was now looking rather embarrassed and buttoning his pyjama jacket. For a moment neither spoke, then Elaine realised that she herself was only dressed in an almost see-through, short nightie. She made an embarrassed explanation and turned to leave.

'No... don't go... Come and sit on the bed,' Paul whispered.

'I'm... I'm not really dressed for a long discussion, Paul.'

He indicated his dressing gown carelessly thrown over a chair back. 'Slip that on, love,' he said.

Hurriedly, Elaine donned the striped, red and black garment. It virtually engulfed her.

'One extreme to the other,' she said, trying to lighten the moment.

Going over to the bed, she sat beside Paul, who had arranged the cushions behind his back and head. She was pleasantly surprised when he encircled her waist with a protective arm and pulled her closer.

'Thank heavens you arrived when you did, Elaine. The woman had totally transfixed and hypnotised me. It was as if I couldn't help myself... How did you know?'

Elaine told him how she had investigated a noise and what she had seen.

'Well, at least you now know what Fatima and I described to you in the tomb was not in our imaginations.'

'Knowing you, I never thought it was, but what are we going to do about Chantal, now that she is possessed by this spirit? My brother, Clive, telephoned me back and said he can't be here until tomorrow night, but he did stress the seriousness of the situation,' said Elaine.

'The trouble is neither you nor I have any knowledge of the paranormal or supernatural. Did he say what we should do with Chantal until tomorrow night, because it's plain that she has no control over the times that the spirit takes her over?' asked Paul.

'No, he just said to keep her as quiet as possible and try to avoid overexciting her.'

'How in blazes are we to do that? We can't leave her here with poor old Noha tomorrow. We shall have to take her to the tomb with us where we can keep an eye on her.'

'And she on you, because it seems to be you she's after. If she is indeed Queen Hatshepsut, I always said you were a ringer for Senenmut.'

'Don't joke about such things, Elaine. It's not funny. I was quite bewitched and out of control back there. If you hadn't arrived, there's no telling what I might have done.'

Elaine raised a smile.

'Oh, I think there was.'

One of Elaine's legs had emerged from the enveloping dressing gown. Paul gave her a playful slap across the thigh.

'I'm glad you think it's funny, Elaine.'

Her face took on a more serious expression.

'If I didn't laugh, I'd cry, Paul… This is all quite beyond my comprehension.'

'Do you mind if I come back to your room with you tonight?'

At first Elaine thought that he was joking, but when she saw the serious look on his face she realised he was in deadly earnest. Before she could reply, he went on, 'Look, Elaine, what if she comes back here after you go? I'm not sure I can handle the power she has within her to control my inner senses.'

Elaine was about to say something about his outer ones needing some control as well, but thought better of it. Obviously he had been seriously disturbed by the event and sarcasm wasn't going to help him. Instead, she held out her hand to him and after climbing off the bed, said, 'Of course you can, Paul. Come on.'

Together they left his room for hers.

The following morning Chantal turned up at breakfast, her usual disagreeable self, with plainly no knowledge of the previous night's visit to Paul's room. One look at her made Paul inwardly thankful for Elaine's timely arrival. He would never have been able to live with the thought of having cohabited with Chantal.

After breakfast and saying goodbye to Noha, the three of them, accompanied by Fatima, left in the jeep for the valley tomb. Paul's intention was to explore the black hole or abyss in the floor of the cavern. With them were extra ropes for the purpose. He had instructed Ibrahim to acquire two helmets with fitted headlights. He hoped the foreman would have accomplished this, for it would leave both hands free for the descent.

The jeep, with Paul at the wheel, bumped off the road onto the sandy rocky floor of the valley. Already the sun was up, casting long weird shadows, as it was as yet very low in the early-morning sky. Paul was very aware of Chantal sitting in the back, cursing every time the vehicle bumped over a large rock or down a gully, which were numerous. She had said very little but both Elaine and Fatima seemed to be giving her a wide berth, only speaking when she actually addressed them, which wasn't often.

Elaine, for one, was feeling very uneasy and wondering if they had done the right thing in bringing Chantal along with them this morning. To be truthful, it was hard, under the circumstances, to see what else they could have done. Chantal was co-leader of the exploration, so they couldn't have insisted on leaving her behind anyway. Elaine hadn't slept very well, although she had at least had the bed, whilst Paul had slept in the chair in her room. Now the nagging thought stayed with her. What if the spirit possessed Chantal again, whilst they were all in the tomb? It was going to be quite hazardous enough, exploring that deep dark hole of an abyss, without having to worry about Chantal, and what she might be doing up top. What on earth did Paul expect to find down there anyway? What if it turned out to be a bottomless pit? She had heard of such phenomena. All these thoughts raced through her head, and she was still lost in them, when Paul braked and bumped the jeep to a stop outside the cavern.

Ibrahim stepped forward, a smile on his face, to inform Paul that he had secured the helmets.

'Which of you is going down, effendi?'

Paul looked at Elaine. 'Are you feeling up to accompanying me?' he asked.

Elaine's tan visibly faded, but she gallantly replied, 'Well, I am your assistant, so I guess I'll have to.'

Before Paul could reply, Fatima spoke up. 'What are you like on ropes, Elaine?' She had instantly picked up on Elaine's dubious hesitation and look of apprehension.

With a weak smile, Elaine replied, 'I guess I'm about to find out.'

'Why put yourself at risk? I've been a gymnast all my life. It's second nature to me… Let me go with Mr Stanton.'

When Elaine remained silent, Paul prompted, 'Well – what do you think?'

There was a long pause before Elaine grudgingly answered, 'Well, I guess she would be of more use to you than me down there, Paul.'

Quickly he took Elaine aside and whispered, 'Perhaps it would be better if you stayed on the surface and kept an eye on Chantal.'

She nodded and with a wry smile admitted that she didn't really fancy either job and would be very glad when her brother, Clive, arrived that evening. Paul agreed with her sentiments about the latter, saying that Clive would be far better qualified to deal with the spirit world than they were. They rejoined the others.

Ibrahim fitted the canvas harnesses with their metal buckles and pulleys to both Paul and Fatima. Today all of them were dressed in grey boiler suits, which would be far more practical in the cavern than shorts and shirts. Paul donned his helmet with the attached high-powered lamp, and Fatima followed suit. He, together with Ibrahim, entered the cavern in single file, followed by Fatima and Elaine, with Chantal, surprisingly quiet for a while, bringing up the rear. By the time the entrance to the abyss was reached everyone was still strung out in a line although this time on hands and knees. There was, of course, no room for anyone to pass.

Paul called back to Ibrahim immediately behind him, instructing the foreman to knock the piton-type pins in. Ibrahim produced the necessary from the back pack on his shoulder and proceeded to hammer them home into the cavern floor. Due to the uncertain prognosis concerning Chantal, Paul had considered it necessary to leave the other two workmen outside after all.

Elaine and Fatima held their hands over their ears, the noise in the confined space, with its shattering echo, being almost unbearable. At last all was silent and Ibrahim confirmed to Paul that the pitons were secure. Paul looked down into the uninviting depths, the lamp on his helmet casting weird shadows, but failing to expose the bottom far below, if indeed there was one.

'Hook on, Fatima,' he called back and passed the end of his own rope back to Ibrahim.

'All secure,' recorded Fatima's confident voice.

'Yours, too, effendi,' confirmed Ibrahim.

Carefully preparing the coil of his rope for letting out, Paul eased himself over the edge, and helped Ibrahim negotiate the diameter of the hole to the other side, thus enabling Fatima to follow by making room for her. By the time he was about five metres down he saw Fatima come over the top and begin to follow him down. He called out some advice to her.

'Don't try and abseil down, Fatima. It's too narrow. Lower yourself down about five metres at a time, then jam your feet into the side and take a rest. That way we won't take too much out of ourselves.'

He heard her grunted agreement and dropped down another five metres himself. They continued like this for some forty metres. Looking up, he could just make out the dim lights at the top beyond Fatima's form some five metres above him.

'How goes it? Are you okay, Fatima?' he called.

'Yes, I'm okay. No problem.'

He smiled at the use of this universal phrase and dropped another five metres. The air here felt both rare and fetid and breathing seemed quite difficult. Still he pressed on with Fatima following him on down. A voice from high up at the top came eerily down to him. It was Ibrahim's.

'Are you all right, effendi?'

'Okay so far,' he called back up the chimney-like structure.

Elaine's voice floated down.

'Be careful, Paul.'

He pressed on down and was suddenly quite alarmed to see that he was a good seventy-five metres down and still no sign of the bottom or foot of the chimney. The light on his helmet showed up the craggy limestone shelves and once a lizard ran over his hand, obviously disturbed by the brightness. At least he hoped it was a lizard. It had disappeared into a crack in the rock face before he could properly identify it.

Suddenly he realised the chimney-like drop was opening out into a much wider chamber and he could hear the sound of water, although he couldn't as yet see anything. He called out to Fatima, warning her of the change in terrain. It did, however, with the increased room, give them the chance to abseil now. He eyed the amount of rope left on his coil. If they didn't reach the bottom within another thirty metres they would have to return. The length of rope would have run out by then, he calculated.

They descended another five metres, then another. Ah, he could see the bottom. They might just make it. He knew they each had one hundred and twenty-five metres of rope. He had never dreamt the shaft would be so deep. Breathing was increasingly difficult, but he couldn't give up now, not when he was this close. A small underground stream ran below him with high rock shelves on each side. He could hear the water gurgling below as it passed the rocks. Soon they would feel their feet on firm ground once again.

Chapter XI

Up on top, at the face of the shaft, Elaine was peering down over the rim. She could dimly make out two tiny pinpoints of light far, far below, almost out of sight now. Inwardly she felt guilty that she hadn't accompanied Paul on the descent; after all, she was the archaeologist, not Fatima. Grudgingly, she had to admit to herself that Fatima was probably of more use to Paul in this instance.

Down in the depths, Elaine was dimly aware that even the pinpoints of lights had disappeared. She turned to Ibrahim, who was standing behind Chantal, and asked him to go back and fetch the compressor.

'If we can get a little more light in here, it will help Paul and Fatima when they come up.'

Ibrahim nodded and crawled back up the low narrow passage to commence his retreat through the main chamber and out. Elaine was left with Chantal in the dimly lit, space-restricted passage. Forgetting Chantal's presence behind her, she lay on her stomach and peered over the edge. There was no sign of life below and not a sound reached her from the depths.

Aloud she murmured, 'I hope they are all right.'

She didn't know why, but she experienced a cold tingling sensation at the back of her neck. Alarmed, she half-turned to speak to Chantal, then sheer panic struck her. Chantal, once again, had taken on the appearance of the Egyptian queen, who, even in the half-light, she could see was half-crouched and watching her with malice. Elaine's first thoughts were to wonder how this could be possible? She had been there all the time. How could she have changed her clothes? Desperate for some rational explanation, she eyed the floor of the narrow defile for some sign of the discarded boiler suit. There was nothing but the rocky floor of the cavern.

'W... why?' was all she could utter from her parched throat.

Chantal, her voice tinged with ice, answered her. 'Why are you with my great love, my Senenmut, oh fair one?'

Elaine found herself replying, without really being aware of what she was saying. 'We came here to investigate a possible tomb.'

'My tomb?' said Chantal, in a half-snarl of contempt for Elaine's fear.

'We found the cartouche of a great queen of Egypt and investigated further.'

'An insignia put there by my loyal handmaiden, Shazar – even now she is down in the hidden depths with my lover.'

'Whatever do you mean? All of this is a riddle to me,' murmured Elaine nervously.

'So you say, fair one.'

Elaine grew increasingly alarmed at the way Chantal was looking at her. Ibrahim and one of his men wouldn't be back for ages as they would have to manhandle the heavy generator through the tomb. She couldn't expect any assistance from them, and Paul would never be able to return in time from the shaft to help her. Trying to be rational and pull herself together she tried to placate the spirit possessing Chantal's body.

'Why, great queen are you buried here in the Valley of the Nobles in an unmarked tomb? Why are you not with the other great Pharaohs of Egypt in the Valley of the Kings?'

'Why indeed,' snarled Chantal. 'That fiend of a stepson had me murdered, poisoned by his minions and dragged here in an ox cart, denied all royal rights for everlasting life.

Tormented I have gone on through the centuries and the millenniums – a captive spirit forever entombed here.'

'So why have you emerged now?' whispered a nervous Elaine, and realised she had once more said the wrong thing.

Chantal flew into a fury.

'This hateful woman, this follower of my wicked step-son, whose body I have occupied, chose to break in here, waking me from a restless sleep. Is it not just that I should use her feeble form to rise again?'

'But wh… why her – if you h… hate her so?' stammered Elaine.

'She deserves punishment for her attachment to Tuthmosis III, of that ignominious name usurped from my father.'

'But surely it is not fair—'

'Not fair!' thundered Chantal, fury exuding from every pore. 'Was what they did to me fair?' she exploded. 'Not content with murdering my earthly body and denying me a passage into the after life, they erased all my great buildings and monuments to raise their own inferior ones.'

Desperately afraid of what the possessed Chantal might do to her, Elaine played desperately for time.

'There are still great monuments existing today to your eternal honour. Your mortuary temple at Deir el-Bahri has been partly restored and your obelisk at Karnak has survived all the attempts to destroy it.'

For a moment the spirit seemed appeased, but it was only moments before she was verbally attacking Elaine again.

'But what of my other great works? I was once called the architect queen, you know… What of them?'

Elaine knew it was foolish to attempt a lie. She tried to speak with a courage she didn't feel, here alone with a spirit of three and a half thousand years before.

'What you say, great queen, is only too true. The man with me, Paul Stanton, is an archaeologist as am I. We have spent most of our lives researching yours.'

'You lie, fair one. The man with you is my love, Senenmut, returned to me, and down there in my innermost sanctuary is my handmaiden, Shazar, with him. She will show him where I have lain all these years.'

Quailing before the onslaught, Elaine moved backwards towards the rim of the shaft, and in a moment of terror lost her footing and felt herself falling backwards into the abyss. Somehow she half-turned and grabbed the edge of the precipice. Even so, she hung precariously to the rocky rim. Both the attached ropes with their pitons were situated on the other side, the side where Chantal now stood, an amused expression on her beautiful face.

With her feet swinging in mid-air and only a void below her, Elaine cried out, 'Help! Help me, Chantal.'

'Why do you call this Chantal? She can't hear you. I have her now. Only I can help you, and why would I do that?'

Elaine's mind worked overtime. Her hold on the rock was only tenuous and she knew it. She dug her knees into the side, trying to drag herself up, but it was impossible.

'Please!' she begged.

'No!' screamed the spirit. 'You are trying to ensnare my lover. I shall not help you.'

'I'm not,' yelled Elaine. 'I'm his friend and therefore your friend, so you must help me or he will be cross.'

'You are a schemer and would trick me. No, it is better that you die and reside here as I have for ever.'

Chantal moved menacingly forward on her knees, and made as if to prise Elaine's fingers free from the rim. Elaine, half-crazed with fear, shrieked, 'Don't be a fool. If I fall I shall knock over your lover and handmaiden as they climb up. All of us will be killed, and you will never see him again... Quick – my hands are slipping. I'm going to fall.'

The wisdom of desperation prevailed. Chantal reached down and with consummate ease plucked Elaine's hands clear and lifted her to safety. For a moment Elaine clung to her, sobbing with relief and shock, then realising what she was holding on to, instantly let go. Then she gasped in amazement. Chantal sank to the cavern floor and, as if in a dream, her clothes once again became a boiler suit like they all wore.

Chantal looked up, blinked and said offhandedly, 'I hope they hurry up down there. We can't wait all day.'

Elaine realised once again the spirit's power had waned and Chantal, disagreeable as ever, was back, but for how long before the queen had her for good?

The attacks were getting longer. One thing for sure, she had never been more pleased to see Chantal, with all her bad temper and ill grace.

Down in the shaft, or rather at the foot of it, Paul assisted Fatima to disengage herself from the rope used for the descent. They stood ankle-deep in water which had made a pool between the rocks. It had come in from higher up in the boulders to their left, and trickled away in a shallow stream to the right of where they stood, in a gentle downward slope. Without the powerful lights on their helmets it would have been impossible to see anything. As it was, the torch beams cast eerie shadows all about them. Even a whisper sounded loud as Paul placed a gentle hand on Fatima's shoulder.

'We shall follow the stream downward... Watch the surface, it's pretty slippery where the water has run over the limestone.'

Fatima nodded in agreement and tested the surface under her feet. 'What sort of thing are we looking for?' she whispered.

'Could be anything or nothing... You watch the terrain

to the left of the stream and I'll watch the right... Sing out if you spot anything.'

In the confined space, with its treacherous surface, both needed to exercise extreme care. A broken leg or wrist down there would be mighty serious indeed and could well threaten their return to the surface. Slowly they edged on down, the water depth varying between ankle-deep and knee-deep. It was uncomfortably cold even through the boiler suits they both wore. As they progressed downward, the roof of the cavern and underground stream became ever higher. There was nothing to see but the sheer rock face on either side of them, where the water had cut a channel through the limestone cliffs. In front of them they could hear the water gurgling away, but as yet couldn't see where.

'Have you any idea where this stream goes, Mr Stanton?' asked Fatima.

'No telling, but in this sort of terrain you often get underground streams. Sooner or later it will probably disappear through a crevice in the rocks. That's my guess anyway.'

Suddenly the sheer cliffsides narrowed and took a twisting turn. The water seemed to bunch up and then dash on downward. Paul, followed by Fatima, edged sideways round the turn. Here it was so narrow that a fat person would have had extreme difficulty in squeezing round the buttress of rock. Once round, they could see that only six metres remained before the water funnelled out through a wide crack at the cliff base, disappearing from their sight for ever.

'What's that at the base, where the water is going under the rock?' asked Fatima.

Paul strained his eyes and tried to follow the beam of his helmet light.

Fatima pointed with her index finger. 'See – there!' she said, excitedly.

Paul crawled forward on hands and knees, totally disregarding the chill of the icy water. Something white glistened under the surface of the silvery water. He focused the beam from his helmet full on it.

'Jumping Jehosaphat!' he cried in his excitement. 'It's a pile of bones.'

Fatima leant forward, pushing down on his shoulders as he knelt to see for herself.

'Are they human?' she asked.

Paul reached down carefully through the shallow water and withdrew the biggest of them. He held it up in front of the light. 'It's a human femur, by God,' he shouted, excitedly.

The echo of his voice resounded back off the cavern to greet them.

'How do you think they got here, Mr Stanton?'

Paul thought carefully for a moment before answering, continually studying the bone he held in both hands.

'Almost certainly someone either fell or was pushed down the shaft. As the body decomposed, the skeleton finally broke up under the effect of the running water, and the stream obviously washed the remains down here, where the aperture in the rocks, luckily for us, stopped them from going further.'

'Can you tell whether the bone was male or female, or how long it has been here?' asked Fatima, in an excited whisper.

'Quite impossible at this stage; the bones themselves will have diminished in size due to the action of the running water. By the length of this femur, I'd hazard a guess, though, that it was female, but as to time, without laboratory tests, I wouldn't have a clue.'

'Can we retrieve the bones and take them back up with us?' ventured Fatima.

'Too risky. We are not equipped to carry anything on

this trip and I don't want to damage them... Time will have already done its share of that,' he said, pessimistically.

'Can we risk taking one up with us?' asked Fatima, hopefully.

'I don't see why not,' affirmed Paul, scratching about under the water with his hand and coming up with a smaller bone. 'Clavicle, collarbone,' he explained and carefully stowed the relic away in his backpack, after wrapping it respectfully in a linen handkerchief.

He was becoming increasingly aware of the bad fetid air and realised he was finding some difficulty in breathing. Decisively he grasped Fatima's arm.

'Come on, we have been down here too long. We should have brought oxygen at this depth to help us breathe. We must get back on up to clearer and cleaner air.'

As they worked their way back up the stream towards the base of the shaft he found that he was veritably gasping for air. Fatima, in front of him, was virtually staggering from side to side.

'Come on, we must hurry, or we shall be overcome down here,' he urged.

Fatima was coughing violently and almost crawling. 'Go on, Mr Stanton,' she gasped. 'I'm done for. Get out while y... you c... can.' Her words were coming in short bursts.

Paul placed an arm round her and under her shoulders. 'Come on, Fatima. You can do it. We have to get out,' he urged.

At the foot of the shaft she fell forward, gasping, onto her knees. A moment later she fell flat on her face into the water, out cold. If Paul hadn't been there, she would have drowned in the shallow depth of the stream. He heaved her into a sitting position with her back pressed up against the rock for support.

With merciful relief, Paul realised that, although the air was still rare, there was a definite draught coming down the shaft from above. He inhaled deeply into his lungs and felt marginally better. Producing a knife from his belt, he slashed free sections of one of the ropes which they had used for the descent. Then, with great difficulty, he lifted Fatima onto his shoulders, so that she was draped round him with her arms and legs over each of his shoulders. It proved even more difficult to tie her securely at the wrists and at the ankles. Finally, he used another section to join both together. By the time this was accomplished, which took considerably longer than it takes to tell, Paul was very nearly exhausted with the effort. Luckily, he concluded, Fatima was lithe and supple, and probably only weighed in the region of eight stone or thereabouts. Even so, the climb ahead of him, some hundred and thirty metres above him up the shaft, was a daunting prospect.

Taking several deep breaths to flood his lungs with what air there was, he grasped the end of the intact rope he had used on the way down. The first section would be the worst, he knew that. He would have to climb, using every ounce of his strength, with nothing to help him. Once he reached the narrow section he would at least be able to jam his feet against the sides of the chimney-like shaft, gaining some relief.

However, by the time he had accomplished this, his arms felt like lead and his shoulders and tummy muscles were virtually screaming their protest at the abuse. It was with the utmost relief that he wedged his feet against the rock wall to take the strain out of his arms. He rested in this position for fully two minutes before setting off upward. Occasionally he heard a low moan from Fatima, draped across his shoulders, and wondered whether she was recovering consciousness.

Just in case, he explained, 'Keep dead still and you will be all right. Move and we are both going to fall all the way down.'

There was no reply, so he concluded she must still be unconscious. Even the low moaning sounds were not coming from her now. With horror, he thought, perhaps she was dead, but realised there was nothing he could do about it – only to continue with the climb. Although it was easier now that he could use his feet to assist him, he was growing ever more fatigued and tired. The ascent seemed to be taking an age, but looking down, he could at least see that he had made progress. A dim light above told him that there was still much further to go to reach safety. More and more he was having to rest now, taking the weight on his feet against the craggy walls. He pressed on and rested alternately in as disciplined a fashion as he could manage. If his strength held out he would make it.

At the face or head of the shaft Elaine peered down. Having somewhat recovered from her terror and shock, she lay flat on her belly, shining her flashlight down into the black abyss. What she saw rekindled her terror. Paul was some twenty metres from the top and on his shoulders he carried Fatima trussed like a chicken.

Before she could even speak, Paul must have sensed the light shining down on them and called out, 'For God's sake somebody come down the other rope and lend a hand. I don't think I can hold on much longer.'

Without thinking Elaine began to lower her legs over the edge, grasping the other free descent rope.

'No, go back,' screamed Paul, looking upwards and seeing that it was Elaine. 'Get Ibrahim, he will know what to do.'

'He's not here. I sent him back for the compressor,' cried Elaine.

Chantal joined her at the edge and lay down on her stomach, looking down.

In a flat, matter-of-fact tone, she exclaimed, 'By the time Ibrahim gets back here, it will be too late. Your Hatshepsut fancier will be exhausted with his double burden and fall to his death.'

Elaine turned to remonstrate with Chantal and even in the half-light was amazed to see the transformation, as once more the work clothes of the archaeologist began to fade and be replaced by those of the Egyptian Pharaoh. The face, too, seemed to change and come alive.

'We shall see about that, lover of Tuthmosis,' she exclaimed, vehemently.

Elaine stared, transfixed, and realised that once again the spirit had gained control of Chantal and was addressing her own earthly medium.

Before Elaine could even fully take in what was happening, Chantal was over the edge and shinning down the other rope like a monkey. Elaine heard her call out to Paul as she continued her descent.

'Hold on, my love, I am coming to your assistance.'

Paul looked up and was too exhausted to be anything but relieved. Elaine watched Chantal come abreast of Paul and Fatima way down in the shaft. She watched as Chantal, working from the other side of the narrow shaft, backed onto Paul in such a way that her shoulders came up underneath Fatima, thus taking most of the weight off him. In this fashion the strange trio gradually edged their way upward.

Although Elaine couldn't hear what was being said, she realised Chantal, or rather her possessor, was continually whispering encouragement to Paul. After what seemed an eternity they were near enough to the rim for Elaine to reach down and assist Paul over the edge with his human burden. Collapsing on his knees, he gasped for Elaine to free the ropes holding Fatima to him. She grabbed the knife from the sheath at his belt and slashed the bonds entwining them and eased Fatima onto her back on the cavern floor.

'Oxygen,' Paul managed to get out between exhausted

gasps.

'We didn't bring the cylinder in. It's outside,' answered Elaine in desperation.

'Give her mouth-to-mouth Elaine. There's no time to go for it,' exclaimed Paul.

'But what about you?' queried Elaine.

'Never mind me. Get to work on her.'

Somehow Paul managed to get authority into his voice, which succeeded in activating Elaine. A moment later she commenced mouth-to-mouth on Fatima. Chantal, still in the attire of the female Pharaoh, began to massage Paul's shoulders and neck, whilst whispering terms of love. This time Paul was too totally weary to resist, and her warm sensuous hands soon began to relieve the miserable ache in his shoulders and neck.

'My brave lover, you have saved my favourite hand-maiden, Shazar, and shall be richly rewarded.'

With relief he heard a coughing and spluttering behind him and realised Fatima was coming back to the land of the living. When he managed to turn and look, she was sitting up.

'What happened to me?' she asked, still in a daze.

Paul started to tell her but Chantal cut in, 'You are indeed a lucky girl, Shazar. My brave Senenmut has undoubtedly saved your life. Any other man would have saved himself and left you to die down there, but not this one. Not my Senenmut.'

With a warm glow in her eyes she looked at Paul adoringly, whilst Fatima could only stammer her thanks.

'You would have done the same for me if the position had been reversed,' Paul replied.

Chapter XII

Fortunately, by the time that Ibrahim and Ahmed arrived, dragging the generator between them, everyone had just about recovered from the traumas and shocks of the day. Luckily, two minutes before, Chantal had once again regained control of her body, and was, as usual, dressed in her boiler suit. Paul was relieved that no further explanation concerning her dual personality would be necessary to the two men.

He was anxious to get the clavicle bone carefully packed and sent away to the laboratory in Cairo for some extensive tests. Next time he would make sure that they had oxygen cylinders and masks. Perhaps tomorrow, or the next day, he would go back for the collection of the rest. He informed Ibrahim that the exploration would be called off for the day and asked him to see that the tomb was well guarded until they all returned the next morning.

'Come on, everybody. Let's see the light of day,' said Paul, as cheerily as he could.

Chantal raised an objection to finishing for the day but was argued down by the rest of them. With bad grace, she submitted to reason.

That evening Paul and Elaine met the Reverend Clive Gilroy, Elaine's brother, at Luxor station, with a taxi.

'Are we glad to see you, Clive,' said Paul warmly.

'Well, it's nice to be popular,' laughed Clive, a genial-looking fellow, with spectacles and a slightly receding hairline. He was a man of average height who obviously, by his slim waistline, kept himself in shape. The face was firm with a high forehead and square jaw, laughter lines enhancing his brown eyes and strong mouth. He was dressed in a sports jacket and flannels, but the first thing Paul noticed was the dog collar he wore.

Elaine warmly hugged her brother. 'Great to see you, Clive,' she exclaimed.

'Have you eaten, Clive?' enquired Paul.

When Clive responded in the negative, Paul suggested a good restaurant.

'Hotel, actually, The Etap – food there is excellent, especially the à la carte. The view is superb too, faces the Nile and is a few hundred metres north of Luxor temple.'

'Never say no to a freebie,' joked Clive.

Paul gave the instructions to the taxi driver and half-turned in the front passenger seat to talk to Clive and Elaine in the back of the vehicle.

'We decided to use a taxi rather than meet you in the jeep, just in case Chantal asked awkward questions. I expect Elaine told you about the problem we have here?'

'Well, I know something about it, but no doubt you will fill me in with a lot greater detail over dinner,' replied Clive.

There was something about the man that instantly inspired confidence and both Paul and Elaine felt a lot happier with his arrival in Luxor.

It was that delightful period just before full dusk when the lights were coming on in buildings all along the Nile. The reflections danced on the surface of the great river and were accompanied by a myriad of lights from the river cruisers. A light wind rustled the sails of the numerous feluccas tacking along on their homebound way. On the promenade, calèches, horse-drawn carriages, trotted to and fro. The half-light hid the poor condition of the horses and gave them an air of romance. All too soon for Elaine they arrived at The Etap and were luckily able to secure a table.

After the starter course, when pleasantries had been

exchanged, Clive smiled and said, 'Well, let's have it. Who's going first? You, sis?'

'No, I think it better if Paul starts; after all, it was he who found her in the tomb first.'

Clive looked at Paul expectantly.

'In your own time. Try to remember every detail you can. It may well be important.'

In turn both Paul and Elaine recounted the various events from the time that Paul had found Chantal in the cavern. Where he forgot a detail or two, Elaine helped out, finishing up with the happenings in Paul's bedroom and of the events of that day.

Paul blushed with embarrassment at Elaine's recounting of the bedroom scene but Clive, good-naturedly, patted him on the arm as if to say he had nothing to be ashamed of, which prompted Paul to show him the well-worn golden cartouche of Hatshepsut which he had found before the encounter with the spirit.

Clive turned it over, studying it in detail.

'And you are quite sure that this one matches the cartouche discovered outside the cavern?'

'Oh, yes, it is the cartouche of Queen Hatshepsut, the female Pharaoh of the eighteenth dynasty,' put in Elaine.

Her brother smiled at his young sister's intensity. 'I am no Egyptologist, as you two are, but that would make it three and a half thousand years old, wouldn't it?' he queried.

'Pretty nigh spot on,' affirmed Paul.

Clive slowly and deliberately sipped his wine and studied both of them in turn.

Elaine, impatient for guidance, exclaimed, 'You do believe us, don't you, Clive?'

'I believe you, Elaine, but it is not a matter that can be resolved in a conversation held over dinner.'

Paul, equally anxious, asked, 'Have you ever met a similar situation, Clive?'

'Every encounter with the supernatural is different and what you have here is a dormant spirit that has never passed over for some reason or other. Your Chantal disturbed it by breaking into a tomb, which had remained closed for over three thousand years.'

'But why did it possess Chantal?' exclaimed Elaine.

'As you have already told me a little of the lady's history, I gather she would have been hostile to the Pharaoh queen,' said Clive.

'Very. She hates everything she stood for,' put in Paul.

'And you don't,' asked Clive.

'He worships her... well, very nearly,' said Elaine, in mitigation of the first part of her sentence.

Clive smiled.

'There – you have it. You have already said Paul looks like the ancient architect who was supposed to be the queen's lover.'

'The spitting image. I am always telling him so, but he won't have it,' stated Elaine.

'Be that as it may. What has plainly happened here is that the ka or spirit, as you call it, of the famous queen, has been disturbed by a very hostile living person in Chantal Shariffe. For that disturbance she has taken her revenge on the good lady. In the bodily sense, now that she has a human form, she has seen Paul and mistaken him for her old lover of millenniums past.'

'Surely this is not possible,' interjected Paul. 'It's too far-fetched for anything.'

'And another thing, Clive. How do you account for her being able to change her image and clothes whilst you watch?' asked Elaine.

'She doesn't. It's as simple as that,' laughed Clive.

'I beg your pardon, Clive, but she does, I tell you. I've seen her do it on three occasions,' exclaimed Elaine, indignantly.

'I didn't say you hadn't, did I? What I said was she doesn't change her clothes or her bodily image. She simply has the power to make you believe it. Mind over matter if you like... You see what she wants you to see,' explained Clive.

'So why has she come back now? What does she want?' enquired Elaine.

'Vengeance for one thing, love for another,' replied Clive.

'How is it that she hasn't completely taken over Chantal? I mean, she only seems to be there for brief set periods...' Paul let the sentence tail off.

'This Chantal you speak of is a very strong character and her own inner strength is resisting the takeover of her body. Gradually, though, she will succumb. The periods of domination will grow in length, until Chantal herself will be no more and the ka, or spirit, will have total control,' explained Clive.

'But that's terrible... horrible,' gasped Elaine. 'In fact, it's murder. We can't allow that to happen.'

'We must face the fact that we may not be able to stop it without divine intervention,' suggested Paul, looking hopefully at Clive for some inspiration.

Clive smiled and said, 'There is nothing divine about me just because I wear the cloth. In fact, there would be many of my calling who would not only rebuke, but demand my resignation for my acceptance of this situation... let alone by assisting you and dabbling with it.'

'Does that mean you are not going to help us?' asked Elaine, anxiously.

'I wouldn't be here if that were the case now, would I, sis? However, I do want you both to realise that I cannot guarantee success, only God can do that, and we shall need all our prayers if Chantal's life, as she knows it, is to be saved.'

'But how can we tackle this? I mean neither Elaine nor I have ever been faced with anything remotely like this situation, Clive, and then there's the other issue – outsiders – what if people other than ourselves realise what is happening and the world press get hold of it... what then?'

'We mustn't let that happen, or Chantal is doomed. She would become a figure of worldwide interest for every pressman and weirdo in the universe.' Clive looked thoughtful and then went on, 'This helper of yours, the woman whose life Elaine says you saved, this Fatima, can she be trusted?'

'I have spoken to her and impressed on her the need for secrecy,' replied Paul.

Elaine looked doubtful.

'We know nothing about the girl at all, Clive. She arrived by chance and needed help... Paul decided to give her a job, although we didn't really need her.'

Clive picked up the censure in Elaine's tone and smiled indulgently.

'Perhaps you had better speak to her on the matter as well then, as you think Paul too easy-going with her.'

'None of this is getting us anywhere,' rebuked Paul. 'I repeat, what are we going to do about it?'

'There is no obvious answer to that, Paul,' replied Clive, 'but I have an idea, if you are both prepared to go along with it.'

Elaine and Paul leant forward expectantly in their chairs.

'Go on,' urged Elaine, 'we are all ears.'

Clive looked from one to the other.

'I can't promise it will work, mind. There is no such thing as certainty in this sort of situation, but I think you will both agree we have to act sooner rather than later. Where is Chantal this evening?'

'As far as we know, back at the apartment in her room,'

volunteered Elaine.

'Good. In that case, as soon as we have finished this delightful meal I suggest we pay your Chantal a visit... One of us, and it had better be Elaine, goes into her room to see her.'

'Why me? Why not you, or Paul, for that matter?' objected Elaine.

'Think about it, sis. From what you both tell me, Chantal hates Paul and she has never met me so that leaves you.'

'And what do I say when I go into the lion's den?' Elaine's voice was heavily weighted towards sarcastic humour.

'You face her with the truth about herself. We need to ascertain first if she is even aware of the possession, and if she is, whether she will allow us to help her rid herself of the alien within her.'

'Supposing she isn't aware, and thinks I'm a raving loony, or worse still, the queen is in control of her, when I go in there?'

'I'm afraid you will have to deal with it as it comes. Paul and I shall be outside. If she is the queen, Paul will immediately join you and try to reason with her.'

'I shall?' exclaimed Paul, incredulously.

'Of course you will. The queen won't want to harm you, for she clearly believes you to be her lover, and furthermore, she won't harm Elaine with you there to protect her.'

Elaine interrupted, 'And what, Clive, will you be doing whilst all this is going on?'

'Listening outside, my dear. Then, as soon as we ascertain that the woman needs help, one of you comes and gets me. After you have introduced me you can both expediently withdraw.'

Elaine looked at Paul for some show of enthusiasm for the plan, but the doubt on his face matched her own.

'Guess we've no option but to try it,' was all he said.

★

Fatima had gone round to the terrorists' hideout that evening. Whilst Elaine and Paul were engrossed in conversation with Clive, she was, in fact, involved in a fierce argument with Khaled. She had told him about the tomb, but not about the bones they had found, or the matter of Chantal Shariffe's possession, but only that one of the archaeologists had saved her life.

'It seems to me, woman, that you are becoming altogether too friendly with these infidels. They are here to rob our country of its treasures. Is that not so?'

'I think you are wrong, Khaled. Anything they find will be handed over to the government,' argued Fatima.

'Exactly – and is this not the government we are pledged as Fundamentalists to pull down…? They are as traitorous as the infidels invading our land.'

Fatima realised she had made a mistake in bringing in the government angle, and tried to recover her composure, quickly adding, 'Do I not bring you news of the infidels and their mission here?'

Khaled snorted.

'Some news! According to you, they have found nothing, only unearthed an old limestone cave. Tomorrow we go in and either take them captive and hold them to ransom, or kill them outright. Either way it makes no difference. When the ransom is paid we kill them anyway.'

'Surely they do no harm here if they haven't found anything? Why not let them go, once the government has paid the ransom for them?' argued Fatima.

'No harm? What do you mean? They are infidels, are they not, and all infidels must die. We are sworn to avenge our forefathers who died at the hands of those infernal

304

crusaders throughout Islam.'

Fatima shrugged her shoulders seeing that arguing was getting her nowhere.

'If you say so, Khaled,' she said, without enthusiasm.

'I do say so and I am our elected and appointed leader here in Luxor, am I not?'

'It would appear so, Khaled.'

Khaled's one eye flashed with temper. He was close to spilling over.

'Woman, you have gone soft. It would not surprise me if you had not cohabited with this archaeologist man you speak of...' A sneer appeared on his face. 'No doubt that is why he saved your life, so that he could have you again, whore that you are.'

Fatima slapped Khaled hard across his face and succeeded in knocking his eyepatch askew, revealing a horrifically chewed-up eye socket. Hurriedly, he replaced it, swearing oaths at her effrontery. It is probable that he would have killed her there and then, with the knife that he had withdrawn from his belt, but for the timely intervention of one of the terrorists, a man called Mohammed.

'Stay your hand, leader. The woman was only defending her honour. She will kill the infidels readily enough when the time comes and you give the order so to do.'

For a moment it looked as if Khaled would turn his wrath on Mohammed, then he glared at each in turn.

'It had better be as Mohammed says, woman, or I shall kill you with my own hands, should you disobey my orders or raise your hand against me again.'

Fatima pulled herself up to her full height and faced him boldly.

'I am a good Fundamentalist and shall not be found wanting when the time comes. Egypt will always be proud of me.'

'See that it is so, woman,' exclaimed Khaled.

'Now I must go back to the apartment of the archaeologists before I am missed.'

Without waiting for leave, Fatima turned on her heel and exited through the door. As it shut behind her, Khaled growled to Mohammed, 'One day I shall kill that woman for her insolence.'

Mohammed said nothing, simply raising his eyebrows. As Allah wills, he thought to himself, and walked away.

*

When Elaine, Paul and Clive arrived back at their apartment they were informed by Noha, the housekeeper, that Mademoiselle Shariffe was still in her room and hadn't been down for dinner. Paul thanked her and diplomatically suggested that she might like the rest of the evening off to go out and visit her sister who lived nearby. To his relief she jumped at the chance and five minutes later took leave of them.

'Do we know where the Egyptian girl, Fatima, is?' enquired Clive.

'Apparently, according to Noha, she was going out for a while and will be back later,' said Elaine.

'No point in waiting then. Off you go, Elaine, and knock on Chantal's door. We have to start somewhere and now seems as good a time as any other,' urged Clive. 'We shall both be listening outside, so don't worry. At the first sign of trouble we shall barge in.'

Elaine climbed the stairs; her feet felt heavy, as did her heart, which was beating madly within her. She halted outside Chantal's door and her mouth went dry. She swallowed hard, brushed an imaginary strand of hair off her forehead and, as boldly as she could, knocked sharply on the door. At first there was no response, then a voice, definitely female, called from within, 'Come in.' She turned the handle and entered. Chantal lay on the bed facing the door with pillows propped up behind her back. There was little or no expression on her face.

'You wanted something, Elaine?' was all she said.

Chapter XIII

How did one broach the subject? How do you tell someone they are possessed by a spirit or ka, of over three thousand years gone by? Elaine felt a moment of panic. Did Chantal know, or was she merely a vehicle for the alien being within her? Elaine could feel Chantal's gaze on her and found trouble meeting it. Where in blazes did she begin? In the event, the decision was taken out of her hands.

'Come and sit on the bed and talk to me, Elaine,' whispered Chantal, in a low sensuous voice.

My God, thought Elaine, remembering what Paul had told her earlier about the woman, she fancies me. She shuffled her feet awkwardly, very unsure of herself. Was this Chantal speaking or the spirit within her? Chantal patted the cushion beside her.

'Come, I won't eat you, at least not yet. I promise.'

Elaine gingerly eased herself onto the bed, trying to distance herself as much as the limited bed space would allow. Chantal leaned across and stroked Elaine's blonde tresses.

'Did you want to talk to me about something? A problem perhaps?'

Elaine was somewhat overdressed, having been out for the evening with Paul and her brother. She was beginning to regret it. Chantal was virtually ogling her. Where she had wriggled herself onto the bed, her tight skirt had ridden up, exposing a fair amount of thigh. She tried to pull it down. Chantal placed a hand over hers.

'Don't cover them, Elaine, your legs are quite beautiful,' murmured Chantal, running a hand over Elaine's thigh.

At least now Elaine knew for sure that this was Chantal

to whom she was speaking.

Recovering her composure and not wishing this confrontation to escalate further, she blurted out, 'I think it is you who have the problem, Chantal.'

'Whatever do you mean?'

'Are you aware that you are possessed by an alien force beyond your control?'

Chantal laughed.

'Why? Because I fancy you? Lots of women would fancy you.'

Obviously Chantal was unaware of the changes that came over her, making Elaine even more unsure of the best approach in tackling the problem... She tried again.

'We have been very worried about you lately. Are there periods when you have felt faint or lost consciousness for short periods... lapses of memory or anything like that?'

Chantal abruptly stopped stroking Elaine's leg and actually looked worried.

'Why? What have you noticed about me?'

'Well, you are not always yourself. In fact, at times you are a different person.' Oh dear, I'm not handling this very well at all, thought Elaine, seeing the confusion on Chantal's face.

Then, to Elaine's amazement, Chantal began to whisper, confiding in her. 'I didn't think anyone had noticed. I think I am going mad. I've tried to pretend that it's not happening, but there are times when I seem to lose consciousness and can't remember anything for ages. That's why I've locked myself away from you all, in case I blacked out again and made an exhibition of myself... Did anyone else notice?'

Elaine felt desperately sorry for Chantal, who had obviously been too proud to seek help. Now it was slightly easier for her to explain.

'No, Chantal, you are not going mad but something is

seriously wrong.'

'How do you mean? I've always been very fit.'

'It's not that, Chantal... It's a spiritual thing... This is not going to be easy for you to accept, but you have been possessed by a spirit from centuries ago.'

Chantal looked aghast and visibly paled.

'How do you know?' she murmured.

As gently as she could, Elaine recounted the events that led up to the present. In all it took several minutes to relate and almost as long for Chantal to accept it. Chantal was quite terror-struck. Gone was the strong dominant character she presented to the world.

'If anyone finds out I shall be placed in a straightjacket and locked away in a mental institution,' moaned Chantal.

Elaine placed a comforting arm round her companion's shoulders.

'No, you won't. We won't let that happen to you. Accept that it's not your fault. What has happened is quite beyond your control, and if you allow us, Paul and I have brought someone to help you.'

'Why would Paul help me? I wouldn't help him if the position were reversed.' For a moment the old hatred re-emerged, and then dissipated just as quickly. Chantal looked lost and helpless. 'This help you speak of...? Where...? What...?' she stammered.

'He's outside now. My brother, the Reverend Clive Gilroy.'

'How can he help me?'

'He's something of an expert in all things to do with the occult, as well as being a cleric.'

'And he's actually here now?' asked Chantal.

'Yes, we sent for him, as it was totally beyond our realms to help you,' affirmed Elaine.

'Then I suppose the least I can do is to see him,' said Chantal, rather reluctantly.

Elaine crossed to the door and called for Clive. He was, of course, waiting near at hand and appeared almost at once. On seeing the dog collar round his neck, Chantal immediately tried to hide the cleavage shown by her low-cut night-dress. Clive pretended not to notice. Elaine introduced him, but Chantal didn't accept his outstretched hand of friendship, but continued to hold her hands crossed over her breasts.

'Elaine says you can rid me of this spirit that has invaded my body,' she exclaimed.

'I am prepared to try, if you will allow me to hypnotise you. I need to reason with the ka within you.'

Chantal looked nervously from one to the other.

'It's all right, I shall remain with you at all times,' said Elaine.

'Very well, Reverend Gilroy, I am ready,' affirmed Chantal.

Clive seated himself on the edge of the bed and took Chantal's hand in his.

'Look into my eyes,' he commanded. In a low voice he continued to address Chantal. 'Hold your other arm out in front of you… Now feel it getting heavier by the second… heavier still… Your mouth is dry and you are compelled to swallow… Close your eyes and feel your arm heavier still… ever heavier… Now you must swallow. It is impossible not to.'

Chantal gulped and swallowed and her arm sunk towards the bed.

'In a moment I shall tell you to open your eyes, but you will not be able to. They will remain closed. You are tired and sleepy, a feeling of total relaxation is coming over you. No one can harm you. A cocoon of soft white clouds surrounds you… Now you will try to open your eyes on the count of three, but you will be unable to do so. One… two… three.'

Elaine watched, half-mesmerised herself. Chantal seemed to be struggling to open her eyes but couldn't.

'You are now completely under my control and I now no longer speak to you but to the invasive spirit that has possessed your body. Spirit – answer if you hear me. Proclaim yourself.'

For a moment there was an ominous silence, then from Chantal's mouth came a deep, full-throated, feminine voice, definitely not Chantal's.

'I am who that I am.'

'That is no answer. Are you ashamed to proclaim yourself, spirit?'

'I am ashamed of nothing, nor have I been these three and a half millenniums.'

'Then proclaim yourself,' ordered Clive.

'Pharaoh of both upper and lower Egypt. I wear both crowns of red and white.'

'Still you deny us your name. Why?'

'Because you are unworthy and of common stock. I have no need to proclaim myself to you or any man not of royal birth.'

'Would you do so if your lover, Senenmut, were here, though he be of common stock?'

'I would do so were he here, but he is not.'

Clive signalled to Elaine to fetch Paul into the room. Quietly, she rose and headed for the door.

'I have sent for him,' he exclaimed. 'Now tell me why you occupy this woman's body?'

'She disturbed my sleep of ages and she is alien to me. I have exacted my vengeance upon her.'

Paul entered with Elaine.

'You see, he is here, as I have promised. Now proclaim yourself before us as you have promised.'

After another long pause, in which the spirit seemed to be battling with itself, there came a solemn statement, 'I am the Pharaoh Hatshepsut.'

'That of the eighteenth dynasty, is that not so?' asked Clive.

'It is so, and ever will be.'

'Why do you still persist in occupying this earth when your body has long since fallen into decay?'

'To avenge my murderous stepson, Tuthmosis, who not only had me killed, but denied me eternal life amongst the gods.'

'He is long since dead, spirit, so how do you expect to exact such vengeance upon him?'

'He denied me a place even on the carved list of Pharaohs and this woman in whose body I must reside, is a follower of the usurper.'

'Do you consider it fair to use another's body?'

'I have no other,' came the matter-of-fact reply from the mouth of Chantal.

'I shall ask you once to leave this woman's body for ever,' said Clive.

'And I, Pharaoh, will laugh in your face, fool.'

'Then prepare to be exorcised.'

Clive produced his prayer book and commenced a string of Latin incantations followed by several signs made with his hands. At the end of this procedure, his fingers drew a giant cross between them.

'Begone to your eternal rest and may God forgive you,' he concluded. 'The blessings of Christ be upon your spirit.'

From Chantal's throat came loud musical laughter followed by the words, 'Pitiful! I know not this God or Christ that you speak of. Bother me not again.'

Try as he might, Clive could not extract any further response from the spirit. After several attempts to do so, there was nothing left for him but to awaken Chantal from her trance. She blinked and focused her gaze on each in turn.

'Well, did you succeed, Reverend Gilroy? Am I cleansed of this spirit?'

Clive looked crestfallen and apologetic.

'I'm afraid not, my dear, but don't give up hope. We shall try again at a later date.'

'Then it's still inside me, this horrid thing.' She began to cry.

Paul had never liked the woman, but even his heart went out to her. In an effort to console her, he said, 'One thing, Chantal, the spirit won't want to harm you. At the moment you're its only vehicle to the outside world.'

Chantal continued to weep.

Everyone except Chantal, who wished to be left alone, adjourned to the apartment's one lounge. Over a cup of coffee the bizarre and difficult situation was discussed at length. In the middle of the exchange of ideas Fatima arrived back. She asked what had happened and Elaine explained as best she could, after introducing her brother. Fatima looked thoughtful for a moment or two, then addressed Clive.

'Surely you used the wrong god in trying to exorcise the queen's spirit?'

Far from being angry Clive was intrigued.

'What do you mean my dear, the wrong god? There is only one God, the Father, the Son and the Holy Ghost, the Holy Trinity.'

Fatima smiled and said, 'For you perhaps.'

'And you, do you not believe?' said Clive.

'Whether I believe or not is beside the point. We are concerned here with the living spirit of a long-dead queen... a queen from over three thousand years ago. Far before the time of your Jesus Christ.'

Clive rubbed his chin thoughtfully, contemplating her remarks before bringing himself to reply. Paul butted in, hotly rebuking Fatima for her presumption in challenging

Clive.

'No, no. Leave her alone. The young lady is quite right. I believe I see where she is coming from,' exclaimed Clive.

'Perhaps you would care to enlighten the rest of us, then,' said Paul.

Clive ignored him and turned to Fatima.

'Go on, Fatima. I shall value your opinion.'

Elaine never seemed to be amazed by her brother's incredible tolerance and open-mindedness. As a minister of the cloth, she would have expected him to have been somewhat annoyed and put out by Fatima's remarks. Instead of which he lit his pipe and sat back, contentedly drawing on it, awaiting Fatima's reasoning.

'Think about it, Reverend Gilroy. When Queen Hatshepsut was walking on this earth, all those thousands of years ago, the only gods were the Egyptian gods – Osiris, Horus, Hathor, Isis, Seth and a host of others. The chief of these would have been Amon Ra… your Jesus Christ was still fifteen hundred years into the future.'

Clive smiled and drew on his pipe again. 'Go on,' was all he said.

'Don't you see, Reverend, she would never even have heard of your god, let alone respond to threats from it, or even encouragement for that matter.'

'Really, Fatima, this is too much,' exclaimed Elaine hotly.

Clive raised his hand to stop any further outburst from his sister.

'No, she has a valid point. Something that I should have thought of myself.' He turned back to Fatima, saying, 'I would be interested to hear more, Fatima.'

'Forgive me for suggesting it, but I think you should hypnotise Mademoiselle Shariffe again, but this time you should try the exorcism using one of her own gods. Amon, or better still, a female one, say Hathor or Isis, her favourites.'

Paul looked amazed and addressed Fatima, 'I didn't realise you knew anything of these things, Fatima.'

'Why would I not, Mr Stanton? I am Egyptian, am I not? The old ways are well known to me.'

Clive held up his hand to Paul and nodded to Fatima to resume.

'You are Europeans of a modern age and must therefore rid yourselves of superficial judgement, and enter into the deep roots from which our religion springs. We should remember that the problems facing ancient Egyptians were much like ours, at least their spiritual ones. Amon Ra was all-powerful. Ra, light of the universe, Amon, spirit of the universe. Coupled together – creative power. All of the lesser gods had their places in our religion and their tasks to perform—' Fatima broke off, suddenly. 'Do you see what I am getting at, all of you?'

Everyone was viewing Fatima in a totally new light.

Clive replied at length, 'There is much wisdom in what you say, young lady, but I seriously wonder if I have enough knowledge of the ways of your ancients to convince the spirit to leave Mademoiselle Shariffe's body, even under hypnosis.' Clive paused for a moment, weighing the possibilities, then resumed, 'In any case it would be far too much of a strain for Chantal to be subjected to another trance tonight, in order to contact the spirit.'

Fatima looked doubtful.

'I don't mean to be offensive, Reverend, but I doubt that you could do it. I mean you could obviously hypnotise the subject and probably raise the spirit once more, but could you persuade the invader to leave the body? It would take a great knowledge of our cosmogony of Heliopolis before creation to achieve that end.'

Far from being put down, Clive looked very impressed.

'If I were to hypnotise Chantal – say tomorrow night –

316

and programme her to your voice, do you think you could do it, my dear? Or could Paul with his great knowledge of archaeology, for that matter?'

Fatima considered for a moment. 'No, I do not think so,' was all she said.

'Then it looks like we are defeated and the spirit will eventually take Chantal over completely,' said Elaine.

'Not necessarily so,' put in Fatima. 'I know of a woman here in Luxor who could achieve such a deed.'

'Then what are we waiting for, Fatima? Who is this magical priestess you speak of?' exclaimed Paul, jumping to his feet.

'She is my older sister, Yasmin Sherin.'

'And would she be prepared to help with this bizarre situation, do you think, Fatima?' asked Clive.

'Obviously we would be willing to recompense her for her trouble,' added Paul.

'I would have to speak with her tomorrow, but I know that she will not accept money… Although she is my sister, she is a strange one, quite a law unto herself, in fact… but I shall try,' said Fatima.

'Then for tonight let us leave it at that. There seems little else we can do for now. I suggest I accompany you all tomorrow, together with Chantal, to the tomb. At least there we can all keep an eye on her. Meanwhile Fatima can go and visit her sister. Perhaps then, if she is willing to help, we can try another session of hypnosis tomorrow night,' suggested Clive.

Everyone agreed that this sounded the best plan. The meeting broke up and everyone left for their own rooms, leaving Clive to sleep on the futon in the lounge.

Chapter XIV

It was about two in the morning when Clive was awakened by a door or floorboard creaking. Always a light sleeper, he was immediately wide awake and astonished by what he saw. Appearing to be quite oblivious of his presence, Chantal, once more in the full regalia of an Egyptian Pharaoh, passed by him where he lay on the futon. Maintaining his silence, he watched as, light of foot, she headed up the stairs of the apartment and onto the landing. Quickly and silently he rose, donning his dressing gown as he went, tiptoeing up the stairs after her.

At the top of the stairs he paused and watched. She had halted at Paul's door and was about to turn the handle. What should he do? One should, he well knew, not awaken a sleepwalker, but this was no sleepwalker. By reason born of necessity, he spoke in a soft voice, almost a whisper.

'Are you lost, great Pharaoh?' he enquired.

Chantal turned, her expression hard for him to gauge. She took her hand from the door handle and approached him.

'Who are you to address your Pharaoh?' she said, coldly.

'A messenger from the god, Anubis, the guardian of eternal life. He who guards your tomb, oh king,' lied Clive, trying a new tactic… It didn't work.

'What tissue of lies is this? You are the Christ person who tried to trick me earlier,' hissed the possessed Chantal.

'I repeat, what do you want here? Are you lost?' he exclaimed.

'I come for my lover, Senenmut, and none shall stop me… Do you not know how many years I have waited?'

'He is not here. The man you think of as Senenmut is an archaeologist, Paul Stanton.'

Fire seemed to almost visibly transmit itself from Chantal's eyes. Clive could feel himself faced with something beyond his control. Slowly he backed away until his back came in contact with the guard rail of the landing. Chantal advanced on him, standing proudly before him.

'You lie, Christ man,' she hissed.

'No, I have only your best interests at heart, Pharaoh.'

'Not true. You seek to prevent my reunion with my lover.'

With this, Chantal took a pace forward and seized Clive by the throat. He was no weakling, but even so, he was unable to tear himself loose from her vicelike grip.

'Die, traitor,' she said, almost spitting the words at him.

The rail at his back pushed into him. The upper half of his torso was precariously balanced. In another moment he would go over and crash down onto the floor below. A man of the church he might have been, but this was no moment for refinement or Marquis of Queensbury rules! Sharply he brought his knee up into Chantal's stomach. With a gasp, she was forced to relinquish the hold she had on his neck. Quick to follow up, he grabbed her round her bare midriff, forcing her back across the landing. Violently wrestling, the pair slithered down the wall onto the floor with Clive on top of her. The position changed as they rolled to and fro across the landing, until once more Chantal had the ascendancy.

All this had taken but a few moments, but the commotion had woken the household. Paul was first onto the landing from his room, followed by Elaine and Fatima. For a moment everyone stood stock-still in shock, and then it was Fatima who was the first to react. She grabbed a heavy vase from a pedestal and stooping down over the tussling couple, brought it crashing down on Chantal's head.

All fight went out of the victim, who until then had been pinning Clive down. She became an unconscious dead weight on top of him. He rolled her over onto her back and shakily got to his feet, whilst, at the same time, explaining to the others what had happened.

Then, to everyone's amazement, they watched the woman lying senseless on the floor change her identity. Gone was the apparel of a Pharaoh of Egypt, back was Chantal dressed only in a short nightie, which had ridden up round her hips. Elaine instantly dropped to her knees and did her best to rearrange the garment a little more modestly. Paul also bent down and took Chantal's limp hand, seeking a pulse.

Fatima, still holding the base of the splintered china jug in her right hand, exclaimed, 'I'm sorry if I have killed her, but she would have killed the reverend if I hadn't.'

Paul looked up after taking Chantal's pulse.

'No, she's not dead, just unconscious. Don't blame yourself. I should have acted quicker myself, Fatima.'

'Do we send for a doctor, or what?' remarked Elaine.

'I think not. She's breathing easily and will come round fairly quickly,' replied Paul.

'It's lucky Noha doesn't live in, or all this would be very difficult to explain,' remarked Elaine.

'That's all very well, but what the blazes do we do with her all day tomorrow, until Fatima's sister can do her stuff… always provided she's willing to try,' added Paul.

'Look, this is all getting very dangerous for everybody,' put in Fatima, placing the cracked vase on the floor. 'We shall have to tie her up for her own good, otherwise she may kill one of us whilst we are sleeping, if she re-emerges as the Pharaoh again.'

'Hold on, Fatima. We can't tie up Chantal. She could have the law on us… She doesn't much care for Paul, as it is,' argued Elaine.

Clive, suitably recovered, gave an embarrassed cough.

'Sorry, it's probably the wrong thing for a man of the Church to say, but Fatima is right... For Chantal's own sake we must keep her where she can do the least damage to herself, or anyone else... Has anybody got anything we can tie her with before she comes to?'

'I'll get some stockings from my room... We can use them,' said Elaine, hurrying off, convinced by her brother's reasoning. A moment later she was back with two brand-new packs, which she broke open.

'Here, give them to me,' exclaimed Fatima. 'I'll tie her.' In less time than it takes to tell, Fatima had Chantal trussed hand and foot. 'How about a gag?' she asked.

'Come off it,' said Paul. 'I draw the line at that... poor creature!'

'No need anyway. Noha won't be coming in until the morning to clean and cook, so we can make an early start and take her with us to the tomb. By the time we return in the evening, Fatima can have her sister here. How does that sound?' said Clive.

'I guess it's the best we can do. I'll take Chantal back to her room. She will at least be more comfortable on the bed. Anyway I'll have to stay with her until she regains consciousness. If she recovers as Chantal herself, someone had better explain to her what has happened, or she'll have a fit or something,' said Paul.

'Well, I think that someone had better be me, Paul,' put in Elaine. 'She will never listen to a word you say.'

Paul scooped up in his arms the body of the still coma-tose woman and headed off, followed by Elaine in his wake. Once he had deposited Chantal in her own room on her bed, he turned to Elaine.

'Are you sure you will be all right left alone with her, Elaine? I think I ought to stay, too.'

'No, I'll be all right... What can she do anyway, trussed

up like that? You go and get some sleep.'

Paul continued to argue.

'Well, okay, but only if you promise to wake me in a couple of hours, then I'll stand watch and give you a break.'

'We'll see,' was all Elaine said.

★

By the time dawn broke the next morning Khaled was in a foul temper.

'Where in the name of Allah had that fool woman, Fatima, got to?' He had expected her to report to him the night before but she hadn't shown up. It occurred to him that she was spending much too much time with the infidels. Why had the senior Fundamentalists insisted on making the woman his second in command? All this nonsense she kept on about taking the infidels prisoners and holding them to ransom. Why had he even listened to her? Like all foreign infidels they should be exterminated once and for all.

Savagely he ran the pull-through along the barrel of a rifle and checked the light reflection to show that it was clean. With a grunt of satisfaction, he laid it down and picked up a Sten. He was well aware that to gun down the infidels wouldn't be easy. The whole valley around Deir el-Bahri and the surrounding valleys were crawling with Egyptian soldiers and police. Since the recent massacre of tourists on the approach to Hatshepsut's mortuary temple, the authorities were only too aware of possible Fundamentalist terrorism. Terrorism indeed! Exterminate all foreigners and put Egypt back to the old ways! All women in their place and fully veiled, not like the modern harlots! Restore proper Islamic laws and force everyone to obey!

Late afternoon would be the time for such an attack. Tourists would be on their way out of the valleys and the troops would be tired after a day patrolling in the heat and not as alert as usual. He and his men would dress as tourists, concealing their weapons. They would trek on foot to the tomb and surprise the foreigners and their Egyptian traitorous workers in the cavern. Round them up and shoot the lot! It would be a fine example to all Egyptians who were thinking of co-operating with infidels.

The guns could be fitted with silencers, so, with luck, no one outside the cavern need know of the planned slaughter. They could dump the bodies at the back of the cavern and be away before anyone was any the wiser. When eventually the remains of the infidels and their helpers were found, he and his men would be long gone. The Fundamentalists could claim the deed at no risk to themselves.

What of the woman, Fatima? If she turned up later that day she could take part in the slaughter.

If she didn't show, he would have her disgraced in the eyes of the Fundamentalists and thrown out of the order. He chuckled aloud. Thrown out, that was a joke. No one left the order. She would be executed without trial for disobeying orders.

'Serve the know-all bitch right,' he exclaimed aloud, relishing the thought.

'What did you say, Khaled?' asked Abou, one of his men, who had been near enough to overhear him.

'Nothing for you to worry about, just thinking aloud.'

That same morning, after a fairly interrupted and sleepless night, Fatima breakfasted with the rest of the archaeological party, but when Paul, Elaine, Clive and the now liberated Chantal left for the valley site, she left to visit her sister, Yasmin, over on the other side of Luxor. Yasmin was not exactly pleased to see her. In truth, she had virtually disowned her younger sister when she had thrown in her lot with the Fundamentalists a year earlier.

'Are you still associating with those Islamic throwbacks?' was her sister's first remark to her.

Yasmin was taller than her sister with a somewhat overbearing and commanding presence. She was dressed in European clothes, a grey pencil skirt and white blouse. Possessed of finely cut, aquiline features, she was not unattractive. Her dark hair was cut in a short modern style, tapering to the nape of her slender neck. Dark eyes flashing, she swept her gaze up and down her sister's frame.

'At least you don't dress like one of them anyway. It's a wonder they haven't put you in a veil and garbed you in black from head to foot.'

Fatima ignored the remarks and tried to remain affable.

'It's lovely to see you, Yasmin. It's been so long.'

It was Yasmin's turn to ignore the overture.

'What do you want? Obviously something, or you wouldn't have come to see me, knowing how I feel about your association with the cursed Fundamentalists.'

'I am in need of your special gifts and talents, Yasmin.'

'Why, when you have always ridiculed them before?' replied her sister. 'What need could a Fundamentalist possibly have for an emancipated, university-educated woman?'

'Perhaps if you will listen to what I have to say, Yasmin,' said Fatima, her voice heavy with sarcasm.

'I'm listening,' came back the equally veiled reply.

Fatima, without being invited, seated herself in one of her sister's armchairs and began to relate, in great detail, the events that had befallen her since she had first met up with the European archaeologists. It was when she came to the part about the spirit's apparition and Chantal Shariffe being possessed that Yasmin suddenly came alive and drew up a chair herself. Up until then she had only shown a token interest. Now she craned forward on the edge of her chair, taking in her sister's every word. She remained so until

Fatima concluded her narrative. Then came a barrage of questions, which Fatima did her best to answer, followed by an ominous silence. Fatima, unable to bear the suspense, broke it.

'Well... what do you think? Can you help us, Yasmin?'

'Us? Who? The Fundamentalists who are dragging Egypt down, or the archaeologists you seem to have been spending so much time with of late?'

The question took Fatima aback. She hadn't really thought about her loyalties, and had quite forgotten, in the excitement of the previous night, to report back to Khaled and the terrorists. She realised her own feelings were now terribly mixed up. With all that had happened, she had simply been carried along with the flow. There hadn't been time to consider her own position. The physical shock, as well as the spiritual one, of actually encountering a spirit from over three thousand years before had completely knocked her sideways.

Then there was the stark fact of her erstwhile hated infidel enemies, one of whom had risked his own life to save hers. She was grimly aware that without Paul Stanton she would be dead. She had, however, taken a vow to work towards everything the Fundamentalists stood for. Surely now she couldn't go back on that.

She recalled the spirit queen, in the guise of Chantal Shariffe, calling her Shazar, her handmaiden. Was there such a thing as reincarnation? The queen certainly believed Paul Stanton to be her old lover, Senenmut, of ages past. All these things and a dozen others assailed her reasoning.

'You do not answer, sister,' goaded Yasmin.

Fatima knew that her sister would see through any lies, so she tried to answer truthfully.

'The help I require from you is for Egypt, both of our Egypts... Yes, I agree the Europeans are desperately in need of your particular talents as a medium too.'

'And the Fundamentalists – what do they have to say about all this?' asked Yasmin.

'They know nothing of these events, only that the archaeologists are exploring a possible tomb, and that I have inveigled myself into their midst.'

'And the Europeans trust you, I suppose?' said Yasmin.

'They have no reason not to,' added Fatima.

'Until you turn on them like the asp that struck down Cleopatra.'

Fatima visibly paled at the venomous remark from her sister and hung her head.

'Look at me, Fatima,' said Yasmin. Leaning forward in her chair, she placed her fingers under the younger woman's chin and gently pushed her head up. 'The truth now. I'll have the truth from you. Where do your loyalties lie? Our parents, had they been alive, would have been ashamed of your association with these Fundamentalists... They shame this very Egypt.'

Fatima could sense her sister's eyes boring into her, almost as if they were exposing her inmost thoughts... Little wonder that her husband, Hassam, had left her two years earlier. She must have scared him just as she was scaring her now.

'Truthfully, I do not know. Never in my life have I been so uncertain. I have always thought the infidels the enemies of our country... Now I am not sure...' Fatima's reply tailed off.

'Well, in that you tell the truth, sister,' exclaimed Yasmin. 'Perhaps it is as well that you search your own soul for an answer.'

'But will you help us, or the woman, Chantal, is lost? Time is running out for her. The defences of her body are growing ever weaker against this powerful queen's possession of her mind,' pleaded Fatima.

'It is at least good that you are concerned for another

326

besides yourself,' said Yasmin. 'Where are the Europeans now and the woman who is possessed?'

'They have taken her to the tomb with them to keep an eye on her,' replied Fatima.

'Then I shall keep an open mind… I promise nothing, understand… You will take me to the tomb this morning and I shall observe for myself this phenomenon you speak of.'

Fatima rose from her chair and hugged her sister, but Yasmin pushed her firmly an arm's length away.

'Not yet, Fatima. You must prove yourself worthy, if I am to acknowledge you as a sister of mine, and a daughter of our late parents.'

During the long night Elaine and Paul had taken alternate stints at sitting with the trussed-up Chantal. Soon after Paul had left Elaine with her, she had recovered consciousness with a very sore head, and was angry and confused at finding herself firmly tied up. Elaine had explained in detail what had happened and that the restrictions were for her own benefit. She was horrified to hear that she, in the form of the queen, had almost murdered Clive Gilroy, and finally agreed that what they had done to her was for the best. Elaine had gone on to explain that they were going to get help for her and eventually Chantal fell into a troubled sleep.

The party, with Chantal now untied, left for the tomb after an early breakfast. On arrival at the valley cavern they found Ibrahim guarding the entrance. He rose at once to greet them.

'The oxygen equipment and extra lighting you required, effendi, are here and the men have taken them inside, Mr Stanton.'

'Good man… I want to take another look at the foot of

that shaft today and we don't want a repeat of what happened last time,' replied Paul.

'Who will accompany you down, effendi?'

Paul looked round. He realised he hadn't thought about it.

'Well, don't look at me. I'm no good at heights or depths for that matter,' laughed Clive, to lighten the moment. Elaine looked nervous.

'I guess it will have to be me then, as Fatima's not here.'

'What's wrong with me going down? After all, I'm the other experienced archaeologist,' exclaimed Chantal, putting the accent on the word experienced.

Elaine ignored the put-down and looked round at the others for their response. Paul shot an unspoken question to Clive, with a glance and raised eyebrows. In Chantal's presence, Clive found it difficult to state his concern and merely shrugged his shoulders. After all, if the spirit emerged again down there at the bottom of the shaft, could it do any worse than if it happened at the face of the cavern?

'That's settled then,' affirmed Chantal.

Paul looked far from happy but nevertheless led off towards the cavern entrance with the rest of the party in his wake. Threading their way through the cavern, they found Ashraf and Ahmed at the head of the shaft, with the oxygen cylinders, masks and extra lighting. After greeting them, he instructed them to go back to the entrance and stand guard and to send Ibrahim back to assist him. No sooner had they left than he whispered to the others that they couldn't afford to have too many people aware of what was going on. He was reasonably sure of Ibrahim's loyalty and could trust the man to remain silent about anything that he might witness.

They waited in comparative silence until Ibrahim joined them. The foreman then helped first Chantal into her gear of cylinder, harness and helmet, then Paul who, addressing

Chantal, said, 'Leave the mask off and the cylinder switched off until we reach the foot of the shaft. We won't need it until then.'

She nodded in affirmation. When Ibrahim had ascertained that the new pulleys and ropes were in place to his satisfaction, he nodded to Paul to seat himself into the home-made bosun's chair. A makeshift gantry had been erected over the abyss by the men. It was a relief to Paul that at least he wouldn't have to repeat his last climb even if something went wrong this time. Once seated, he buckled himself in, and went through a final check on the oxygen and harness, lastly checking the mask to make sure there were no blockages.

'Lower away, Ibrahim. I'll give three tugs on the rope when I'm down, then you can pull the chair up and let Chantal down to join me.'

'Very well, effendi.'

With a creaking of rope on wood, Paul began to feel himself moving. He switched on the light on his helmet and shone the powerful flashlight in his hand downwards. Its beam gave an eerie reflection, casting shadows back off the narrow walls of the shaft. Soon he was on his own, the whispered sounds of the other voices disappearing somewhere above him. Only the constant creaking of the gantry accompanied his descent. At least, he reflected, it was effort-free on his part, but even so it seemed to take ages before he found himself at the base.

Rapidly he unbuckled and climbed free of the uncomfortable seat. First he switched on his oxygen cylinder and donned the mask, then gave three tugs on the rope. He watched the contraption disappear upwards into the blackness of the shaft, then turned away to explore.

He worked his way through, following the tiny stream until he came upon the pile of bones bleached white by the ever-present ice-cold, running water. Producing a bag made of canvas, he carefully unfolded it and lay it on the rocks. Then, one by one, he diligently removed each bone in turn from its resting place, trying to identify it as he went about the macabre task. It occurred to him that it was a strange phenomenon. If the bones had been here in the water for over three thousand years, they surely should have worn right away to nothing. Given that the water was ice-cold it might have helped, but surely... The logical conclusion was the water had to be fairly newly arrived. His thoughts were rudely interrupted.

'The water only began a few weeks ago.'

The voice behind him so startled him that he almost dropped the bone that he was holding. He turned and was amazed to see once again the figure of the Egyptian queen in all her regalia as Pharaoh. Suddenly he realised with horror that not only was he down here alone with her, but her last remark showed an ability to read his mind. She stood there, a smile on her face, carrying the oxygen cylinder and mask in her hand. Of the helmet there was no sign. On her head was the double red and white crown of ancient Egypt, the vulture and cobra plainly evident in the beam of his torch.

Paul's mouth almost fell open with shock, but her next remark brought him back to something like normal.

'Why bother with my ancient bones when you have me here in the flesh, my love... I have long since left them to rot and decay.'

Paul gulped, then tried to change the subject.

'Put your mask on quickly and turn that cylinder on or the bad air down here will kill you, Chantal.'

She threw back her head and laughed, saying, 'Why do you keep addressing me as Chantal, when it is merely her body I use?' She looked down at herself. 'A worthy body, is it not, even if not as glorious as mine once was. The flesh that once contained those bones you are so carefully preserving was indeed something, was it not, my Senenmut?'

In the beam of his torch her eyes flashed provocatively, alive and vibrant. Why was the bad air down here not affecting her? How was she breathing so easily without the aid of oxygen?

'It has long been my only home. I do not require your mortal air.'

With horror he realised it was true – she could read his inmost thoughts.

'You may not, but Chantal does, or she will die and you will have no body to support your spirit.'

Again the soft musical laughter.

'And which would you care to lose, your Chantal or your great love... your queen?' She was moving ever nearer towards him. He seemed powerless to move. Reaching up she removed his mask. 'There,' she whispered, 'you can do without it for a little while, I'm sure.'

Her face was close to his now, a beautiful face and he could catch the aroma of exotic perfume. Those beautiful haunting eyes bore into his, making him feel bewitched. Now her arms encircled him, crushing him into her. Almost savagely she reached up with one hand behind Paul's neck and pulled his head down. Her lips engaged his and he felt his head swim, knowing not whether it was the lack of air or something else. She was not cold as he had expected but her flesh burnt fiercely at his touch.

Another moment and he was going to be lost. Suddenly it dawned on him she was going to kill him and keep him there with her for ever. Terror struck at his very stomach.

Chapter XV

By ten o'clock that morning Khaled, with the non-arrival of Fatima, had worked himself into a fury. He turned to Mohammed and the rest of his men.

'Change into the clothes that have been allocated to you... We must all appear to be tourists, so keep your guns well out of sight. I shall walk in front with a raised green umbrella, just like we have seen the infidel guides do.'

This remark was followed by weak laughter from the men.

Mohammed appeared surprised and exclaimed, 'But, leader, you said we would go in the late afternoon. It is as yet two hours short of midday. Why the change in plan?'

Khaled's one good eye glared almost through him. 'Do you question my orders, Mohammed?' he snarled.

'No, leader, I was interested, that's all... I meant nothing by it.'

'The infidels have been left alone long enough. There is no knowing what treasures they have plundered from our country... Be quick now, men. We leave in ten minutes.'

Everyone trailed off to search for the assortment of tourist-like clothes with which they had each been issued. Ten minutes later they were all dressed and assembled ready to pull out.

'Leave what you can't carry. We shall not be coming back here. As soon as our task here is completed, we shall leave Luxor for the safety of Nubia,' ordered Khaled.

'Where is our second in command, Fatima Sherin? Should she not be with us?' enquired Wael.

Khaled shot him a glance of bitter venom.

'It is possible she is in the tomb cavern with the other infidels. When we get there we shall know for sure that the woman, as I have always expected, is a traitor,' snarled Khaled.

'But I heard you yourself tell her to infiltrate their party, leader, and find out what was going on,' protested Mohammed.

'Silence! I shall not be questioned. The woman has chosen not to report back and that is enough for me. I conclude that she is a traitor to the Fundamentalist brotherhood.' As everyone moved out, Khaled was conscious of a low muttering amongst them. 'Enough!' he roared. 'We shall be on the street in a moment or two. Look and behave like the sheep packs of idiot tourists that we so often see traipsing around our country.' With this he held the furled green umbrella above his head. 'This way, gentlemen,' he said, loudly enough for any bystander to overhear.

The small column moved out, looking like a party of common-or-garden travellers the world over.

Fatima arrived with her sister, Yasmin, at the cavern entrance. They had travelled the first part of the journey by taxi, then trekked along the valley floor on sandalled feet. Ahmed, who was seated on a rock with Ashraf, leapt up to challenge them.

'Effendi Stanton, he say no one to enter.'

Fatima smiled at him, saying, 'Surely you recognise me, Ahmed. I am one of Mr Stanton's party and this is my sister,' she said and waved her hand towards Yasmin by way of introduction.

'Well, I suppose it's all right to let you go in... What do you think, Ashraf?' he said, turning to the other man.

Ashraf grunted his affirmation.

'You will have to wait whilst I light a pair of hurricane lamps for you, mademoiselle,' said Ahmed. He hurried away behind a rocky outcrop and a few moments later returned with the two lamps.

Fatima and Yasmin each took one, graciously thanking him.

'Come on, sister, I shall show you the way,' said Fatima, leading off towards the cavern entrance.

No sooner had they entered than Yasmin stopped dead in her tracks, looked to the right and left. Sensing that her sister had halted, Fatima turned to face her.

'What's the matter, Yasmin?'

'There is a strong presence here. I feel it,' exclaimed Yasmin.

Fatima was puzzled.

'Do you mean an evil presence?'

'Not necessarily so. It is uncertain, like a lost soul searching for something,' replied Yasmin, seemingly sniffing the air and still looking to right and left.

Fatima decided, as she did not understand her sister, to ignore the statement and pushed forward.

'Come on, Yasmin. I'll take you to them,' was all she said.

Through the darkened passages and chambers the pair gradually felt their way, holding their hurricane lamps before them. Finally they arrived at the entrance to the narrow passage containing the shaft entrance. Peering in, Fatima could see Elaine and her brother, along with the foreman of the workers, Ibrahim. They were all on their knees peering down into the shaft.

'Has Mr Stanton gone down?' called out Fatima. 'I have my sister, Yasmin, here with me.'

Clive answered, 'Yes, and Chantal is down there with him.'

Everyone in the eerie silence heard the gasp from Yasmin. A moment later she had pushed her sister aside and crawled on her hands and knees down the low passageway.

'From what my sister tells me you should not have allowed Mademoiselle Shariffe to accompany him.'

Even in the dull glow of the hurricane lamps she could see the embarrassment on the faces of Elaine and her brother. Ibrahim just looked totally confused by this turn of events. Elaine tried to make an excuse but it tailed off miserably. She was well aware she should have raised more of an objection when Chantal had volunteered. Clive admitted cowardice as his motive.

'I'm afraid I just don't care for heights, my dear.'

'If I am right, your colleague is in great peril,' exclaimed Yasmin.

'How can you be sure of that?' asked Elaine.

'Fatima here has told me what has happened to date, and I fear you are dealing with something you know little about... Even the minister here is out of his depth.'

The dramatic tone of Yasmin's voice caused Elaine to feel the goose pimples rise on her own flesh. Clive was the first to respond.

'What do you suggest we do?'

'I must go down there at once,' said Yasmin, creeping forward to the edge of the abyss and peering over. 'Can you lower me down?'

Ibrahim countered, 'At the moment the chair is at the bottom and I would have to bring it up for you.'

'Then do so at once, please.'

Ibrahim looked at Elaine for confirmation. Elaine nodded her affirmation. She was feeling perfectly wretched that she had let Paul down. It should have been her down there. She addressed Yasmin.

'I shall follow you down,' she said, coming to a sudden decision.

'No you won't, sis. We only have one more tank of oxygen and one more mask,' pointed out Clive.

'Then get it buckled onto me whilst this man brings up

the chair,' urged Yasmin, jerking her thumb at Ibrahim.

'No. It had better be me that goes if we only have one tank,' stated Elaine.

Yasmin looked at Elaine with something like profound wisdom in her eyes.

'Who do you think will be the most use down there, you or me? What do you know of the occult?'

Seeing that she had no case to push Elaine backed down.

'Okay, Yasmin, you have a point.'

She helped the elder of the two Egyptian girls buckle on her harness with its heavy oxygen tank, then handed her a helmet and mask, by which time Ibrahim had brought the bosun's chair creaking up through the well-like shaft. It came to rest, swinging ominously.

Ibrahim handed Yasmin into it and buckled her in, saying, 'Remember, mademoiselle, three pulls on the rope when you want to come up.'

Yasmin said nothing but simply nodded. A moment later Ibrahim began to let her slowly descend. Soon her head disappeared below the rim. Everyone craned forward, watching until the light on her helmet was a mere speck, then there was nothing, only silence.

Some ten minutes must have passed when the silence at the shaft face was broken by a guttural command in poor English.

'Come out here, all of you.'

Such was the shock that Elaine nearly overbalanced and fell into the abyss.

'In heaven's name, who are you?' gasped Clive, peering back down the low passageway at a crouched figure menacingly pointing a Sten gun at them. A moment later he turned as he felt something pushed into the small of his back. It was Fatima, a small pistol gripped tightly in her hand.

'Do as he says, or I shall fire,' she commanded.

Elaine looked at her in horror.

'What the devil are you playing at, Fatima? Is this some sort of bad joke?'

The voice floated down the narrow passageway. It was the man.

'Don't waste my time. Out here, all of you.'

Fatima jerked the gun menacingly at all three of them. There was nothing for it but to obey the command. On hands and knees they crawled out. First Elaine, then her brother, then Ibrahim, followed lastly by Fatima complete with pistol.

'It is as well that you are still with us, Fatima Sherin,' snarled the newcomer, an evil-looking fellow with an eyepatch over one eye.

'What do you mean by this outrage? Who are you and what are you doing here? The men outside have orders to admit no one,' exclaimed Clive. He was prevented from speaking further by a vicious backhanded slap across the face from the unwelcome visitor.

Elaine stepped forward to help her brother but was halted by the Sten being menacingly levelled at her stomach. She could see that behind him in the chamber were several men, all carrying guns. On their knees at their feet were Ashraf and Ahmed. She realised with horror that they could expect no help from that quarter. Deep down, she knew at once that these were the fanatical brotherhood of Fundamentalist terrorists. Unless she could think of something quickly there was little hope of mercy from these people. The one with the eyepatch proceeded to introduce himself and she wasn't at all surprised when her suspicions were confirmed.

Clive was still rubbing his face ruefully and Ibrahim looked lost and bewildered. Elaine swung on Fatima.

'And you… you're one of them! We trusted you and Paul even saved your life. How—'

She got no further. Fatima stepped forward and struck her a blow in the stomach. Clutching herself, she crumpled to the floor. The man with the eyepatch laughed. Elaine would always remember that laugh. It was like stones passing across a sieve, totally mirthless, setting one's nerves on edge. She knew that they were near death.

'Where are the others? We know from your men that there are three more in here... two women and a man. We have reason to believe he is your leader... Out with it! Where are they?' Khaled jabbed his Sten into Clive's midriff. Elaine was still curled up on the floor writhing in pain. Pointing his Sten at Elaine, he addressed Clive. 'I shall count to three and if you haven't told me where the others are, I shall shoot this European bitch. One... two...' The bolt clicked back ominously.

'All right, hold it. I'll talk,' Clive exclaimed, nervously.

'Well?'

The man's tone was unmistakably full of malice and venom. Clive knew he had little option. He saw that they were all going to die at the hands of these killers, but it wouldn't do any harm to play for time.

'The others are all down in the shaft... They have to bring the gold up, you see, and there's quite a lot of it. Very heavy stuff, gold.'

Elaine looked up through tear-filled eyes at her brother, guessing what he was trying to do.

'Yes, not only gold, but emeralds, too,' she gasped out.

'If you are lying to me?' said Khaled, swinging the gun barrel from one to the other of them.

'Why would we do that? You have the guns. What could we do?' argued Clive.

For a moment Khaled turned to look at the others, then at Fatima. 'Is what they say true, woman?' he snarled.

Cold fear hit Elaine's stomach. She had completely for- gotten Fatima behind her. Of course, the girl knew there was nothing down there but bones. Now they were finished for sure. In desperation she looked at Clive. Then came an even greater shock with Fatima's reply.

'What they say is true, Khaled. Gold and emeralds beyond your wildest dreams. All down there waiting for us.'

'Why have you said nothing of this before, woman?' he fired the question at Fatima.

'Because I had to make sure first, and now I have.'

'Was it not because you thought to keep the riches for yourself?'

'No, everything is for the brotherhood,' countered Fatima.

So, if Fatima was going to give us away, she would have done so, thought Elaine. A glimmer of hope was showing, but why had Fatima hit her so hard? Obviously to make it look good to these terrorists.

Khaled seemed to be thinking, weighing up everything she had said.

'You say three people are down there? Two women and one man.'

Fatima confirmed this to him.

'Lie on your bellies all of you, like the vermin you are, infidels,' he commanded.

So this was it, thought Elaine, the swine is going to shoot us all in the back, just like the terrorists did at Deir el-Bahri, a few months ago. My God, she mused, these could be the very same assassins.

With Elaine, Clive and Ibrahim measuring their length on the cold rocky floor, Khaled issued another order, this time to Fatima.

'Check them all out, woman. See that none are carrying arms.'

Fatima made an elaborate show of complying, running her hands over each in turn.

'Not even a knife between them, Khaled.'

Next Khaled wanted to know how to reach the bottom of the shaft. Fatima explained the use of the bosun's chair.

'No, we shall wait for them to come up and take the gold from them,' he said and laughed. 'Then kill them like the dogs they are.'

'You will have a long wait then,' mumbled Elaine, from her position, with her head down facing the ground.

Khaled strode across, grabbed her by the hair and forced up her head.

'What do you mean, a long wait, infidel bitch?'

With her throat stretched tight it was difficult to speak, but Elaine knew her life depended on her wits. Pray God Fatima was still on their side and would pick up the cue.

'They will be down there all day stacking the mass of treasure. This evening they will bring it up.'

Khaled looked unconvinced.

'Why, if there is so much treasure to lift, would two women be down there to do it and not the man?'

Whilst Elaine searched for a convincing answer, Fatima beat her to it.

'The area is restricted down there. Some of the crevices are so small that only a woman can get in to retrieve the gold.'

'And you have seen this for yourself, woman?' Khaled exclaimed.

'Yes. A man would never be able to enter some of the niches,' replied Fatima.

'Can you work the chair contraption and lower me down?' he asked Fatima.

'Easily. I have seen the man, Ibrahim, do it.'

'Come then. You shall let me down into the shaft.' With this he turned to the gun-toting Mohammed and said, 'Guard these people well. When we have all the treasure up and the other three here also, we shall exterminate these vermin.'

'Why not kill these now, leader? Save us time and energy looking after them,' argued Mohammed.

'Silence! Do as I say. I shall not be contradicted,' snapped Khaled. 'We may yet have need of them.'

Fatima crawled into the passageway leading to the shaft entrance. 'Follow me, Khaled. You will not be able to stand up straight in here,' she called back over her shoulder.

With a grunt, Khaled dropped to his knees, still with the Sten in one hand and crawled in her wake.

Elaine, lying face down on the hard rocky floor, experienced a new terror with the departure of Fatima. The three of them were now left alone with the terrorists. What if they decided to disobey their leader and kill them now?

The man, Mohammed, who seemed to have assumed command on Khaled's absence, walked round and round her. She couldn't see his face, of course, but she felt sure that it would probably have an evil leer on its swarthy countenance. Then she felt his hands going all over her and squirmed desperately to avoid his invasive touch.

'Leave my sister alone,' shouted Clive, in a futile but gallant effort to protect her.

'Silence, dog,' roared Mohammed and hit him a painful blow with the butt of the Sten on the back of his neck.

Clive gasped with pain but still continued his protest. Another voice cut in. It was Wael, one of the terrorists.

'You had better do as our leader says, Mohammed. Leave them alone until he returns. He may want the yellow-haired one for himself before he kills her.'

Elaine could feel her whole body tightening up like a coiled spring with tension. Her mouth dried up and fear clutched at her stomach. These fiends were discussing her as if she were an animal for their amusement.

Then, with relief, she head Mohammed mutter, 'Perhaps you are right, Wael. He can be an evil devil if crossed.'

For the moment anyway, she relaxed anew, but for how long?

Chapter XVI

Whether or not it was the scarcity of air, Paul felt the resistance draining out of him. The presence of the beautiful queen and the aroma of her perfume was becoming quite intoxicating. Without his mask he knew he would eventually succumb and die in the bad air, but he seemed quite powerless to resist. He wondered why she didn't seem to need her mask, and was so full of life and energy, when his powers to fight her off were fast receding. Her hot lips found his throat and her tantalising fingers were somehow inside the boiler suit he wore, although he hadn't felt her undo the press studs that kept the garment together.

Gasping for air, he felt himself pushed back against the rock, almost oblivious to a sharp craggy protuberance pressing into the small of his back. Her hands were both inside his jumpsuit now and round the back of his hips. She pulled him forward to meet with her eager vibrant body and ran her lips down his bare chest.

Somewhere in the deep recesses of his mind he thought, This is Chantal Shariffe. I can't do this. With the last vestige of his strength he brought his knee up and thrust her away. She tumbled onto her back, half in the small trickling rivulet of water. The historic kilt of the Pharaoh of Egypt rode up round her hips and he could see that she was nude underneath. Firm brown thighs terminated in a pretty bush of curly black pubic hair. She looked up and saw where his gaze had alighted. Those dark eyes flashed an invitation and she laughed that soft musical, so enticing sound that seemed to come from deep within her.

Paul pulled himself together and grabbed up his mask

from where she had laid it on the rocks. Clamping it over his nose and mouth he took several deep breaths and immediately felt a whole lot more human.

As her soft laughter was replaced by a sly smile, she exclaimed, 'I see you want to fight for it like we did all those centuries ago.'

He watched as she gracefully slid up the face of the rock like a serpent until she was in a standing position. She flicked out her tongue and wetted her ruby lips provocatively and Paul was forced to bite his own, to retain tight control over his emotions. Holding her arms low, a sensuous smile still on her face, she advanced and gradually circled him. Paul kept turning to face her. At least now that he had the mask back on, receiving oxygen, he could think and act again.

'Take that ridiculous thing off,' she commanded. 'I don't like it.'

Then, with a flying leap, she was upon him, wrapping those long slender legs round his waist. Paul grabbed her wrists to prevent the mask being pulled off his face. She struggled and fought with the strength of a tigress. The encircling legs felt like steel bands round his waist. Unable to use his hands, he bit her savagely on the neck, as she tore the mask from him.

'That's more like the old Senenmut, my love. Again! Again!' she gasped in ecstasy.

Temporary rescue came in a strange form. A voice from behind them interrupted their unique wrestling tryst. It came as a pail of ice-cold water, such was the shock to both, down there in that dark cavern. Ceasing their struggles abruptly, they turned to face the newcomer.

A woman unknown to both stood, hands on hips, facing them. She had removed her mask to address them and now repeated the words slowly and deliberately, holding the mouthpiece in her hand.

'My name is Yasmin Sherin and I am here to help you, Pharaoh.'

Clearly Egyptian of origin, she was, Paul guessed, about thirty or thereabouts, and striking rather than beautiful, with jet-black hair. He knew for sure, he had never seen her before, so was as amazed as the possessed Chantal at the woman's appearance out of the dark gloom. From Chantal's mouth came the challenge.

'How dare you enter here? I do not need your help, whoever you are… Begone and leave us alone.'

The newcomer replaced her mask, took a couple of deep breaths and removed it again.

'If you are to reach the eternal land of your forefathers – Osiris, Horus, Isis, Hathor and all the rest – I may be your only way, Pharaoh.'

'Presumption on your part, Yasmin Sherin, or whatever you call yourself… Who are you, a commoner, to address your Pharaoh?'

Yasmin appeared unmoved, never taking her eyes off the woman she addressed.

'Are you not a restless spirit, journeying for these thousands of years, down here in this dark place, when you should have taken your rightful position amongst the gods?'

'You seem to be well informed, commoner. It is because of my evil stepson, Tuthmosis III of that name, that I was murdered and my body left here to rot in this dark hole,' came the reply.

Yasmin continued. 'And do you choose to remain down here for ever in your misery and take this poor man with you?'

She pointed at Paul, who stood with his back to the rock, totally bemused by developments. Who on God's earth was this woman and how did she get here? Then he remembered the surname. This must be Fatima's sister. Yes, that was it. She had called herself Yasmin. Hadn't

Fatima said her sister had special powers?

'I, Pharaoh, have need of him and wherever I go he shall accompany me.'

Yasmin tried a new approach.

'He is not the man you seek, Pharaoh.'

'Do you presume to tell me whom I seek?' The spirit accentuated the word 'me' with a contemptuous shrug of her shoulders.

Yasmin started to address her once more, but was quickly cut short, when Chantal leapt forward with the speed of a panther to grasp the newcomer's neck. Seeing what was happening, Paul rushed to the rescue. Grabbing Chantal by the waist, he proceeded to haul her off Yasmin. In the confined space in the semi-darkness the three of them battled anew, weaving about like drunks in an alley. Although Paul succeeded in breaking Chantal's hold on Yasmin's neck, such was her grip that he was unable to separate the two women.

Up at the head of the shaft, Fatima was engaged in the act of lowering Khaled down the dark, narrow, funnel-like well. She was sorely tempted to cut the rope and send him hurtling down to his inevitable death. Reason prevailed. If she did this, his dying scream would echo and reverberate throughout this accursed place. In no time at all Mohammed or one of the others would come to investigate. She remembered that she had said nothing of the bad air down there, and that without oxygen he wouldn't survive long. Then another thought struck Fatima. When he reached the bottom of the shaft he would still have the Sten and could easily take one of the other three's masks to survive. Knowing Khaled as she did, she knew he wouldn't think twice about it once he realised the situation for himself.

She thought of bringing the bosun's chair up, but there was no way she could lower herself down, due to the way

Ibrahim had rigged it. The only way of getting down there, to help the man who had earlier saved her life, was to abseil down the rope. She knew from past experience that, due to the narrowness of the shaft, it would amount to half-abseiling and half-sliding down the rope. Very much aware that when she arrived without oxygen, she wouldn't last long before passing out in the bad air. She was equally conscious that she couldn't allow her sister, whom she herself had persuaded to help, to die either, not if it was in her power to stop Khaled murdering them. With a small shred of relief, she remembered the small derringer pistol she had concealed on her person. Luckily it didn't show under the roomy boiler suit she wore.

She felt the rope go slack and realised that Khaled had reached the bottom and unbuckled himself from the bosun's chair. With no more time to think about it, she reached out and grabbed the rope, and lowering herself over the rim, she began the descent.

'Break it up, all three of you, and up against the rock face,' commanded a rough male voice, in broken English with a heavy Middle Eastern accent.

Paul, Chantal and Yasmin recoiled from one another's grasp as if struck by lightning, such was the impact of yet another strange voice down there in the confined space. It would be impossible to say who was the most surprised. Even Khaled lowered the Sten momentarily in surprise at seeing Chantal dressed in her attire of an Egyptian Pharaoh. Seeking to take advantage of this and instantly realising that the newcomer was no friend, Paul advanced on the half-distracted Khaled. Quick to recover, the Egyptian swung the gun on him.

'Oh no, you don't. Back with the others against the wall,' commanded Khaled.

There was nothing for it but to comply. Paul backed away to join the women against the cold rock.

'Where's the gold and emeralds?' snarled Khaled, looking to left and right of them.

Totally bemused, Paul answered, 'What gold? What emeralds?'

'Come on, man, you can't fool me. The woman, Fatima, said you were down here preparing to bring them to the surface.'

Paul didn't know what was happening, but it was clear this man was some sort of robber and could only mean harm to them. He was equally aware that if he held out long enough and played for time the fellow would succumb to the air down here and pass out. He stalled.

'We haven't located it yet, but we know it's here. Perhaps you would like to help us look?'

Khaled's one good eye scowled. In the poor light, with his dark eyepatch, he looked even more sinister.

'You lie, infidel. Show me where the gold is hidden. It is the property of the brotherhood not yours.'

So that's it, thought Paul. He's one of the Fundamentalists. His astute mind put two and two together. These people always ran in packs, therefore there must be more of them up top in the cavern above. That must be why they had received no warning about this. Elaine and the others must be captives too. Almost assuredly Elaine would have warned him if that hadn't been the case.

Khaled reiterated his command concerning the gold. 'Bring it here at once,' he ordered.

Paul thought of jumping him, but realised in this confined space, even if he himself succeeded, one of the two women, or both, might get hit. A ricochet off these rocky walls would prove just as fatal.

'Put that instrument down, whatever it is,' commanded Chantal's spirit governor.

Paul realised with something like amazement that, of course, she would never have seen a gun or anything like it.

'You! Why are you dressed like that?' snapped Khaled, turning his attention to Chantal.

'Because I am your rightful Pharaoh and you offend me by your ugly ill-mannered presence.'

This latter remark was received by a mirthless laugh.

'You think to dress up as an ancient Egyptian to mock us, we, the Fundamentalists, the very spirit of old Egypt, we who would turn Egypt back to the old and rightful way of life,' exclaimed Khaled.

It was Chantal's turn to laugh, although much more attractively.

'The old ways, you say. What do you then call a Pharaoh from over three thousand years ago?'

'What nonsense is this?' bellowed Khaled, the echoes reverberating from the rocky walls…

The mocking echoes reached Fatima's ears as she arrived at the base of the shaft. She recognised Khaled's gruff voice at once and realised that he had located the others. Silently, with both feet now on terra firma, she reached inside her boiler suit and withdrew the small derringer. With the other hand, she picked up a loose rock and crept forward, following in the direction of the sounds. Just before the last turn, she heard the voice of the possessed Chantal.

'Dog! I shall have you executed for your insolence.'

This was followed by Khaled's laughter, if that was what you could call the sound his gravely tone uttered.

'It is you, fancy-dressed woman, who will be executed, just as soon as I see the gold. Executed for the good of Egypt and for the honour of the Fundamentalists brotherhood.'

Paul noticed that Khaled caught his breath at the conclusion of the sentence and realised that if he could play for time a little longer, the stale dirty air down there would work for them, but he still couldn't for the life of him understand why it wasn't affecting Chantal. Both he and

Yasmin still had their masks in place. Almost at the same time as this was going through his head, the same thought must have entered into Khaled's brain.

'Why do two of you wear masks and not her?' he pointed at Chantal.

'Pharaoh needs no such frivolity,' replied Chantal.

Khaled jerked the gun from one to the other and began to sway a little. He seemed to be trying to work something out.

Paul countered, lying through his teeth, 'We are both asthmatic and need a little oxygen.'

For a moment only, the ploy seemed to work.

'Show me where the gold is, infidel, if you wish to live a moment l… longer.' Khaled's speech was becoming slurred and he stumbled over the last word.

Fatima crept round the last turn and then stepped back in a hurry. Khaled had his back to her, but she was sure that of those facing her, Chantal had seen her even if only for a split second. A second later the spirit's voice floated round the bend in the tunnel confirming her worst fears.

'What is my handmaiden, Shazar, doing down here? Come here, girl. I need you at once.'

She remained pressed up against the rock, derringer tightly gripped in her right hand, the piece of limestone in the other. With her cover now blown, it was certain Khaled would come to investigate. How long, she wondered, could she hope to hold out without oxygen? Already she could feel her chest tightening and her throat drying out. She had passed out before down here and realised that it wouldn't be long before she repeated the act. Fatima was beginning to experience that light heady giddiness that preceded such an attack. One thing saved her. Khaled, after all, was a professional killer and obviously believed Chantal was trying to trick him, making him turn round so that they could rush him.

Fatima heard him exclaim, 'Fool, woman, you don't really think I would fall for that one. It's the oldest trick in the b... book.' Again he stumbled on the last word. Fatima realised, if she was ever going to act, now was the time. Khaled, after all, had been down here a few minutes longer than her, so in reality she had the upper hand. Gun in hand, she crept round the corner and advanced on Khaled's back, which was still turned towards her.

'There she is,' cried out Chantal. 'I told you, it's Shazar.'

The expression on Chantal's face was so triumphant and the tone so convincing that, in spite of himself, Khaled half-turned, with Fatima still some three metres short of him. Fatima could still have shot him in the back, but somehow, although she hated the man, she herself was a Fundamentalist and couldn't bring herself to murder him in cold blood.

Khaled, seeing the pistol in one hand and her upraised hand gripping the rock, obviously thought she had come down to help him.

'I told you to stay at the head of the shaft and to bring me up when I gave you the signal, woman.'

'It occurred to me that you might need help, Khaled, so I decided to come down myself.'

'You mean you wanted some of the gold for yourself... but no matter. Now that you are here and obviously know where the gold is, you c... can s... how me.' At long last the reality of the masks was dawning on Khaled. His one good eye glinted in the reflection of the lights on the helmets of Paul and Yasmin and an evil smile creased his face. 'You two take off those tanks on your backs and masks f... from y... your f... faces.' He swayed on his feet and even the barrel of the Sten wavered. 'Q... quickly n... now,' he half-mumbled. Then, sensing that he was in imminent danger of passing out, shouted at Fatima, 'Shoot the infidel d... dogs. W... we have no n... need of them n... now that y...

you are here.'

Without more ado, Fatima leapt forward and smashed the rock against the side of Khaled's head. Almost in slow motion, he seemed to crumble, half falling into the trickling water; the Sten flew from his grasp and clattered onto the rocks.

Paul, seizing his moment, leapt forward to retrieve it and swung it onto the fallen Khaled. There was no need, the man was out cold and blood trickled from a severe gash from his temple.

'He won't be troubling us in a hurry. Good girl, Fatima. You saved our lives,' said Paul, enthusiastically. Then he saw her begin to sway and the sight brought him back to grim reality. Snatching the mask from his face, he placed a supporting arm round Fatima's shoulders and clamped the mouthpiece over her nose and mouth. 'Breathe!' he exclaimed.

It didn't take long for Fatima to recover once the oxygen began to react on her. Whilst he had been administering to her, Yasmin had sought out the mask and tank jettisoned on arrival by the possessed Chantal.

'Here, put this on her and take back your own mouthpiece,' commanded Yasmin, taking control of the situation. Then, glancing at Chantal in her Pharaoh's apparel, she added, 'She obviously doesn't need it!'

Once the tank and harness had been buckled onto Fatima, she addressed all of them.

'You are all far from out of the wood yet. Even if we get out of here and up into the top cavern, we shall be faced with eight terrorists of the brotherhood – and all armed.'

'My God!' exclaimed Paul. 'Elaine's up there and her brother, besides my workmen. If they have…' The words tailed off.

Fatima put a consoling hand on Paul's arm.

'They were being held captive by the brotherhood when

I left to come down here after Khaled. I can't guarantee anything, but I don't think they will do anything until Khaled returns. Unfortunately, Miss Gilroy is blonde and attractive and they might decide to pleasure themselves whilst they are waiting.'

'We have got to get up there fast,' exclaimed Paul, moving back towards the direction of the foot of the shaft.

Whilst all this was going on, Chantal had stood, hands on hips, looking vaguely puzzled, her gaze resting on each in turn.

'What in the name of Osiris is going on?' she demanded.

It was Yasmin who answered. 'You might say we are all faced with our version of Tuthmosis III.'

The effect on Chantal was electric. 'And he is up there?' she screamed.

'Yes, and he means to kill us all and put this very Egypt back to the dark ages,' replied Yasmin.

'Not twice he will not. The gods have given me a second chance to even old scores,' affirmed Chantal.

Paul looked at the Sten he held in his own hands and at the derringer in Fatima's.

'Well, we have two guns. It's a start.'

'Yes, two guns and one held by an amateur. Against eight fully armed, professional terrorists and just to make things more difficult they are holding five hostages. That's if they haven't killed them already,' said Fatima, sarcastically.

'Oh yes, I was forgetting, just for a moment, you are one of them… these professional killers, my sister,' exclaimed Yasmin with equal sarcasm.

'What do you mean?' gasped Paul. 'She just saved our lives.'

Yasmin looked meaningfully at her sister, who looked rather embarrassed, before replying, 'Yes, it's true. I was one of them, but let us say I have seen the error of my ways and I now realise that you people are not my country's enemies… I am truly sorry.'

Paul placed a consolatory arm around Fatima's shoulders.

'I think you have proved that once and for all,' he said, warmly, sensing her remorse.

'This is all very well, but what are we to do now?' pointed out Yasmin.

It was Chantal, or more realistically, the Pharaoh Hatshepsut, who answered. It was in a firm resolute tone that she addressed them.

Chapter XVII

'These strange weapons you seem to place so much faith in – these guns as you persist in calling them – they are beyond my comprehension.' Chantal gave the prostrate form of Khaled a vicious kick with her sandalled foot. Then, bending, she removed the black eyepatch exposing a gnarled eye socket in his villainous face. 'I think my need of this will be greater than his.' With this, she set off for the foot of the shaft.

Paul rushed after her, to try to stop her.

'Wait! You can't go up there unarmed.'

He placed a restraining hand on her bare shoulder. She shook it off firmly.

'No, do not try to stop me. I have been the means of your death once, my love. It shall not be so again.'

Paul fell back, greatly puzzled, as Chantal reached the bosun's seat, which swung gently on the end of the rope at the shaft's base. Gripping the rope firmly in both hands, Chantal turned to face them.

'With no one up there to work the mechanism I shall have to climb.'

Before anyone could even begin to restrain her, she swung herself agilely onto the rope and began to climb hand over hand, like a monkey, gripping the rope between her feet. She was soon lost from Paul's gaze in the enveloping darkness.

He turned to face Yasmin and Fatima. 'I should have stopped her,' he mumbled.

'It would have made no difference and probably she has a better chance than you...' Then, looking doubtful,

Yasmin added, 'That's if she remains the queen long enough, before Chantal's inner self again regains control of her body.'

Paul realised he hadn't even thought of that aspect and inwardly cursed himself for not trying harder to restrain the determined spirit. If Chantal suddenly re-emerged in her own form and found herself suspended up there on that rope... The thought died where it had begun. Almost assuredly Chantal couldn't climb and would crash back down the shaft to certain death. Strangely it was as if Yasmin could read his thoughts.

She added, 'However, I do not consider it likely, now that she thinks Tuthmosis is up there, I think nothing will stop her from exacting vengeance for her untimely death so long ago.'

Fatima interrupted, 'But the brotherhood up there...? Surely they will shoot on sight?'

'And Elaine and the hostages?' ventured Paul. 'What of them?'

Yasmin looked from one to the other, before replying, 'I cannot, it is true, give you all the answers, but all I can say is she has a better chance than you of succeeding. These men up there are all superstitious.'

Paul reached for the rope and gently moved it, feeling its tension or lack of it.

'She has completed the climb anyway and is clear of the rope. Time now for me, I think, to join her.' Tucking the Sten through his tank harness to leave both hands free, he addressed the two women. 'Stay where you are, both of you, at least until your air is almost out. It will last for some time yet. If I am successful I shall shout down and bring you up by the bosun's chair...' His voice almost tailed off. 'If you hear nothing, then I am afraid you will both have to climb up and take your chances. Fatima still has the derringer.' Grasping the rope, he added, 'Fatima, you had better go back and check on Khaled. The last thing you want is him at your backs.' With this last remark he began the ascent and was soon lost to their sight.

'He is right, Yasmin. We must check on Khaled,' whispered Fatima. The two sisters crept back to where they had left the prostrate Khaled. 'No need for worries there, anyway,' affirmed Fatima, kneeling beside her erstwhile leader and taking his pulse, or rather, confirming the lack of it. 'Quite dead,' was her matter-of-fact statement.

'Then say thanks that you have finally seen the light, sister, and returned to the living, instead of this accursed band of Seth worshippers,' exclaimed Yasmin.

'We never worshipped Seth,' denied Fatima hotly.

'You might just as well have done,' said Yasmin.

Fatima let the matter drop and took her sister's arm. Together they crept back to the foot of the shaft. Fatima felt the rope.

'He's still on it,' she murmured.

Back up in the top cavern the terrorists were becoming restless and beginning to argue amongst themselves.

'Khaled should have returned by now,' whined Wael. 'There is something eerie about this place, I tell you.'

'What I want to know is why they haven't come up with the gold and jewels,' muttered another.

'I think we should just shoot these infidels and leave this place,' ventured a third.

'Quiet, I say,' roared Mohammed. 'With Khaled and Fatima away, I'm the leader here.'

'That's a point,' moaned Wael. 'Where's Fatima? She was only going to assist Khaled down. She must still be at the head of the shaft. Maybe she can throw some light on what is happening.'

Mohammed seemed to consider for a moment before trusting himself to reply.

'Very well. Go and investigate, Wael, and take Abou with you. See what our second in command, Fatima, has to say.'

Wael nodded to Abou and the two set off into the dark interior. No sooner had they departed than the dissent broke out again.

'At least give us the blonde infidel woman to have some pleasure with while we wait for Khaled's return, Mohammed,' Elaine heard one voice argue.

'Yes, I shall be first,' cried out another, excitedly.

Elaine felt her blood turn to ice water.

'As the senior here, I shall be first,' snapped Mohammed. 'Two of you get the woman on her feet and strip her.'

Elaine screamed as rough hands pulled her to her feet and Clive bellowed like an outraged bull in defence of his sister's honour. All this brought him was a heavy blow with the barrel of a Sten across the back of his head. He fell back, temporarily knocked senseless. The two members of the brotherhood half-pulled, half-carried her, screaming and kicking, to where Mohammed stood, hands on hips.

'Strip her!' ordered the stand-in leader.

Eager hands reached for the top of her grey boiler suit, but never reached it. A blood-curdling male scream rent the air, reverberating and echoing through the limestone cavern and then faded away to nothing. The terrorists were stopped dead in their tracks, one of them still with his hand on the collar of Elaine's suit. He looked at Mohammed.

'In Allah's name, what was that?'

Mohammed looked as confused as the rest. Every eye turned towards the direction of the interior. Even Elaine forgot her immediate peril, as each of the terrorists reached for and pointed their Sten guns at an unseen enemy. It seemed like minutes but, in fact, was only seconds before the ominous silence was broken by the gasps and hurried steps of someone returning in desperate haste. In blind panic the man, Abou, ran into the outer cavern, so out of breath he was almost unable to speak. Mohammed slapped Abou's face with a savage backhander.

'What happened in there? Why are you so panic-stricken? Where is Wael?'

'Wael is... dead,' spluttered Abou.

'What do you mean, he is dead? How can he be?' snapped Mohammed.

'The Pharaoh queen, she killed him,' screamed Abou. 'She will kill us all.' He was veritably shaking with fear now, perspiration pouring down his face.

Mohammed slapped him again, even harder this time, and every one of the terrorists gathered round him. 'Talk, man!' snapped Mohammed. 'Pull yourself together and explain yourself.'

Abou looked round at the anxious faces of his compatri-ots gathered round him and seemed to gain some courage. He began to relate what had befallen him and his colleague.

'We did as you instructed. We went to the head of the shaft to find Fatima... Crawled on our bellies, we did, but we couldn't find Fatima anywhere. We even called her name. Then it happened—'

'What happened, man?' exclaimed Mohammed, impa-tiently.

'She happened. The woman Pharaoh. Appeared from nowhere, seemed to come out of the very ground. Her face was staring straight at Wael as he looked over. He barely had time to raise his gun. She reached out and pulled the barrel towards her. Wael just fell into the abyss... Pitched right forward and disappeared he did, just like that. I shall never forget his scream until my dying day... All the way down he screamed... Fell into a bottomless black hole, I'd say.'

'Nonsense, man. Get a hold of yourself. This was obvi-ously some sort of infidel trick and you fell for it,' warned Mohammed, although he looked far from convinced himself.

'I tell you I saw her clearly. Full Pharaoh regalia. Double red and white crown of Egypt, vulture and cobra. It had to be the queen… Hatshepsut, I tell you. The one whose mummy was never found. This is her tomb and she's returned to kill us all.'

He began to cry like a baby, convulsing with terror and shock, unable to speak further. The group looked edgy and unsure of themselves, furtively looking to left and right. Elaine now was quite forgotten. With their attention diverted, she quietly crept away to skulk behind a pile of stalactites and boulders. From this position she saw a chance to slip away into the darkness without anyone seeing her depart. From there, knowing the terrain, she was able to reach the cavern entrance. For a moment only, she blinked in the strong sunlight and then ran as she had never run before. With all these soldiers and police around the valley, she reasoned, it shouldn't be too difficult to find help. Perspiration ran down her face and down her back in the stifling heat, but she heeded it not and blindly ran on.

Back in the cavern, Mohammed suddenly noticed her absence. Thinking first that one of the men had carried her off behind the rocks, he made a silent count of his colleagues. It finally dawned on him that she had escaped from them.

'Dolts! Imbeciles! Call yourself professionals?' he screamed. 'You have allowed the infidel woman to get away.' As the other terrorists virtually cowered before him, he issued a new command. 'There is now no time to wait for Khaled. We shall shoot these four men and leave before the blonde one brings troops back.'

'Stand them up against the rock over there, all four of them,' yelled another, pulling the still groggy Clive to his feet. Ibrahim, Ashraf and Ahmed were similarly pulled to their feet, shaking with abject fear, knowing they faced their immediate end.

'You will never get away with this,' protested Clive.

All this brought him was a vicious jab in the ribs from a gun barrel.

As one, everyone turned as a sharp command from the direction of the interior hit them like a pail of ice-water.

'Make not a move any of you common vermin, sons of whores, begotten by lowly serpents.'

Mouths dropped open in both shock and awe, as emerging from the darkness into the light, stepped forward the undoubted apparition of an Egyptian Pharaoh. Two of the terrorists dropped their guns and fell onto their knees, prostrating themselves before the eerie apparition. Mohammed, however, made of sterner stuff, raised his Sten and pointed it at her, nervously fingering the trigger.

'Put down that fool toy. Would you desecrate my last resting place with the obscene noise that infernal thing makes, son of a camel thief!'

Mohammed looked unsure but still clutched the gun menacingly.

'What trick is this? Who are you, woman?' he countered.

'Woman! Woman! How dare you call your queen and your Pharaoh woman?'

Mohammed gave an evil smile. 'We shall soon see how real you are with a dozen or so holes punched through you. I shall let a little daylight through you and we shall see whether you are a ghost or not.' He raised the Sten anew.

'Use that toy and my troops will be awakened and rush in to destroy you, Tuthmosis,' she exclaimed, fixing a cold unshakeable stare upon him.

It occurred to him then that it was strange that she knew his nickname, Tuthmosis. All his friends had always remarked on his likeness to the statues of the ancient Pharaoh, Tuthmosis III. Puffing up his chest he matched her gaze.

'The greatest Pharaoh of all Egypt, the Napoleon of our country. His glorious deeds are legend. I am honoured that you so call me before you die.' His finger tightened on the trigger, knuckles whitening at the pressure. 'Die, queen impostor, whoever you are, in the name of Tuthmosis.'

The staccato chatter of a Sten echoed and reverberated round the confines of the cabin, but it was Mohammed who pitched forward onto his face, his blood staining the rocky floor. The gunfire had come from the blackness behind the Pharaonic queen but to the terrorists cowering on the floor it looked as if the apparition had struck their leader down. Screaming with terror, they edged away and ran back towards the entrance, disappearing round the bend. A moment later, Paul, Sten in hand, emerged to join Chantal. Their eyes met for an instant, recognition showing in hers.

'Another debt I owe you, my love,' she murmured.

'I think it is we who owe you, queen,' he answered.

She smiled and came into his arms. Paul was forced to relinquish the Sten. It clattered noisily to the floor and was quickly retrieved by Ibrahim. There was no need now to have bothered, all the terrorists were gone.

Paul held her firmly and was more than aware of the enticing exotic perfume she wore. He had to remind himself that this was really the hated Chantal Shariffe he held in his arms. Then the noises from outside reached them, a hail of machine-gun fire and awful screams followed by much shouting and then silence.

Five minutes later an Egyptian army officer, with about five or six men behind him, entered the chamber. With them was Elaine Gilroy. Paul wondered how he was going to explain away the Egyptian Pharaoh, but then he suddenly realised she had vanished, and in her place he was left with his arm round and supporting Chantal, once again clad in her boiler suit. She blinked, looked thoroughly confused, then seeing who was holding her, rapidly detached herself from Paul.

'Luckily for you people this lady', said the captain, pointing to Elaine, 'was able to warn us.'

'Did you get them all, captain?' asked Paul.

'To the last man, but we were forced to shoot them all. Perhaps you can inform me what happened here, sir, as none of them are left alive to tell us.'

'Later, captain, but first I need to get two of our party up from the lower cavern… two young ladies,' explained Paul.

'Very good, sir, but when you have done that, perhaps you will be so kind as to give me a detailed report about what's been happening here?'

Paul nodded, and having ascertained that Elaine and Clive, besides Chantal and his workers, were none the worse for their experiences, he left again for the shaft.

When he arrived there, he was surprised to find Elaine had crawled along the tunnel after him.

'Thought you might need some help, Paul,' she ventured.

Still on his knees he turned and embraced her.

'I was worried sick about you up here with those murderous swine.'

'I wasn't too happy about it, myself,' said Elaine with a half-laugh.

Without realising quite how it happened, their lips met in a long lingering kiss, as they swayed precariously near the edge of the abyss. It was Paul who finally broke clear.

'Thank God you are all right anyway, love. Now we had better see about getting Fatima and Yasmin up out of there.' He looked down and shouted into the dark shaft. 'One of you sit on the bosun's chair and buckle yourself in. I'm going to bring you up.'

Far away he heard a very faint answer, 'Okay.' He waited about a minute, then tested the rope's tension. Feeling the weight on the end, he began to bring the first one up very slowly. Three minutes later Yasmin's face appeared over the edge. Elaine helped her unbuckle and get her feet on terra firma, then the makeshift chair was lowered down again. Paul noticed that it was considerably heavier coming up than it had been with Yasmin in it. Four minutes later he found the reason. Fatima had brought up the bag of bones about which he had in all the excitement quite forgotten. In answer to the questions of both girls, he was able to inform them that the terrorists had all been accounted for and the immediate danger was over. Fatima looked dejected.

'I suppose you will now hand me over to the authorities as one of them, Mr Stanton? It's no more than I deserve.'

Paul smiled.

'I don't know what you are talking about, Fatima. You are a trusted member of my team.'

Fatima's eyes almost shone with gratitude in the dark. 'How can I ever repay you, Mr Stanton?' she murmured.

'I think you already have, when you saved the lives of both your sister and Chantal down there, and mine too, as it happens.' Then Paul suddenly remembered the two bodies down in the lower cavern – Khaled's and Wael's. 'Guess I shall have to tell the army about them,' he mused.

Turning again to Elaine, he suggested that she took Chantal, Fatima, Yasmin and Clive back to the apartment whilst he paid off Ibrahim and his workers. He would join them just as soon as he gave the army a full report for the record.

'You take the jeep and I'll cadge a lift from the army chaps,' he added.

Once everyone was out in the daylight, Paul watched Elaine drive off with her passengers, everyone looking fairly numb with shock. He then spent the next half-hour making a statement for the army. When he had answered all Captain Hassam's questions to the best of his ability, the young military man informed him that he would have to do it all again for the police.

When Paul's face showed his exasperation, Hassam laughed and exclaimed, 'Don't worry, sir. There's no immediate need. We shall clear up here and bring up the bodies of the two terrorists from the lower cavern you told me about.'

'Thanks, captain. My foreman, Ibrahim, will show you the shaft entrance and will help you in any way he can. Then, when you finish here, perhaps I can cadge a lift with you back into Luxor.'

'Certainly, sir, if you don't mind putting up with a truckload of dead bodies,' quipped Hassam.

Paul laughed.

'I think I prefer this particular bunch in their present state to that which faced us before.' Whilst Hassam was getting his men organised, Paul took Ibrahim aside and whispered, 'Under the circumstances, I think it better if neither you nor your men mention the apparition that you saw, or anything to do with it. The fewer people who know about that the better, I think. See that Ashraf and Ahmed understand that. I shall see that their silence, and yours for that matter, is well rewarded. Tomorrow I want you to begin filling in the tomb entrance. I want it permanently closed and shall issue the necessary report to Mr Ali ben Mustapha of the Egyptian Antiquities Authority.'

To his surprise, Ibrahim raised no objection to what amounted to the termination of his contract, simply agreeing that he felt it would be for the best.

'As you English say, Effendi Stanton, let sleeping dogs lie... eh?'

Paul paid him and his men off to the end of the week.

'That should give you ample time to seal the tomb off properly.' As he watched the three workers go into the tomb accompanied by Captain Hassam and three of the soldiers, he thought to himself, If only the matter of Chantal and the spirit possessing her could as easily be resolved.

He sat in the warmth of the sun until the recovery party re-emerged with their grim and macabre cargo. He watched with a strange detached and unfeeling emotion as the cadavers were loaded with the rest onto the military truck. He asked himself why he should feel anything else. These dead men were all cold-blooded murderers. This time, luckily for him and his party, they had failed in their mission, gambled for greed and lost.

Hassam called him over when everything was battened down, saying, 'Perhaps you would like to sit in the front with the living, sir?' Hassam waved a hand to the passenger side of the lorry. 'A bit of a tight squeeze, but I expect you won't mind for the short trip back into town...' Then, as an afterthought, he added, 'Oh, by the way, I called up the police on my mobile and they will be coming round to your apartment in the morning for a civil statement... I hope that's all right?'

Paul nodded and climbed up beside the driver.

Chapter XVIII

Paul found everyone waiting for him on his return to the apartment. By the time he had filled everyone in with the later developments, all except Chantal, who sat morosely in a corner of the room, seemed to have recovered from their ordeal. Clive turned to address him.

'Whilst you were tidying things up with the military, Yasmin and I have been discussing what should be done here and, I think, although as a churchman I can't understand why, she is right.'

'What is she saying?' said Paul, anxiously.

Clive took Paul by the arm and led him outside.

'Why all the secrecy?' questioned Paul.

'For obvious reasons I don't want Chantal to hear, or rather the spirit within her,' answered Clive.

'Okay, I'm listening… Shoot!' exclaimed Paul.

'Do you think you could get permission to enter the Valley of the Kings tonight after sunset, Paul?'

'I don't know… probably – but for what reason?' Puzzlement was written all over Paul's face.

'A funeral – a royal one,' remarked Clive.

'I think you had better explain what you are up to, Clive.'

'Very well… I can't guarantee it will work, but Yasmin has put the plan forward and I'm prepared to go along with it. At first I thought it was too far-fetched for anything, but now on reflection I consider it's the best chance we have.'

'Chance of what?' exclaimed a confused Paul.

'Of removing the possessive spirit that occupies our Chantal and helping it on its way to its true resting place amongst the ancients.'

'How can you, a churchman, a man of God and the Holy Trinity, believe this? Surely you believe only in one God?' argued Paul.

Clive smiled.

'We are not talking of what I believe in. We are only interested in what the spirit controlling Chantal Shariffe believes in... Do you see what I'm getting at?'

'Yes, but why do you want to visit the Valley of the Kings after sunset tonight?'

'Yasmin believes we have a chance if we take Chantal not only to the valley but to Hatshepsut's original tomb, the one that she had prepared for herself and her beloved father. There is a chance, no more than a chance, that the spirit within Chantal will recognise the tomb as her rightful last resting place.'

'And?' prompted a bemused Paul.

'And then I shall hypnotise Chantal and try and contact the spirit once more.'

'You didn't have much luck the last time, when you tried that,' said Paul, being devil's advocate.

'This time I have Yasmin to help me and she understands these strange phenomena much better than I. Having put Chantal under, I shall simply programme her to Yasmin's voice and hand over to her. From then on it's all in her hands,' reasoned Clive.

'Is there nothing else we can try? This all sounds far out to me.'

Clive turned his palms upwards and looked to the heavens.

'I'm open to suggestions, Paul.'

'Very well. It shall be as you wish. I shall make some telephone calls to the authorities and see if I can get the necessary permission for a night entry into the valley, but I don't think they will be very pleased about it... less still, if I told them the true reason for the request. I shall just say we need to do some special research that can only be done after sunset.'

'Good man! Go to it, Paul. There's no time to waste. The longer this possession goes on the greater the risk to Chantal's mental health.'

Paul spent the next half an hour making several telephone calls. As he had expected, the authorities were not too keen on the idea, but after much persuasion he finally wore down their objections, and they reluctantly agreed to his request for a night entry into the Valley of the Kings.

The remainder of the daylight hours were spent in discussion and Paul had the housekeeper, Noha, make up an early dinner for everyone. Once everything was cleared away he let her go off home early. The fewer people knowing about this the better, he concluded. For this reason he decided to visit the west bank home of the valley, the long way round, over the new bridge further down the river. The whole group of them, travelling on the ferry after dark, might cause speculation they could do without.

Everyone, except Chantal, waited patiently for sunset. She seemed to have lost interest in everything and everybody, and still sat morosely in the corner of the room, curled up in an old armchair, her legs drawn up under her.

It was a beautiful Egyptian sunset when it came. Elaine watched through the window, marvelling at the colours reflected in the slow-moving waters of the Nile, red and gold gradually turning to purple. Little feluccas tacked across the broad stretches of the river homeward bound. She watched with interest as a Nile river cruiser deposited its passengers further down along the riverbank. The lights from the buildings were reflected in the water as darkness closed in, dancing like a thousand fireflies on the surface of the dark river. Paul came up behind her and slipped his arms round her, joining his hands together around her waist.

'It's time,' he whispered, interrupting her thoughts.

'Shall we all be able to get in the jeep, Paul?' she answered, bringing her head back to rest on his shoulders.

'With six of us, it's going to be a tight squeeze,' he replied, 'but we can just about manage. I'll drive... Clive's the biggest of you all, so we shall put him in the front passenger seat, and wedge Chantal between us on the utility bucket seat. That way we can keep tabs on her... Leaves you, Fatima and Yasmin to manage in the back. Okay?'

'Guess we can all cope,' agreed Elaine. 'Once we get to the valley it will all be on foot anyway.'

And so it proved. They travelled approximately seven miles alongside the Nile on the east bank and then, crossing by the new bridge, they reached the west bank. It was quite dark by the time the crowded jeep progressed on to the gates of the valley and came to a halt. Immediately two armed guards advanced from the sentinel's box. Upon Paul's explanation it became clear that the guards had been informed of their arrival. The senior of the two guards explained that they would have to leave the jeep outside the gates and proceed on foot. He opened a small side entrance for pedestrians and ushered them through, asking if they wished for someone to guide them.

Paul quickly informed him that this would not be necessary and slipped the fellow a few Egyptian pounds. They set off up the valley. The first part was a concrete road, which swept forward for about four hundred metres before making a turn into the valley proper. Here it narrowed and climbed more steeply.

They passed several deserted wooden stalls, which, during the daytime, would have been occupied by the various pedlars and hawkers selling postcards and souvenirs. Now they looked strangely out of place, stark and angular in the newly risen moon's glow. Then came several tomb entrances with their bare concrete archways; over them were steel grids now locked for the night.

Further up, Paul, in the lead, left the marked trails and headed away from the East Valley. Elaine recognised the tombs of Rameses I and Sethos I. After this it was tough going on a little used sandy track which climbed steadily. Chantal never spoke during the entire ascent or even enquired where they were taking her. Clive and Yasmin supported her, one on each arm, and she trudged on like an automaton between them.

Elaine found herself wondering whether the tomb would be closed with a steel grid like the rest of them. She said as much to Paul.

'Definitely not,' he assured her. 'After all,' he reminded her, 'it has nothing worth taking within it. Not even the beautiful coloured walls will be evident here, just bare limestone rock.'

She recalled her earlier visit, which now seemed an age ago, but, she realised, was a matter of days only.

From the time they arrived at the entrance to KV20, their objective, the official tomb of Queen Hatshepsut and her father, Pharaoh Tuthmosis I, forty-five minutes had passed. She saw now why Paul had been so sure it wouldn't be locked. Who but someone coming here for a specific reason would venture up here?

A strange dry wind seemed to get up, coming from nowhere. Elaine could feel the material of her white cotton dress stretch tight across her thighs. It was almost as if the wind was coming from the tomb entrance itself to meet them. She realised this was impossible and must be her imagination, but it was an eerie feeling nevertheless. Glancing at the others, she noticed that, with the exception of Chantal, they were all looking uneasy. Paul produced from his backpack a couple of hurricane lamps and some torches. After lighting both lamps he took one himself and handed the other to Elaine. Every member of the party was handed a flashlight.

'Okay, everyone, we are going in now. Try and keep close together. This tomb is like nothing you will have seen before, so try not to be alarmed. It will be a long time before we reach the lower burial chamber. During the descent you will probably notice the tomb has a huge curve and, in fact, comes back on itself. When it finally levels out, if it were possible to keep going, we would come out on the other side of the valley, right into Hatshepsut's mortuary temple at Deir el-Bahri in fact.'

Elaine, close behind Paul, remembered it from her last visit with him, but she realised it must be coming as a shock to her brother, Clive, and the others. She looked back at Chantal behind her. If the woman recognised it, she gave no sign, simply trudging on.

After a lengthy flight of steps they reached the first undecorated chamber and Paul paused for a few moments for everyone to catch up, then proceeded on down yet more steep steps. Even knowing where they were going to finish up, Elaine felt as if she were visiting the bowels of the earth. They went past a row of slotted apertures, which Paul called out were for the beams to have been placed to ease the sarcophagus on its downward journey. Then came an archway cut into the rock and beyond it a passage cutting across their own descent. Paul led them past it and gradually everyone was aware the corridor-like passage was continually curving away to the right, finally coming into a large antechamber, which was also undecorated.

Just when most of the party thought they had arrived, Paul was off again, still going downwards. Eventually, in what must have seemed like an age to everyone, they were in another chamber with three bare rooms going off it.

'This is the final burial chamber, where once there were fifteen limestone slabs all inscribed with scenes from the

Amduat. We are finally at our destination,' said Paul, in a low voice.

The light from the hurricane lamps and flashlights threw strange eerie shadows from the rocky walls, making Elaine only too aware of their own bizarre purpose for being there. She gave an involuntary shiver and wondered how the others were being affected.

Clive gently eased Chantal forward and then turned her round to face him. Her face was expressionless and Elaine thought she resembled someone in a trance already. Clive raised his eyebrows towards Paul in an unspoken question. Paul nodded solemnly in response.

The former then produced a crystal prism on a stainless-steel chain and raised it in front of Chantal. Her eyes fastened on it and remained there. Ever so gently, almost imperceptibly Clive began to swing it from side to side. In a low authoritative voice he addressed Chantal. Her eyes followed the crystal prism from side to side, seemingly unaware of the presence of the onlookers. Clive continued to address her, in such a low voice that Elaine, standing behind and to the side of him, couldn't discern the words. Finally the prism came to rest and with it the fixed glazed eyes of Chantal centred upon it. In a much louder voice Clive commanded the latter to close her eyes.

'On the count of three you will try to open them, but you will be unable to do so, as you are under my control... One... two... three.'

Everyone watched with bated breath as Chantal appeared to be battling to open her eyes, but was unable to do so.

'You will now respond only to the voice you will next hear. Do you understand?' There was no answer. 'If you understand, answer I will,' said Clive.

'I will,' came back an almost inaudible reply.

'Very well then. The next voice to speak to you will be

the goddess, Hathor,' exclaimed Clive.

Elaine forced herself to suppress a gasp of shock. She hadn't known what to expect but the reality of this escapade and her brother's audacity nearly bowled her over. Clive nodded to Yasmin who stepped forward to take his place in front of Chantal.

'Do you know me, Pharaoh?' came the deep solemn tones of Yasmin's voice. 'I am the one with the ears of the cow.'

'Why do you address me as Pharaoh?' replied Chantal, in what was unmistakably her own voice.

'I speak not to you but to the one within you, the Pharaoh queen,' exclaimed Yasmin.

This was met by an ominous silence and Yasmin repeated the sentence. Again there was silence, and then just when Elaine thought the project doomed to failure, the deep mellow tone of the spirit possessing Chantal rang out.

'Why do you bother me? Have I not been tortured enough?'

Yasmin's eyes never left Chantal and she spoke again, methodically and slowly.

'I come not to bother you, Pharaoh, but to assist you.'

'How can you, a mere mortal, help me?' came back the spirit's answer.

'Not at all, unless you have the courage to show yourself.'

'Why should I?'

'Because I am Hathor, your divine mother, and through me you can find everlasting peace,' urged Yasmin.

'Can you prove that of which you boast?'

'Only if you are prepared to show yourself, Pharaoh. Only then can I prove to you I am that which you worship.' Again there was an ominous silence, broken once more by Yasmin. 'Show me the courage that once you bestowed on Egypt, oh valiant queen, the courage that made you both respected and loved by your people.'

'Words, words, empty words... Where is your proof? You would, like my stepson, Tuthmosis, seek to trick me and destroy me.'

Paul sensed rather than saw the slight loss of confidence in Yasmin's expression and voice.

'I seek only to help you.'

'Proof, I say, proof,' cried out the spirit voice.

Paul suddenly remembered for the first time the golden cartouche he had found on that first day in the cavern, the cartouche, which he had meant to send on to the authorities in Cairo, but, in the excitement that had followed, he had clean forgotten. Reaching into his breast pocket, he handed it to Yasmin. Eagerly she grasped it and then held it high above her head.

'Here, Pharaoh, is the proof you seek. Your own golden cartouche. Show yourself and you shall behold.'

Then an amazing thing happened. A wisp of smoke, which rapidly became a cloud, appeared, obscuring everyone's vision in the confined burial chamber. When it slowly cleared there was a strong acrid smell, and Elaine felt her own eyes stinging. In a crumpled heap on the floor lay Chantal. Mercifully Elaine could see she was still breathing. It was, however, the apparition behind Chantal that took everyone's attention.

Standing tall and straight, just as she looked in all the sculptures and reliefs of her, stood Queen Hatshepsut. The same broad intelligent forehead and handsome features resolutely stared back at Yasmin. Elaine realised with shock that she was able to discern the shapes of the rocky tomb, directly behind the queen. It was as if someone was projecting a film image, and yet it stood clear, in three-dimensional shape off the background.

'Where are your cowlike ears?' exclaimed the queenly spectre.

'Where is your faith, Pharaoh? Surely you know I can take many shapes... a cow, a mortal woman, an animal... anything I choose.'

So convincing did Yasmin sound that Elaine almost found herself believing that she really was the goddess, Hathor, holding the cartouche so that it faced the queen.

'Your cartouche, is it not, Pharaoh?'

The queen looked uncertain and now quite bewildered.

'It looks like that of mine,' she said, doubt creeping into her voice.

'It does not look like yours. It is indeed yours. How, unless I am who I say I am, would I have this, Pharaoh, when you yourself haven't?'

Slowly the queenly apparition held out her wraithlike hand. Yasmin boldly stepped forward and Elaine found herself marvelling at the Egyptian girl's courage. On reaching the queen she placed the cartouche in her hand. Elaine was flabbergasted. She had expected the object to drop through the transparent filmy hand, but it remained in space, held there in fingers of gossamer.

Yasmin stepped back.

'You are now reunited, oh Pharaoh, with your rightful identity.'

The queen turned the golden object over and over in her hands, pure joy written all over the handsome face.

'Now, Pharaoh, Isis awaits you... All that remains is for you to seek her blessing,' exclaimed Yasmin.

It was then that the queen seemed to notice Paul for the first time. She turned to face him, saying, 'Come with me, my love, into everlasting eternity.' She held out her right hand, having transferred the cartouche to the other.

Paul stood rooted to the spot. Yasmin stepped in quickly.

'This man is not Senenmut, your lover, although he greatly resembles him... At the end of your journey you will find him, the man you fashioned your dynasty with. The man whom you bestowed both your love and favour upon. An architect who built to your eternal glory for love of you.'

'And a man whom I forsook and betrayed, to my eternal shame,' answered the queen.

'You will find, when you reach the other side, that he has forgiven you and even now impatiently awaits your arrival in the east.'

The expression of the wraithlike queen turned to joy and then, almost as quickly, to doubt and despair.

'But how, Hathor, am I to journey to the everlasting land of the gods? I see no golden barque to convey me there.'

'You need no golden ship, Pharaoh, only belief in the eternal life ahead.'

Still suspicious, the queen ventured, looking from one to the other of the tomb's occupants, 'Who then are these people in their quaint unusual dress? Why are they here?'

'They are here', answered Yasmin, 'to bid you farewell from this arduous earthly existence. As you see, the walls of your tomb are undecorated and unfinished because of your untimely mortal demise. These loyal subjects are of a new age, but nevertheless have great knowledge... far greater than any hieroglyphs on any walls could contain. This knowledge you will take with you to meet the rising of the sun.'

Then a strange thing happened. The queen stretched out her right hand towards Yasmin and said, 'Will you lead me there, dear Hathor, to join with the gods?'

Yasmin boldly stepped forward to meet her and took the transparent hand in her own.

'Take heart, oh queen, I cannot go with you, for I have work here in this mortal land, but in thought I shall be with you always.'

Elaine watched in amazement as the wraithlike hand was clasped round Yasmin's hand.

'Has the time come? And will Isis be there waiting to receive me? I fear my heart was never weighed against the feather. Suppose it is the crocodile god?'

Elaine knew that the queen was referring to the ancient process of mummification, where the Pharaoh's heart was always weighed against a feather, to ascertain its purity and right to enter into eternal life with the gods. She waited with bated breath for Yasmin's answer. She didn't have long to dwell on it.

'I, Hathor, your earth mother, have guaranteed your purity to Isis and even now she awaits your coming, great Pharaoh. Have no fear, your heart is pure.'

The phantom queen seemed to be overcome with a great warmth. For the first time there was a look of peace that seemed to transform her features. In that cold barren tomb it was as if all could feel the warmth. She reached upwards with both arms aloft, as if to embrace an unseen presence, and then, almost before their very eyes, began to fade into a red mist, which turned to gold and enveloped her wraithlike figure. Time seemed to stand still. Deep down there in the forsaken tomb arose a sweet scent of summer jasmine. Then even the golden mist was gone, leaving only the bare rocks where the apparition of the queen had stood a few seconds before.

On the floor of the tomb, Chantal Shariffe stirred, sat up and rubbed her eyes. She looked at each in turn before, in her own aggressive tone, exclaiming, 'What the hell are we all doing here?'

Yasmin looked washed out and exhausted and began to sway on her feet. Clive and Paul rushed forward to support her.

'Is it over?' gasped Clive.

'Yes. She has found peace now and passed over to her

rightful existence,' murmured Yasmin.

'Will someone tell me what this is all about?' snapped Chantal.

Chapter XIX

The following morning back at the apartment Elaine and Paul were left in no doubt that Chantal Shariffe was no longer possessed. She was back in her usual disagreeable and aggressive character, finding fault with everything and everybody. Strangely, she seemed to have little or no recollection of the happenings of the past few days, only that the whole expedition and excavation was a total flop and they had found nothing.

Paul told her he had given orders to have the cavern sealed and work would have already begun on it. She had replied that she had already told him as much, and would be leaving for Cairo that morning, saying that there was urgent work awaiting her experience as a foremost archae-ologist.

Elaine sensed Paul's relief that Chantal had no memory of events and wasn't surprised that he showed no sign of argument with her, simply agreeing that the cavern had exposed little of real interest.

Half an hour later she had packed and left. As the taxi pulled away, Paul watched from the window and muttered, 'I liked her much better when she was the queen.'

'You would,' chuckled Elaine, trying to lighten the mood. 'That way she fancied you.'

Clive entered, also packed and ready to leave. Elaine tried to persuade him to stay on.

'Sorry sis, but I really ought to get back to Cairo. Every-thing will be piling up in my absence.'

Elaine looked disappointed but let it go at that. Paul shook his hand firmly, warmly thanking him for all his help in the matter.

'Don't thank me, thank Yasmin. She really is something else that one,' exclaimed Clive.

Elaine rang for a taxi for him, which arrived within three minutes. Both she and Paul stood on the steps of the apartment and waved goodbye as the vehicle drove off with him towards the station. She turned to Paul.

'Well, I guess it's just you and me now.'

Paul followed her back inside, Fatima having gone back with her sister to Yasmin's house, when they had returned the night before from the valley.

Elaine put the kettle on, it being Noha's day off. Having silently and thoughtfully watched it boil, she made a couple of instant coffees, took one to Paul, and sat down beside him on the sofa.

'What time are the police coming?' she said, making conversation.

'The army captain just said they would be round this morning... didn't give a time,' replied Paul.

'What are you going to tell them?' asked Elaine.

Paul looked thoughtful and took his time replying.

'Well, luckily Chantal can't remember anything other than thinking the excavation was a flop, so we don't have to worry about her talking. Fatima, due to her terrorist activities in the past, will want to keep a low profile and Yasmin, I am sure, is a deep one, and will keep all of this to herself.'

'How about Ibrahim and the men? They saw Chantal when she was possessed. Won't they talk?'

'No way. They are all too superstitious and will expect harm to come to themselves if they opened their mouths.'

'Clive won't say anything, I'm sure of that... Anyway, it wouldn't look good for him in the church, if he did,' put in Elaine.

Paul laughed.

'Anyway I don't think anyone would believe him if he did. Even now, I'm finding it hard to believe myself, having seen with my own eyes. Until last night I've always been a confirmed atheist but not any more... My beliefs have been shaken to the core, or should I say the lack of them... beliefs, I mean.'

Elaine nodded.

'I see what you mean... Even now I'm finding it hard to take everything in.' Then suddenly she gasped, 'The cartouche... What happened to it?'

It was Paul's turn to look shaken.

'It was in the queen's hand when she disappeared into the mist,' he said, half to himself, then aloud, 'There was certainly no sign of it when we left the royal tomb.'

'Then it must have gone with her to... wherever,' muttered Elaine.

'I guess you could say it was hers anyway. If anyone had a right to it, she did,' said Paul.

The doorbell rang. Elaine jumped up to answer it and a few moments later re-emerged with two policemen, one in uniform, and an older man in plain clothes. Offering a hand, the elder of the two introduced himself, then the other man.

'I think you were expecting us, sir. A formality really. Luckily for you all the terrorists were caught and killed, although a woman was reported to be with them, and she hasn't been apprehended as yet. When we do come up with her she can expect short shrift... These Fundamentalists are ruining our country's economy.'

'Quite so, Inspector,' said Paul, with a little cough and an apprehensive look at Elaine.

'However, sir, if you care to give me a statement in your own words... then perhaps you, miss,' he added, glancing at Elaine.

Paul relayed in detail all the events concerning the terrorists, but, of course, omitted anything to do with other events. When questioned, Elaine verified Paul's statement.

'And this woman terrorist – neither of you saw her then?' prompted the inspector.

'I am sure if there had been a woman there, other than those in our own party, either Elaine or myself would have seen her. No, most certainly, Inspector, there wasn't a woman with them. Anyway, surely it wouldn't be very likely would it? I mean – a woman terrorist?'

'Perhaps not, then, sir. It's possible we could have been misinformed… Well, if there is nothing more you can tell us, we won't take up any more of your time. I understand you have given orders for the excavation site to be permanently closed… best thing, sir, if you don't mind me saying. Leave the past alone, I always say. Although I don't expect you two as archaeologists to agree with me,' the inspector added.

Paul smiled and got up, offering his hand.

'Let me show you out, Inspector, if there's nothing else.'

When they had gone, Paul turned to Elaine. 'Perhaps you would like to help me pack up the bones Fatima brought up. We should send them on to the Cairo museum for forensic tests.'

'Have you heard anything yet about the clavicle you sent on before?'

'No, too early. Extensive tests have to be made, but we owe the authorities that much, so we had better get these off to them.'

Elaine laughed.

'Although this time, I think, even after their tests are concluded, we shall know a great deal more than they will.'

'Very true,' agreed Paul.

As it was Paul's responsibility to see that the excavation site was properly sealed, both he and Elaine remained in Luxor for a few days. When Ibrahim reported to him that the work was completed, they joined the workmen at the site. After a thorough inspection Paul thanked the men. It was just before sunset.

'Will you be wanting us for anything further, effendi?' said Ibrahim, hopefully.

'Perhaps, in the future. Who knows?' Paul responded.

After the men had left, Paul found Elaine deep in thought, sitting on a boulder facing the now sealed cavern. 'A penny for them,' he said, coming up behind her.

'I was just thinking it's hard to imagine that any of this actually happened, and even funnier that we shall be the only people to ever know about it... Then with those terrorists appearing we were lucky to escape with our lives, thanks to your intervention with that Sten gun... I really thought our last moments had come.'

It was Paul's turn to gaze into space, before replying, 'It was she who saved you, not me, you know.'

'What do you mean?'

'Well, think about it. The terrorists were suddenly faced with an ancient queen of Egypt and remember they are a superstitious lot. That Mohammed fellow was about to have a confrontation with her, when I fired out of the darkness behind her. They never even saw me, so they obviously thought it was she who had killed Mohammed and not me... That's why they all ran out in terror. The queen's vengeance on the past, I call it.'

'Or the queen's love for you is another way of putting it,' added Elaine.

'The man she thought I was, you mean.'

Elaine smiled and said, 'I think you miss her really.'

'I might miss Hatshepsut, but I certainly don't miss Chantal Shariffe.' Turning, Paul gazed wistfully in the direction of the fast sinking sun on the horizon. 'Can't help wondering where she is now, though... this eternal never-

never land amongst the immortals.'

Elaine climbed off the boulder and joined him. Standing next to him, she kicked off her sandals and jiggled her toes in the soft sand. Looking up at him she said, 'Wherever she is, I'm sure she has found the peace she has searched for all of these years.'

'And the man, Senenmut? Do you think she has found him?'

'I'm sure that he will be waiting there for her. Such love transcends millenniums, or so the legends would have us believe,' ventured Elaine.

'From what we have experienced ourselves here in Egypt, who are we to doubt legends?' said Paul, still watching the sunset.

The sun was a large red ball of fire with a background of golden and purple streaks. In a few moments it would be gone. Already shadows had enveloped them, where they stood. Elaine could, however, still feel the warmth of the desert sand on her bare feet and knew that, after a long, sultry, Egyptian night, it would rise again in the east, just as glorious as ever... How she would miss this Egypt. She said as much to Paul.

'You don't have to, you know,' he said, very softly.

'But surely now that our work is finished and once we make our final report to Ali ben Mustapha in Cairo, we shall be going back to England?'

'I won't – and you don't have to – that's unless you want to, that is,' Paul said, a nervousness she hadn't heard before creeping into his voice.

'But we've nothing to stay for now... have we?' Elaine found herself blurting out.

Paul turned and reached for her, and clasping his hands round her slender waist, he drew her towards him. Gazing into her blue eyes, he murmured, 'I'm staying in Egypt and wonder if you want to stay too?'

'Why would I do that?' Elaine replied coyly, forcing him to come out into the open.

'Because I love you and want to spend the rest of my life here with you by my side, here in Egypt... Marry me, Elaine?'

She decided to tease him a moment longer. After all, he had made her wait so long.

'Well, if that's the only way I can keep Egypt, then I guess I'll have to,' she said, laughing at his doleful expression. Then, unable to stand his hurt expression a moment longer, she reached up and clasped her hands round his neck. 'You fool, Paul. Of course, I'll stay and marry you. I've always loved you right from the moment I first met you. I guess you must have been the only one not to have realised it. Even my parents did, when they saw us together.'

Their lips met in a long, sensuous and loving kiss; both could feel the warmth of the other through their thin cotton attire. In the background, somewhere far away, came a cry from a minaret, the call of Egypt and Elaine had heard it. The queen had finally brought them together.